Praise for

THE LETTER

'A wonderful, uplifting story' Lesley Pearse

'Autumnal Sunday afternoons were invented to read
heart-tugging novels like this' *Red*

'This moving love story had everyone talking . . . Get
set to be hooked' *Look*

'A beautiful story . . . I didn't want to put it down'
Reviewed by Fran

'A moving story of love, loss and hope' *Bella*

'You will find it hard to put down. I cried buckets of
tears reading it' *Books With Wine And Chocolate*

'Beautifully written and incredibly poignant.
You cannot fail to fall for this story'
The Last Word Book Reviews

'The story kept me gripped . . . A breath of fresh air,
and just what I needed after a long day in the office'
Here.You.Me

Praise for

THE SECRET

'An emotional and intriguing read . . . Keeps you guessing right to the end' *People's Friend*, 5*

'Gripping' *Good Housekeeping*

'Heart-warming and optimistic' *Jen Med's Book Reviews*

'A gripping and moving family drama that will tug at the reader's heart' *Writing* magazine

'Pulled me in right from the first page . . . I really enjoyed this book' *Rea's Book Reviews*

'I so thoroughly enjoyed this book, it was filled with all kinds of mystery, family secrets, [and] characters that really stood out' *Read Along With Sue*

'One that you just HAVE to finish' *Hollie in Wanderlust*

'A wonderful and memorable read that will stay with me for a long time' *By The Letter Book Reviews*

Turn

THE KEY

And unlock the past . . .

Kathryn Hughes is the bestselling author of *The Letter*, *The Secret* and *The Key*. She lives with her husband near Manchester and has a son and a daughter.

Stay up-to-date with Kathryn's latest news on her website at www.kathrynhughesauthor.com, by following her on Twitter @KHughesAuthor, or find her on Facebook at www.facebook.com/KHughesAuthor.

By Kathryn Hughes

The Letter
The Secret
The Key

Early praise for

THE KEY

'A heartbreakingly powerful read' *Sun*

'A wonderful, enthralling story; one that I didn't want
to end' Lesley Pearse

'I relaxed and I sat back and I devoured it' *Bibliomaniac*

'The pages just flew through my fingers . . . I savoured
this book till the last page' *Book Inspector*

'A very atmospheric, heartbreaking and intriguing read
that will shock and surprise you' *Alba in Bookland*

'Well-crafted fiction . . . you will absolutely need a few
Kleenex!' *Mama Loves to Read*

'Emotional, heart-wrenching at times and deeply
affecting' *Books, Life and Everything*

THE KEY

Kathryn Hughes

REVIEW

First published in 2018
by HEADLINE REVIEW
An imprint of HEADLINE PUBLISHING GROUP

First published in paperback in 2018
by HEADLINE REVIEW
An imprint of HEADLINE PUBLISHING GROUP

2

Cataloguing in Publication Data is available from the British Library

ISBN 978 1 4722 4884 8

Typeset in Garamond MT by Palimpsest Book Production Ltd,
Falkirk, Stirlingshire

Printed and bound in Great Britain by Clays Ltd, Elcograf S.p.A.

HEADLINE PUBLISHING GROUP
An Hachette UK Company
Carmelite House
50 Victoria Embankment
London EC4Y 0DZ

www.headline.co.uk
www.hachette.co.uk

This book is dedicated to the memory of
James and Mary Thomas.

Prologue

November 1956

I've been half walking, half running since I crept out of the house; my chest heaves and my breath escapes in ragged gasps. The streets are deserted and I'm grateful for that small mercy. I won't be forced to explain myself to our inquisitive neighbours. Behind closed doors, someone is frying onions, and the sweet smell wafts in front of me, the tantalising aroma reminding me that I've not eaten. Ahead of me a ginger tom strolls out from behind a hedge and sits down on the pavement, the glow from the gas lamp illuminating his orange fur. As I draw closer, he stands up and moves towards me, his tail erect except for the tip, which curls over. He tilts his chin upwards and mews a greeting to me. Normally I might have bent down and given him a little tickle, but not tonight. There's nothing normal about tonight.

I round the corner, and as the park gates come into view, I'm momentarily surprised by how quickly I've arrived here. With a glance behind me, I push open the rusty iron gate, the ancient hinges squeaking in protest.

The sound cuts through the still night air, sabotaging what was supposed to be a stealthy entrance, but I do feel safer now that I'm in the sanctuary of the park and begin to slow my pace a little. Not too much, though; it's important to keep moving. There's no room for complacency. The pungent smell of the stagnant, weed-filled water tells me the lake is just around the corner, and I lengthen my stride until it comes into view. The water laps on the shingle beach and a couple of swans doze beside an upturned rowing boat.

The cold almost chokes me as I take my first tentative step into the icy water. The stones beneath my bare feet are sharp, and a piece of slimy pondweed wraps itself around my ankles. I turn around and look at the shoes I kicked off only moments before. They are lying on the shingle about a foot apart, and one is upside down. I inwardly chastise myself for my uncharacteristic sloppiness. They should be placed neatly side by side just as my mother always taught me. She will be disappointed, for in a few moments, those shoes will be all that's left of me. It's the only reason I took them off.

My feet ache with the cold, but I take another couple of steps. Now the water is up to my knees. My skirt billows around my legs, the only movement in the dark, tranquil lake. I've been here many times before, but never at this time, never like this. The sky is clear and black; very black. There's only a crescent moon, and the lack of light allows the stars to pepper the night sky. From somewhere in the trees an owl takes flight, screeching as it glides just above the surface of the lake. It startles me, and I stumble backwards but manage to remain upright. I take a few calming breaths. I can still see my feet through the murky water; tiny feet, size three and bone-white.

Another few steps and the water is up to my waist. I feel like I'm suffocating already. There's blackness all around, not just in the sky but in the water, in my heart and in my head. There's sadness too. There's always been sadness. I wear it like a cloak. A great big heavy cloak that swamps me, a cloak I am unable to shrug off. I'm in a rush to get it over with now. Just another couple of strides and peace will be mine. I gaze down at the sleeping baby in my arms but I don't feel anything. I didn't expect to. The screeching starts again, shrill and desperate, but I don't need to turn round to know it's not the owl this time. It's something else.

1

September 2006

She watched him as he stood in front of the hall mirror, brushing imaginary flecks of dandruff from the shoulders of his beige camel coat. His sandalwood cologne floated around on the breeze from the open window. He was still a handsome man. Age had not withered him, and although his hair was now white, it was enviably thick, while his dark eyes held a sparkle that had not been dimmed in spite of his grief.

'Morning, Dad. You off to the cemetery, then?'

He gave her a thin smile. 'Yes, Sarah. Where else would I be going?'

She adjusted the knot in his tie and gave him a peck on the cheek. 'It's been six months, Dad. You don't need to go every day.'

'I know I don't *need* to, Sarah. I want to.' He bent down to give his already-polished shoes one last buff with the soft brush he kept on the hall table. He straightened up and looked her directly in the eye, his tone gentle, almost pleading. 'It would be nice if you came with me once in a while.'

She suppressed an impatient groan. She couldn't bear having the same conversation over and over again. 'I don't need to keep going to Mum's grave in order to remember her.' She thumped her chest. 'I carry her in here every moment of every day.'

He sighed, picked up her hand and kissed it. 'As you wish, but we need to think about planting some bulbs soon. I want there to be lots of colour during the drab winter months. I'll get some snowdrops, I think. They come out early, don't they? And then some crocuses and daffodils. At least the bloody rabbits won't chew their way through those.' He gave a small chuckle. 'Eh? What do you think?'

Sarah unhooked her bag from the newel post and slung the strap over her shoulder. 'All right then, I'll pick some up from the garden centre on my way back.'

He raised his eyebrows. 'On your way back from where?'

'Dad,' she said, dragging the word out. 'You know very well where I'm going.'

'Oh please tell me you're not still snooping round that place.'

'I'm not snooping. It's called research.' She regretted her sharp tone when she saw the hurt look in his eyes and softened her voice. 'And you're a primary source, Dad. Have you any idea how valuable that is to a historian? You want my book to be a success, don't you?'

'An historian now, are you? I thought you worked at the local library.'

'Yes, Dad, that's my job. We all have bills to pay, but this book's my passion and your input could mean the difference between it being a good book and an absolutely brilliant one.'

'I've told you before,' he said, his voice weary, 'I don't want to talk about it.' He jabbed his finger towards her. 'And don't come running to me when you're done for trespassing.'

'It's not trespassing, it's urban exploration.' She noticed his tight jaw and the change in his breathing. She tugged gently on the sleeve of his coat. 'Please, just tell me what it was like in there,' she whispered. 'I promise if it gets too uncomfortable we'll stop. Just tell me as much as you want to.'

He opened the front door and sighed irritably at the rain bouncing off the driveway. Picking up his umbrella from the hall stand, he brandished it at her like a sword. She took a startled step backwards.

'I've already told you as much as I want to.'

'Yeah, which amounts to precisely nothing.'

He opened the umbrella and held it over his head. 'Some things are best just left in the past, Sarah. And that's my final word on the matter.'

She watched as he strode off down the path, willing him to turn round and give her an apologetic wave. Without her mother around to dilute his moods, he could be unbearably cantankerous. Mum had been good for him. She'd never allowed him to sulk and could lift him

7

out of a black mood with just a well-timed quip, usually at his expense, her infectious laugh making it impossible for him to be down for long Sarah was certain that he had loved her mother. She'd witnessed his devastation at losing her, his pit of grief so deep that she feared he would never find the strength to crawl out of it. His daily visits to her grave had become an obsession rather than routine. And yet she felt there was something missing. Not enough to negate their marriage or diminish their love for each other; just something that wasn't quite right. She likened it to completing a thousand-piece jigsaw but then finding that you've only got nine hundred and ninety-nine pieces. That one missing piece spoils the whole effect. It's still clear what the picture is, but your eye will always be drawn to the little space where that missing piece should be. And Sarah didn't know why, but she had the uneasy feeling that the missing piece had something to do with Ambergate Lunatic Asylum.

She'd been coming to Ambergate for months now, but every time she rounded the corner and the stunning building came into view, the sheer grandeur of it made her gasp. She'd seen stately homes less well-appointed. Constructed from the finest limestone, the facade appeared lavish, pretentious even, the octagonal cupola of the clock tower rising majestically over the arched doorway. No expense had been spared in the construction of the asylum, and although many of its more valuable features had long since been pilfered, some sections of the fine glazed wall tiles remained along with the stained-glass windows that adorned the ballroom. It was derelict now, of course, most of its windows smashed and the stonework crumbling beneath the invasive tendrils of ivy.

Sarah pulled a book from her bag and stared at the black-and-white photograph taken around the turn of the last century. *Ambergate County Lunatic Asylum c.1898.* She read the paragraph below the photo.

Constructed between 1870 and 1872 to a design by renowned architect Sir Leonard Groves, Ambergate County Lunatic Asylum was originally built to care for 1,000 patients from the Manchester, Liverpool and Chester areas. By the 1950s it housed over 1,500 patients, resulting in severe overcrowding. In line with a national effort to reduce the stigma associated with the words 'lunatic asylum', the name was changed to Ambergate Mental Hospital in 1925. A further name change was effected after the passing of the 1959 Mental Health Act, which decreed that the word 'mental' be omitted from hospital names. Ambergate Hospital closed its doors in 1997, and the building has been derelict ever since, some of it falling prey to arsonists and vandals.

Spots of rain fell on the pages and she thrust the book back into her bag before picking her way along the sweeping driveway. She arrived at the metal security hoard-ings and stared at the warning sign advising people not to venture any further. It stated that the site was monitored twenty-four hours a day, and depicted a particularly aggressive-looking Alsatian, its long fangs dripping with saliva There were no dogs here, though, it was only a deterrent, and the monitoring was carried out sporadically by an old guy, rumoured to be a former patient, who wandered the grounds occasionally shouting profanities and shaking his fist in the direction of anybody who dared to ignore the signs.

Sarah lifted the hoarding out of its concrete base, creating a small gap she could squeeze through. She waited for a second, scanning the grounds, holding her breath to make it easier to hear any unfamiliar noises. The breeze rustled the leaves on the trees and a pigeon cooed softly to its mate, but otherwise there was nothing. The security really was a joke.

She crossed the weed-ridden front lawn, the long wet grass reaching the top of her thighs, and arrived at the foot of the stone steps leading up to the main entrance. She gripped the once-ornate handrail, now merely a rusting eyesore, and climbed to the partially boarded-up front door, on which someone had hilariously daubed a pentagram in bright red paint. She pushed on the rotten wood and it yielded without much force, allowing her to step over the threshold and into the hallway.

The overwhelming atmosphere inside was one of decay.

Mildew covered the walls, and pigeon droppings speckled the floor. The stench of urine permeated the air, and Sarah covered her nose with her hand. Broken bottles, cigarette butts and the remains of a disposable barbecue indicated that some sort of gathering had taken place. It might be somewhere for bored teenagers to gather now, but Sarah could only imagine the horrors that had gone on within these walls. Her father, however, had valuable first-hand knowledge and it infuriated Sarah that he was unwilling to share it.

She scratched at the flaky varnish on the banister and surveyed the staircase. The floorboards were rotten, though, and she knew it would be madness to attempt to climb them. Double swing doors lay ahead, the hinges squeaking as she pushed her way through. A seemingly endless corridor stretched out in front of her, plaster hanging off the walls, the floor strewn with splinters of wood. She crouched down and pulled the floor plan out of her bag, smoothing it out on the ground. There was over four miles of corridors, so she'd adopted a method-ical approach to exploring the building and had carefully highlighted the areas she had already covered.

Once she'd got her bearings, she replaced the floor plan and retrieved her notebook. Rain trickled in through the gaps in the rafters, accentuating the mouldy stench and general rotting ambience of the derelict building. There was silence, apart from the rhythmical plip-plop of the raindrops. She shuddered and took a furtive three-sixty survey of her surroundings. She would never get used to the eerie walls with their unsettling graffiti, the creepy corridors and the long-buried secrets that her father seemed determined would remain that way.

She froze at the sound of a scuffle coming from a side room. Rats. She'd encountered them before, and no matter how many times she'd told herself that they were more scared of her than she was of them, it made no difference. She still hated the scurrying blighters with their long hairless tails and beady black eyes. She stamped her feet and, feeling slightly stupid, shouted at them to bugger off. Silence descended once more and she laughed quietly to herself. *That showed them.* But as she stared at the opening to the side room, its door hanging off its hinges, the darkness inside pointing to a lack of windows, she heard it again. A shuffling of feet, far too heavy to be a rat. She swallowed hard. 'Hello. Is . . . is there anybody there?'

A hooded figure emerged from the gloom, arms outstretched and moving towards her in a zombie-like fashion. She expelled a breath of relief. 'Nathan, you bloody idiot. What're you trying to do to me?'

He pulled down his hood and grinned at her. 'Sorry, I couldn't resist.'

'What are you doing here at this time anyway?'

'Too wet to be on the streets today. I chose to give it a swerve.'

'I thought beggars couldn't be choosers?'

He shrugged. 'Got any fags?'

She ferreted around in her shoulder bag. 'No, I haven't got any bloody fags.' She thrust a package towards him. 'Here, have these and be grateful.'

He unwrapped the silver foil and crammed a cheese and ham sandwich into his mouth. 'Fanks,' he mumbled. 'I am grateful, honest.' He pulled the sandwich apart and peered inside. 'Could've done with some pickle, though.'

They sat down side by side on the hard floor as Nathan munched his way through her sandwiches. Their paths had crossed a few weeks earlier, when Sarah had stumbled upon him asleep in one of the wards. At first she'd thought it was just a bundle of old clothes, until she had prodded him with her foot. He'd been sleeping rough following a series of blazing rows with his parents, after which he'd stormed out vowing never to return. Since then they had become friends of sorts, although at twenty years his senior, she did have the instinct to mother him, in spite of the fact – or maybe because of it – that she had no children of her own. Her thoughts turned to Dan and the familiar bitterness washed over her. She shook her head to clear away the memories. It didn't do to dwell; what's done is done.

She watched Nathan wolf down the last of the sandwiches, crumbs settling along the fine blond hair on his top lip. 'Nathan?'

'Mmm?' He continued to chew noisily.

'Why won't you let me help you?'

He pointed to his cheeks, puffed out like a hamster's. 'You are helping me,' he mumbled.

'No, Nathan, that's just a sticking plaster. I mean really help you. Get you back on your feet again.'

'I'm all right.'

'Winter's coming. What're you going to do then?'

'Dunno, stay here, I suppose?' He looked up at the ceiling as a large raindrop landed on his head. 'Maybe go to London.'

'You're only eighteen. You've got your whole life ahead of you.'

He scoffed. 'That's what worries me.'

She glared at him. He was a stubborn so-and-so all right. Considering he'd been living rough for a couple of months, he could've looked a lot worse, though. His body odour had the distinctive tang of an overripe Stilton, but his blue eyes were bright and his skin was surprisingly smooth for one who did not have regular access to a razor. His blond fringe was too long and he had a habit of shaking his head in order to flick it out of his eyes.

She delved into her bag again and brought out a bottle of water. He looked at the label. 'I don't suppose there's any chance you've filled this with vodka, is there?'

'Spoken like a true down-and-out.' She shook her head. 'What do you think?'

He unscrewed the cap and took a long drink. 'What're we exploring today then?' he said, changing the subject.

She knew when she was beaten, but it wouldn't stop her trying again another day.

She placed the floor plan between them and pointed to a long corridor with numerous rooms off each side. 'This one is it today.'

He struggled to his feet, unfurling himself to his six-foot height, his jeans barely clinging onto his bony hips, and held out his hand. She took it and he heaved her into a standing position. She brushed herself down, flicking off bits of grit and dust. 'Thanks.'

They walked side by side along the corridor, passing wards still full of metal-framed beds, complete with stained mattresses, the horsehair stuffing spilling out onto the cracked tiled floors. In one side room stood an old dentist's chair in its reclined position, rusty instruments still on a tray beside it. They came to a corridor of tiny rooms, each barricaded with a thick steel door. Sarah closed one eye and squinted through a peephole. 'Looks like a padded cell.'

'Bloody hell, I wonder what they were used for. 'Ere, I wonder if your old man was ever shoved in one of those. He was a nutter, wasn't he?'

'Nathan!' she admonished. 'My father was not mentally ill. Why would you jump to such a conclusion? People were sent to asylums for all sorts of spurious reasons back then; not everyone was mad, and in any case my—'

He grabbed hold of her arm. 'This one's open. Will you lock me in?'

'What on earth for?'

'I just want to see what it's like. Go on, it'll be fun.'

'Fun? You need to get out more, Nathan.'

He heaved the door open and entered the tiny room. The floor was spongy and the walls were lined with canvas and padded with horsehair.

'Are you sure you want to do this?' asked Sarah, closing the door behind him.

His reply was muffled. Sarah looked through the peephole, but the blackness had swallowed him. She counted to ten before opening the door again.

He stepped out, grinning. 'That was awesome.'

She cringed at the use of the adjective. Clearly Nathan had led a sheltered life if he thought ten seconds standing in the darkness of a padded cell was awesome. Poor bugger.

'Come on, you.' She pulled him out but couldn't help smiling at his beaming face. 'We've got work to do.'

They'd reached the end of the corridor, the atmosphere now cool and clammy. There were only two tiny windows, high up on the wall ahead, which did not let in nearly enough light.

'What now?' asked Nathan.

'I'm sure there should be a door round here somewhere.' Sarah studied the floor plan again. 'Yep, there should definitely be a door along this wall.'

She stood, hands on hips, surveying the corridor. Her

gaze settled on a large wardrobe, one of its doors completely missing, the other one clinging on by a single hinge. She moved towards it.

'Hang on a minute. Look at this, Nathan.'

The back of the wardrobe was also missing. They both stared at the door behind, the blue paint peeling off in large curls. 'There it is,' declared Sarah. 'I knew there should be a door here.'

Nathan stuck his head inside the wardrobe and twisted the knob on the door. 'Blimey, all we need now is a lion and a witch.'

He heaved the wardrobe out of the way and Sarah charged at the door with her shoulder, then, when it failed to give, kicked at it with her boots.

Nathan intervened. 'You'll hurt yourself, Sarah. Here, let me.' He turned the handle patiently, listening for a click, and after a few jiggles the door opened. 'It just needed a little coaxing, that's all. There's no need to go at everything like a bull in a china shop.'

As their eyes adjusted to the gloom, they both stared up at the narrow wooden staircase behind the door.

Nathan grimaced at Sarah and gestured with his arm. 'After you.'

'You're such a gentleman, not to mention a coward.'

'Well it does look a bit creepy.'

'Says the man who sleeps in a derelict lunatic asylum every night.'

She tentatively tested the strength of the first stair, then, satisfied that it would take her weight, crept up to the top.

'What can you see?' called Nathan from below.

'There's another, smaller door, really low. I'll have to bend down to get in.'

'Wait for me, then, you can't go in on your own.'

They both crouched at the top of the stairs as Sarah turned the handle. The key was still in the lock and without much effort she was able to push the door open into a small windowless attic space. She reached into her bag, pulled out her pen torch and moved the dim light around the room, its beam lighting up layers of dust and cobwebs. A single bulb hung from the ceiling, covered in an opaque layer of grime.

Nathan pointed to the far side of the room. 'There's something over there.'

Sarah made her way across to where stacks of suitcases were piled up under the eaves. 'Nathan,' she breathed. 'Come over here. I've found something.'

He shuffled over to join her, his lanky frame making it awkward for him to move. He spoke in hushed tones. 'Why are we whispering?'

'Look at all these cases.' She pulled down the top one and blew off a cloud of dust. A brown luggage label was tied to the handle with a piece of frayed string.

He peered over her shoulder. 'Is there a name?'

She squinted at the label. 'No, just a number, 43/7.

Here, hold this.' She passed him the torch and with her thumbs tried to flip up the catches either side of the handle, but they were rusted and stiff. 'Damn, I think it might be locked.'

Nathan intervened. 'Here, let me have a go.'

Seconds later, he had managed to pop the catches and he slid the case over to Sarah. 'I'll let you open it.'

'Thanks.' She wiped her clammy hands on the bottom of her sweatshirt, knelt down and gently eased the lid of the case open. 'God, this hasn't been touched for years.'

She had almost lifted the lid clear when it suddenly exploded like an airbag from a dashboard. She scuttled back in alarm as Nathan jumped and banged his head on the wooden rafters.

'What the hell is that?' she exclaimed.

Nathan slung his arm across her body and shone the torch on the case. 'I've got this.' He edged forward and poked at the mound of white material with his toe.

Sarah pushed him out of the way and bent down to touch the fabric. 'Feels like silk.' She picked it up and shook it free, the folds of the material creased with age. 'It's a wedding dress.' She ran her fingers over the row of tiny pearls on the neckline. 'It's beautiful, but I wonder what on earth it's doing in here. It's been worn, too, judging by the yellow stains under the armpits.'

'She was a big lass,' Nathan observed. 'A family of four could go camping under that thing.'

He picked up a black-and-white photograph from the case. 'And look at this.'

They both studied the picture of the young man in uniform. He had his back to the camera but was looking over his shoulder, grinning into the lens, a cigarette hanging from his lips. He had the rugged good looks of a forties film star. At least he would have done if someone hadn't gouged his eyes out. Sarah held the photograph up and shone the torch behind it, the beam piercing the holes where his eyes should have been. 'Blimey, he must have *really* upset someone. This is absolutely fascinating. Let's have a look in some of the others.'

The attic space was long but low, the piles of cases wedged under the woodworm-infested eaves varying colours and sizes but all with a brown luggage label hanging off the handle. Sarah dragged down another case and flicked it open. She thumbed through the musty clothes, wrinkling her nose at the stale smell. Nathan pulled out a moth-eaten old jumper. 'Hey, looks like I've found myself a new wardrobe.'

Sarah glared at him. 'Don't you touch any of this stuff, do you hear me?'

He held his palms aloft. 'All right, I was only joking.'

Sarah rubbed her chin, frowning in concentration. 'We need to be methodical with this lot.' She scanned the room. 'There must be twenty-odd cases here, each with a story to tell.' She grabbed Nathan by the arm, her voice an excited whisper. 'This is a gold mine, Nathan. You mustn't tell anybody about it.'

He shrugged. 'Who'm I gonna tell?'

She took her camera out of the bag and flicked up the flash, snapping furiously at the stacks of suitcases. 'This is going to make a great cover for the book.' She knelt down and rocked back on her heels, scrolling through the photographs she had just taken.

Nathan hovered over her shoulder. 'I'll help you if you like.'

She studied him in the half-light, his pupils dilated, his mouth pulled into a wide smile. She'd never seen him look so animated. 'Thanks. I'd like that.' She hesitated. 'I'll pay you, of course.'

'That's not why I offered. I *want* to help you, that's all. I don't expect anything in return.'

She patted his knee. 'You're a good lad, Nathan.'

She stood up as straight as the low roof would allow and massaged her neck. 'We can't do much in this gloom. I'll come back tomorrow with a couple of lanterns and we'll start properly then. She packed away her camera. 'Why don't you come home with me, at least for a bath and a hot meal?'

He shook his head. 'I can't, I've told you before. Please just leave it.'

2

The rain had eased off by the time she arrived home. Her father was in the front garden, pulling up weeds, still wearing his shirt and tie, his sleeves neatly rolled up to the elbow. 'I'm back,' she announced, unnecessarily. 'How was the cemetery?'

He wiped his brow, leaving a faint smudge of soil across his forehead. 'Not too bad. I took a stiff brush to the headstone, got some of the muck off; bloody birds had been doing their business all over it.'

She turned to go indoors but stopped when he called her name. 'Sarah, have you given any thought as to when you might move back into your own place?'

She hesitated, searching for any hidden meaning behind his words. 'Well, I'm not sure. I thought you liked me living here. Are you saying you want me to go?'

His tone was matter-of-fact, dismissive almost. 'Well, you can't stay here forever, can you? I've got to learn to be on my own again.' He paused and loosened the knot in his tie. 'And so have you.'

It was the first time he had mentioned her situation in

such blunt terms. He knew only too well how much she hated living alone in her soulless apartment. She couldn't talk about this just now. She stared at him and changed the subject.

'I found something really fascinating at Ambergate this morning.'

He visibly bristled. 'Sarah . . .' he warned.

'No, it's all right. I know you don't want anything to do with it. I'm just telling you. I found a pile of old suitcases in an attic. I'm going to document the contents for my book.'

She didn't wait for a response but skipped over the threshold, leaving him standing there deep in thought, a worried crease across his forehead.

'Are you familiar with spreadsheets?' Sarah flipped open the laptop and sat cross-legged on the attic floor beside Nathan.

'I'm homeless, not thick.'

She had placed two battery-operated lanterns on the floor at either end of the attic space, which gave off sufficient light in which to work. 'Sorry. Here, look at this. I've made a sheet with these column headings: Label Number, Description of Case, Contents. All we need to do now is populate it.'

'Sounds simple enough. Give it here then.'

She passed him the laptop, then shuffled over to the case they had opened the day before. 'We might as well start with this one as it's already open. I'll call out the details and you type them in, okay?'

He gave a salute. 'Yes, boss.'

'Right, label number 43/7.'

Nathan tapped away on the keyboard.

'Description of case,' she continued. 'Navy blue with brown leather reinforced corners. Contents, one white silk wedding dress, one black-and-white photograph of a young man in uniform.' She picked up an item between her thumb and forefinger and held it at arm's length. 'One pair of . . .' She peered into the case again. 'No, several pairs of knickers, all white . . . well, whitish.' She sighed. 'God, this is a glamorous job.'

After two hours, they had documented and photographed around half of the cases. None had contained anything more exciting than clothes, books and toiletries, but all were poignant in their own way. How did one pack for a stay in a lunatic asylum, and why had all these people left without their possessions? Sarah rubbed her face and reached over for the cool bag she had brought. 'Time for some refreshments, I think.'

She pulled out a bag of crisps and lobbed them at Nathan. 'Here you go.'

He caught the packet. 'Cheers.'

'Have you saved that document?'

He tutted and looked up to the rafters. 'Yes, I'm not daft.'

She studied him through narrowed eyes. 'You did go to school, then?'

He shoved a handful of crisps into his mouth. 'Sometimes,' he said eventually. 'Other times, I bunked off.'

'Where?'

'Where what?'

'Where did you go to school?'

'A comprehensive, All Hallows, it's not round here.'

'You a Catholic, then?'

'What? No. Jesus, Sarah, what's with the inquisition?'

She poured two cups of tea from the Thermos. 'I'm only making conversation, Nathan, no need to get all defensive.'

He took a cup from her. 'I'm sorry. I just don't like talking about the past. I was . . . bullied at school. It holds very bad memories for me.'

'Must've been tough.'

'Yeah, it was.'

She left a pause, watching him as he gnawed at the skin around his thumb. 'Why don't you go back home, Nathan? I'm sure your parents must be frantic with worry. I know if it was my son who—'

He cut her off. 'You don't know anything about it. There's no way they'll be spending one second worrying about me. Please,' he implored, 'just leave it. You're wasting your time.'

She left a pause, waiting for him to calm down. 'Why are you so angry, Nathan?'

'I'm not,' he sighed. 'I'm sorry I bit your head off, okay.

It's just . . . Oh look, I'm fed up of talking about me. Tell me something about you now we're such good friends. Are you married?'

She absently massaged her finger where her wedding ring used to be. 'No, not any more.'

'Oh, sorry . . . Er . . . how long were you married, then?'

'Ten years.'

'Wow, that's a long time. What happened?'

She flicked him playfully on the arm. 'Nosy bugger, aren't you?'

'But it's all right for you to give me the third degree?'

She brought her knees up to her chest and laid her forehead against them. Closing her eyes, she allowed a vision of Dan into her head. It was painful to remember him, but the thought of forgetting him was even worse. 'We had everything, Dan and I. At least that's what it looked like from the outside. A big house, fancy cars, a hectic social life, two foreign holidays a year, all the shallow things that seem to make other people envious. But we really did love each other.'

'Sounds great. Where did it all go wrong?'

She gave a rueful smile. 'We didn't have the one thing we craved and longed for.'

He raised his eyebrows. 'Which was?'

'A baby.'

'Oh.'

'We spent a small fortune on IVF, but the cost couldn't

only be measured in financial terms. The emotional cost was far greater. I knew I'd become obsessed with having a child, so obsessed, in fact, that I ignored every other aspect of our marriage.'

Nathan pulled a face and placed his hands over his ears. 'Where's this going?'

She laughed. 'I'll spare you the details, Nathan, but nine months ago, Dan suddenly announced that he'd never wanted children and he'd only gone along with all the IVF nonsense, as he called it, for my sake.'

'The heartless bastard.'

'Yep. Needless to say, our marriage collapsed and I'm single again at the age of thirty-eight with any hope of ever having a baby diminishing with every passing month.'

'Is there any chance of the two of you getting back together?'

'Hmm, I'm not sure his pregnant girlfriend would go for that.'

Nathan spluttered on his tea. 'What?'

'Oh yeah, Dan moved on with alarming speed. Found a girlfriend almost half his age who he managed to impregnate within two months of their first meeting.' She shook her head. 'You couldn't make it up.'

'You'll meet someone else,' Nathan said. 'You're very attractive for a . . . well . . .' He faltered as he struggled to find the right words.

'Very attractive for an older woman, were you going to say?'

Nathan smacked his forehead. 'Aargh, sorry. I'm no good at this.'

'Where am I going to meet anyone? I divide my time between my job at the library and wandering round this place.'

'These things happen when you least expect them to.'

She fell silent, picked up a stick and began to trace circles in the dirt on the floor.

'Sarah?'

She took a deep breath and snapped the stick in two. 'It's so hard to imagine being with anyone else. Dan and I were together a long time. No matter how much I know he's hurt me, it's still difficult just to switch off my feelings for him. It would be easier to hate him, but I can't.' She heaved herself up. 'Come on, that's enough of my woes. Let's crack on, shall we?'

In a well-worn routine, she hefted down another case, placed it on the floor and sat down in front of it. 'Right, label number 56/178. God knows what all these numbers mean. There's no rhyme or reason to them. Okay. Description, brown leather, somewhat battered.' She attempted to flick up the catch, but it was stuck fast. 'Damn, I think this one's locked. How annoying.' She turned to Nathan. 'Do you have a Swiss Army knife or anything?'

He patted himself down theatrically. 'No, I must have forgotten to pack one when I stormed out.'

Ignoring his sarcastic reply, she shoved the case to

one side. 'We'll have to deal with that one another time, then.'

Two hours later, all the cases had been opened, documented and restacked, and they were both stiff from sitting on the bare floorboards in the cramped attic. Sarah stretched her arms over her head and yawned. 'Thanks for all your help, Nathan. I do appreciate it.'

'My pleasure. I've not exactly got a busy schedule.'

She stared at the only unopened case. 'A pity we can't get into that one, though. I hate leaving a job unfinished.' She fiddled with the catch again. 'I'll bring a hair grip or something tomorrow. Nathan?'

He was on his hands and knees, holding a lantern in front of his face, squinting in the fading light. He ran his hand along the rough floorboards, his fingers digging between the grooves.

'What are you doing?'

'I saw something.' He put the lantern down and used both hands to try and work the floorboard loose. 'There was something glinting in the light.' He fumbled around, cursing as a splinter of wood pierced his finger. 'Ouch.'

Sarah shuffled over to him. 'Let me have a look.' She took hold of his hand and ran her thumb over the end of his finger. 'I need to get that out.' She pressed hard, easing the tiny fragment of wood out from under his skin.

'Ow, that hurts.'

'Oh don't be such a baby. Here,' she showed him the splinter, 'it's out. Now, what were you looking for?'

He sucked his finger and nodded towards the floorboards. 'There's something wedged in there.'

Sarah followed his gaze, bending down to get a closer look. 'You're right.' She picked at the object with her fingernail until she managed to flick it out. They both stared at the small brass key. 'Well, well, well,' said Sarah. 'It looks like we won't be needing that hair grip after all.'

She pulled the last case towards her and slipped the key into the lock. After a bit of jiggling around, the catch popped open with a satisfying click. 'Bingo,' she whispered.

She lifted the lid and gave a low whistle. 'Well, this is a bit different.' The painting that sat on top of the rest of the contents was almost as large as the case itself. She glanced at her watch, aware of the advancing hour. 'Okay, one watercolour, unframed and signed by . . .' She pulled her reading glasses down from the top of her head. 'Signed by Millie . . . Millie McCarthy, I think it says.'

Nathan looked up from the keyboard, his eyes wide. 'At last, a name. I wonder why she was in here.'

Sarah continued to pick through the contents, dictating to Nathan. 'A pebble painted with a pink flower . . . a hairbrush.' She ran her fingers through the soft bristles and pulled out a strand of fair hair. She was holding the DNA of someone who had lived and quite possibly died here. The hairbrush was part of a set, pink padded silk on the back with a mother-of-pearl handle and a matching mirror. 'Correction,' she said. 'A hairbrush and mirror set.' She could hear Nathan tapping the delete key. She paused to let him catch up. 'Oh, look at this.' She held up a knitted teddy, made from odds and sods of different-coloured wool. An unexpected lump formed in her throat and she found it difficult to carry on.

'What's up?' asked Nathan.

'Nothing,' she sniffed. She composed herself before continuing. 'One hand-knitted teddy.' She propped the soft toy in the lid of the case. 'One . . . two . . . three floral dresses and . . . Oh my God.' She picked up the tiny blue jacket and held it to her nose. 'One baby's matinee jacket, blue.'

Nathan was unmoved. 'How do you spell that?'

'B-L-U-E,' she replied absently.

'Yes, thank you, Sarah. I meant that other word. The matinee whatsit.'

'Oh, M-A-T-I-N-E-E.'

'Anything else in there?' he asked.

Sarah stroked the soft wool, then held it to her cheek. With the other hand she swept the bottom of the case, her fingers alighting on a piece of paper, which had been folded in two. She put down the jacket and opened the note.

The first four words had been printed in capital letters and she didn't need her reading glasses to absorb the full impact of them. 'What in the name of . . .?'

Nathan stopped typing. 'What's up?'

She turned and wordlessly passed him the note.

'What's this?' He frowned as he read the words, a puzzled look crossing his face. 'Jesus Christ,' he whispered.

3

November 1956

She remembered the last time she had walked through these gates and down the potholed drive, edging her way towards the intimidating grandeur of the building. On that occasion too she had been sick with nerves, her lips dry and flaky but no saliva with which to moisten them. She glanced at the navy sky. With daylight still an hour away, the early-morning mist had not yet lifted and the grass verges sparkled with frost. She pulled her cape tightly across her chest and blew out a deep calming breath, which crystallised before her eyes as it met with the cold air.

As she rounded the bend and the imposing building came into view, the water tower dominating the skyline, her nerves were quelled by the tiniest frisson of excitement. On her very first day in the classroom, her tutor had informed them that all the Victorian asylums had been built at the end of long winding tracks, surrounded by high walls, hidden from the public. Growing up in the shadow of Ambergate, or 'The Big House', as they had all called it, she had heard a fair few horror stories over the years, and her young imagination had conjured up images of half-naked inmates, with caveman hair and wild eyes, hiding in the shrubbery, unintelligible sounds coming from their drooling mouths. Nobody in her family had known with any certainty what went on behind these walls, but she could hear her mother's threatening voice in her ear as she scolded Ellen or her younger brother: *You two drive me insane, I swear I'll end up in Ambergate*, or, if they had been particularly naughty: *I'll get the men in white coats to cart you off to The Big House if you don't behave.* Even the threat of a good hiding was preferable to that terrifying fate.

As she approached the main entrance, her thoughts turned to all the unfortunate people housed within this vast warehouse for the insane, many of them abandoned and forgotten by their families. She set her mouth into a grim line of determination and adopted a more purposeful stride as she climbed the stone steps and dug her thumb into the button by the side of the door. The bell rang long and shrill, and before she'd had time to adjust her cap, the door was opened by a small woman in a tweed suit who peered at her over her wire spectacles. 'Good morning.' She raised her eyebrows. 'Name?'

'Oh . . . good morning. My name's Ellen. Ellen Crosby.'

The woman opened the door a little further, allowing Ellen to cross the threshold. The clinical smell of disinfectant and over-boiled cabbage hit the back of her throat.

Memories of the last time she'd been here flooded back. It was the day of the entrance examination, and she'd been led to a classroom at the end of a seemingly endless corridor. The room was airless and stuffy, the only sounds coming from her pen scratching on the paper as she wrote, and the occasional knocking of the water hammer in the pipes.

She had only managed to complete around two thirds of the paper, so was somewhat surprised when a few weeks later a letter arrived offering her a position as a student psychiatric nurse. Maybe it had something to do with the fact that she'd been the only one taking the exam. She'd spent the previous four years working in a clothing factory, and although the pay was good, the hours were long and the work monotonous. Whilst it was true that her mother appreciated the money her daughter brought into the family home, she knew that Ellen had always harboured a desire to go into nursing. For her sixth birthday, Mrs Crosby had made her daughter a simple nurse's uniform and the young girl had not taken it off for two whole weeks. With the war still on, it hadn't been easy to get the materials, but Mrs Crosby had sacrificed an old pillowcase and a pale-blue blouse, which admittedly had seen better days but was good for a few more years yet. And it was Mrs Crosby who had left the paper open on the kitchen table showing the Situations Vacant column. She had drawn a red ring around 'Psychiatric Students Wanted – No Academic

Qualifications Needed'. The warning bells should have gone off right then.

'I said you're to start on Γ10. Long stay.'

Ellen stared at the woman, who was now holding a clipboard. 'What? Oh, sorry. Of course. Which way is that?'

'I'll get someone to come and show you momentarily. You can wait here for now.' She gestured to a wooden pew, and Ellen perched on the edge and rested her bag on her knee. She'd been too nervous to eat breakfast, and now her stomach rumbled, the hollow sound echoing round the room. She rummaged in her coat pocket for a mint to take the edge off.

'Student Nurse Crosby?'

A rather rotund woman with a doughy face extended a chapped hand towards her. Ellen shook it, the calloused palm feeling more like leather than skin. 'Yes, that's me, how do you do?'

'Very well, thank you. I'm Sister Winstanley. You call me Sister, all right?' Without waiting for an answer, she turned and headed back in the direction she had come from. 'Follow me.'

Ellen trailed behind, marvelling at how a woman of Sister Winstanley's size managed to walk at such a brisk pace when surely her thighs must be chafing together.

Sister's office was situated at the end of the ward, and as Ellen trotted through, she stole a glance at the shapes slumbering in the beds either side of her. There didn't seem to be any privacy for the patients, no curtains to pull round and no more than a foot or two between each bed. Despite the fact that the place looked spotless, there was a fusty smell in the air, no doubt coming from the bodies stagnating beneath the sheets.

'Have a seat.' Sister made it sound like an order as she gestured towards the chair in front of her desk. 'Now, have you had breakfast?'

Ellen shook her head. 'No, I couldn't . . .'

'Tell me, how do you expect to make it through a fourteen-hour shift on an empty stomach?'

'Well, I couldn't force anything down, I was too—'

Sister held up her palm. 'Please don't say nervous. This is no place for the fearful, you know. You need to be strong, assert your authority and start as you mean to go on.' She banged a fist down on the desk, causing her cup to rattle in its saucer. 'Never mind the six weeks you've spent in training school. That was a doddle. You've arrived at the coal face now.' She paused to let her words sink in. 'You sure you've got the stomach for it?'

Ellen straightened in her chair and tilted her chin upwards, forcing a note of conviction into her words. 'Oh yes, Sister, yes I have.'

Sister stared at her for a few seconds, her frown registering a slight doubt. 'Good, then we'll get along fine.' She stood up, a trace of a smile on her lips. 'Couple of boiled eggs do you?'

*

Ellen had just finished scooping out the last of the egg when she was startled by a presence in the doorway. She could hear Sister at the other end of the ward telling another patient not to stand in the chamber pot. She turned and smiled at the patient hovering nearby. 'Good morning. My name's Nurse Crosby. And you are . . .?'

The old lady stared through her, the whites of her eyes yellow and her irises a shade of murky blue. Her mouth caved in around her toothless gums, giving her the look of an emaciated gargoyle. Ellen stood up and took hold of the old lady's liver-spotted hand, the translucent skin making the veins beneath resemble a relief map. 'Can I get you something?'

The old lady continued to stare; didn't nod or shake her head, nothing. Her thin cotton nightdress had come undone and was gaping open at the front. Ellen retied it to preserve her modesty. The woman might not care that she was exposing herself, but Ellen did. Sister Winstanley appeared in the doorway, a murderous look on her face. She took a firm hold of the patient's arm. 'How many times? You're not to get up until you're told to. Now back to bed, Gertie, go on. I'll fetch your teeth shortly.' She tutted at Ellen. 'It's like herding cats sometimes.'

The old lady shuffled wordlessly back to her bed, feeling her way along the wall. She walked with an exaggerated limp, dragging her left leg.

'Why's she in here?' asked Ellen.

'Old Gertie?' Sister shrugged. 'I'm sure I don't know.

It's not my job to know. I'd have to look it up. Been here forty-odd years, I believe, but I've never heard her speak yet.'

Ellen did a quick mental calculation. 'You mean she's been here since before the war – the first one?'

Sister rubbed her chin and eyed Ellen up and down. 'She's well looked after, she gets fed three times a day, a bath as often as we can manage it, sometimes a walk if we've got time.'

'You make her sound like a dog.'

'Look, *Student* Nurse Crosby,' Sister put her hands on her hips, 'it's your first day so I'm going to let that one pass. You have to understand that some of these patients could not function on the outside. They're completely institutionalised and it would be cruel to turf them out. They wouldn't last a day.'

'But—'

'Enough, you're testing my patience now, and I've not got time to stand around debating the issue.' She ran her hands down her stiff starched apron and softened her tone a little. 'We do our best for them, you know. Where would Gertie be without us, eh?'

Ellen glanced at the old lady, who was now sitting on the edge of her bed, picking at the skin around her fingernails. She had undone the ties on her nightdress again, exposing herself for the whole ward to see.

'Why don't you start with toileting Gertie?' Sister said.

Ellen nodded. 'All right, I can do that.'

'And don't take all day about it; we've thirty-odd patients to get up and dressed before breakfast.'

Ellen approached Gertie, helped her off the bed and linked one arm through hers. 'Come on then, Gertie, let's get you to the bathroom, shall we?' There was no response. She guided the old lady into the toilet block and gestured towards a cubicle. 'Will this one do?' Still silence as Gertie backed into the cubicle, hoisted up her nightdress and settled herself on the toilet seat.

Startled to see there was no door on the cubicle, Ellen turned away to give her some privacy and busied herself straightening up the towels. The lumps of carbolic soap in the sinks were cracked and ingrained with dirt, and she made a mental note to ask for some more. She turned around as she heard Gertie coming out of the cubicle.

'All done? I'll just flush the . . .' She faltered, momentarily stuck for words. 'Oh, dear God, what have you got there?'

Gertie held out her palm. It was smeared with brown streaks, as was the front of her nightdress and the walls of the cubicle.

'What . . . Oh God, that's dirty . . . Gertie.'

Nothing she had learned in training school had prepared her for this. She grabbed the old woman's hands, thrust them under the hot tap and lathered up the dubious-looking soap. Then she took one of the towels off the rail, soaked it in hot water and swabbed the walls of the toilet cubicle, the stench causing her to retch as she tried to breathe through just her mouth. She was certainly regretting those boiled eggs.

'Gertie, that was very naughty,' she chastised, fully aware that she sounded as though she was speaking to a child.

Sister bobbed her head round the door. 'What on earth is taking so long? I told you we've . . .' She shook her head as she looked at the brown stains down the front of Gertie's nightdress. 'You turned your back on her, didn't you?'

Ellen bit down on her bottom lip and nodded. 'I wanted to give her some privacy.'

Sister sighed. 'There's a reason we don't have doors on the cubicles, you know. You can't take your eyes off these nutters for a second.'

Ellen blinked away the unwelcome tears. 'I'm sorry, I won't do it again.'

Sister smiled. 'Looks like you've learned this lesson the hard way, so we'll say no more about it.'

'Thank you, Sister, and again, I'm really sorry.'

'Hmm, you'll laugh about it one day, believe me.' Sister clapped her hands. 'But not today. Come on, chop, chop.'

By eight o'clock, the patients were all seated at the long dining table, identically dressed in their shapeless brown dresses. A tower of blackened toast was placed in the middle, and immediately hands grabbed from all directions, scattering it across the table.

'One at a time,' yelled Sister, collecting up the toast

and restacking it. She turned to Ellen. 'Student Nurse Crosby, would you mind handing round the plate? Honestly, it gets more like a chimps' tea party in here every day.'

Ellen passed the toast around the table as another staff nurse filled up the cups with weak tea. Sister doled out some rather unappetising greyish scrambled eggs, and calm descended as the patients tucked into their breakfast. They didn't interact with each other; there was no small talk, no conversation, just the sound of them noisily chewing the rubbery toast and slurping the tea, most of which ended up in the saucers.

Ellen circled the table, her hands behind her back, nodding and smiling in turn at the patients. Some of them returned the smile; others just grimaced and looked away. She noticed that Gertie had finished and was now rocking back and forth in her chair, drumming her fingers together. 'Gertie, would you like the last piece of toast?'

Before she had even finished speaking, the old woman sitting next to Gertie reached for the toast herself. Gertie picked up a fork and brought it down like a dagger on the back of the other woman's hand. She screamed in agony as blood spurted from the wound and splattered the tablecloth. Sister was on the scene in seconds. 'For crying out loud, Gertie, you don't make this easy for yourself, do you?'

Ellen stood anchored to the spot, rigid with horror, her mouth agape in a silent scream.

'Student Nurse Crosby!' Sister snapped. 'See to Rita, will you? I'll deal with this one.'

She placed her hands under Gertie's armpits and hauled her to her feet. Gertie kicked her legs as though she was riding an invisible bicycle, but she was no match for the formidable bulk of Sister Winstanley. The other patients began mumbling to themselves, or maybe to each other, it was impossible to say as Rita's screams drowned them all out. She clutched her injured hand to her chest and turned her fury on her assailant. 'You mad cow, you want locking up, you do.' There was no trace of irony.

Sister Winstanley intervened. 'Thank you, Rita. I'll handle this now.' She barked at Ellen, 'Count the cutlery back in, will you; there should be thirty-two forks and thirty-three knives, including the one stuck in the margarine.' Then she called for the staff nurse on duty, and together they dragged Gertie the length of the corridor, her feet barely touching the floor. Throughout the entire episode, the old woman had not uttered a single sound.

4

By the time she'd dragged her aching body up the stairs
to her first-floor bedroom in the nurses' home, Ellen was
fit to drop. Although the rest of the shift had passed
without incident, she had been deeply traumatised by what
she had witnessed with Gertie and couldn't bear to think
about the old woman languishing in the padded cell for
the rest of the night. Sister had assured her that she would
be checked on periodically and given something to eat.
They weren't monsters, she'd said. Ellen wasn't sure if she
was referring to the staff or the patients. In the dim light
of the hall, she fumbled in her handbag for her room key,
desperate to kick her shoes off and collapse onto her bed.
Unable to locate the key, she tipped her bag upside down
and picked through the contents on the hall floor.

'Hey, whatcha doing down there? Need any help?'

She stared at the feet standing beside her pile of clutter:
highly polished brogues, with the laces tied in a double
knot. She let her gaze travel upwards and cocked her head
as she scrutinised his face. He looked vaguely familiar;
she might have seen him before – in the students' bar if
memory served – but never here in the nurses' home,

and certainly not on the girls' corridor. She struggled to her feet, her face flushed and tears not far away. 'I can't find my key. I know it's in here somewhere.'

His knees cracked as he crouched down and began to sift through her things. It only took a few seconds before he straightened up again, triumphantly holding the key.

'Is this what you're looking for?'

Ellen exhaled with relief. 'Oh, thank you. It's been such a long day, I can barely seem to function.'

'I know the feeling. First day on the wards, was it?'

Ellen felt her bottom lip beginning to quiver, and not trusting her voice, she merely nodded.

He extended his hand. 'Douglas Lyons, second-year student.'

She reached out and shook his hand. 'Ellen Crosby, first-year student . . . obviously.' She gave a small laugh. He had an open, friendly face with a broad smile, and his blond hair was tousled as though he had run his fingers through it. 'I can't place your accent. Where're you from, Douglas?'

'Please, call me Dougie,' he invited, before continuing, 'My family's in Manchester now, but I was born in New York. My mother's from England, but she met my dad in the States and we lived there until I was nineteen. Mom was really homesick at first and they hadn't intended to stay that long, but then came the war in Europe and they decided it would be safer to stay put. We came back six years ago, when my grandma fell ill.'

Ellen stared up into his glacier-blue eyes. She hadn't expected him to answer with his life story and was conscious they were still holding hands. 'Well, I'm very pleased to meet you, Dougie, and thanks again.' She bent down and began to gather up the detritus from her handbag.

Dougie crouched next to her, their heads only inches apart. She could smell his cologne, fresh and dewy, like a pine forest after a downpour. 'Here, let me.' He scooped up the contents and handed the bag back to her. 'Well, I'd better get off this floor before the night matron puts in an appearance.' He lifted Ellen's hand and brought it to his mouth, delicately skimming her skin with his lips. It was a shockingly bold move, she thought, but that was Americans for you. Not that she'd ever met one in the flesh before. Then with a half-bow he turned and bounded down the stairs, leaving his aftershave lingering in the stale air of the hallway. She sniffed the back of her hand: carbolic soap. Considering the day she'd had, it could have smelled a lot worse.

She had not thought it possible to sleep so soundly. She'd been expecting a fitful night's rest filled with nightmares about marauding mental patients threatening to stab her, so she was somewhat startled when the bell of her alarm clock roused her from her sleep. The mustard candlewick bedspread lay in a crumpled heap on the floor. She stared at her uniform hanging on the back of the door, her stout black shoes neatly placed under the wicker chair.

She heaved herself out of bed and ran a sink of hot water. Whatever the day held in store, it could not be any worse than yesterday.

Back on the ward, she was relieved to see Gertie lying in her bed, her eyes wide open, staring at the ceiling, apparently none the worse for her ordeal in the padded cell, although it was difficult to know with any certainty. Sister Winstanley was being briefed by the night staff as Ellen entered the office and hung up her cape.

'Gertie's back on the ward.'

'Yes, Sister, I noticed.'

'You'll need to keep an eye on Rita. She won't exactly be welcoming her with open arms, and we don't want a riot on our hands.' Sister laughed as she took in Ellen's worried expression. 'Welcome to another day in paradise. Can you make a start on the teeth?'

Of the thirty-two patients on F10, eighteen of them wore false teeth. The night staff had cleaned the teeth and left them soaking overnight in individually marked glasses. Ellen collected the tray and began to make her way round the beds. It was a ghastly sight: eighteen glasses of false teeth, with their pale pink gums, bobbing around in sterile cleaning fluid. She felt like an extra in some low-budget horror film. She approached Gertie's bed first and gently touched her on the shoulder. 'Time to get up, Gertie. I've brought your teeth.'

The old woman stirred and Ellen helped her into a sitting position.

'How are you this morning?' No answer, of course. Close up, Ellen could see that Gertie's eyes were blood-shot and puffy, with mauve semicircles underneath. She looked as though she had been punched. Ellen pushed the thought from her mind. It was too horrific to contemplate. This was a hospital, a caring environment, not a maximum-security prison.

She set the tray on the end of Gertie's bed and inspected the labels. She found Gertie's glass and placed it on the cupboard beside the bed. She couldn't be sure if what happened next was deliberate or some sort of reflex action, but either way, Gertie's leg shot out from under the sheet and sent the tray crashing to the floor. Although it seemed to happen in slow motion, Ellen was not quick enough to grab it, and now seventeen sets of false teeth lay on the floor, their mocking rictus grins contrasting with the polished wood.

She stared silently at the hideous mess, wondering how she was going to get it all cleaned up before Sister found out. She was too late. As seemed to be the case whenever anything went wrong, Sister Winstanley materialised by her side in a second. 'What in God's name has happened here?'

Ellen glanced at Gertie, who stared impassively ahead. 'It was my fault, Sister. I don't know, it just . . . slipped.' She could feel the heat of embarrassment rushing to her face.

'Find an orderly to help clean this glass up, and then rinse the teeth under the tap.'

'Won't they need sterilising again?'

'You think we've got time for that? Just rinse them off and then hand them out.'

'But . . . but I don't know which teeth belong to which patient.'

'Then you'll just have to try them out for size. But don't take all day about it; if they end up with the wrong teeth it's not the end of the world. Half of them won't even notice.'

Ellen recoiled in disgust. The thought of having to wear someone else's teeth was enough to make her gag. She turned to Gertie, now sitting up in bed, cradling an empty glass. She ran her tongue over her lips, giving them a moist sheen before smiling at Ellen, revealing a perfect row of sparkling clean dentures.

5

Almost two months had slipped by since the last time she'd been home, but as Ellen surveyed the street where she had grown up, she was satisfied to see that nothing had changed. The gas lamps still brightened the greasy cobbles, and scabby-kneed kids still sat on the kerb, hunched over in little groups, sharing their childish gossip. She knew she should have warned her mother she was coming to visit, but it had been a spontaneous decision, and with no telephone there was no way of letting her know she was on her way. After her tumultuous start to life on the wards, she now had the luxury of a couple of days off, and the urge to return home to the sanctuary of her family was too strong to resist, even though she knew it would send her mother into a flap.

As she pushed open the front door, the smell of her mother's steak and kidney pie wafted through from the kitchen. Even though it would be more kidney than steak, it was enough to get her juices flowing.

'Mum,' she called out. 'It's me. Surprise!'

Mrs Crosby was sitting on an upturned fruit box by the fire, darning needle in hand and her cheeks aglow with the heat from the flames. She struggled to her feet as she greeted her only daughter. 'Ellen, love, why didn't you say you were comin' 'ome? I would've made summat special. Oh God, I hope there's enough to go round. Never mind, eh, Bobby can 'ave a couple of butties instead. I've got some bloater paste in t' larder. I'm sure he won't mind giving up his slice of pie for his big sister, and he'll still be able to drink t' cabbage water, won't he?'

Ellen smiled at how well she knew her mother. She was in a flap all right; she hardly drew breath.

They embraced, Ellen revelling in the comforting, familiar smell of her mother's skin. Mrs Crosby used the same brick of bright green household soap for scrubbing her husband's grubby shirt collars as she did to cleanse her own face. Maybe the slathering of cold cream she applied every night was enough to counteract the drying effect of the soap, because she was certainly glowing, with a radiant complexion the envy of some women ten years younger.

'It was a spur-of-the-moment thing really,' Ellen answered as she sank down into the only chair in the room – her father's chair. Mrs Crosby cast a nervous glance towards the door.

'It's all right, I'll get up when he gets in.'

'Well you know 'ow tired he is when he gets home from work, and I like him to get settled before he has his tea. You know, close his eyes for a while.'

51

Ellen shook her head. 'Was there ever a man who was looked after so well as my father?'

Mrs Crosby was on the defensive. She wiped her hands down her housecoat. 'Well, he works so hard for this family. It's back-breaking work, y'know, delivering coal, and he never stops all day; he even eats his butties on the go.'

'Mum, I'm only teasing you.' Ellen craned her neck to look through to the kitchen. 'Where is our Bobby anyway? It's getting dark.'

'Playin' outside still. I'm surprised you didn't see 'im. P'raps he's gone down to the rec for a kickabout. He'll be 'ome when he's 'ungry, I expect.'

Ellen adored her little brother, and the feeling was mutual. He was only eight years old, and the age differ-ence could easily have been a barrier, but a special bond existed between them. He had been devastated when he'd learned that Ellen was going away and had literally had to be peeled off her as she'd said her goodbyes.

'I've missed him. How he's doing?'

Mrs Crosby perched on the fruit box. 'Up to his usual mischief,' she sighed. She moved the fireguard away and picked up the poker. As she prodded at the fire, a flash of orange sparks rose up from the coals. 'I popped round to Hilda's last week to borrow a couple of spuds, and you know 'ow she likes to gas. Anyway, by t' time I got back, the little bugger was in the kitchen leaning on t' table, gawping into my mixing bowl.'

Ellen frowned. 'Had you been making a cake then? Was he eating the mixture?'

Mrs Crosby snorted. 'I wish! No, there was a bloody goldfish in there.'

'A goldfish? Where the heck did that come from?'

'Oh, the rag-and-bone man came and our Bobby rushed out to pet his 'orse as usual. Well, while he's out there, he spots a bucket of goldfish, doesn't he? The old guy says he can have one if he has anything for him. Bobby scurries back inside and comes out with my best coat, which I'd hung on the banister.' Mrs Crosby folded her arms across her chest and shook her head. 'The worst of it is, I haven't even finished payin' for it yet.'

In other circumstances this might have been a faintly amusing story, but Ellen knew very well how scarce money was in this household, and new clothes were a rarity. That coat would have been meant to last her mother for years. 'Can't you get it back off him, explain the mistake?'

'Too late. By the time I caught up with him, he'd already sold it.'

Ellen grabbed her handbag. 'Here, let me give you some—'

Mrs Crosby stood up. 'You're a good girl, Ellen, but we don't need your money. You keep it, you've earned it. We'll manage.' She changed the subject. 'Tell me about you. What's it like at t' hospital.'

'It's . . . challenging, but I'm getting used to it. I've been on a long-stay ward so far, but I'm moving to an acute-admissions ward on Monday, which should be better.' She stretched her arms above her head and yawned, the fire making her sleepy. 'There are some sad cases in that place, Mum. One old dear has been there for forty-odd years and she never speaks to anyone, not one word, ever.'

'Goodness me. She's a proper nutter, then?'

'Well, that's not a medical diagnosis, Mum, but yes, she must have problems. I'm going to look up her admission records when I get a chance and see why she's there. Everybody seems to have forgotten.'

A gust of wind blew in a swirl of crusty leaves as the door was flung open. Ellen's young brother was in such a rush to get in, he tripped over the threshold. He picked himself up and inspected his knees, then, satisfied that there was no damage, asked his mother, 'What's for tea, Mam? I'm starving.'

Mrs Crosby laughed. 'You're always starving. Tell me something I don't already know.' She ruffled his hair, then stood back and folded her arms as she regarded him.

'What?' asked Bobby.

She didn't reply; merely smiled and tilted her head over towards their father's chair.

He followed her gaze. 'Ellen! You came back!' he shrieked. He rushed over and scrambled onto her knee.

'I'm just visiting because I missed you so much.' She pulled him closer and kissed his forehead. He nuzzled into her chest.

'I had a goldfish, but it died.'

Ellen glanced at her mother.

'Oh yes, I didn't mention that, did I? The bloody thing only lasted a day.'

6

Reporting for duty on the acute ward felt like her first day at school all over again. There were so many new faces and names to learn. After a couple of days off, though, and with renewed vigour, Ellen felt ready to embrace the next challenge.

Whilst everybody seemed to have given up on the patients on the long-stay wards, including the patients themselves, here there appeared to be a more proactive attitude to nursing. On the long-stay wards it seemed more about containment than cure, somewhere to wait whilst eking out the last scraps of life. On this ward, though, the patients were given all the latest treatments and medication and some were expected to make a recovery. The doctor even put in an appearance. Some things were the same, of course: beds too close together, no doors on the toilet cubicles, baths placed side by side without a partition in between. Maybe the stench of decay was not quite so overpowering, but there was still a detectable smell of ammonia beneath the Dettol and Mansion Polish.

'Morning, Student Nurse Crosby.'

It seemed a mouthful, but Ellen had learned she would

not be known simply as Nurse Crosby until she had qualified.

'Morning, Sister . . .?'

'Atkins,' the woman supplied as she checked the label on a medicine bottle and placed it back in the cupboard. She was as tall and thin as Sister Winstanley was short and round, with her greying hair pulled into a tight bun. 'Welcome to the ward. Shall we start with a brew?' She nodded towards the battered teapot in the corner. Sister Atkins had a long face, with sharp cheekbones, bereft of make-up except for a slick of red lipstick, which seemed at odds with the rest of her plain appearance.

'Yes please.' Ellen could hear her mother's voice. *Never say no to a cup of tea and never pass up the chance to use the toilet* was her sage advice.

'We've got a new one coming in today, so I'd like you to take care of the admissions process.'

'Me? But . . .'

'Don't worry, it's quite simple.' Sister Atkins took a sip of tea, leaving a greasy red stain on the rim of the cup. 'Been on long stay, have you?'

Ellen nodded. 'Yes, it was . . . eventful.'

The other woman smiled. 'So I heard.'

Ellen's face coloured. The incidents with the toilet and the teeth had spread like measles round the social club and the nurses' home, and she could not walk down a corridor without someone giving her a knowing smile or a nudge.

Sister Atkins patted the back of Ellen's hand. 'Don't worry about it. Moments of light relief are scarce around here. Anything remotely funny is seized upon, retold and no doubt exaggerated.' She turned to the pile of notes on her desk. 'The new admission is due to arrive around ten, so I'd like you to go and prepare a bed, the one between Pearl and Queenie, then go to the stores and put together a new clothes bundle: nightdress, day dress, knickers and stockings. Try and find a dress that's not been boiled to death if you can.'

All the communal clothes were washed at scaldingly high temperatures to ensure that every vestige of vomit, sputum and other obnoxious bodily fluids was removed. Inevitably, it meant that the clothes shrank and were extremely drab and ill-fitting; itchy, too, if the way the patients clawed at their own skin was anything to go by.

Ellen returned with a stack of starched white sheets and began to make up the bed, beginning with the rubber sheet, which she pulled tightly over the mattress. She had no idea if the new admission was incontinent or not; it was just standard procedure. She glanced over at Queenie, who was lying on her own bed, fully dressed but with what appeared to be a hand-knitted cape draped over her shoulders and tied at the neck with a satin bow. Queenie was watching her carefully through narrowed eyes, her rust-coloured hair a frizzy ball of tight curls and her green eyeshadow looking as though it had been applied by a particularly heavy-handed toddler.

'Morning. I'm Nurse Crosby . . . Student Nurse Crosby.'

Queenie swung her legs over the side of the bed. 'Am I gettin' a new neighbour then?'

'Yes, she's due in shortly. I hope you'll make her feel welcome.'

'Depends on whether she's a right lunatic or not.'

Ellen slotted the pillow into its case and bashed it into shape. 'I don't know what the matter with her is, but I'm sure you'll get along if you try hard enough.'

Queenie changed the subject. 'When can I go home?'

'Well, that's up to the doctor, isn't it?' Ellen sat down next to her on the edge of the bed. 'How long have you been here?'

Queenie shrugged. 'Dunno, what year is it?'

'It's 1956, November.'

Queenie counted on her fingers. 'Well, I've been here since me father died in 1952, in the February it was, you probably heard it on the wireless and saw it in the papers. He'd not been well but we didn't know it was that serious.' She sighed and shook her head. 'I wish she'd just stayed there and never come back.'

Ellen was struggling to keep up. 'You wish who had just stayed where?'

'My sister, Elizabeth.' Queenie stared blankly ahead, tears not far away. 'If she'd just stayed in Kenya, I wouldn't be here now.'

7

She wasn't sure what to pack, or indeed how long she would be away. How many sets of underwear would she need, how many books should she take? The suitcase lay open on the bed, its brown checked lining now faded. She wandered over to her dressing table and picked up her mother's hairbrush, running her hand over the soft bristles. She'd spent many hours brushing her mother's auburn locks until they shone so brightly Amy imagined she could see her own reflection staring back at her. She took the brush and dragged it through her own hair, the static causing it to crackle and stick out. She knew she would never be as beautiful as her mother had been, but that didn't mean she shouldn't make an effort, especially today of all days. The set had been a wedding gift from her father, and she knew her mother had treasured it.

Her eye caught the gold carriage clock on the mantelpiece. She wandered over and picked up the watercolour that was propped up behind it, once again marvelling at the delicate brushstrokes that had been coaxed into producing such an evocative painting. The shades of gold, russet, ochre and sage combined to convey such a vivid depiction of the landscape that it made Amy gasp each time she looked at it, for even now she always discovered something new. At the sound of her father's voice bellowing up the stairs, she hurriedly plopped the painting on top of the clothes and other bits and pieces in the case. Then she closed the lid and fastened the catches.

'Amy. Are you ready?'

She stood at the top of the stairs, the suitcase hanging by her side. 'Is it time already? I thought we could have a spot of lunch before . . .'

Peter Sullivan stared at his daughter, a flash of irritation passing across his face. 'Amy, please don't make this any more difficult than it needs to be.' His voice was weary, each word cloaked with regret.

She grunted as she laid the suitcase on its side and pushed it down the stairs. It shot down like a sledge, causing her father to leap out of the way as it reached the bottom. She descended the stairs and picked up the case. It was worth one more try. She wouldn't make things easy for him. 'Is this really necessary?'

Noticing his glance towards the kitchen door, she followed his gaze to where Carrie stood, her hands clutching at the door frame. As they both stared at her, she folded her arms across her chest, obviously in no mood to argue. 'It's the only way, Amy, unless of course you want me to press charges.' Her gentle delivery seemed at odds with her defiant stance.

'There'll be no need for that, dear.' Peter spoke with a

firm tone, but as he went to kiss her goodbye, he tenderly tucked her blond curls behind her ears and stroked her cheek. Then he took hold of her shoulders and kissed her forehead, leaving his lips there for a few seconds. Unable to witness the intimacy between them, Amy pulled open the front door and strode off down the path.

She had never been the best traveller, and as they pulled up outside the entrance to Ambergate, she felt decidedly sick. She swallowed the saliva that flooded her mouth and tried to think of biting into a lemon. Imagining that bitter taste on your tongue was supposed to quell the nausea. It didn't work. Her father had driven too fast down the bumpy driveway, the Morris Minor's suspension no match for the potholes, and now he was already on her side of the car, wrenching the door open for her. It was as though he couldn't wait to be rid of her. He offered her his hand, which she brushed away, alighting from the vehicle under her own steam with as much dignity as she could muster. The car's flatulent exhaust had choked out some obnoxious fumes and she covered her mouth with her sleeve.

'You look a bit peaky,' he announced, taking the suitcase from her. 'Are you feeling all right?'

She glared at him, ignoring his ridiculous question. Of course she wasn't feeling all right. How could he be so insensitive?

Once inside the hospital, the feeling of nausea only

intensified. The clinical smell barely masked something else she was not able to identify with any certainty but guessed to be rancid cooking fat. Over the clattering of china she could hear someone moaning, the sound starting off low and then rising to a crescendo. Her thoughts drifted back to her days on the farm and the time the big old bull was suffering from an impacted bowel. He hadn't protested as much as whoever was making that dreadful racket. Honestly, was there really any need for all this? She turned to her father.

'Perhaps there's another way. I mean . . .'

Although he spoke softly and with compassion, his words left her in no doubt that he couldn't be swayed. 'It's for your own good, Amy, and that's the last I'll say about it.'

'But . . .'

'Amy, please. I love you, I'll *always* love you, but you need help.' He squeezed her arm, digging his nails in, a level of physical aggression he had never shown before, and his cold, dry eyes confirmed there was no point in arguing any further.

A jangling of keys heralded the unlocking of the door to the ward, and a young nurse beckoned them in.

'I'm Student Nurse Crosby,' she announced. 'I'll be dealing with your admission. Please come this way.'

Amy stared at the long ward looming in front of her, metal-framed beds barely wider than a coffin, windows obscured by thick bars. The suffocating atmosphere of desperation and lost hope made it difficult to breathe, and she had a sudden urge to charge out of the building and gulp in a lungful of fresh air, enough to last her for however long she was going to be forced to stay in this place. She could feel the panic beginning to rise; it started with the tingling in her toes, then rose slowly, steadily, like mercury in a thermometer, and she knew it wouldn't stop until it had reached boiling point. She swivelled round to address her father once more, appeal to his soft side, the one he'd had before *she* had calcified him. It wasn't fair, she hadn't done anything wrong; why would no one listen to her?

'Where's my father?' she demanded of the young nurse.

The nurse stared at her own feet, the hesitation in her reply exposing her discomfort. 'He . . . he's already left.'

'What? No! There's been a terrible mistake, I shouldn't be here. Please, you've got to believe me. It's all *her* fault.'

She wrenched her suitcase from the clutches of the nurse and belted towards the door, skidding on the highly polished parquet and sending a trolley full of medicines crashing to the floor. Her breathing came in short gasps as she grabbed the handle and twisted it. Her moist palms could not get the required purchase, and as she pushed and pulled, the door rattled in its frame but remained stubbornly shut.

A firm hand grasped her shoulder and she cried out in shock and pain. 'Get your hands off me.' She wriggled free and dug her fingernails into the space between the door and the frame, trying to prise them apart. She started yelling then. 'Help, help. I can't . . . I can't breathe, let me out, I need to go home.' She dropped to her knees and shouted through the gap at the bottom of the door. 'You can't do this. Father . . . come back . . . please.'

The edges of her vision were blurred, the creeping blackness smothered her and she knew she was going to swoon. She stopped screaming for a moment. What had made her think of such an old-fashioned word? Victorian ladies used to swoon after an attack of the vapours. She wondered if they had any smelling salts here, and was just about to ask when she felt a sharp prick in her upper arm, followed by a dull ache and a thud as her head hit the hard floor.

8

'When she comes round, I want you to take down all her details: height, weight, hair colour, a full description.'

Ellen frowned. 'Why do we need that? We know what she looks like.'

Sister Atkins didn't bother to hide her impatience. 'Don't they teach you anything in that so-called training school? It makes it easier to track them down if they go AWOL. You'll also need to check her for lice, on her head and down below, and give her a bath, and her hair's too long – use the scissors in my desk drawer – but before you do all that, label her suitcase and take it to storage. Attic room 12.'

Ellen was exhausted just listening to the instructions.

The walk to the storage room was more of an expedition than a quick errand, giving Ellen time to reflect on the new admission. Amy Sullivan was only a young girl; she couldn't have been any older than Ellen herself, and yet their circumstances were poles apart. Working on the long-stay ward had been bad enough, but those patients had reached the end of their lives and, let's face it, were simply waiting to die. Amy's life was just beginning, and yet here she was incarcerated against her will, a young girl with her whole future ahead of her.

Ellen glanced down at the directions Sister Atkins had given her. *First door on the right after the refractory ward, then second left after the kitchens, then all the way to the end of the corridor. Door is on the left at the end, a blue one.* Ellen had already been walking for twenty minutes, the suitcase now weighing heavily in her hand. She wondered if she would find her way back by following the directions in reverse. Perhaps she should have left a trail of breadcrumbs.

Finally she found the blue door, yanked it open and climbed the steep staircase to another door at the top, much smaller than the first one, meaning she had to bend down to enter the attic room. She fumbled around for the light switch. The dim, unshaded bulb hanging from the middle of the room provided barely enough light, but as her eyes adjusted to the gloom, she saw the suitcases stacked on top of each other, various shapes and sizes, all containing remnants of a life left behind. She couldn't stand up to her full height and her hunched-over position made it awkward, but she managed to wedge Amy's case on top of a stack of others.

The cobwebs hung heavy with dust and there was a lingering smell of mothballs, but after the chaos of the ward, it was peaceful up here and Ellen had the urge to sit a while and gather her thoughts. She looked at the labels on the cases and wondered what had become of their owners. She remembered Gertie then, forty-odd years stuck in this place, her life simply erased. Perhaps she had a suitcase here somewhere that would reveal more than Gertie herself was prepared to.

After a dressing-down from Sister Atkins for taking so long with the suitcase, Ellen sat on the end of Amy's bed, pen in hand, poised to take down the admission details of her new patient. The young girl was propped up on her pillow, arms folded tightly across her chest, a defiant look on her face. 'Where are my things?' she demanded.

Ellen tried to reassure her. 'I've taken your suitcase to storage; don't worry, it'll be safe there.'

Amy picked at the shapeless gown covering her slender frame. 'I'm not wearing this, I want my own clothes.'

'Sorry, all patients have to wear the hospital-issue clothes. Now, can you tell me your full name?'

'Yes, of course. I'm not bloody stupid. Amy Amelia Sullivan. When can I speak to the person in charge?'

Ellen glanced towards the nurses' station. Sister Atkins was busy attempting to get a rather difficult patient to finish her breakfast. Every time Sister raised the spoon of grey porridge to the woman's lips, she clamped her mouth shut. Sister Atkins whipped her hand across the patient's face, the sharp slap echoing off the bare walls. Then she pinched her nose between her fingers until her reluctant charge was forced to open her mouth. Sister shovelled in the porridge and wedged her hand under the patient's chin.

Ellen turned back to Amy. 'Look, a word of advice. Please don't make any trouble for yourself. You saw what happened when you created a scene before. You want to spend your time here drugged up – or worse?'

Amy fell silent and covered her face with her hands. 'My chest . . . it feels so tight, like a boa constrictor is about to make me his lunch.'

Ellen peeled Amy's hands away and held them in her own. 'Just breathe deeply for me, all right? I know this is a bit strange for you, but the sooner you accept that you're here, the sooner we can concentrate on making you better and getting you home again.' She gave Amy's hands a reassuring squeeze. 'That's a good girl. Look, I'm new here too.' Amy began to speak, but Ellen cut her off. 'Oh, I know our circumstances are different, but let's find our feet together, shall we?'

Amy nodded. 'I'm not mental, you know.'

'I'm not saying you are. Now, what's your date of birth?'

'Is that a trick question, to see if I'm a certified lunatic or not?'

Lord above. 'No, it's the standard admissions process.'

Amy sighed. 'Twenty-fifth of January 1937.'

Ellen hesitated before she wrote it down. She and Amy had been born only a week apart. 'Now, can you stand up whilst I measure your height.'

'I'm five foot three.'

'Well if you don't mind, I need to check.'

Amy threw off the thin cotton sheet and stood by the side of the bed as she allowed Ellen to measure her.

Ellen filled in the card. 'Yes, five foot three. Right, hair colour?'

Amy climbed back onto the bed. 'Butterscotch. My mother always said my hair was the colour of butterscotch.'

Ellen scanned the admissions card. 'I don't have a box for that, I'll just have to put light brown. Eye colour?'

'Chocolate.'

Ellen smiled. 'Let me guess. Your mother always said your eyes were the colour of chocolate.'

'Are you making fun of me?'

'Gosh, no, I'm sorry. I'll just tick brown, then. Now, I need to check you over for . . . um . . .' She cleared her throat. 'Lice.'

'What? I've not got lice; where the hell do you think I've come from?' The girl had the face of a cartoon fawn, her big eyes framed with long, sweeping lashes, but the sudden flash of anger had hardened her pretty features. 'Get me the person in charge, now,' she demanded.

'I'm afraid it won't make any difference; she's the one who gave me the instructions.'

As though sensing some drama, Queenie shuffled over and flopped down on her bed next to Amy's. 'I hope we don't have a troublemaker in our midst.'

'Who asked you?' snapped Amy. 'Just keep your beak out.'

'You need to learn some manners, young lady. Don't you know who you're talking to?'

Ellen intervened. 'Now, now, ladies, let's all calm down, shall we? Queenie, would you mind giving us some privacy?'

'Oooh,' Queenie sing-songed. 'Hark at you, Nurse. Only been 'ere five minutes and already throwing your weight around. I might have to bring you down a peg or two. How about a stretch in the Tower, eh? See how you like that.'

Amy raised a finger to her own temple and made a circular motion. 'Completely cuckoo, I assume?'

'Delusional,' Ellen confirmed. It was time to stamp her authority. 'Come on, we'll go to the bathroom, get you into a nice hot bath and I'll check you over for . . . well, you know.'

Two high-sided Victorian baths stood next to each other on the tiled floor. Ellen turned on the huge taps, the water gushing out in a torrent. She added a capful of Dettol and swirled it around with her hands, then turned to Amy. 'Could you remove your dress, please?'

Amy hoisted the garment over her head and tossed it on the floor, leaving her naked from the waist up.

'Thank you, and . . . your knickers.'

'You want a good gawp, do you? Do you fancy girls, then?'

Ellen refused to be riled, although she wasn't sure how

to handle this sudden truculence. 'No, I don't. I'm just doing my job.'

Amy pulled down the baggy knickers and stepped out of them. She bent down, hooked them onto the end of her forefinger and held them aloft. 'Where do you want them?'

'Over there, with the dress.'

Now completely naked, Amy stood with her hands on her hips and thrust her shoulders back. 'Come on then.'

Unnerved by the confrontational stance, Ellen forced herself to take a step forward. 'Could you just stand with your feet apart, please?'

She picked up a small comb, then bent down and gently parted the girl's pubic hair. She would not be rushed, would not let this girl think she was uncomfortable with the task in hand, even though she would rather have stuck pins under her own fingernails. As she worked the comb through, trying to calm her trembling fingers, she sensed Amy's legs stiffen and her stomach muscles tense.

'All done, you can climb into the bath now.'

She supported the girl at the elbow as Amy lifted her leg over the high-sided bath, and pretended not to notice the solitary tear that slid down the side of her nose. Kneeling down and picking up a small pan, she scooped up bathwater and poured it over Amy's head. She lathered up the carbolic soap and massaged the suds into her hair.

'What the hell are you doing?'

'Washing your hair.'

'With soap? Are you mad? I'll never get the comb through it.'

'There's no shampoo here, I'm afraid.' She rinsed off the soap, Amy's hair hanging in long tendrils down her back. Stripped of its natural oils, it was now squeaky clean. 'I need to cut it, it's too long.'

'Over my dead body. You're not coming anywhere near me with a sharp implement.'

Ellen ignored the protest as she gathered Amy's hair into a ponytail. It would be a shame to cut it off, but she knew that if she did not obey Sister's instructions, not only would she be in yet more trouble, but Sister Atkins herself would then hack it all off with far less style and finesse. She gripped the bundle of hair in one hand whilst surreptitiously reaching down with the other for the scissors. Then as efficiently as the blunt instrument would allow, she snipped off the length of Amy's hair.

Back in Sister's office, Ellen left the completed admission card in the wire basket on the desk, ready to be added to Amy's records later.

'What a flamin' performance that was.' Sister Atkins appeared, tossed the empty breakfast bowl onto the food trolley and rubbed her hands together. 'That'll teach the little bitch to try and bite me.'

Ellen peered round the door and saw that the patient who had been subjected to the force-feeding was now lying on her bed, her arms stretched wide above her head, her wrists strapped to the metal frame with bandages, her gagged mouth only capable of uttering the most guttural of sounds. She flailed her legs, causing her dress to ride up and expose the baggy knickers all the patients had to wear.

Ellen began to protest, but the shock had rendered her speechless. 'I . . . I don't . . .'

Sister Atkins stood with arms akimbo and skewered her with a stare. 'You don't what, Student Nurse Crosby?'

'Well, I mean, that's not very . . . well they didn't teach us any of that in school.'

'Now look here. I'm in charge of this ward, not your bloody tutors. They haven't been near a patient in years.' Sister waved her arm in a sweeping arc. 'You've got to show these lunatics who's boss, or before you know it they'll be taking over and we'll all be doomed.'

'But look at Amy,' Ellen protested. 'She's only a young girl; she shouldn't see that, she'll be terrified.'

Sister Atkins snorted. 'If early indications are anything to go by, that girl's more than capable of handling herself. A feisty one she is, and no mistake.' She softened her tone a little and placed a conciliatory hand on Ellen's shoulder. 'I was just like you once, believe it or not. Oh yes, when I first started here, I thought I could change the world too. You think things are bad now, but back in the thirties it was far worse. On one of my first shifts, me and another student nurse were sent to the refractory ward, where the most dangerous patients were kept locked away in side rooms. We were told to stick together, but my colleague had other ideas. She thought we could get the round done quicker if we split up, and before I could protest, off she went. I was terrified, I don't mind admitting. We only had to collect the chamber pots, but these were the most disturbed patients in the whole hospital. I've never worked so fast in my entire life, and by the time I reached the end of the ward, my colleague was nowhere to be seen. I thought, bloody charming that is, she's left me and gone back to the main ward.' She dropped her voice a little. 'But she hadn't. A massive search was undertaken, but it wasn't until that afternoon that they found her under one of the patient's mattresses.'

Ellen was transfixed. 'Oh, that's awful.'

'An understatement if ever there was one.' Sister's brittle tone was back. 'So if I tell you a patient has tried to bite me, forgive me if I seem to be a little harsh in response.'

Ellen bent her head and stared at the floor. 'Yes, Sister, I'm sorry.' Apologising was all she seemed to do these days. 'Was she all right . . . your friend, I mean?'

'She most certainly was not all right.' Sister Atkins left a suitably dramatic pause. 'She'd been strangled.'

9

The social club heaved with bodies, a fog of cigarette smoke hanging above their heads, the sound of raucous laughter a reminder that they were all human beings with a life outside the asylum. This was the place where staff came to unwind at the end of a long shift, a place to let go of pent-up frustrations in the company of other people who knew exactly how you felt. Students who had never touched a drop before suddenly found themselves ordering pints with whisky chasers, doubles at that.

Ellen pushed her way through the throng and shouted her order to the bar steward. 'Two fingers, please, Jack.'

He sloshed the whisky into a glass and slid it across the bar. She downed it in one, the sharp taste making her eyes water as she spluttered, 'Same again, please.' She thumped her chest.

Jack smiled. 'That bad, is it?'

She grimaced as she took the second drink, made her way to a nearby table and pulled up a low stool. It really wasn't the place to come if you wanted peace and quiet, but she just needed a few moments to let the drink work its magic. She thought about her mother, the woman who battled all life's hardships without turning to hard liquor. In fact she only drank once a year, a small glass of sweet sherry on Christmas Day, taken one minute after midday and not a moment before. Thinking of home brought on an unexpected rush of sadness. Ellen let her head loll back against the wall and closed her eyes, the glass resting in her lap.

'This one taken?'

She opened her eyes as Dougie pulled up another stool. 'No, please join me, and let me get you another when you've polished that one off. It's the least I can do after you helped me the other week. Where've you been, anyway?'

'Back in school, unfortunately.' He took a long swig of his pint. 'I've sure missed this place, though.'

'Have you really?'

He laughed. 'You'll get used to it. The classroom's a pretty dull place after the excitement of the wards.'

'Hmm, that's one word for it, I suppose.' She gulped down the rest of her drink, trying not to imagine her mother's disapproving stare.

'Let *me* get these and you can tell me all about it.' Dougie rose from his stool, took her glass and elbowed his way to the bar.

He was taller than most of the other students and had no problem in shouting his order over their heads. He returned with the drinks, his face flushed and a fine emulsion of sweat on his top lip. He lifted his chunky cable-knit sweater over his head and blew a cooling plume of air over his own face. The shirt underneath rode up, giving Ellen a glimpse of his well-defined torso, with a line of golden hair travelling down from his belly button to . . . oh dear God. Her face on fire, she pushed the thought from her mind and looked the other way.

'Well that sure is better,' he declared, tossing the heavy jumper onto a vacant stool. 'Now, how's it been? Come on, don't spare any details.'

'I'm surprised you haven't heard already; everybody else seems to have done.'

He shook his head. 'I've kept a low profile; been revising, you see. Why, what's happened?' He edged closer and folded his arms on the table between them. 'Come on, honey, you can tell your Uncle Douglas.'

She hung her head and picked at the beer mat, eventually lifting her eyes to meet his inquisitive gaze. 'I'm beginning to wonder if this job is right for me. I seem to be a laughing stock round here.'

'I'm sure it's nothing personal. Student nurses are fair game, I'm afraid.' He leaned in closer and lowered his voice. 'When I was a first-year student, my charge nurse sent me over to the female side of the hospital to collect some supplies from Matron. I was terrified of that woman, I don't mind admitting. She ruled the place with an iron fist and never bothered with the velvet glove. Her voice only had two levels: bellowing if she was in a good mood and thundering if she considered you to be a halfwit.'

Ellen took a sip of her drink. 'I'm sure you could never be considered a halfwit, Dougie.'

'Oh no? I looked down at what the charge nurse had written and asked Matron for a box of fallopian tubes.'

Ellen snorted on her drink and covered her mouth with the back of her hand. It was a few seconds before she could speak. 'Oh Dougie, you didn't.'

He leaned back in his chair, holding his palms up. 'As I said, fair game, us students.'

Sister Winstanley from the long-stay ward lumbered towards them, a pint in each hand, froth cascading down the sides. Broken veins mottled her cheeks. 'Evening,' she nodded. 'Sorry, I've forgotten your first name.'

'It's Ellen.'

'Right, listen. Old Gertie's been moved to the sick ward. I thought you'd like to know, as you seemed to take an interest in her.'

'What's the matter with her?'

Sister Winstanley shrugged. 'I don't know what the diagnosis is, but she'd started bringing up blood and the doctor says there's fluid on her lungs. She can't breathe right, either.'

'Has she said anything?'

'Don't be daft, of course she hasn't. Not one word for donkey's years; what makes you think she's going to start talking now? I've never 'eard her voice yet.'

'I'll pop in and see her when I get the chance.'

Sister Winstanley laughed. 'You're a proper soft one, you are, but you'll be wasting your time.'

She caught the eye of a colleague over in the corner and bustled off, leaving Ellen and Dougie alone again.

'What was that all about?' he asked.

'Oh, there's a patient on long-stay who hasn't spoken a word for years.'

'Good Lord, how incredible.'

'Apparently she did speak to begin with but nobody seems to remember her doing so.'

'How long has she been here?'

'Forty-odd years, they tell me.'

Dougie traced his lips with his forefinger, his brow furrowed. 'Why don't you look up her admission records?'

'I've checked the filing cabinet in Sister's office, but there's no file there for her. She's been here that long, it's as though she's part of the furniture instead of a human being with feelings.'

Dougie drained his pint and set his glass down. 'Come on, sup up, as they say round these parts.'

Ellen rose from the stool and gathered her bag. 'Why, where are we going?'

Once outside in the frigid air, Ellen wrapped her arms around herself, her breath billowing around her face. She blew out hard, as though trying to extinguish candles on a birthday cake. 'When I was a kid, I used to pretend I was smoking when the air was this cold.' She placed her forefinger and middle finger to her lips and sucked on her imaginary cigarette before breathing out again. 'It used to make me feel so grown up to see all the smoke.'

Dougie ferreted in his back pocket and pulled out a packet of Capstan. 'D'ya want one for real?'

Ellen wafted away the packet. 'Oh blimey, no. It seemed very exotic when I was a kid, but the reality's somewhat different. It just made my eyes water and my throat sore.'

'You obviously weren't doing it right. D'ya mind if I do?'

'Not at all, go ahead.'

She watched as he struck a match and cupped his hands around it, the yellow glow lighting up his face for a second. The phosphorous smell hung in the air.

'Are you warm enough?' he asked. Without waiting for an answer, he slung his jumper-clad arm around her shoulder and pulled her closer. 'Come on, let's pick the pace up a bit.'

By the time they arrived at the hospital, they were both breathing heavily from the exertion of the brisk walk. Ellen's lungs ached from the onslaught of icy air. 'My . . . my chest hurts,' she gasped.

'You'll feel better once we get inside. Come on.'

She surveyed the villa in front of her. It stood to the right of the main building and was almost as impressive as the hospital itself, but on a much smaller scale. The leaded windows set into stone frames and the elaborate cornice on the clock tower hinted at a degree of craftsmanship usually reserved for only the most eminent of palaces.

'This is the administration block. It's where most of the patients' records are kept, along with staff records, past and present,' Dougie explained.

Ellen squinted at the clock. 'Will there be anybody here at this time?'

'There's always someone here, Ellen. Follow me and I'll introduce you to Fred.'

He propelled her towards the wooden front door and pulled back the thick iron knocker. After three loud raps they could hear the sound of keys jangling on the other side, and the door was eased open a crack.

'Evenin', Fred.'

The door creaked open a little further and a tiny man with wispy white hair peered over his spectacles. 'Who goes there?'

'It's me . . . Dougie. How've you been, Fred?'

The old man gave a chortle and beckoned them inside. 'Douglas, my friend, come in. You all reet?'

'Aye, that we are,' Douglas mimicked, his American accent temporarily quashed. 'This is Student Nurse Crosby, she needs some help.' He turned to Ellen. 'This here is Fred, used to be a patient here many moons ago and now can't bring himself to leave us, can you, Fred?'

The old man took a playful swipe at Dougie. 'A cheeky Yank, you are. Now come in an' we'll 'ave a snifter.'

Fred's office was uncomfortably hot. It stank of

paraffin and was lit by a heavily shaded Anglepoise lamp. His newspaper was spread out on the desk, a half-empty bottle of whisky on the table beside it. He poured out two more glasses and refilled his own, then held it aloft. 'Nice to see yer again, Douglas. It's bin too long. Now what can I do for yer?'

Ellen spoke up. 'I'm looking for the admission records of Gertrude Lewis. She's been here for forty-odd years and that's about all I know, I'm afraid.'

Fred narrowed his eyes. 'Hmm, that name sounds familiar. Perhaps our paths crossed whilst I was in 'ere proper like.' He scribbled something down on the edge of his newspaper, then shoved the end of the pencil into his mouth. 'Forty-something years? So we're looking at an admission year of, let's see, 1916, would be forty years, but you think it's more than that?'

'Yes, I believe so,' said Ellen. 'I'm sorry I don't know the exact year. Do you think you can help us still?'

'It's what I'm 'ere for, in't it?'

He heaved down a monstrous leather-bound ledger, its pages yellowed with age. He ran his finger down a column, flicked over the page and repeated the process. 'Hmm . . . yes, 'ere we are, that's the one.' He made another note in the margin of his newspaper, then opened a mahogany cabinet on the wall. Row upon row of keys dangled from brass hooks. He selected one and tossed it over to Dougie. 'Room 10, upstairs, first on yer left. The records 'ave been archived.'

*

The room was packed with wooden shelves, only the narrowest of aisles in between, and there was a grittiness beneath their feet, the result of year upon year of collected dust, the musty smell reminiscent of second-hand book-shops.

'Phew, where do we start?' asked Ellen as she surveyed the endless boxes packed together. 'I can't actually believe Gertie's records have been archived. She's still a patient, for goodness' sake. She's not dead yet.'

'It looks worse than it is. It's all alphabetical.' Dougie pointed to the first row of shelves. 'That's A to C, so we can forget that one.' He marched ahead down the next aisle. 'This one's D to F; we're getting closer.'

Ellen skipped an aisle and ventured down the next one. 'Here we are,' she called. 'I'm in J to L.'

Dougie appeared by her side and together they traced their fingers along the boxes, carefully scrutinising the names on the yellowing labels. 'Langton to Lipman,' read Ellen aloud. 'This must be the one.'

Dougie heaved it down from the shelf, the sheer weight of it taking him by surprise. 'Let's take it over to the table.'

Ellen lifted the lid and peered inside at the tightly packed files. She licked her forefinger and began to flick through them one by one. 'Here it is, Gertrude May Lewis.' She wrestled the buff file free and spread it open on the table. Dougie pulled up a chair and they sat side by side, their heads only inches apart as they pieced together Gertie's history.

Ellen pointed to the admission date. 'Look at that, 1 September 1912.'

'There you go then,' said Dougie. 'She's been in here for . . .' He began to count on his fingers.

Ellen saved him the trouble. 'Forty-four years.'

He seemed impressed. 'That's quick math.'

'Maths,' she corrected. 'You've surely been here long enough to know that?'

'But . . .' He stopped when he noticed her teasing smile.

Ellen continued studying the file. 'She was born on 12 August 1871, so that makes her, what, eighty-five now and . . . forty-one when she came to Ambergate.' She shook her head and gazed at the ceiling. 'She's been here for half her life.'

Dougie angled the file so he could get a closer look. 'Says here she was admitted with a diagnosis of intellectual insanity and melancholia.'

They pored over the file in contemplative silence as they learned the scant details of Gertie's admission. Found wandering the streets of Manchester in stockinged feet, without a single penny to her name, she'd been brought in by the local police constable after he could find no good reason to keep her in his cells. The notes described her as being five foot six, of slight build, with waist-length brown hair.

'God, she's a shadow of her former self. She must only be about five foot now, and her hair is coarse and white.'

'She is eighty-five,' reasoned Dougie. 'I'm sure her hair

would've been white by now even if she'd spent her entire life cocooned in luxury.'

'Mmm . . . I suppose you're right.' Ellen continued to read. 'Hang about, according to this, she's married.' She frowned at Dougie. 'How odd that she appeared homeless when she was admitted. Perhaps he'd chucked her out.'

'Yeah, that could be it,' agreed Dougie. 'Maybe that's why she went loopy.'

'It says here she had a course of ECT that began in April 1940.' Ellen raised her eyebrows. 'What's that?'

'Electroconvulsive therapy,' he confirmed. 'Electrodes are placed on both sides of the patient's head, and up to a hundred and fifty volts passes through their brain.'

'Lord above, that sounds gruesome.'

'It's got a lot better,' said Dougie. 'At least the patient is anaesthetised nowadays and given a muscle relaxant.'

Ellen picked up the notes and read aloud. '"The patient has responded well to the latest course of ECT and did not protest as much, which is a positive step. She displays all the signs of retrograde amnesia, having no memory of the treatment itself. During the last administration of ECT on 8 September 1940, the patient suffered a double fracture of the left leg during a particularly violent convulsion. At the time of writing (16 September 1940) she refuses to speak to anyone and seems introverted and withdrawn. Her mood is apathetic but she is no longer complaining, so I conclude that the ECT has been successful and recommend no further treatments.

However, there is nothing medically wrong with her that prevents her from speaking, so she remains certified."'

'That's so sad,' said Ellen, placing the notes back in the file. 'She hasn't uttered a word for sixteen years. That can't be right. I'm going to see her tomorrow and I don't care what Sister Winstanley says. This place has let her down and it's time someone did something about it instead of just idly standing by.'

Dougie smiled at her determination. 'You do that, Ellen. Someone's gotta fight Gertie's corner, and I can't think of anyone better.'

10

'Good morning, Sister Atkins, how are you today?'

'Very well, Dr Lambourn, yourself?'

'Can't complain.' The doctor blew on his hands and rubbed them together. 'I say, it's nippy out there this morning.'

Sister Atkins thrust a mug in his direction. 'Here, get yer 'ands round that.'

'Thank you, Sister.' He began thumbing through the files on her desk. 'I need to see the new admission – what's her name, Amy something?'

'Sullivan,' she confirmed. 'You'll need to be firm with her. She's a troublesome one if you ask me.'

Dr Lambourn continued to flick through the files, then looked up. 'Well I didn't.'

'Didn't what, Doctor?'

'Ask you.'

She pursed her lips and gave him a contrite stare. 'Of course, Dr Lambourn. I apologise.'

He nodded. 'No harm done, Sister.'

It was all very well being approachable and friendly with the nursing staff, but sometimes they overstepped the mark and needed reminding who was actually in charge around here. The staff nurses and sisters were mostly older than he was and he found their flirtations mildly amusing, sometimes pitiful. Through the office window he caught sight of a young nurse gently brushing a patient's hair, smoothing it down and smiling as she chatted.

'A new recruit, I see.' They were always easy to spot.

Having recovered from the doctor's slap-down, Sister joined him by the window. 'Aye, that's Student Nurse Crosby. She's very . . . shall we say enthusiastic?'

Dr Lambourn tucked a file under his arm. 'I'll go and introduce myself. Which bed has Amy Sullivan been allocated?'

'The one between Pearl and Queenie.'

Dr Lambourn smiled knowingly. 'Lucky girl.'

He approached the nurse from behind and gave a small cough. 'Ahem, I don't believe we've met.'

The girl twisted round to face him. Her dark hair had been scooped into a tidy bun beneath her cap, save for a stray strand that hung down the middle of her forehead. She attempted to blow it out of the way as she wiped her hands down her apron.

'I'm Dr Lambourn and you are Student Nurse Crosby, I believe.' He held onto her sweaty palm, amused by the rush of heat to her neck.

'Yes, that's right, it's Ellen. I'm very pleased to meet you, Doctor.'

'And how are you settling in?'

'Well it's not too bad. I'm a quick learner.' She hesitated and dropped her voice a little. 'Since you're here, I wonder if I may have a word.' She glanced at Pearl sitting in the chair, her ample frame spilling over the sides. 'In private?'

'I can still 'ear you, you know. I may be daft, but I'm not deaf an' all.'

'Sorry, Pearl. Don't worry, it's not about you. I'll be back to finish your hair shortly.'

Dr Lambourn guided her to the end of the ward. 'Well, what is it?'

'There's a patient in the sick ward who I really think needs to see a doctor. Not a medical one, one who can . . .' She tapped her own temple with her forefinger. 'Sort her out.'

'A psychiatrist?'

'Yes, that's it. I was wondering if you could pay her a visit?'

Sister Atkins had not exaggerated this girl's enthusiasm. 'Tell me, Student Nurse Crosby, when were you put in charge of this hospital? The last time I checked, student nurses ranked one above the old boy on the refractory ward who empties the chamber pots for three-pence a week.' Although his words were spoken with the hint of a wry smile, they were enough to cause her hands to fly to her mouth and the words to come spluttering out.

'I . . . I'm sorry, Dr Lambourn, I didn't mean . . .'

He placed his hand on her shoulder. 'Rest assured that

this patient of yours will be receiving the very best care this hospital has to offer. You don't need to worry or take it upon yourself to recommend treatment.'

She nodded. 'I understand.' His potent aftershave was making her eyes water.

'Good, now can you tell me where I can find Amy Sullivan?'

'Yes, she's in the day room, Doctor.'

Ellen returned to Pearl and resumed brushing her hair more savagely than she intended.

'Ow,' protested Pearl.

'I'm sorry, Pearl.' She laid the brush down and took a strand of Pearl's hair between her fingers instead, gently teasing it into a loose curl.

'He's gorgeous, isn't he?'

'Who is?' asked Ellen, genuinely puzzled.

'Dr Lambourn. He looks just like Clark Gable, without the daft 'tache, of course. 'Ere, how old do you think he is?'

Ellen blew out her cheeks. 'I've no idea, I didn't really look at him that closely. Thirty-ish, maybe a bit younger, I would guess.'

'I think he has some foreign blood in him, Mediterranean perhaps.'

'Well, I suppose he does have a rather swarthy complexion. Anyway, it's none of our business where he—'

'He's not married, you know,' Pearl interrupted.

'So what, Pearl? I couldn't care less if he's married or not. It's of no consequence to me.'

Pearl chuckled to herself. 'That's what they all say.'

He saw her in profile first, silhouetted in the window as the low morning sun shafted its beam across the carpet. She sat with her hands in her lap, one thigh crossed over the other, making circular motions with her raised foot. Her 'Ambergate Special' haircut exposed her slender neck. Whoever had cut it had not done a bad job. He'd seen a lot worse. He touched her shoulder. 'Amy Sullivan?'

She gazed at him, her deep brown eyes opening slightly wider at the sight of him. 'Yes.'

His heart started to gallop, as though he had suddenly exerted himself, instead of merely standing transfixed and immobile. He took a few steadying breaths, then loosened his tie.

'I'm Dr Lambourn.' He reached down, picked up one of her hands and attempted a handshake.

She pulled her hand away and folded her arms across her chest. 'When can I go home?'

He'd lost count of how many times he'd been asked that question over the years. He gave the same answer he always did. 'When you're better.'

'For God's sake, there's nothing wrong with me, surely you can see that? I'm not like that bloody nutcase in the next bed, who thinks she's the Queen of England, or that Pearl woman, who's completely off her rocker. I shouldn't be here. I *wouldn't* be here at all if it wasn't for *her*.'

Dr Lambourn pulled up a chair and sat down opposite Amy in the bay of the window. He put his file down on the window seat, leaned back and steepled his hands together. 'Can you remember what it feels like to be happy, Amy?'

The question seemed to take her by surprise, and she opened and closed her mouth again before answering. 'Define happiness.'

He thought about this. 'It's a difficult thing to define. You have to be unhappy to understand it.'

'Well I should be a bloody expert then.'

He nodded. 'Some people pursue happiness, others create it.'

She glared at him, not bothering to hide her contempt. 'So you're saying it's my own fault that I'm stuck in here?'

'I'm not saying that at all, although it's interesting that that's what you inferred.' He noticed her balled-up fists and white knuckles. 'Why are you so angry?'

She let out a mirthless laugh and clapped her hands together, slowly, sarcastically. 'Oh well spotted, Doctor. Years of medical school have obviously paid off.' She stood up, and the shapeless dress slipped off one shoulder, exposing her collarbone. She hoisted the dress back in place. 'I've had enough of this. I'm going back to my bed.'

He stared after her retreating figure, clenching and unclenching his jaw as he mulled over his new young patient. If she was as difficult as this at home, he could appreciate why her father had brought her in, but it didn't take an expert to realise there was a lot more going on beneath the surface. He picked up her file and strode back along the ward, ignoring Pearl's plaintive cries as he passed the end of her bed.

'Dr Lambourn, you said I could go home this week, why haven't you come to see me? How much longer do I have to stay here? Dr Lambourn, are you listening to me?'

The beds in the sick ward were much farther apart than the ones on the long-stay ward; there were fewer patients here and none outstayed their welcome, most of them leaving feet first. Ellen approached Gertie's bed and stared at the old woman curled up in a foetal position, her mouth agape and a wet patch of drool on the pillow beside her. A faded floral curtain fluttered on the breeze coming from the open window. The staff nurse had told her that Gertie was in a lot of pain and that sleep was difficult. She seemed calm and peaceful now, though, and as Ellen gazed at her sleeping form she decided it would be unfair to wake her.

She sat down on the chair beside the bed and pulled out the copy of *My Weekly* she had bought especially for Gertie. It reminded her of home. Ellen's father visited the newsagent every Tuesday and bought a copy for his wife, along with a two-ounce tin of Old Holborn for himself. Mrs Crosby was not fond of money being spent on her, even though the magazine only cost threepence, but Ellen knew she devoured each new issue, particularly its endless supply of knitting patterns.

She studied the model on the front of the magazine in her delightful gaily embroidered jumper and thought of her mother. Mrs Crosby would no doubt love to knit the garment for herself, but Ellen knew she would not squander valuable wool on anything so frivolous, not with a young boy to clothe, one who wore out jumpers at an alarming rate. She flicked past the recipes for Christmas gingerbread and mock chicken casserole and settled down to read the first story. She had not made it beyond a sentence or two when, without warning, Gertie burst into a violent coughing fit, making her jump. The magazine slid to the floor.

She poured a glass of water from the jug on the bedside cabinet. 'Gertie, it's me, Ellen . . . I mean Student Nurse Crosby.' She pulled the old lady into a sitting position, surprised by how little she now weighed, and propped her up on the pillows. Gertie continued to cough, her eyes watering as she spat the resulting blood-splattered phlegm into a sputum mug. Ellen raised the glass of water to her cracked lips. 'Here, drink this . . . That's better, isn't it? How are you feeling, Gertie?'

Gertie gave no indication she had even heard the

question. Undeterred, Ellen ploughed on. 'I've had a look at your case notes. I'm not supposed to really, but what harm can it do, eh? I know how long you've been here, Gertie, and it must seem a big frightening world outside those doors, but you may be able to get out if only you'll start talking again. I've spoken to a doctor, and he didn't promise anything, but . . .'

She noticed that Gertie had closed her eyes. 'Can you hear me?' She tapped the back of the old lady's wrist. 'Gertie, I know you were married once.'

Gertie's eyes flew open, and she fixed Ellen with a stare so penetrating she was forced to look away. She stared at the third finger of the old woman's left hand: no wedding band and no indication that she had ever worn one. No telltale indention of the flesh, no pale silvery skin.

'Where's your husband now, Gertie? Is that why you're in here? Did he leave you?'

With an almost imperceptible nod of her head, Gertie pulled the sheets up to her chin, rolled onto her side and closed her eyes.

11

Although Ambergate housed both male and female patients, the two sides were run as separate entities and patients were not permitted to mix on the wards. This segregation of the sexes often led to frustration amongst the inmates, who would find ingenious ways to arrange clandestine meetings whilst the staff turned a blind eye. Out on the airing courts, where the patients took their daily exercise, one enterprising girl, Belinda, had set up a nice little earner for herself, allowing male patients tending the market garden to down tools and fondle her through the gate in exchange for a cigarette or two. At first, Ellen had intervened to stop these unsavoury trysts, but Sister Atkins had explained that even mental patients needed to relieve themselves. 'I find it as disgusting as you do,' she'd told Ellen. 'But it calms them down, makes them easier to handle.' She'd winked. 'And that can only be good for us nurses, right?' Ellen had nodded and soon learned to look the other way.

It was apparent this morning that the rain had set in for the day, and Ellen bemoaned the fact that the patients would be even more fractious and difficult without a break in the monotony of their routine. Sister Atkins swept her forearm over the window to clear the mist and peered out at the torrential downpour. 'It's barely spitting,' she declared, glancing at her watch. 'Right, come on then, you lot, we're going outside.' She looked at Belinda, who was sitting on the edge of her bed, her hand moving rhythmically between her thighs. 'For Christ's sake, not here, please, Belinda.'

Belinda looked up, a glazed expression on her face. She smiled, revealing a row of huge yellow teeth that would not have looked out of place on a carthorse. 'I need to go outside, Sister.' She cocked her head and slid her forefinger slowly in and out of her mouth. 'You know what I mean?'

'I just said we're going outside, and if you weren't so intent on pleasurin' yourself, you would have heard me, you disgusting little whore.' Sister strode over and hoisted Belinda off the bed, with a clip round the back of her head for good measure. 'Go and wait in the day room.'

Outside, on the airing court, Ellen stood with her back pressed against the wall, the eaves offering some meagre shelter. The patients walked round the perimeter, the track worn down with the passage of endless shuffling feet, following each other like sheep. Ellen was reminded of the tiger at Belle Vue Zoo. Even though he had a large enclosure with trees, rocks and a small pond in the middle, he only ever paced around the fence line, snarling at visitors as he went past.

She watched as Belinda said something to Amy, who reacted with a hard shove in the girl's chest, sending Belinda staggering backwards. Ellen made to intervene, but Belinda seemed to have got the message and instead turned and headed towards the far corner of the court. Ellen could hear her whistling to a figure in the distance. He was hunched over digging at the vegetable patch, but he straightened up when he heard the female voice calling his name. With a glance towards his charge nurse, he ambled over, his hands thrust deep into his pockets as he approached the fence. He must have been seventy if he was a day, his bald head shiny with rain and cross-hatched with shaving cuts.

'Payment first,' demanded Belinda.

He fished out two cigarettes and looked her up and down. 'Top and bottom.'

Belinda grabbed the cigarettes, tucking one behind each ear. She looked over her shoulder at Ellen, a salacious grin on her lips, as she slowly unbuttoned her dress.

Ellen set the huge communal make-up box on the table in the middle of the day room. 'Right, who wants to go first then?' It was always preferable for a staff member to apply the make-up. The patients tended to be heavy-handed with the rouge and the kohl, often ending up with clown-like faces that only accentuated their manic appearance. She picked up the stubby pink lipstick. 'Amy, do you want some?'

Amy looked up from the book in her lap. 'No thank you, I'm not going to some stupid dance. I've been here two weeks now and I want to see a doctor. You can't keep me locked up forever.'

Ellen sighed. The young girl had been repeating this mantra day in, day out since she arrived, but there was no way she was going home yet. It wasn't a choice; her father had signed her over and the family doctor had backed him up. 'You don't need to wear the make-up, but you will be going to the dance.'

Amy slammed the book shut and dropped it onto the window seat. 'A lunatics' ball? Are you seriously expecting me to shuffle round a dance floor with that mixture of ungainly, pathetic creatures?' She nodded towards the window. 'I've seen the way they traipse round the grounds, hardly able to walk straight, let alone manage a waltz.' She folded her arms. 'I'm not going and you can't make me.'

Pearl waddled over, her puffy feet swollen like dough that had been left to prove and was now spilling over the edges of her shoes. 'Well I'm going. Can you do me?' she huffed, plonking her twenty-stone frame in a chair.

Ellen picked up the pot of face powder and began to blend it over Pearl's face. She had flawless skin already, but all her features were crowded into the middle of her moon face.

'Gimme some lipstick too, will yer, and can I put my wedding dress on?'

Sister Atkins shouted over from the door. 'How many times, Pearl, we don't have your bloody wedding dress here. You can wear the hospital-issue dress like everybody else. Honestly, I don't know where you think you are sometimes. This isn't Butlin's, you know.'

'Purse your lips for me, Pearl.' Ellen applied the pink lipstick carefully and stood back to admire her handiwork. She felt sorry for Pearl. Only in her mid thirties, she had been in and out of Ambergate for the past twelve years. A chubby girl with modest looks, she'd had no trouble saving herself for the man she was going to marry and could scarcely believe it when the handsome GI with the exotic accent asked her to marry him on only their second date. Her mother had been beside herself with excitement and had managed to procure some parachute silk, from which she made the most exquisite wedding dress for her daughter. The neighbours had all mucked in and handed over their ration coupons, thus enabling Pearl to have a three-tier fruit cake, swathed in royal icing and decorated with pale pink sugar paste rosebuds.

Ken had announced he had to go away for a couple of months but would be back for their wedding. Caught up in the excitement and swayed by his declarations of love, Pearl surrendered her virginity to him before he left. When the big day finally arrived, she waited patiently at the altar for over an hour, ignoring the mutterings of the congregation, until she was forced to admit that he wasn't coming back. She retreated to her bedroom with the top tier of the cake and refused to take off the wedding dress for two whole weeks.

Sister Atkins had recounted Pearl's story to Ellen with obvious glee, but it wasn't until she got to the punchline that she broke down in hysterics. Apparently Ken had bedded Pearl and agreed to marry her for a bet. A mental breakdown followed, and Pearl had turned to food for comfort before being brought to Ambergate by her frazzled mother.

Ellen finished brushing Pearl's hair and pushed her fringe to one side, securing it with a clip. 'There you are, Pearl – beautiful.' She ignored the sarcastic snort from Sister Atkins. 'Who's next?'

'I can't find my tiara.'

Amy glared at Queenie. 'Oh for God's sake give it a rest. Your name's Gladys and you're not and never will be Queen of England.'

'Please, Amy,' warned Ellen. 'Queenie means no harm.'

The patients' ball was one of the few occasions when the sexes were encouraged to meet and interact with each other, so the dance hall was almost full by the time Ellen arrived with her entourage. She'd been ordered to chaperone Pearl, Queenie, Belinda and Amy, but judging by the way the patients were lined up, men on one side and women on the other, the job would not be too onerous. She spotted Dougie on the other side of the hall and gave him a cheery wave. He had taken off his white coat and dispensed with his tie, his beige shirt open at the neck and a pair of green braces holding up his trousers.

'Who's that?' asked Amy.

'His name's Douglas Lyons; he's a second-year student nurse.'

'Mmm . . . I think he's giving you the glad eye.'

Ellen glared at Amy. 'Don't be ridiculous, he's just a friend and you need to stop being so insolent.' She surprised herself with her sharp tone.

'Ooh, touched a nerve, have I?'

'Be quiet.' Ellen ran her hands through her hair as she saw Dougie approaching.

'Evening, Ellen, your first lunatics' ball, I assume?'

Amy crossed her arms. 'Charming. I can't speak for this lot, but I can assure you that I'm no more of a lunatic than you are.'

Dougie turned to her. 'I do apologise, that was rude of me, but I sure meant no offence.' He placed his hand on her forearm. 'Please forgive me.'

Amy moistened her lips and smiled coyly as she cocked her head to one side. 'That's quite all right, I forgive you, Douglas.'

Ellen interjected a little more savagely than the situation warranted, 'It's Nurse Lyons to you.' She grabbed Amy's arm and squeezed it tightly. 'Come on, let's go and sit with the others over there.'

Dougie called after them, 'Tell Pearl I'll be over later for my dance.'

*

The room was cavernous, with ceilings as high as a cathedral's, so much so that the music from the gramophone sounded hollow as the needle scratched its way around the surface of the record. A few of the male patients had been herded onto the dance floor, and they swayed awkwardly in their ill-fitting suits, which were obviously subjected to the same boiling regime as the women's dresses. With trousers at half-mast, lumpy shoulder pads and jackets that had not been buttoned up in the correct sequence, most of them looked as though they had been shipwrecked.

Ellen rested her gaze on a tall, gangly chap who circled the dance floor with an unusual high-stepping gait, his head bent so low his chin rested on his chest. He stopped, lifted his head slightly and launched into an animated conversation, gesticulating wildly, spittle flying as he became more and more agitated. It was impossible to tell what had sparked his wrath, because he was speaking to an empty space. Dougie sidled up to him and placed an arm around his shoulders. Ellen smiled at the immediate calming effect this had on the patient. Dougie patted him on the arm and steered him in her direction.

'I'd like to introduce you to Alroy Bennett,' he announced. 'Affectionately known to all as Uncle Alroy.'

Ellen extended her hand. 'I'm pleased to meet you . . . Uncle Alroy. My name's Nurse Crosby,' she replied, daringly dropping the 'Student'.

'Uncle Alroy is one of our long-stay patients,' Dougie

explained. 'Been here for nearly forty years, haven't you, Uncle?'

'I've been shot at, you know.'

Ellen took a step back. 'Oh my goodness.'

Dougie laughed. 'Yes, Uncle, but not recently.' He whispered an aside to Ellen. 'Although that could be arranged.' He turned back to Alroy and clapped him on his back. 'Uncle was injured in the trenches in the First World War.'

Uncle Alroy tapped his own head. 'Aye, I've still got shrapnel floating round me brain. Left for dead I was, until the burial party found me and carted me off to the 'ospital.'

He appeared to spot someone over on the other side of the room and gave a salute before he marched off to greet them.

'Poor old sod,' said Dougie. 'He can seem normal for days, but then the madness returns. They've tried everything, but he's completely institutionalised now.' He lowered his voice to a whisper so Ellen had to strain to hear over the music. 'Did you notice those indentations either side of his head?'

Ellen nodded. 'They're hard to miss.'

'Pre-frontal leucotomy in 1942,' Dougie confirmed. 'The doctor drilled holes in his skull to access his brain, then poked around a bit and declared him cured.'

'Good heavens, that sounds barbaric.'

Dougie shrugged. 'I'll say, but he's a lot calmer now than he used to be by all accounts, so who knows? Anyway, there was a reason for bringing him over. He remembers your Gertie. She used to be a lovely singer, apparently, and knew her way round the dance floor too.'

'Really? Oh, I'd love to talk to him.'

'I thought you might. Listen, when you go off duty tonight, come to the ward. I'm on until morning, and I'll clear it with the charge nurse. I'm not promising anything – Uncle Alroy's a bit unpredictable, as you've noticed – but it's gotta be worth a go.'

'Thank you, Dougie, you're so kind.'

The strains of 'Moonlight Serenade' echoed round the room. 'Uh oh, that's my cue.'

Ellen watched as Pearl lumbered across the room, her arms outstretched towards Dougie. Taking one of her hands, he guided her gracefully onto the dance floor. He glanced at Ellen over his shoulder and winked. 'See you later,' he mouthed.

12

There was something serene about a ward at night, even at Ambergate. After the inevitable chaos of the daytime, the low lighting and comparative silence provided a soporific ambience. Dougie put his finger to his lips as he unlocked the door and beckoned Ellen in. She crept past the charge nurse's office and noticed he was fast asleep with his legs up on his desk, his mouth open, an annoying clicking sound stuck in his throat.

Dougie nodded in the charge nurse's direction. 'You can tell who does all the work round here.' He walked softly down the middle of the ward, his shoes making barely a sound. The last thing a nurse wanted at this time of night was to wake the patients with the sound of his clodhopping.

'Uncle Alroy's in the day room. Don't worry about keeping him up; he tends to drift off around three.'

She found Alroy sitting in a straight-backed chair, his escape blocked by a food tray bolted to the arms. 'What's he doing in a toddler's high chair?' she whispered.

Dougie appeared a little uncomfortable. 'He can't sleep, so unless he's . . . contained, he'll spend all night wandering up and down the ward, picking fights with God knows who. Nobody will get any sleep if he's allowed to roam freely.'

Ellen nodded towards the office. 'Including your charge nurse?'

'Believe me, Ellen, the patients don't want to get on the wrong side of him. He has his own way of dealing with them and it's not pretty.'

'Can't you give Alroy something to help him sleep?'

'He's already had his paraldehyde; he loves the vile-tasting stuff for some reason, but I think he's immune to it now. He's had enough to put an elephant out; I can't give him any more.'

He took her arm. 'Come on, come and say hello.'

The old man lifted his head as he heard them approaching. If he recognised Ellen from earlier, he didn't show it. He reached out and picked a piece of imaginary fluff off her shoulder, brought it close to his eye and rolled it between his thumb and forefinger. The familiar smell of the paraldehyde lingered on his breath.

'You remember Nurse Crosby from the dance? She's come to talk to you about Gertie.'

'Who?' His voice was gruff and his eyelids heavy.

'Gertie,' confirmed Ellen.

Uncle Alroy's tone was impatient. 'I know who Gertie is; I meant who are you?'

Dougie laughed. 'I need to get back on the ward. I'll leave you to it.'

Ellen pulled a chair alongside the old man, grimacing as the wooden legs scraped across the floor, cutting through the silence. 'So, you remember Gertie, do you?'

He fixed his eyes on her, the irises mottled with age. 'Aye, course I do. She was quite a looker back in the day, and I 'ad a bit of a crush. By t' time I arrived, she'd been here for eight years or so, if I remember correctly, but I wouldn't bank on that. Looked out for me, she did. Came over and chatted when we were allowed. She's a good bit older than me, though.'

'How old are you, Uncle Alroy?'

He gazed up at the ceiling as though trying to work out a particularly difficult conundrum. 'Eee, I'm buggered if I know.'

'Tell me what you do know then. About Gertie, I mean.'

'It's a sad tale. It's why it's stuck with me. That and the fact she must have told me the same thing about a hundred times. She was fond of repeating herself, that one,' he chuckled.

Ellen pressed him for more. 'I'd love to hear her story.'

'Aye, well, she was working as a chambermaid at that posh hotel in town – The Midland, do you know it?'

Ellen gave a low whistle. 'I'll say, it's quite a landmark. I've never been inside, mind.'

Alroy rested his chin in his palm. 'No, me neither. Anyhow, one day, a young chap comes to stay. He'd come from America on business. He was a stock buyer, you know, horses and that, and he'd been up in Scotland looking at Clydesdales. He came down to Manchester and took a bit of a shine to our Gertie. As I said, she was quite a beauty back then. He was a bit younger than her, but they started courting, and the next thing you know, they're getting married. Well, Gertie was forty-something by this time and Edgar was only in his thirties, but she told The Midland what they could do with their job and they set sail to start a new life together in America.'

Ellen edged forward in her seat. She could not imagine Gertie on the arm of her young American husband. 'How exciting for her. So, what happened next?'

'Treated the crossing as a honeymoon, they did. They could only afford steerage, mind you, but it was an adventure all the same for Gertie, who'd never been out of Manchester.' Alroy sighed and rubbed his bleary eyes. 'Well, you know the rest.'

'I'm sorry?'

'Which one of us is crazy here?'

'I'm not following you.'

'Ship hit an iceberg, didn't it?'

The memory of Gertie's notes flashed up. She'd been admitted in September 1912.

'You mean she was on the *Titanic*?'

'Aye, she made it into a lifeboat, but poor old Edgar was still on the ship as it slid beneath the water. He jumped into the sea, but it was freezing – I mean, obviously, there were icebergs an' all. According to Gertie, there was still room in her lifeboat but the officer in charge wouldn't go back to pick up the men in the sea. Said they would be overrun and sink themselves.'

'How terrible.'

Alroy nodded his agreement. 'And Edgar's body never did wash up.'

'So Gertie couldn't even give him a burial. You know she was found wandering the streets before she was admitted?'

Alroy nodded. 'She never got over losing him, if you ask me.'

Ellen chewed on her thumbnail, deep in thought, her brow furrowed in concentration. 'How did she get back to Manchester?'

'A couple of weeks after the sinking, she had to board a ship to bring her home. You'd think she'd be terrified of getting on another boat, but she wasn't. She told me she half hoped that one would sink too, taking her with it this time. She'd given up, didn't think she could carry on without 'im.'

Ellen took hold of Alroy's hand and ran her thumb over his swollen knuckles. 'Thank you, Uncle Alroy. You've been a great help.'

'My pleasure.' He placed his hands on top of his head and began to pull at his hair. 'I've been shot at, you know.'

Ellen crept back down the ward, mulling over Gertie's tragic story. Dougie was sitting at a desk in the corner, the Anglepoise lamp directed onto his newspaper. 'All done? How was it?'

She bent down so her eyes were level with his. 'Dougie, I really need you to do me a favour.'

He chewed on the end of his pencil and tapped his paper. 'Hmm . . . sure . . . Four across, Scottish land-owner, five letters?'

'Laird.'

He counted out the letters. 'Oh yeah, clever girl.'

'Never mind your bloody crossword. Dougie, please listen to me,' she urged. 'Can you meet me in the students' bar tomorrow night, say six o'clock?'

He looked up from the paper. 'Sure, what's the matter?'

'I'll tell you all about it tomorrow.'

'Great, it's a date.'

She threw a backward glance over her shoulder and shook her head. 'It's not a date.' Still, she couldn't help but smile.

The next evening, he came through the door at exactly six o'clock. He wiped his feet on the mat and shook the droplets of rain from his hair, showering the group of students who were huddled round a nearby table. 'Oi, Douglas,' said one of them, wiping his eyes, 'you're not a bloody Labrador.'

'Sorry, pal,' he apologised.

Ellen laughed to herself at the exchange, then stood up and called across to him. 'Dougie, over here. I've got you one in.'

He meandered over and sat down opposite her, taking a long, grateful gulp of the beer. The foam settled on his top lip and Ellen marvelled at how he could be oblivious to it.

'Dougie.' She mimed wiping her lips. 'You've got . . . you know.'

He ran his tongue over the beer moustache. 'Thanks.'

'When're you due back on?' she asked.

He pushed up his sleeve and squinted at his watch. 'Not until eleven, but I should really get some shut-eye before then.'

'Oh, I'm sorry, you should've said. Look, I won't keep you long.' She picked at the beer mat, pulling it apart as she spoke. 'I know what happened to Gertie.'

'I'm glad Alroy was useful. Tell me.'

'Oh yes, he revealed quite a lot actually.'

She filled him in on what Alroy had told her, his eyes widening as she reached the end of the story.

'Good God, that's quite a tale. Poor old Gertie.' He shook his head and took another swig of his pint. 'How is it you think I can help you, though?'

Ellen shuffled uncomfortably in her seat. The beer mat was now a pile of confetti. 'Would you come and see her?'

'Well, yes, if that's what you want, but I'm not sure what good it will do.'

'She's not got long left, Dougie. I just think if she hears your accent it might remind her of Edgar and send her on her way with some semblance of peace.'

Dougie spluttered on his pint, the beer coming out of his nose. 'Ellen, I'm not impersonating a dead guy, no matter how well-meaning your intentions.'

'I'm not asking you to impersonate anybody. Just be yourself, reassure her.'

She noticed his features soften a little and dared to venture further. 'Perhaps tell her you'll be waiting for her on the other side; nothing too specific, of course.'

'Wait . . . waiting on the other side! Have you taken leave of your senses?' His voice had risen a couple of octaves.

She drained her drink, plonked her glass on the table and stood to leave. 'No, you're right, it's mad, completely mad. Forget I even mentioned it.'

13

Amy gazed out of the window of the day room across the vegetable patch and over to the airing court on the male side. She watched as a lone figure, swamped in a trench coat, scrabbled around in the dirt for dog ends. She'd noticed that some of the male patients at the ball had blackened fingertips and noses as a result of smoking cigarette butts. What a desperate existence they led. She squinted at the male nurse in charge, one foot up against the wall, casually smoking a cigarette himself. It was the American one she'd met at the dance. She couldn't imagine why someone as charismatic and charming as he would choose to work in a desolate place such as this. Some people really had no ambition. She turned as she heard someone calling her name.

'Amy, come on, it's time to get ready.' Nurse Crosby – Ellen – made it sound as though she was preparing for a glamorous night on the town instead of visiting time in a lunatic asylum.

Reluctantly Amy heaved herself off the chair and ambled over to her. 'I *am* ready.'

Ellen looked her up and down, frowning at the egg-yolk

stains on her front. 'Let's get you a clean dress, shall we? We can't have your father seeing you like this. And your hair could do with a wash. Come on, let's get you in the bath.' She clapped her hands as she walked down the middle of the ward. 'Those of you who are expecting visitors, please come with me.'

A small queue of patients formed behind her as they followed her to the bathroom. Sister Atkins had already filled the two baths, and Ellen stood between them, arms akimbo, her face flushed from the rising steam. 'Come on, don't hang about, we've not got all day.'

Obviously used to this procedure, several patients clamoured to go first, stripping off their dresses and underwear without the slightest trace of embarrassment. Seventeen days Amy had languished in this place, and she'd only had one bath in all that time. She was suddenly desperate to rid herself of the accumulated grime, but she wasn't quick enough, and Pearl and another patient took the first two baths. Water sloshed over the side as Pearl lowered herself in.

'It's like bathing a baby elephant,' said Sister Atkins as she poured water over Pearl's head. Without ceremony, the first two patients were sluiced down, scrubbed and then ordered to stand up and climb out. Sister Atkins wiped her brow. 'Next.'

Amy stepped forward with a weak smile. 'I'll undress when the bath's ready, if you don't mind.'

Nurse Atkins stared at her. 'It is ready.'

'But . . . but it's the same water that Pearl used.'

Sister Atkins turned to Ellen, who was busy with another patient. 'Have you 'eard this one 'ere?' She nodded towards Amy. 'Wants fresh water, can you believe?' She moved closer to Amy, their faces only an inch apart. 'Now listen to me,' she spat. 'I don't know who you think you are, but we're not running a spa here. We've not got time to empty the water out between each patient, you silly little girl.'

'But this isn't hygienic; it's more like a sheep dip.'

Sister Atkins snapped. 'Right, that's it. Get to the back of the queue.' She shoved Amy hard in the chest, sending her stumbling backwards. She slipped on the scummy water that Pearl had displaced and hit her cheek on the side of the bath. For a moment she was stunned by the sharp pain and fought against the fuzziness that threatened to envelop her. She raised her hand to her cheek; it felt hot, and already she could feel her eye swelling, but she would not cry out. She would not give Sister Atkins that satisfaction.

Amy waited in a side room with a few of the other patients who were expecting visitors. She'd never been in this part of the building before; it was obvious that it was the public face of the hospital. There was carpet on the floor, for starters, albeit in a hideously garish pattern; a fire had been lit in the grate, and the logs crackled as the scent of burning pine filled the room. There was even a tall plant standing in a brass pot, its fronds green and lush. Pot plants were not allowed on the ward, as some patients had a habit of eating the soil.

She didn't stand to greet her father, merely offered him her cheek as he bent to kiss her. If he was shocked by her appearance, he did an admirable job of concealing his feelings.

'Sister filled me in about how you slipped and fell in the bathroom.' He reached out to touch her cheek, but she flinched and pulled away.

'I bet she did.'

The nurses had wrestled her into a clean dress, but she still stank and her hair was lank and greasy.

'You've had your hair cut, I see.'

'Oh yes, they have a lovely salon here. You can even get a manicure.' She ruffled both her hands through her short hair, leaving it sticking out at all angles. She glared at her father. 'They hacked it off with a pair of blunt scissors.' She drew a deep, shuddering breath; she would not cry, but her voice was barely a whisper. 'You've got to take me home. I promise I'll—'

'Amy, please,' he warned. 'The doctor says you're not well.'

'Don't make me laugh! I've seen him once, and then all he did was try to provoke a reaction, goading me into an argument.'

'Let's be honest, Amy, you could start a riot in an empty house.'

He sounded weary as he wrung his hands together, and she noticed the first signs of grey at his temples. Two vertical lines had appeared between his eyebrows, and even though the light had been snuffed out in his eyes long ago, they now held a vacant expression, as though he had lost the will to care. She loved him so much, every fibre of him: the way he looked at her, the memory of his smell and shape as she'd clambered onto his lap by the fireside. As a child, there was nowhere she would rather have been. Except for her mother's lap, of course. That wasn't quite as comfy, it was true, not with her bony legs, but her hair was long and soft, and as Amy snuggled her head into her mother's chest, she would take a strand of her hair and run it across her top lip, revelling in the coconut scent and silky texture, until she drifted off to sleep.

It was too hard; there was a golf ball lodged in her throat and she felt a hot tear slip down her cheek, stinging her skin as it ran over the graze. 'I just miss her so much, Daddy,' she whispered. She clamped her hands over her face so he wouldn't have to witness her tears, and felt him lean forward and pat her knee.

'So do I, Amy. So do I.'

'You do forgive me, don't you?'

His voice came out hoarse, barely audible. 'You know I do.'

After the visitors had departed and the patients had returned to the ward, Ellen busied herself with closing down the visitors' room. She raked over the fire until the embers were dispersed and pushed the chairs to the side of the room. Picking up the dustpan and brush, she was on her knees sweeping up the biscuit crumbs when she felt a tap on her shoulder.

'Oh, goodness me, you made me jump.' She struggled to her feet and addressed the visitor. 'Can I help you?'

'I'm so sorry to startle you. I'm Amy's father.'

'Yes, I remember.' She held out her hand. 'How do you do?'

He twisted his cap in his hands. 'I'd like to give you something. It's to remain on my daughter's file, which I trust is confidential.'

'Well, yes, of course. What is it?'

He rummaged in his jacket pocket and pulled out an envelope. 'It's a letter to the . . . doctor. The one in charge of our Amy.'

Ellen took the creamy envelope and nodded. 'I'll make sure Dr Lambourn gets it.'

Amy's father studied his shoes, never once looking up as he muttered his thanks and left the room.

14

Every breath she took seemed laboured, a coarse rattle as she inhaled, a hissing sound as she let go. Ellen filled a bowl of warm water and gently wiped a cloth over Gertie's face. The old lady had reached the end of the road, and Ellen was determined she would depart this world with as much dignity as possible. Gertrude May Lewis had come to the asylum a broken-hearted woman who had never recovered from the death of her husband, had never had the chance to love again and was now facing her final journey. Ellen had no idea what would be waiting for her at the end of it, but if there was such a thing as heaven, a place where you were reunited with your loved ones, then she would see to it that Gertie was looking her best.

'There you are, Gertie,' she soothed as she patted the old lady's cheeks dry. Then, with a furtive glance towards Sister's office, she pulled a compact out of her pocket and dabbed powder over Gertie's face. 'Aren't you going to look nice when you see Edgar again, hmm?'

The old lady lay propped up on two pillows, staring directly up at the ceiling. At the mention of Edgar's name, there was a barely noticeable flicker in her eyes. Ellen pulled out her tweezers and began to pluck the coarse hairs from Gertie's chin. She tipped a bottle of English Lavender onto her finger and dabbed the scent behind Gertie's ears. Finally, she brushed what was left of the old lady's white hair, skilfully arranging it so it covered most of her pink scalp. 'There you are, Gertie, don't you look a picture?'

She wafted the thin sheet covering Gertie's body to let some fresh air under the covers, wrinkling her nose as she did so. The English Lavender was clearly not up to the job of masking the purulent odour. She folded back the sheet and lifted Gertie's nightdress. On the bony protrusion of the old woman's hip was a festering necrotic bed sore, the flesh around it blackened and oozing pus. Ellen covered her mouth with her hand and pinched her nose as she went to fetch a bowl and a cloth.

After swabbing the wound and applying a puff of zinc powder, she took the old woman's hand and held it in her own. It was cool to the touch, the thin skin silvery, the nails yellow and ridged. 'I'm so sorry the system has let you down, Gertie. I know all about Edgar, and I must say he sounds like a wonderful young man. You've been denied a lifetime of happiness together, but he's waiting for you now, I'm sure of it. You can let go.'

Gertie's eyes were closed, her breathing shallow, but her mouth bore the trace of a faint smile. Ellen could feel her own eyelids beginning to droop. She'd had a long day and should really be getting some sleep. She leaned forward, placed her arm on the bed and laid her head in the crook of her elbow. She would just grab a few minutes.

She had no idea how long she had dozed, but she was woken by a hand on her shoulder. Groggily, she looked up and saw Dougie smiling down. 'Hello, you,' he said, sitting on the edge of the bed. 'You look shattered; why don't you call it a night? I'll take over here.'

Ellen rubbed the sleep from her eyes. 'You came? I thought you said . . .'

He shushed her with a finger to the lips. 'I thought: what the hell, what harm can it do?'

'Thank you, Dougie,' she breathed. 'Will you talk to her?'

He nodded. 'Course I will.' He turned to Gertie, and Ellen marvelled at the effortless way he spoke, his tone reassuring and sincere. He was a natural.

'How are you, Gertie my love?' He winked at Ellen. She knew he was exaggerating his accent for the old lady's benefit and she could have hugged him.

He took hold of Gertie's hand, running his thumb over the back of it. Then he reached up and caressed her weathered cheek, all the time gently murmuring her name. Ellen was mesmerised by his tenderness.

'Ask her if she remembers you,' she said quietly.

He took a step backwards and whispered in Ellen's ear, 'I'm not Edgar. I told you I wouldn't pretend to be.' His voice was tinged with kindness. but she knew he meant it.

'I'm sorry. I got caught up in the moment. You're just so . . .'

'I'm just Dougie, doing a friend a favour.'

'I know, and I'll be eternally grateful.'

She stared down at Gertie's sleeping form, her chest barely rising with each breath. 'She looks peaceful now, doesn't she?'

Dougie nodded. 'I wonder if she can hear us.'

Right on cue, Gertie opened her eyes and lifted her hand. Her mouth opened, then closed, her lips twisting and gurning. Ellen picked up a glass of water. 'Here you are, have a little drink.'

Gertie shook her head and brushed the glass away. With a monumental effort she raised her hand and beckoned Ellen to lean in closer. Ellen bent down, her ear close to the old woman's mouth. 'What is it, Gertie? Do you want to say something?'

It began with a few rasping sounds from deep within Gertie's throat, her vocal cords evidently having trouble responding to what they were being asked to do, but as she took her final shuddering breath, her first words for sixteen years echoed in Ellen's ear.

Ellen straightened up, gently closed Gertie's eyes and turned to face Dougie, her own voice barely a whisper. 'She spoke.'

'What?'

'She spoke, Dougie.' She allowed herself a small smile.

'What did she say?'

'She just said . . . *thank you.*'

Dougie held his arms wide, and she didn't hesitate as she collapsed into them, burying her face in his white coat. 'Thank you, Dougie. That was all because of you.'

15

Dr Lambourn ran his hand over his chin, the stubble reminding him that he needed to purchase a new blade. He adjusted the knot in his tie as he heard the door brush across the carpet and stood to greet his patient.

'Here's Amy, Dr Lambourn,' the nurse announced as she pushed her young charge into his office.

Amy glared at the nurse. 'Don't shove me. I'm quite capable of walking into a room unaided.'

The nurse rolled her eyes. 'She's all yours, Doctor.'

He indicated the chair opposite him. 'Please have a seat.'

She slumped down, her eyes blazing with undisguised fury, and he was glad the enormous mahogany desk stood as a barrier between them. He'd encountered all manner of patients in his time, had been physically attacked on more than one occasion, but none of them had unnerved him as much as this young girl did. He clasped his hands together and laid them on the desk in front of him. It would not be helpful to either of them if she noticed they were shaking. He took a sip of water and cleared his throat.

'How are you feeling, Amy?'

She rocked back in her chair, placed her hands behind her head and studied the ceiling. 'It's been a month, Dr Lambourn. Why are you keeping me here?'

'It's for your own good.'

'Well it's not working. I'd be better off at home. My father said he's forgiven me.'

Dr Lambourn glanced down at the desk drawer. It was slightly open and he caught a glimpse of the creamy envelope, *The Doctor* written in copperplate on the front. He closed the drawer and turned the brass key.

'Tell me about your earliest memory, Amy.'

'Why? What's that got to do with anything?'

He smiled. 'Just humour me.'

She sighed and folded her arms. 'What's the difference between God and a psychiatrist?'

He tapped his pencil on his pad. 'I don't know, please enlighten me.'

'God doesn't think he's a psychiatrist.'

He nodded slowly, her words affecting him more than he cared to show. 'Very good, Amy.'

She twisted a strand of hair round her finger, her lips stretching into a smirk. Her huge brown eyes had softened, and even though they were framed with dark circles, she radiated a beauty that he'd never witnessed in a mental patient before.

'Let's get back to the topic, shall we? Your earliest memory.'

Without warning, she rose from her chair and wandered over to the window. She spoke with her back to him, as though not wanting him to witness her emotion. 'I was happy, in the beginning at least. I know you're expecting a sob story about a deprived childhood filled with cruelty and neglect, but it wasn't like that all.' She ran her fingers along the velvet curtain, caressing the soft pile. 'I was only two when the war began, not that I remember it, of course, but I do remember my great-aunt's farmhouse where we went to live, just my mother and I. Dad was away fighting.' She turned to face him. 'Have you ever lost anybody, Dr Lambourn?'

The question threw him, and he took a couple of seconds to regain his composure. 'This is about you, Amy, not me.' He could feel the vein in his temple throbbing. 'Please carry on.'

'I wish I could remember more of those days. When I think about the farm, I get a physical ache here.' She thumped her chest. 'It's a yearning, a real sense of longing to turn back the clock. It's beautiful down there, have you ever been?'

He shook his head. 'Been where?'

'West Wales. The coastline is spectacular – wild unforgiving seas and windswept moors in the winter, flower-strewn cliffs and sunny skies in the summer.' She licked her lips. 'I can almost taste the salt. Oh, and the smell of the fields, freshly cut hay; even the farmyard with cowpats dotted around smelled like heaven to me.'

'It sounds idyllic.'

'Oh, it was.' She extended both arms and spun round on the spot. 'We were there for the entire war, Mummy and I, completely sheltered from what was going on in Europe and the rest of the world. We didn't even have a wireless. We'd get the odd letter from my father, sometimes just a pre-printed postcard where he'd ticked a box saying he was quite well or something like that. I was too young to miss him, though, and besides, I was kept busy.

'Once I was old enough, I spent the mornings at school, and when I came out, Jess, my great-aunt's Border collie, would be waiting for me with the handle of a basket in her mouth. We would skip home together, stopping to collect the hens' eggs from the shed in the field behind the cottage. My mother would be in the meadow, painting, her easel sticking up from the long grass, surrounded by wild flowers, buzzards soaring overhead. Then we'd go inside and I'd have a glass of milk, straight from the cow's udder. Still warm, it was. Then Mummy would heat up the griddle pan and make Welsh cakes.'

He had never seen her so animated, her eyes shining and her mouth lifted into something approaching a smile. 'And after the war?'

He might as well have pulled the rug from under her feet. Her face clouded over, her shoulders sagged and she flopped back into the chair. 'I don't want to talk about it.' She clamped her hands over her face, breathing deeply.

He stared at his watch, waiting for the second hand to

go round the dial twice before he spoke again. 'Amy.' She didn't even flinch. He stood up, moved round to the other side of the desk and knelt down in front of her chair. One by one he lifted her fingers away from her face. Her skin was blotchy and the light behind her eyes that had been present a few minutes ago had been extinguished. 'I can't help you if you won't cooperate.'

'It's too hard to think about, never mind talk about, Dr Lambourn,' she whispered. 'Please don't make me; it won't help.'

He was so close to her, he could feel the heat radiating from her body, could smell her breath, sweet like pear drops. He placed his finger under her chin and forced her to look at him. Her eyes were so dark, it was hard to make out her pupils. 'Do you trust me, Amy?'

She exhaled deeply and switched her gaze to the window whilst she considered his question. 'I don't trust anybody, Dr Lambourn,' she said eventually.

She was a powder keg of conflicting emotions. Vulnerable and childlike one minute, tempestuous and confrontational the next.

He returned to his seat behind his desk and picked up his phone. 'Tea for two, please, Sister Atkins, and some biscuits too.'

Five minutes later, the young student nurse entered the room carrying the tea tray, Sister Atkins obviously having delegated the menial task. 'Thank you, Nurse, you can leave it over there.' He indicated the small table by the fireplace.

He turned to Amy. 'Shall we?'

She stood up and he dragged her chair over to the fireplace, taking the chair opposite for himself. They sipped their tea in silence, contemplative rather than awkward, the stillness occasionally shattered by a loud pop from the crackling fire.

Dr Lambourn drained his cup and leaned back in his chair. Amy nibbled round the edge of a biscuit, crumbs spilling onto her lap. She absently flicked them onto the carpet before resting her head on the antimacassar and closing her eyes. 'I was eight years old when the war ended,' she began. 'I must have been the only person in the country not to celebrate. I knew we'd have to return to Manchester and I would have to share my mother. I couldn't remember my father. I hadn't seen him since I was two years old, so he was a stranger to me. It may sound harsh, but I honestly couldn't have cared less if he'd never come back. But my mother was beside herself with excitement. The house had been locked up for six years, and we spent many weeks cleaning, airing, titivating until I was sure the King himself must be coming to visit.

'I was sitting on her knee and we were reading a book together when my father finally came through the door. He was still in his uniform. I remember his face was dirty, and when he took off his cap, his hair was flat and greasy. I thought a tramp had wandered in off the street. My mother recognised him instantly, though, and she shrieked and stood up so quickly that I slid off her knee and landed on my bottom on the stone floor. She didn't even notice. They held each other for so long, I was certain they must have forgotten all about me, but then they managed to peel themselves apart, and my father came over, bent down and held his arms wide. I wasn't sure what to do, but he scooped me up and held me so tight, I thought I would suffocate from lack of air and the fumes of some kind of engine oil that came off his skin. His cheek was rough with stubble and I turned my head to try and get away, but he just laughed and put me down in the chair.'

Dr Lambourn sat and listened in silence. It was the longest she had spoken and he was reluctant to interrupt her with questions. Instead, he smiled and gave a slight nod of his head, indicating that she should continue.

'I helped my mother to fill the big tin bath by the fire in the kitchen whilst my father sat in the chair and watched. She wouldn't let him do anything; insisted that he just rest. When he was ready to climb in, I was sent upstairs. I could hear them both laughing and giggling, and then it went quiet and I couldn't hear them at all.'

She leaned forward and reached for her cup of tea, spitting the cold dregs back into the cup before continuing. 'When he was all clean and shaved, I sat on my father's knee for the first time I could remember. He dug in his pocket and pulled out a brand-new threepenny bit. He held it between his thumb and forefinger and right before my eyes he made it vanish. I had never seen anything like it before, and I couldn't believe this magical man was my father. Then he reached behind my ear and brought out the threepenny bit. I was so shocked, I couldn't think of anything to say. He laughed and kissed the top of my head and I knew then everything was going to be all right. He was my father and he had more than enough love for both me and my mother.' She smiled. 'I wasn't a difficult child, Dr Lambourn, in spite of what you may think.'

'I'm sure you weren't, Amy. Please carry on.'

'I'll admit I did have a bit of a paddy that evening at bedtime, though. For the past six years I'd slept in my mother's bed with her, and now suddenly I was being told to sleep in my own bed in another room. I couldn't believe it. I felt betrayed, and I stomped up the stairs without kissing either of them goodnight. I couldn't sleep, and lay awake until I heard them coming up. One of them opened my bedroom door and peered in. I pulled the eiderdown over my head and pretended to be asleep.

'I used to love bouncing on my mother's bed. The springs were old, and as I jumped up and down, they used to squeak in rhythm to my bounces. I could hear them squeaking as I lay under my covers, and I wondered why on earth my parents were bouncing on the bed. I mean, surely my father must be tired, and weren't they a little too old for that anyway?'

Dr Lambourn gave a small laugh. 'How does that make you feel now, Amy?'

She shrugged. 'They were in love. They always had been, ever since they were sixteen. Neither of them had ever had eyes for anybody else. The kind of love that only comes along once in a lifetime, for the lucky few, that is.' She paused and took a shuddering breath. 'That's what made it more difficult when . . .'

'When what, Amy?'

She screwed up her eyes and rubbed at her temples. 'When I killed her.'

The pen he had been holding slipped through his fingers and landed on the floor. He was glad of the few seconds' respite as he bent down to retrieve it. 'You killed your own mother?'

She nodded. 'She was nine months pregnant at the time: a baby boy . . . my little brother. He died too.'

Her matter-of-fact tone alarmed him. 'How did you . . . I mean, can you tell me what happened?'

'Not really, no. I can remember the aftermath, sitting in the front room, my father sobbing and hardly able to look at me. My arm was in a sling and I had a graze on my forehead. There were lots of people there who I didn't recognise, all drinking cups of tea, as if that was the solution to every problem.'

Dr Lambourn stared at the empty cups and saucers on the table between them. 'Are you able to carry on?'

'With life or my story?'

'With your story, Amy.'

She stared at the ceiling in what he guessed was an effort to contain the tears. 'I remember seeing the dog on the other side of the road. She was just like Jess, who I hadn't seen for almost a year, and even though I knew deep down it couldn't possibly be her, I just ran out into the road. All I can remember is someone screaming, a car horn blaring and my mother's body spread-eagled on the bonnet of the car.'

Dr Lambourn looked down at his pad. He'd been so entranced with her story, he hadn't written down a single thing. 'It sounds as though it was a tragic accident. Why do you think it was your fault?'

'She died trying to save me. If I'd not run out into the road, she'd still be here now, and I wouldn't be stuck in this place with my father hating me.'

'He doesn't hate you, Amy. And you did say he's forgiven you.'

'He says that with his mouth, but not with his eyes.'

He was silent for a moment. There would never be a good time to ask his next question. 'Why did you take the baby into the lake, Amy?'

She glared at him, her face covered with a veil of confusion. 'What lake? What baby?' She stood up with such force, the chair tipped backwards and crashed to the floor. As she swept out of the room, a bauble fell off the Christmas tree in the corner and shattered on the tiled hearth.

16

Ellen scanned the torn-off scrap of paper she had been handed by Sister Atkins. 'What's this?'

'Doctor's orders, that's what.'

She stared at the ward sister. She'd been too liberal with the lipstick again, and red flecks coated her front teeth.

'Amy's to have ECT?' she asked, her voice rising with horror.

'That's what it says, doesn't it?'

Ellen thought back to Gertie's records. She'd suffered a broken leg as a result of that particular treatment.

'Is it safe? I mean, I've heard some terrible—'

She stopped and spun round as she heard Dr Lambourn's voice. 'Questioning the doctor again, I see, Student Nurse Crosby. I don't know why you even bother going to that training school; you obviously know better than anybody else already. Perhaps you could teach me a thing or two. After all, I've only got a diploma in psychological medicine.'

Sister Atkins stifled a smile, obviously revelling in Ellen's discomfort.

'I'm sorry, Doctor, it's just that—'

'Hmm, another thing you're good at – apologising. You've certainly had plenty of practice at that.' He leaned in so close, she could smell the toothpaste on his breath.

Sister Atkins took pity and stepped in. 'Make sure that Amy doesn't have anything for breakfast this morning, please, Student Nurse Crosby.'

Dr Lambourn regarded Ellen thoughtfully. 'Actually, you can accompany Amy to the ECT suite; you might learn something.'

'Me? Oh, I'm not sure I'd . . .'

She noticed Dr Lambourn's raised eyebrows and left the sentence hanging. 'I mean, yes, of course, Doctor.'

Amy was sitting in her favourite window seat in the day room when Ellen found her. The watery December sun cast a shaft across the carpet, dust motes dancing in the beam. 'Amy, come on, it's time to go.'

She didn't look up. 'I'm not going anywhere.'

'We've been through this. Dr Lambourn has recommended treatment to help you.'

Now she glared at Ellen. 'By frying my brain?'

'It's not like that, and in any case, it's not up for discussion. Detained patients are not required to give their permission for treatment.'

Belinda wandered over in an effort to help. 'Don't be scared, it's not that bad. I've had it loads of times and look at me, I'm fine.' She ran her fingers through her hair, leaving it standing on end, crossed her eyes and stuck her tongue out to one side. 'Thee,' she lisped. 'I'm all cured now.' She laughed maniacally as she sloped out of the room.

Dr Lambourn was waiting for them when Ellen wheeled Amy into the electroconvulsive therapy suite. He clutched the lapels of his starched white coat. 'Good morning.' He handed a list to Ellen. 'Can you confirm these points please, Nurse.'

Ellen looked down the list. 'The patient has not eaten; as you can see, she doesn't wear spectacles, and neither does she have any false teeth to remove.' She handed the list back to him.

'Thank you.' He turned to Amy and patted the back of her left hand, studying the veins. The anaesthetist nodded and inserted the tube through which the anaesthetic and muscle relaxant would be delivered. Amy lay still, her eyes glazed and unfocused, all her fight drained away.

The anaesthetist sported a mad professor look, round spectacles perched on the tip of his nose, long strands of thin grey hair swept back from his face. 'Amy,' he said. 'Count backwards from ten, please.'

She licked her lips and sighed. 'Ten, nine, eight, sev . . .' She closed her eyes as her small voice trailed off.

'Student Nurse Crosby, please apply the conducting jelly to the bitemporal areas.'

Ellen raised her eyebrows.

'The temples,' sighed Dr Lambourn, not bothering to mask his impatience.

She could feel the tears welling as she smoothed the jelly onto Amy's head with trembling fingers. With its dark brown walls, the room was too small and claustro-phobic, and there was a strange smell, a kind of obnoxious gas that travelled up her nose and settled in the back of her throat, making her feel woozy. She glanced up as she heard the door open and two other nurses entered the already overcrowded room.

The anaesthetist nodded at Dr Lambourn, who turned his attention to the wooden box on the trolley beside Amy. There was an array of dials and switches, which he fiddled around with until he seemed satisfied. He lodged a rubber gag in Amy's mouth, then picked up two elec-trodes and placed them on the jellied areas of her scalp. Ellen clamped a hand over her own mouth as she waited for the doctor to flick the switch that would deliver the shock. She felt herself swaying, and she grabbed onto the trolley as eighty volts of electricity passed through Amy's brain. In spite of the two nurses holding her down, the girl's body convulsed, every limb jerking violently, and she practically levitated. Once she was still, the anaesthe-tist removed the gag and clamped an oxygen mask over her face for a few seconds.

Dr Lambourn smiled at Ellen. 'There, that wasn't too bad, was it?'

'Not for me, but what about her?' She nodded at Amy. Her body was now relaxed and her chin glistened with drool.

'She'll come round in fifteen minutes or so and she'll probably have an intense headache. It's a side effect that can't be avoided, unfortunately, but it won't last.'

'And long-term?'

His eyes narrowed and he adopted a headmasterly tone. 'Amy has difficulty remembering things, things that are important to aiding her recovery. Whilst it's true her memories may be scrambled after this treatment, in some cases patients actually have improved memory following ECT because of its ability to remove the amnesia that's associated with severe depression.'

She noticed a tiny nerve flickering on his bottom lid. He clasped Amy's file protectively to his chest. This did not look at all like a man who believed the words that were coming out of his mouth. She seized her chance. 'So you're saying it's a bit of a lottery, then?'

He seemed to choose his words carefully before answering. 'Are you always this difficult, or do you some-times have a day off?'

'I don't think it's a bad thing to question certain methods if they seem a little barbaric, with haphazard results.'

He exhaled sharply through his nose. It might have been a snort of laughter, the derisory kind, of course. It was all too apparent that he did not find her amusing in any way. 'Stick to giving bed baths and enemas and leave the important stuff to actual doctors.' He strode out of the room and slammed the door behind him.

The anaesthetist afforded Ellen a small smile, then shrugged his shoulders and busied himself with his instruments of torture.

She had an overwhelming desire to find Dougie. She needed to see a friendly face and hear reassurance that everything would be all right. She walked briskly along the polished corridor to the male side of the hospital, praying that he would still be on duty. It was hard enough to get to grips with her own shift patterns, never mind anybody else's. She rapped on the locked door of the ward and peered through the square of reinforced glass. She groaned inwardly as the overweight charge nurse lumbered towards her, his huge set of keys bumping against his thigh. He selected the appropriate key and opened the door. 'Yes?'

'Is Nurse Lyons still on duty?'

'Who wants to know?'

She was in no mood for silly games. 'I do.'

He smiled and beckoned her in. 'He's in the day room.'

'Thank you.'

She walked the length of the ward to the day room at the end, not needing to turn around to know that the charge nurse was ogling her bottom and the eyes of every male patient were boring into her, as though she was some strange exhibit in a Victorian freak show.

Dougie was seated at a small square table, with his back to the door, hunched over with his head in his hands. The young boy sitting opposite him reclined in his chair, his arms folded and a self-satisfied smile on his face. 'Checkmate,' he declared.

Dougie shook his head. 'You've bloody won again!'

The lad beamed, two dimples denting his smooth cheeks. His jet-black hair had been shaved on one side, and although it was now growing back, Ellen could still make out the scar beneath the stubble.

'Hello, Dougie.' She smiled at his chess partner.

'Goodness, Ellen, what brings you here?' Dougie motioned towards the boy. 'This is Edward, and he's just beaten me yet again.' He began to scoop up the chess pieces. 'Go on with you, Ed, get out of here.'

Edward picked up the black king, kissed the top of it and tossed it in the air. Dougie stuck his hand out and caught it. 'Same time tomorrow?'

Edward rubbed his chin. 'I'll have to check my diary.' He rose slowly to his feet, grabbing the edge of the table for support. Dougie went to stand up, but Ed waved him away. 'I can do it, thanks.' He walked unsteadily towards the door, tiny shuffling steps, his arms outstretched ready to grab onto anything that would keep him upright. When he was almost there, he lurched for the frame as though it were a life raft. He looked back over his shoulder, his face crimson with the effort. 'Told you,' he beamed.

When he'd left the room, Ellen settled down in the

chair Ed had vacated. 'That's so nice of you to keep letting him win, Dougie. Good for his self-esteem, I expect.'

'Letting him win? I wish he'd let *me* win once in a while. I've never been able to beat him yet.'

Ellen couldn't keep the surprise out of her voice. 'Oh, I assumed . . .'

'Yeah, I know what you're thinking. I'm such a bad chess player I can't even beat a mental patient.'

'What's he in here for? I noticed the scar on his head, and he obviously has difficulty walking.'

'Head injury, knocked off his bike. Been here several months.'

'But he shouldn't be in a mental hospital, surely?'

'I don't make the rules, Ellen. He still has fits, you see.'

'Oh, the poor lad. He's so young, too.'

'He's twenty-one, actually, it was his birthday last week. His mom brought him a cake, bless her. She visits him every week, always brings a pear.'

'A pair of what?'

Dougie laughed. 'A pear to eat.' He glanced at the clock on the wall. 'She's due in this afternoon.'

Ellen picked up a white pawn, rolling it between her fingers. 'I had to take a patient to ECT this morning.'

He held his hand out for the chess piece and she dropped it onto his palm. 'You found it tough.' It was not a question.

'God, Dougie it was awful. I mean, how can it be right to torture a patient that way?'

He replaced the lid on the chess set. 'Do you know, Ellen, I've asked myself that question many times over the last couple of years, but I've also seen a great improvement in some patients. That's all I can say. I can only speak as I find.'

'I questioned Dr Lambourn about it, you know, asked if maybe there was another way . . .'

'Ooh, you didn't?'

'Don't worry, I've learned my lesson. He already thinks I'm too big for my boots.'

Dougie patted the back of her hand across the table. 'Nothing wrong with showing a little enthusiasm, chuck.'

She smiled at the northern endearment. He might have picked up the vernacular, but his accent made it sound as though he was taking the mickey.

She stood to leave. 'I'd better get back to the ward, see how Amy is.'

He stopped and raised his eyebrows. 'The young girl from the ball? Is she the one who had the treatment?'

'Yes, that's her.'

His expression was difficult to read. His forehead creased into a slight frown as he parted his lips and drew a long breath. 'Poor lass,' he muttered.

The lunchtime smells still lingered on the ward: stale lard competing with overripe stewed apples. And cabbage. There was always the smell of cabbage, even when it wasn't on the menu.

Amy lay on her bed, flat on her back, staring up at the ceiling, her mouth encrusted with dried saliva. Pearl knelt on one side of the bed, Queenie on the other, each holding one of Amy's hands. Ellen was touched by the show of compassion. 'That's kind of you, Pearl. How is she?'

'Not spoken. 'Ere, help me up, will you? I knew it was a mistake to kneel down here on this 'ard floor.'

Ellen heaved Pearl up by the arm, her face reddening with the effort.

'Thank you, Nurse.'

'Pearl, Queenie, I'll take over here now. You've both been very sweet and I'm sure Amy appreciates your kindness.'

The two women linked arms and ambled off to the day room.

Ellen stroked Amy's forehead. 'I expect you're hungry, aren't you, having missed breakfast an' all?'

There was no response, and as she stared down at Amy's face, she clenched her teeth in frustration. Amy was a pathetic version of the vibrant, feisty girl who had entered the asylum only a few weeks ago, her spirit crushed and her hope diminishing by the day.

'I . . . I . . . want to see my father.' Her voice was small and croaky, like she'd inhaled a cloud of bonfire smoke.

Ellen bent down so she was inches above the other girl's head. 'I'll have a word, you just leave it with me.' She called across to the bed opposite. 'Belinda, come and sit with Amy, will you?'

'No, I'm busy. You can fu—'

'Belinda! Get over here now.'

Ellen knocked on the door of Dr Lambourn's office, her armpits prickling with sweat, her heart thumping as though she'd just run a marathon.

'Come in.' The disembodied voice sounded friendly enough, but she knew that as soon as she crossed the threshold, any bonhomie would evaporate.

'Dr Lambourn, may I have a word?'

He rubbed his temples. 'Oh God, not you again. What is it now?' He held up his hand. 'No, don't tell me. You've come up with a revolutionary new way of dealing with lunatics that doesn't involve digging around in their brains or subjecting them to electric shocks as though they were pigs in a slaughterhouse. Am I right?'

Her arms dangled by her sides, but she clenched her fists before she answered, keeping her voice steady. 'Nothing like that, Dr Lambourn. I just wondered if we could arrange for Amy's father to visit later. She's asking for him, you see.'

'She's asking for him?' His voice was level, but she detected a menacing undercurrent.

Ellen swallowed. 'That's right.'

'And you think it's all right for the patients to issue instructions round here, do you?'

The first stirrings of dread wheedled their way into her stomach. 'Well, I just thought . . .'

'That's your trouble, you spend too much time thinking.'

He pulled open his desk drawer, took out an envelope and thrust it towards her. 'I suggest you read this.'

Her fingers felt as fat and useless as sausages as she fumbled with the envelope she had seen once before. She scanned the letter quickly before her eyes could focus on the words.

1 December 1956

To the doctor in charge of Amy Amelia Sullivan

I, Peter Sullivan, father of the above-named patient, wish to make it clear that my daughter is to remain in your care indefinitely. This is the most difficult, heart-breaking decision I've ever had to make, but I am committing her to the asylum as she is no longer fit to live in my home. She is a danger to herself, and more importantly, she is a danger to my family. Her actions have proved that she is of unsound mind, and having her live at home is a risk I am not prepared to take. I do not believe she is evil, but I have no desire to see her again until she is fully recovered – however long that takes. I will always love her, but to see her this way is too painful for me. Please treat her kindly.

Yours faithfully,

Peter Sullivan

Dr Lambourn sat with his chin resting on his hands, his head perfectly still but his eyes following her every move.

Ellen folded the paper in two and dropped it onto his desk. 'Does she know her father won't be visiting?'

He shook his head. 'I haven't told her yet, and I see no immediate need to.'

'But she'll be crushed . . .'

'Student Nurse Crosby, there are things you do not know, things you don't need to know.' He paused and picked up his pen, using it to tap a large book on his desk. 'Are you familiar with the work of Sigmund Freud?'

'No, not really . . . I've heard of him, obviously, but . . .'

'Carl Jung?'

She shook her head and studied the carpet.

She heard him slide his chair back, and suddenly he was at her side, his arm draped casually across her shoulders as though they were friends. His pungent cologne filtered into her nostrils. 'Go back to the ward, Ellen,' he whispered. 'And leave Amy to me.'

17

Christmas was still her favourite time of year. Her mother had always made an extra effort, and the sheer excitement of running down the stairs on Christmas morning to find her stocking hanging over the fireplace remained with her all these years later. Although it was never exactly bulging – after all, there was a war on – there was always a home-made gift, the best kind, presents Amy still treasured to this day. The handkerchief embroidered with her initials; the smooth flat pebble her mother had collected from the beach and painted with a picture of the pink thrift that adorned the cliffs near their cottage; and her favourite one of all: a small multicoloured teddy her mother had knitted from odds and sods of wool and stuffed with her old stockings.

She remembered sitting on the arm of her mother's chair as she knitted a pale blue matinee jacket for the new baby – her brother, for they had known for certain it would be a boy. Her mother had done something with her wedding ring on a chain, dangling it over her swollen belly. It had swayed from side to side, or maybe it had spun round, Amy couldn't remember, but either way her mother was overjoyed at this apparent confirmation that she was carrying a son.

Amy stared out of the window, the sun low in the sky but dazzlingly bright as it reflected off the white fields, the trees drooping under the weight of the heavy snowfall. That poor little boy, her baby brother, never did get to wear that matinee jacket, and her father had slept with it under his pillow for years after.

'Amy, get up, we're going for a walk.'

She hadn't heard him come in, and his sudden command interrupted her reverie. Perhaps it was for the best; it didn't do to dwell, that was what they'd kept telling her. It was different in here, though. The bloody doctor was always wanting her to talk, make her relive her painful memories.

'A walk?' She gazed up at Dr Lambourn, already kitted out in a thick coat and fur hat that made him look like a Russian spy. He clapped his hands together, the leather gloves producing a loud slap.

'Yes, come on.' He held out the coat he'd had draped over his arm, inviting her to step into it.

She rose slowly, turned her back to him and slipped her arms into the sleeves. He pulled her hair out from under the collar, the contact causing an involuntary shiver.

'Your hair's grown back a little, I see.'

She turned to face him as she buttoned up the coat. 'I expect they'll be wanting to hack it off again then.'

*

Outside in the grounds, she had the urge to run and run and never look back. She wanted to dance around in the virgin snow, mess up its pristine surface. Maybe she would have tried if Dr Lambourn had not taken it upon himself to link his arm through hers, as though they were lovers out for a stroll in the crisp winter wonderland. She stopped walking and looked up at his face. His cheeks were reddened with the cold and his hat had slipped down so it almost covered his eyes.

'Am I just an experiment to you, Dr Lambourn? I mean, I don't see you out walking with Pearl or Queenie or even Belinda.'

He snorted. 'Belinda! God forbid.' He pulled out a handkerchief and wiped his eyes. There were no tears, though; it was just the effect of the cold air. 'You intrigue me, Amy, and I think I can help you. Have you heard of Sigmund Freud?' He propelled her forward, their footsteps squeaking on the thick snow.

'Yes,' she replied warily. 'Something to do with dreams, wasn't he?'

Dr Lambourn laughed. 'He was the father of psychoanalysis. He encouraged patients to talk freely about their experiences, particularly in early childhood. He wanted to investigate the mind, especially the subconscious one, so yes, you are partly right about the dreams.'

'Is this why you keep trying to get me to talk?'

'I'm interested in uncovering the hidden cause of your mental problems, yes.'

She stopped abruptly. 'I'm not mental, Dr Lambourn. Why don't you start with someone who is?' She gestured towards the building. 'That place is full of nutters more deserving of your time.'

'Most of them are too far gone.' He clutched her chin in his hand, forcing her to look at him. 'There's hope for you, Amy.' He planted his finger in the middle of her forehead. 'But we need to find the key to unlock what's happening up here. The key to your freedom isn't on a ring attached to Sister's belt. It's in here, in your own head. Please let me help you.'

He held onto her chin, though not in a threatening way; in fact his leather-clad forefinger caressed her cheek. Perhaps she should trust him. Since the ECT, her memories were less scrambled; he'd been right about that at least. But the last thing she wanted was to go through that again.

'No more ECT.'

He released his grip on her chin, placing his hands firmly on her shoulders instead. 'No more ECT, I promise.'

She gazed off into the distance, studying the building she was now forced to call home. The water tower dominated the skyline and icicles hung like spears from the cracks in the guttering. Would it really do any harm to be a part of his experimental psychoanalysis? After all, what did she have to lose?

'And you're qualified to practise this psychoanalysis, are you?'

'More or less.'

She raised her eyebrows. 'More or less?'

'I'm a fully qualified psychiatrist, Amy. You don't have anything to fear. This psychoanalysis is a bit different but you're in safe hands.'

She sighed. 'All right, Doctor. I'll be your guinea pig.'

A smile of relief played on his lips. 'You won't regret it, Amy. We'll start after Christmas.'

They walked on in companionable silence, the wind freezing their faces, their lips numb with the cold, until they came to the front of the building, where the stone steps were upholstered with a thick cushion of snow. Several men clustered at the bottom, all leaning on their shovels. A nurse appeared and began to issue instructions. 'Ed, you clear the steps, please, starting at the top. Push the snow from left to right so that it falls through the railings.' He turned to the other men. 'You lot start on the driveway.'

Young Ed climbed up to the top, one step at a time, like a toddler learning to use stairs. Grasping the handrail for support, he took a few deep breaths and then began to shovel the snow. His slight frame and apparent unsteadiness were no barrier to hard work, and within seconds he'd cleared the top step entirely and moved down to the second one. Dr Lambourn and Amy waited patiently at the bottom.

When the steps were clear, the young man gestured with a sweep of his hand, indicating that they should proceed. 'Thank you, Ed,' said Dr Lambourn.

Amy acknowledged his hard work with a smile and a nod of her head. Ed beamed and doffed his cap. 'Take care now, miss, I wouldn't want you to slip.'

Dr Lambourn ascended the steps first and stamped the snow off his boots. Amy reached across to the hand-rail and scooped up a handful of snow, moulding it into a perfect ball. Ed was bent over his shovel, turned away from her as she launched the missile, which landed squarely on the back of his head, the snow disintegrating and running under his collar.

He straightened up with a start. 'Oi, watch out.' He looked around for his assailant and noticed Amy rubbing her hands together and smiling. 'You?'

She suppressed a small giggle, but then as she saw him bend down to pick up a fistful of snow of his own, she squealed and darted into the hallway, slamming the door behind her just in time. Hearing the loud thud on the wood as the snowball landed, she leaned against the inside of the door and laughed. For the first time in years she felt the spontaneous eruption of joy, the laughter that had been buried for so long bursting forth like champagne bubbles from a bottle in a torrent she was unable to stop.

18

The ward had never looked so resplendent. It wasn't just the festive adornments, but the fact that the place had been meticulously sanitised, with every cobweb, every stain and every troublesome patient removed. The directive from the new medical superintendent had arrived the week before. The ward was to be opened to visitors two days before Christmas in order that families could spend time with their loved ones and go home safe in the knowledge that they were receiving the best possible treatment the hospital had to offer.

'As if we haven't got enough to do,' snorted Sister Atkins as she read the memo.

Ellen kept quiet. Sister Atkins really had nothing to complain about. After all, she would no doubt delegate the work to Ellen and the other student nurses.

With the scrubbing, polishing and scouring all done, Ellen's hands were chapped and red raw, her nails a stumpy shadow of what they used to be. Amy appeared at the door to the day room holding a tray.

'Where shall I put these?'

The kitchen had sent up a batch of hot mince pies,

which, along with the carols playing on the gramophone, added to the Christmas spirit and even injected a modicum of normality. Ellen took the tray and placed it on the sideboard, rubbing away a small patch of beeswax with her sleeve. 'Somebody didn't do a very good job here,' she muttered.

'How do I look?' asked Amy, twirling round on the spot. 'I want to show my father that I'm on the mend and that I won't let him down again.' Although still wearing the drab hospital dress, she had tied a ribbon around her slim waist and fashioned a piece of tinsel into a brooch. She had brushed her hair and even added a slick of pale lipstick, which completed the transformation.

Ellen busied herself with the sprigs of holly she had collected from the grounds. Their shiny dark green leaves stabbed her fingers and drew a droplet of blood. She thrust her finger into her mouth and sucked noisily, the distraction giving her the perfect opportunity to ignore Amy's question.

The patients were all assembled in the day room as the visitors began to arrive. They milled around sipping cups of tea and eating the pies as though they were in a grand country house being entertained by the lord and lady of the manor. Ellen wandered around the room with the teapot refilling cups and making idle chit-chat. She noticed Amy glancing towards the door, looking for her father, her features darkening every time a new visitor arrived for another patient. But Ellen·knew he wouldn't be coming through the door, not today, not tomorrow or any day in the future. Dr Lambourn had insisted that Amy should not be told about the letter her father had written. Said it would not be conducive to her recovery. Did Ellen want to be responsible for Amy not getting better? Could she live with that on her conscience? It was true that Amy had seemed a little brighter these past few days, not as argumentative or obstreperous. Ellen had no choice but to heed the doctor's instructions.

Queenie was in her element. Her younger sister had come to visit and Queenie was busy promenading her around the room, introducing her as Princess Ethel to anybody who was interested and plenty who weren't.

'For God's sake,' Amy muttered to Ellen. 'You'd think they'd have knocked that nonsense out of her by now. Honestly, it's not right that I'm locked up with people like that.'

'She's harmless enough, Amy.'

She changed the subject. 'My father's not coming, is he?'

Ellen shoved half a mince pie into her mouth, giving herself time to formulate a careful reply. She swallowed the lard-laden pastry and dabbed her mouth with her apron. 'It's beginning to look that way, Amy, but don't lose heart. You just concentrate on getting better, and then when you're out of here you can go and see him.'

Amy grabbed the tinsel brooch and pulled it off her dress, tearing a hole in the fabric. 'I knew he wouldn't come. She's brainwashed him, you see.' She untied the ribbon from her waist and placed it around her neck. Ellen saw the danger immediately. It hadn't registered at first, but there was no way Amy should have been allowed to get her hands on that ribbon. She was a 'red-card' patient, a potential suicide risk, and an investigation with severe repercussions for whoever was responsible would surely follow if Sister found out.

Amy pushed her way through the throng and settled herself on the window seat, staring out over the garden. The snow was beginning to melt, and huge dollops of it slid down the roof like melted ice cream. Ellen sat down opposite her and took hold of her hand.

'There's hope for you, Amy. You mustn't give up.' She fingered the satin ribbon for a moment before gently pulling it from round Amy's neck and slipping it into her own pocket.

19

If Ambergate Mental Hospital had had such a thing as a social calendar, then the Christmas ball would surely have been the highlight. The patients had spent the previous week making paper chains, which now hung around the room suspended between the wall lights. A huge Christmas tree had been commandeered from somewhere, and even though its branches were almost devoid of needles, it added to the festivities in its own pathetic way.

The disappointment over the non-appearance of her father at yesterday's visiting had waned somewhat, and for the first time since her admittance, Amy felt a little more optimistic. Dr Lambourn had promised to help her get better, and even if he was using a method he was not qualified in, who was she to argue? She didn't know the difference between a psychiatrist and a psychoanalyst anyway, and she didn't really care. As long as it meant she wouldn't have to endure another round of ECT, she would agree to anything.

The dance floor was crowded with the shuffling bodies of identically dressed patients pretending to have a good time. Extra cigarette rations had been given out and the fug of blue smoke hung in the air like a toxic cloud. Amy wafted her hand in front of her face as her eyes began to smart. She watched as Queenie hauled Pearl around the dance floor, barely able to reach her arms around the other woman's bulk. She looked up as she felt a tap on her shoulder. A young male nurse held out his hand. 'Care to dance?'

She recognised the accent and wrinkled her nose. 'Sorry, I've forgotten your name.'

'Nurse Lyons, but for tonight, it's Dougie.' His hand was still outstretched.

She shook her head. 'You don't have to, really.'

'I want to.'

She stood up and smoothed her dress, suddenly conscious that she looked just like every other lunatic in here. There was no doubt that this was a pity dance, one he would regale his friends with later, laughing at her expense.

He held her at a respectful distance, but still close enough for her to catch the lemony scent radiating off his skin. He was much taller than she, but there again, everybody was. She stared straight ahead at his chest, his shirt unbuttoned a little to reveal his hairless skin. He guided her expertly round the room, but she was thankful that he didn't try to engage her in conversation, which she knew would just be forced. He was only doing this because it was part of his job.

As the record came to an end, he held her at arm's length and smiled. 'Thank you, ma'am.' Then he took her by the hand and guided her back to the chairs lining the sides of the room. 'That was a real pleasure.'

She regarded him with faint amusement. 'You're a good nurse, Dougie, and an even better liar.'

As the evening dragged on, she became more and more desperate to return to the ward. The stench of sweaty bodies never afforded the luxury of regular baths, never mind deodorant, was overpowering, and the heat almost unbearable. She loosened the buttons on the front of her dress and blew onto her chest. She let her head loll back on the wall behind her and closed her eyes, not even bothering to open them when she felt someone plonk themselves down on the seat next to her. The music had been cranked up and the strains of 'Winter Wonderland' sounded tinny as the gramophone struggled to cope.

'Hello again.'

She opened her eyes and rubbed her ear. 'There's no need to shout, I'm only here.'

'Sorry, I didn't think you'd be able to hear me above the racket.'

She turned to get a better look at him. 'Oh, it's you. How's your head?'

He rubbed his hand self-consciously over the back of his head. 'Getting there. Since the operation to remove the pressure on my brain, it's been a lot better. Not so many fits, but still the occasional headache.'

'Eh? What *are* you going on about?'

'Some bloke in a truck knocked me off my bike in the summer, didn't even stop, left me for dead, he did. I was making the last delivery of the day an' all. Spuds and carrots and what 'ave you all over the road. Still, I'm on the mend now, as long as no one chucks a snowball at my head.'

She felt the colour rise in her cheeks; nothing to do with the heat, though. 'I'm really sorry. I had no idea. I mean, how could I possibly . . .'

She stopped as she saw him smiling. His sombre expression of a moment before was replaced with a cheeky grin. He stood up and gestured towards the dance floor. 'I'll forgive you if you'll dance with me.'

The thought of squeezing in between the heaving mass of bodies was not an appealing one, but he looked at her so sweetly, his dimples reminding her of a little boy. And he wasn't mental. Like her, he shouldn't even be in this place. He was waiting for her answer.

'I'd love to, thank you.'

'My name's Edward Hooper.' He extended his hand. 'But everyone calls me Ed.'

'Amy Sullivan,' she offered in return. 'Everyone calls me Amy, amongst other unsavoury names.'

He held her closer than the nurse had done, and he was much smaller, only a few inches taller than Amy herself. It made eye contact on the dance floor difficult to avoid.

She felt his hand in the small of her back, and in spite of herself, she relaxed into his arms. He seemed a little shaky on his feet, and she wondered if she was actually holding him up, but for a few seconds it was as if nobody else existed, and she forgot about where she was and allowed herself to be transported elsewhere. Back to the church dances she used to go to, where the vicar would take it upon himself to chaperone couples, thrusting his arm between them if he thought they were dancing too close together.

As the music came to an end, she was smiling at the memory. Ed leaned towards her, their foreheads touching briefly. 'Thank you,' he whispered.

They pulled away from each other, but Ed kept hold of her hand in his own moist palm as he led her back to the chairs. She felt lighter than she had in months, maybe even years, as though the big black cloak of despair she had worn like a second skin had been cast off and left in a heap on the dance floor.

20

'Did you have a nice Christmas, Amy?'

She was reclining on his couch, a red velvet affair that was new to his office but that had evidently had a previous life in which someone had seen fit to stub out cigarettes on the upholstery. She stuck her finger into a burnt hole and absently pulled at the stuffing. 'What sort of a question is that, Dr Lambourn? I was stuck in here, so what do you think?'

He tapped his pen on his pad. 'Just trying to relax you before we get started, that's all.' He noticed her picking at the couch. 'Would you mind not doing that, please?'

She tutted and folded her arms across her chest. 'Right, what do you want to know?'

'What would you like to tell me?'

'Do you always answer a question with a question?'

He raised his eyebrows. 'Do you?'

She swung her legs off the couch and made to stand up. 'This isn't going to work, Doctor. There's nothing to tell, there's nothing wrong with me. So what if I sometimes feel so heavy it's like I'm wearing a suit of armour? So what if the anger burning inside me makes me feel as though my skin is on fire? So what if I step off the bottom stair and there's nothing there but a swirling black pit of nothingness?'

She started to finger the cigarette burn again, the only sound coming from Dr Lambourn's pen as he scratched away furiously on his pad. He underlined something several times before he spoke. 'Very good, Amy, very good indeed.'

'Are you married, Dr Lambourn?'

The sudden change of subject seemed to unnerve him. 'No, but . . .'

'Girlfriend, then? Surely a good-looking bloke like yourself isn't short of female company?'

'Amy, this is not about me. Stop trying to change the focus of our session.' His tone was forceful but not unkind. 'Now, tell me about the lake incident.'

She swung her legs onto the sofa and lay back, her hands clasped across her stomach. 'You're like a dog with a bone, Doctor.'

'Whatever it takes.'

She closed her eyes and several minutes passed before she spoke again. 'It was cold, icy cold, and so, so dark. I should have been frightened, I suppose. I mean, there could have been all kinds of nutters lurking in the bushes.' She opened her eyes and looked at the doctor. 'Then again, they're all in here, aren't they?'

He gave her a small smile. 'Please carry on.'

'I don't know, I just wanted to inflict the same depth of pain on her as she had on me.'

'Do you want to tell me who has hurt you so much, Amy?'

She spoke as though she had a bitter taste in her mouth, as though she could not bear the words on her lips. 'My stepmother.' She could feel the familiar rage building and she swallowed hard before she spat out the name. 'Carrie.'

'Carrie?' repeated Dr Lambourn.

She heard him scribbling away again. 'Can we not say her name any more?'

He paused and seemed to consider his answer, as though the question was an important one and not just a simple request. 'As you wish. For now.'

'After I killed my mother—'

Dr Lambourn interrupted immediately. 'Amy, it was an accident, we've been through this. Please stop torturing yourself.'

She sighed. 'All right then, after my mother died in a tragic accident . . .' she stopped and looked pointedly at him, '*that I caused*, my father and I eventually grew closer together. Oh, it wasn't easy at first; in fact it was terrible. I'd been told by relatives not to cry in case I upset my dad. As though it was all about him. I'd lost my mother, for God's sake. She was there one day and the next day she'd gone. How could someone so beautiful and talented, so alive and vital, just cease to exist? I was never allowed to grieve, so I spent many years bottling things up, too afraid to mention her in case I set Dad off. We never spoke about her. It was like she was being slowly erased from our past, like she'd never existed, and I didn't like it.'

A tear seeped out from under her closed lids and she flicked it away with her finger. 'And then there was the baby . . . they couldn't save him. They tried, but it . . . he . . .'

Her voice trailed off as more tears came. She covered her face with her hands, ashamed that Dr Lambourn was witnessing the depth of her sadness. He pulled his handkerchief from his pocket and handed it to her. It had been pressed into a perfect square, and was so white and pristine that she hesitated for a moment before unfolding it and holding it to her nose. The smell of soap powder mingled with a hint of his cologne. She found it strangely comforting.

His voice was hoarse when he spoke, as though he had been the one to break down in tears. 'Why do you hate your stepmother so much?'

Her words came out on a deep sigh. 'Because she made my father happy.'

'Were you not pleased that he was happy at last?'

She shook her head. 'I wanted to be the one who made him happy.' The handkerchief was now a crumpled ball in her sweaty hands. 'After I killed . . . after my mother died, we clung to each other, my father and I, physically and emotionally; there was no room for anyone else. How could there be? The void left by my mother was just too big to fill. But we still had each other and we both knew what the other was going through.'

She stopped talking and flapped her hand in front of her face. 'It's so hot in here – would you mind opening the window?'

He nodded and lifted the heavy sash a couple of inches, scaring off the two pigeons that had been huddled on the window ledge. An icy blast cut through the heat of the room. 'Please continue,' he said.

'She was so beautiful, my mother.'

Dr Lambourn smiled. 'You take after her, then.'

'Oh no,' she said dismissively. 'My mother was *really* stunning. Film-star looks, you might say. And such a talented artist, landscapes. She even sold a few of her paintings. A couple of them were bought by another painter who'd also studied at the Manchester School of Art, L. S. Lowry. You've probably heard of him.'

Dr Lambourn looked up from his pad. 'Yes indeed. Impressive.'

'She didn't make a lot of money but she really was on the cusp of something special. He called her an exceptional talent.'

The temperature of the room had plummeted. 'Are you cool enough now, Amy? I'll close the window, then maybe we can talk about Carrie.'

'No!' she shouted. 'No, no, no.'

He stopped and stepped away from the window. 'As you wish, I'll leave it open.'

'I'm not talking about the bloody window,' she raged. 'I told you not to say her name and you didn't listen to me.' She stood and faced him, not bothering to hold back the sobs as she pummelled his chest with her fists. 'You didn't listen to me.'

He grabbed her wrists and held them tightly. She was no match for his strength and all her fight drained away as her knees began to buckle. He circled his arms around her body and held her close, gently stroking the back of her head. 'We'll leave it there for today, Amy. You've done very well.'

As her sobs subsided, she blotted her nose with the handkerchief then handed it back to him. He put his palms up. 'Please,' he said. 'You keep it.'

She nodded and silently stuffed it up her sleeve, a weak smile on her lips. 'Thank you.'

21

Amy cupped her hands and blew a warm cloud of breath into her palms. She had always suffered from bad circulation and her fingers were stiff and blue with the cold. She trudged around the airing court, where the snow had all but melted, leaving just the odd pile of brown mush. The biting wind gnawed at her cheeks and whipped around her exposed neck. She turned up the collar on the wholly inadequate coat they'd provided her with, the thin fabric worn away in parts, the torn lining neither use nor ornament. She had a perfectly good coat at home: bright red, fitted at the waist, with huge buttons all down the front and a black fur collar. She smiled at the stir it would create if she were allowed to wear it in this miserable place.

It had been two weeks now since her last session with Dr Lambourn and she had not seen or heard from him since. No doubt he had grown fed up of her, tired of her tears, which always seemed to unsettle him. The second she showed any emotion he always abruptly ended the session.

She stopped by the gate in the wall and stood next to

Belinda, who was gazing through the bars. 'Waiting for your rendezvous?'

'Eh?' A stubby cigarette protruded from Belinda's yellow teeth.

'Never mind,' replied Amy, recoiling from her stale breath.

Belinda called through the bars of the gate to where a few of the male patients were digging over the vegetable patch. 'Oi, you with the spade. Got any fags? You can have a little fiddle in return.' She pulled her dress open to reveal her saggy breasts, blue veins clearly visible beneath the pasty skin.

'For God's sake,' Amy muttered under her breath. 'Where's your dignity?'

The lad with the spade looked up and scratched his head. 'Are you talking to me?' he shouted.

Amy recognised Ed's voice immediately. 'Leave him alone, Belinda, you dirty slut. He's only a boy.'

'Gonna make me, are you?' Belinda sneered.

'If necessary, yes.'

Belinda snorted. 'I'd like to see you try.' She balled her hands into fists, but Amy was too quick, and she just had time to delight in the shocked look in Belinda's eyes as her fist connected with her cheek. Belinda stumbled backwards, cracking her head on the wall behind her before she slumped to the ground.

Amy rubbed her knuckles as she smirked at the pathetic figure on the floor. She could hear Ed calling her name but had no time to answer before she felt Sister Atkins grab her from behind and force her arm up her back. She heard a bone crack and was sure her shoulder had dislocated. The pain was blinding, and had Sister Atkins not been holding her up, she would have collapsed in a heap next to the blubbering Belinda.

'I've had just about enough of your nonsense.' Sister Atkins spoke through gritted teeth, flecks of spittle landing on Amy's cheek. In spite of the pain in her shoulder, she longed to wipe her face, but Sister Atkins now had both arms firmly wrenched behind her back.

'Belinda, get up,' ordered Sister Atkins.

Belinda staggered to her feet, blood dripping from both nostrils, her greasy hair framing her snarling features.

'Now listen to me, you two, I don't want any trouble on the ward. You leave it out here, do you hear me?'

Both girls were silent. 'I said, *do you hear me*?' raged Sister Atkins.

Amy stared at Belinda through narrowed eyes. 'Yes, Sister.'

'Belinda?'

Belinda folded her arms and scuffed at the dirt with her toe. 'Yes, Sister,' she mumbled.

Sister Atkins released her grip and shoved Amy hard in the back. 'This is your final warning.' She turned and marched back inside, leaving the two of them alone, the palpable hatred simmering between them.

Amy turned to move away, but Belinda grabbed a fistful

of her hair and spoke into her ear. 'You haven't heard the last of this. You'd better watch your back.'

'Oh, do your worst. I'm not scared of you, you pathetic trollop.'

She elbowed Belinda in the ribs and stormed off to the other side of the airing court. A group of women stood in a huddle, falling silent as she strode past. 'Show's over,' she snapped.

'Do you want to tell me what that was all about this afternoon?'

She glared at Dr Lambourn and shook her head. 'No, I don't.'

'Amy, I'm trying to help you, really I am, but you don't make it easy. I'm giving you a lot of my time, more than I'm giving to my other patients. Why do you think that is?'

'I know, you've already told me. You think the others are all certified lunatics who are too far gone to respond to this kind of help. Either that or you fancy me.'

He closed his eyes, tried to compose himself before replying. 'I shall not dignify that last comment with a response. Now, we shall continue where we left off at our last session.' He glanced down at his notes. 'Thinking back to when you took your stepmother's baby . . .' He paused to check she was listening. 'When you took Carrie's baby?'

She stiffened at the mention of the name, knew he

was deliberately trying to provoke a reaction. She would not give him the satisfaction, would not make this easy for him. Her mouth was dry and she fought to keep her voice steady. He was never going to let this drop, so she might as well get it over with. Besides, it was comfy here on his couch in the quiet haven of his office, away from those savages on the ward. It wouldn't do any harm to humour him.

'I think you were right, Doctor. I had blocked that night from my memory. It would have been my mother's birthday – her fortieth, but nobody else had remembered.' She looked at Dr Lambourn, her face a picture of incredulity. 'Can you believe that? My father hadn't even remembered it was his wife's birthday. I mean, they'd been together since they were sixteen, but all he was interested in was cooing over his new baby. He didn't even think about his other baby who'd been so tragically killed. I just didn't fit into this family any more, there wasn't room for us all. I thought about running away, but where would I have gone, and in any case, why should I be driven out of my own home?'

'Let me see if I understand this correctly,' interrupted Dr Lambourn. 'Your father and Carrie eventually married and had a baby together.'

'Eventually? That's a laugh. They married only five months after they met.'

'I see. And how long after that did the baby come along?'

175

'Nine months,' she scoffed.

'Boy or girl?'

'Does it matter really? What's the point in all these questions?'

'Boy or girl?' he insisted.

She sighed impatiently. 'Oh for God's sake, all right then. A girl.'

'Thank you. Now back to the night in question.'

'Lord above, you sound like a police officer.'

'You do realise, Amy, you could have gone to prison for attempted suicide, not to mention murder. I think you owe a great debt to your father for bringing you here instead.'

'I must send him a thank-you note.'

'You don't know how lucky you are. Only last week I recommended a chap be admitted to Ambergate for treatment after he was found half strangled next to the decomposing body of his late wife. He couldn't carry on without her and had tried to take his own life so they could be together again. The magistrates disagreed with me, however, and he's now doing six months in Strangeways instead.'

She picked at the bobbles of lint on her dress, flicking them between her fingers, her disinterest obvious in her bored features.

He massaged his temples, trying to stay calm. 'Amy, what happened that night?' He paused. 'In your own time.'

He fell silent and stopped writing, hardly daring to breathe. The silence between them grew until it became suffocating and impossible to ignore. Amy was the first to crack.

'I wanted to punish them both for forgetting my mother's birthday,' she began softly. 'I wanted them to feel the same pain that I had to live with every day of my life. They were both downstairs in front of the fire, crammed into the same armchair, the one my mother and me used to sit in. A string of nappies hung over the fireplace, steaming away, and they were just sitting there, their foreheads touching, him running his finger down the side of her cheek. They were completely oblivious to me standing there in the room. I just felt invisible, that they wouldn't even notice if I disappeared forever. It should have been my baby brother's nappies hanging there to dry, and it should have been him fast asleep in his cot upstairs. It was all wrong.'

She paused and rolled a ball of lint in her fingers. 'I decided to go away that night, never come back, make them feel guilty for what they had driven me to. But they didn't care about me. I knew they wouldn't grieve if I never came back. It was what they wanted, me out of the way. The guilt might have gnawed away at them for a little while, but they wouldn't actually miss me, wouldn't feel the all-consuming pain of loss.' She stopped and smiled. 'That was when I decided to take the baby with me. They cared about her, you see. And then my stepmother would know the agony that I had to endure every single day.'

'You are one troubled young lady, Amy Sullivan.'

'And you're very good at stating the obvious, Dr Lambourn. How many years were you in medical school?'

He ignored the question. 'Continue, please.'

'I crept upstairs, taking care to miss out the step that always managed to make a loud creak if you went anywhere near it. I pushed open their bedroom door, and the hinges groaned so loudly I was sure they would both come bounding up the stairs. But no, they were so wrapped up in each other they probably never even heard anything. The baby was asleep in the crib beside their bed, just her little pink face peeping out from the mound of blankets she'd covered her with. I scooped her up as quietly as I could and rocked her from side to side until she settled. Then I hurried back down the stairs, crept out of the front door and made my way to the park.'

'Intent on ending your own life as well as the baby's?'

'I suppose so. I wasn't thinking straight, wasn't really thinking at all. I just knew I wanted all the pain to go away. My stepmother . . . Carrie . . .' She pulled a face as though she'd just taken a bite out of a lemon. 'Carrie was the archetypal wicked stepmother who hated me, thought I was in the way and just wanted my father all to herself. Well, I thought, she can have him, but I'm taking her baby with me, then she too will know the excruciating pain of losing someone you love so dearly.'

'On the contrary, Amy, it sounds as though you had given the situation a great deal of thought.'

She stayed silent for a minute, a frown of doubt creasing her forehead. 'Perhaps you're right.' She threw her hands in the air. 'Anyway, what does it matter now? They found me and had me carted off to this place. She got what she wanted in the end. She won.'

'How do you feel about Carrie now?'

Her eyes widened, the fury appearing from nowhere. 'I hate her. She's an evil, bitter woman who turned my father against me, but he was either too blind or too stupid to realise it. I don't even know what he sees in her; she's an old hag who couldn't hold a candle to my mother. She's a witch, even looks like one, with her sunken eyes, pointed chin and warts. She's only missing a black cat and a broomstick.' She shook her head in disbelief. 'But for some unfathomable reason, she made him happy. I could have done that, Dr Lambourn. I could have made him happy.'

She rose from the couch and wandered over to the window, absently running her finger through the dust along the sill. She stared out, her warm breath condensing on the glass. 'My father's not coming back to see me, is he, Dr Lambourn?'

'No, he isn't, Amy, he's not coming back, not yet anyway.'

She turned round, her face inscrutable apart from the tears that glistened on each cheek. 'I knew it,' she whispered. 'I knew it.'

22

Sister Atkins peered at Ellen over her spectacles. 'The new superintendent's at it again, I see.'

'Oh heck, what's he up to now, Sister?'

She thrust a piece of paper across her desk. 'Read it for yourself.'

Ellen squinted at the pale typewritten script, then held it directly under the desk lamp for a better view. 'His secretary needs to learn when to change the ribbon, I know that much.'

She read the memo twice over, not finding it difficult to imagine the depth of Sister's consternation.

'It sounds like a positive move to me.'

Sister Atkins raised her eyes to the ceiling. 'I might have known you'd see it that way.' She slapped her hand down on the memo. 'Unlocking the wards? I've never 'eard anything so crazy in all my life. Allowing them more access to the grounds? Letting them mix?' Her voice had risen so high, it had nowhere left to go.

'Well, he says he instigated these things at the last hospital he worked at,' countered Ellen. 'It must have been a success or else he wouldn't be trying it here. And it's only certain wards that won't be locked. The most dangerous patients and long-stay ones will still be contained.'

Sister shook her head, but whether it was with disbelief, exasperation or reluctant acceptance, Ellen could not tell.

Ellen continued to look for positives. 'He says the patients became less disturbed and easier to handle when they had a little more freedom. Surely that can only benefit all of us?'

Sister stayed quiet, her elbows on her desk and her hands in her hair, inadvertently working her bun loose. She screwed the memo into a tight ball and tossed it into the bin on the opposite side of the room, the tinny echo shattering the awkward silence as it hit the metal bottom. 'That's what I think of the New Directive for the Enhancement of Patients' Well-being.'

She rubbed her hands together as though the balled-up memo had contaminated them in some way. 'When I was training, we were told not to encourage the patients to fraternise. We didn't want them ganging up on us, you see.' She punched her fist into the air. 'Divide and conquer, that was our motto.' She shook her head. 'It's all right for his nibs, sitting in his plush office dictating memos as though they're going out of fashion, but it's the likes of me and you who are going to have to deal with his fancy ideas and pick up the pieces when it all goes wrong.' She reached for the matches, lit a cigarette and took a long, calming drag as she rocked back on her chair and stared at the ceiling.

Ellen backed slowly out of the room, but hesitated in the doorway. 'Sister, I went home this weekend, and my mother baked a cake.'

Sister Atkins had her eyes closed, making no attempt to even appear interested. 'Mmm . . . I'll alert the press, shall I?'

Ellen detected the sarcasm but ploughed on. 'It's for Amy . . . it's for her . . .' She floundered, wishing she'd caught Sister in a better mood. 'Well, it's her birthday today. She's twenty.'

Sister Atkins glared at Ellen now, the cigarette still stuck between her lips. 'And you've baked her a cake?'

'Not me, no. My mother baked her a cake.'

'Don't split hairs, Student Nurse Crosby. What exactly is it you think we're running here?'

Ellen felt the familiar clamminess in her palms. 'I thought it would be a nice thing to do, that's all.'

Sister regarded her with a thoughtful stare and Ellen could almost hear the cogs turning. 'What sort is it?' she asked eventually.

'Chocolate.'

She squinted through the cigarette smoke. 'Make sure you cut me a slice then.' A faint smile traced her lips. 'Go on with yer, get out of here.'

The day was mild but damp, a smell of woodsmoke filtering over from the vegetable plot. Ellen had asked Amy if she would like to go for a walk in the grounds during visiting time. It was a move designed to take the girl away from the wards, for they both knew she wouldn't be receiving any visitors, birthday or not. Not a single card had arrived for her.

Ellen swung the wicker basket by her side as they walked together in silence. A group of male patients were picking out weeds from between the furrows, the soil much easier to work now the temperature had risen. A male nurse threw some more wood on the fire, which immediately quashed the flames and sent a plume of thick grey smoke into the still air. He coughed and flapped his arms around.

Ellen laughed and hoisted the basket into the crook of her elbow. 'Morning, Dougie.'

His eyes streamed as he squinted to look at her. 'Ellen, how're you? What a surprise. What brings you out here?'

She nodded towards her companion. 'It's Amy's birthday and Sister gave me permission to accompany her on a walk around the grounds.' She patted the basket. 'I've got cake.'

'Well, many happy returns, Amy.' He leaned forward awkwardly, then stopped, thrusting his hands into his pockets instead.

Amy managed a smile. 'Would you like to join us for tea and cake? We've got a Thermos, too.'

Ellen noticed the glint in her eye, the coy smile. She tugged on Amy's arm. 'Come on, Nurse Lyons has plenty to do here without us distracting him.' She propelled the girl forward and called over her shoulder, 'Bye, Dougie.'

'For future reference,' he replied, 'I'd have loved a bit of cake.'

They walked on in silence until they reached the old cricket pavilion, where they could perch on a bench on the veranda, which afforded them a little shelter from the mizzle in the air. Ellen unpacked the cake and poured two cups of stewed tea from the flask.

'He's nice, isn't he?' Amy took a sip of the hot tea.

'Who is?'

'Dougie. He's so handsome, and he's got a lovely way with the patients, so very kind. And his accent, well, he sounds just like a cowboy.'

Ellen studied Amy as the girl began to dissect her way through her chocolate cake, lifting off the layer of hard chocolate and nibbling it like a hamster before finally taking a mouthful of the sponge.

'He's very professional, yes, but don't confuse professional care with any feelings you think he may have for you.' Her words had come out more harshly than she had intended, and she regretted them immediately she saw the hurt in Amy's eyes. 'Look, I'm sorry,' she apologised. 'I didn't mean to snap like that.'

Amy smiled. 'It's all right. I realise he wouldn't look once at me, let alone twice.' She stood up and brushed the crumbs from her dress. 'In any case, I already have an admirer in here.' She paused and stared across the field to the main building, with its countless windows behind which all manner of human life had been left to wither and die. 'And he's my ticket out of this hell-hole.'

23

The weeks crawled by, each day dictated by the same monotonous routine. Even if you weren't insane before you entered Ambergate, you certainly were if they ever let you out. Not a day went by without some sort of altercation, argument or drama, though, often orchestrated by the staff for their own amusement. Ellen had been horrified by some of the tales Dougie had told her. Life on the male side of the hospital was certainly brutal, violence was commonplace and so-called cures questionable to say the least.

She made her way over to the corner of the social club, grimacing at the squelch beneath her feet, the carpet sodden with years of spilled beer. The top of the table was coated with a sticky residue, the origin of which Ellen could only guess at. She called to Dougie as he approached. 'Fetch a cloth, will you, this table's disgusting.'

He returned with a grey dishcloth and swabbed the table. Ellen wrinkled her nose. 'Hmm . . . marginally better, I suppose.'

She noticed his quiet demeanour as he sat down and fiddled with the sodden beer mat. His usual effervescence had evaporated and he looked as though he hadn't slept in a month. 'Are you all right, Dougie? You look so tired.'

He made a valiant effort to perk up. 'Oh, sure, just been one of those days.'

'Every day's one of those days in here. D'you want to tell me about it?'

He hesitated. 'No, you don't wanna hear my problems.'

'Then why did I ask?'

He took a long slug of his pint. 'We had a new patient in today, Brian's his name. His wife brought him, said the doctor had insisted he come in for treatment but she wasn't so sure.'

'What's the matter with him?'

Dougie exhaled deeply and looked shiftily left and right, lowering his voice before he answered. 'He's one of . . . those.'

Ellen frowned. 'One of those what?'

Dougie bent his wrist. 'You know, a . . . homosexual.' He mouthed the last word.

'But you said his *wife* brought him in?'

'That's right, they've been married for five years. He loves her deeply and I can see in her eyes that she feels the same way. It's a mutually tender, caring love.'

'I'm not following you, Dougie. Why's he in Ambergate?'

'His doctor referred him. He thinks he needs treatment to be cured.'

'Cured? Is that even possible? I mean, he's not ill.'

Dougie shrugged. 'We'll see. The aversion therapy

began today. He was shown pictures of naked men and then given an electric shock.'

Ellen plonked her drink down. 'Good Lord. The poor bugger. That's barbaric, that is.'

'I agree, it's bloody awful, but he loves his wife so much, he's willing to go through it just for her. They've never consummated the marriage.'

Ellen felt her face redden and fiddled with the necklace at her throat. Dougie obviously noticed her discomfort.

'That's nice,' he observed, changing the subject.

'Mum sent it for my birthday. It's not an expensive one, but she would have saved for many months to afford it, so it's special.'

'Ah, that's grand. When was your birthday then?'

'Last month.'

'Oh,' Dougie exclaimed. 'You should have said.'

'I just did.'

'I mean, you should have said something before now.' He stood up and held out his hand. 'Come on.'

They sat on the wall side by side, the smell of warm vinegar and newspaper print wafting between them. Ellen unwrapped her bag of chips, her mouth watering at the tempting aroma. 'Thanks for this, Dougie.'

He nodded towards the wooden chip hut. 'It's hardly The Midland.'

'I know, but it's nice to do something normal for a change. It's easy to forget there's a big wide world outside the hospital.' She popped a hot chip into her mouth. The orange light from the gas lamp illuminated the swollen puddles, the result of an earlier downpour.

A scabby dog wandered over and sat down on the pavement in front of them. He cocked his head to one side, his big brown eyes never straying from Ellen's hand as she dipped into the bag and brought out another chip. 'Ah, look at him, he's starving.'

'He's a scruffy mutt all right,' replied Dougie, tossing him a chip. 'You can see all his ribs.'

The dog wolfed the chip down in one go and resumed his begging position.

'It didn't touch the sides, that chip. He barely tasted it.'

Ellen licked her greasy fingers one by one and screwed up the newspaper. 'Thanks again, Dougie. Best birthday meal I've ever had.'

He gazed into the distance, a wistful look on his face.

'I said thanks, Dougie.'

He jolted back to the present. 'I'm sorry. I was just thinking about Brian and his wife. What he's prepared to go through to make her happy, that's true love, no mistake.' He turned to face her. 'But do you know what the really tragic thing is?'

Ellen shook her head.

'She's already happy. She loves him just the way he is.' He forced a smile. 'Fancy a walk?' He jumped off the wall and stood in front of her. 'Come on.'

He placed his hands on her waist as she shuffled off the wall, guiding her gently to the ground. He left one hand there, resting on her hip, and gazed down into her face. She hardly dared breathe as she felt his fingers touch her cheek. Emboldened by her apparent acquiescence, he ran his hand round the back of her head and drew her to him. She felt his hand entwined in her hair and closed her eyes, waiting for the gentle brush of his lips on her own. When it came, she let out a small sigh, opened her eyes and smiled at him.

'You've no idea how long I've wanted to do that,' he said, pulling away.

Her heart was thumping so loudly, she was sure he must be able to hear it. 'And you waited until I stank of chips before you made your move.'

'Nothing wrong with that.' He leaned forward and kissed her again, more deeply this time. She stumbled backwards, her body captive against the wall as he covered her face in warm kisses.

The starving dog had been forgotten until he let out a piercing whine that startled them both.

'Bloody hell,' exclaimed Dougie. 'That's gratitude for you.' He bent down and patted the dog's head. 'Wait here a sec,' he said to Ellen.

He disappeared into the chip hut and returned moments later with a steaming hot bundle. He placed it on the wall and unwrapped a sausage, which he began to pull apart with his fingers, wincing as the hot meat burned his skin.

He blew on the pieces, the steam dispersing with each breath. 'What *are* you doing?' asked Ellen.

He looked genuinely surprised. 'I don't want the poor dog to burn his mouth.'

He put the sausage down on the pavement and the grateful dog devoured his meal as Ellen and Dougie watched. 'Best threepence I've ever spent,' Dougie declared, slipping his arm around her shoulders.

She leaned her head against him. 'You're a big softie, Douglas Lyons.'

He kissed her hair. 'You'd better believe it.'

24

Another skirmish had broken out in the day room. Although the chairs were not labelled, the patients tended to gravitate to what they regarded as their own chair, and woe betide anyone who dared to sit in the wrong one.

'Excuse me, Belinda, you're in my chair.' Amy forced a note of politeness into her voice and smiled sweetly.

Belinda didn't even bother to look up. 'Get lost, yer stuck-up cow.'

Nobody could argue she hadn't tried the friendly approach first, and Amy was almost glad that Belinda had reacted in this way. It gave her a good excuse for what happened next. She launched herself at the other girl from behind, one arm securing her in a headlock, the other hand grabbing a fistful of her hair. In one quick movement she heaved her out of her seat and sent her sprawling to the floor.

Belinda clattered into a table, sending china cups flying everywhere, dregs of tea soaking into the carpet. She sat on the floor, snarling like a rabid dog, then scrambled to her feet and flew at Amy just as Sister Atkins appeared at the door.

'Jesus H. Christ! It's like the Wild West in 'ere. I'm going to need to get saloon doors fitted.' She pulled Belinda off Amy and gave her a firm smack on the back of her head. 'I don't want to know who did what to who first. You're both as bad as each other.' She turned and smacked Amy on the back of her head too. 'There, just to show I don't have my favourites.' She pointed at the broken crockery. 'Now get this lot cleared up immediately.'

Belinda and Amy knelt down and silently picked up the pieces of broken china, stacking them onto a tray. Pearl and Queenie, sitting nearby, watched on in stunned amazement.

'Sorry,' said Belinda.

Amy, still on her knees, placed her hands in the small of her back. 'What did you say?'

'You 'eard. I'll not say it again.'

Amy relented. 'Me too.' She stood up and wandered over to the disputed chair in the bay window.

Belinda followed and took the chair opposite. 'It's shit in 'ere, int it?'

Amy could not argue with that sentiment. She looked at her foe with thinly veiled pity. She had no idea how long Belinda had been at Ambergate, but the experience had clearly ravaged her. 'Why are you here, Belinda?'

The defiance of a few moments ago vanished. 'Me dad,' Belinda whispered. 'He don't want me no more.'

Amy felt a pang of empathy. She could certainly relate to that. 'Threw you out, did he?'

Belinda chewed on her thumbnail, her hooded eyes filled with sadness. 'Something like that. I think I just got too old for 'im.'

'What on earth are you talking about? You can't be much older than I am.'

'I'm twenny-three now,' Belinda sniffed. 'But he likes 'em younger, you see. Came 'ere when I was sixteen.'

Amy was in too deep to stop now, even though every instinct was telling her to get up and walk away. 'What do you mean, Belinda?' she asked, fervently hoping the girl would return to her usual hostile self and tell her to mind her own business.

'He used to come to my bed nearly every night. I would lie awake waiting for him to get home from the pub, and when I heard 'im clomping up the stairs, me 'eart would soar. I knew I wouldn't have to spend the night on me own, see?' She paused and shook her head. 'I hated that, hated having to sleep on me own. I don't like the dark, me. Sometimes he would disappear for days and I would 'ave to look after meself, but there would never be any food. Once I ate the stale bread off next door's lawn. The bloody birds were better fed than I was.'

Amy swallowed, entranced by the story but hardly daring to push for more information. 'And that's all you did then, sleep together?'

Belinda ignored the question. 'I was always cold in bed. He never wanted me to wear a nightie, said it got in the way, but when he cuddled up to me afterwards, I was warm then, I liked that.' She tilted her head back and stared at the ceiling. 'His hands were rough. He's a brickie, y'know, but he was never actually rough with me, always gentle when he stroked me. He loved me so much.'

'I think you're confusing love with something else, Belinda,' Amy said quietly.

'What d'ya mean?' Belinda snarled, the anger never far from the surface. 'You don't know nuthin' about him. He never hurt me. My friend's dad used to beat her black and blue. Once he smashed her head against the wall and cracked the plaster. He was so mad, he stuck the poker in the fire, and when it was red hot, he held it against her bare back. My dad never did anything like that to me, so don't you—'

Amy held up her hands. 'All right, calm down.' She waited until Belinda's breathing had returned to normal. 'Tell me why you're in here then.'

'Me ma buggered off when I was a bab, so it was just me and him. I don't remember nuthin' about her, but I've seen a picture, like, and she was pretty, so I must take after her.'

Amy studied the other girl's greasy hair, cadaverous complexion and prominent teeth, which meant she was never able to fully close her mouth. It would be difficult to imagine a less attractive specimen. God only knew what her mother had looked like. 'That's nice,' she replied. 'Perhaps you reminded your father of her.'

195

Belinda considered this. 'Nah, he hated her. She's a selfish cow. I'm nuthin' like that.'

Amy nodded. 'So . . . I hesitate to ask again, but why *are* you in here?'

'Be patient,' Belinda snapped. 'I'm coming to it.' She folded her arms and put her feet up on the table between them, as though she was going to come out with a nice bedtime story. 'He met someone down the pub – a woman, I mean. She worked behind the bar, always stank of ale. Before I knew it, he'd moved her in with us, can you believe?' She shook her head in bewilderment. 'I just couldn't understand what he saw in her, she was such an ugly cow.'

Amy could only imagine what Belinda's definition of ugly looked like. She thought about her own stepmother, the familiar bitterness threatening to choke her. Perhaps she and Belinda weren't that different after all. 'And she made your father happy?'

'Oh yes,' Belinda scoffed. 'She did that all right. Brought her daughter to live with us, didn't she? She was only seven years old.' She turned her head to the window, unable to look at Amy, lowering her voice to barely a whisper. 'He never came to my bed after she moved in. I assumed he was with the ugly cow, but no, he was in the little 'un's bed.' She turned back to Amy. 'It was her who had taken my place, not her bloody mother.'

Amy let out a long sigh. 'Belinda, your father was abusing both of you, surely you can see that?'

'No! That's not true. He loved me, made me feel safe, did nice things to me.'

Amy shuddered. 'Jesus, Belinda.'

'Anyway, what does it matter now? When I created a fuss, he threw me out, just like that. But no way was I taking it lying down. Chucked a brick through the window, didn't I?' She laughed at the memory briefly before her expression darkened again. 'I'll admit I was screaming like a madwoman, threatening all kinds, so he had me carted off to this place.' She wiped the back of her hand savagely across her cheek, as though annoyed that she had allowed the tears to come. 'Two policemen dragged me off as though I was an animal, my dad shouting, "Lock 'er up, I never want to see her again!"'

Amy reached across and took hold of Belinda's hand. She snatched it away. 'I don't need your pity.'

'Suit yourself. I was only trying—'

Belinda stood to leave. 'Well don't bother.'

Amy stared after Belinda's retreating figure as she flounced out of the room. It was no wonder she was willing to exchange her body for a few ciggies. The girl craved the physical contact that had defined her childhood. What a tragedy she had mistaken this for love.

The sky had turned navy by the time Amy rose from her seat. She was alone, the cacophony of clattering china heralding the start of tea in the dining room. She rolled her head, the bones in her neck cracking as the tension eased. Her eye was drawn to something under the chair opposite. With a quick glance towards the door, she got down on her hands and knees and pulled out a sliver of broken saucer about three inches long. She turned it over in her hands, running her finger over the severed edge. It was sharp and pointy, the kind of thing that should be given over to Sister Atkins immediately.

She lifted the seat cushion off her chair and opened the zip. Carefully she eased the shard of china inside the cover and squashed it into the foam. Turning the cushion over, she placed it back on the chair and sat down again. Perfect. She might never need it, but it wouldn't hurt to have a little insurance policy.

25

She hesitated outside Dr Lambourn's office, her knuckles poised to rap on the door. She knew her neck was flushed, and in spite of herself, she could feel the heat colouring her cheeks too. She ran her fingers through her hair. It was shoulder-length now, and although not restored to its former glory, it was feeling a little softer now that the fabled new superintendent had introduced shampoo to the wards. Amy had yet to meet him, but she was grateful for his positive incremental changes. She ran her hands down the front of her dress, smoothing out the fabric, wondering when he would get round to revamping the communal wardrobe. Still, it didn't really matter to her. She wasn't planning on staying around much longer.

She licked her lips and tasted the lipstick she had applied earlier. With a deep calming breath, she finally knocked on the door.

'Come in.'

He didn't look up straight away, but carried on writing on his pad, the other hand supporting his head as he bent over his desk.

'Morning, Dr Lambourn.'

Her light tone caused him to look up, the surprise evident on his face. 'Well, good morning, Amy. You sound a lot brighter today.'

Uninvited, she plonked herself down on the seat opposite and crossed her legs. 'I feel it, Doctor, and it's all down to you.'

She saw the flicker of embarrassment and stifled a smile.

He stood up and gestured towards the couch. 'Shall we?'

'Ooh, Dr Lambourn, what on earth are you suggesting?'

He loosened the knot in his tie. 'Stop it, Amy. It doesn't suit you.'

She lay back on his couch and folded her hands in her lap as he flicked through his pad, the silence broken only by the loud ticking and mesmerising pendulum of the grandfather clock in the corner.

'I believe there was another altercation in the day room recently.'

She bit down on her lip. Trust him to start with a negative when she was feeling so much better. She wouldn't rise to it, though. It was important to remain cheerful and not return to her usual obstreperous self. She waved a hand dismissively. 'It's all forgotten about. It was nothing.'

'Very well then, if you insist.'

She shifted her weight and made herself more comfortable. 'I do.'

'All right.' He drew the word out, his tone disbelieving. 'You've been here for four months now, Amy. Tell me about your hopes for the future, your plans for when you leave here.'

Her heart quickened. This was new territory; he was usually delving into her past, making her think about things she had filed away in the dark recesses of her brain. She would have to tread carefully and tell him what he wanted to hear.

'I need to take responsibility for my actions,' she began. 'I owe my father an apology, of course, but also my stepmother . . . Carrie.' She screwed her eyes up and held her breath for a moment. 'I need to realise that my mother's death was not my fault and that my father is entitled to happiness.' She was into her stride now, the words tumbling out almost parrot fashion. 'None of this is Carrie's fault; she couldn't help falling in love with my father, and whilst I accept that I will never have another mother, there is no reason why my father shouldn't have another wife.'

She turned her head to look at him, and although he had his hand over his mouth, she could tell from his eyes that he was smiling. He didn't speak, though, merely nodded his encouragement, giving her the confidence to continue in the same vein. 'I'm determined to be happy again . . . meet someone, have a family of my own some day.'

'It's what your mother would have wanted for you.'

She hesitated for a second, annoyed that he was making an assumption. She kept her voice steady. 'Yes, I believe she would.'

She swung her legs off the couch and shuffled to the edge so that their knees were almost touching. 'Do you think I'm pretty, Dr Lambourn?'

He raised his eyebrows, the sudden change of subject catching him off guard. 'It doesn't matter what I think, Amy.'

'It does to me.'

'I'm afraid I'm not going to answer that question.'

She knew she had ruffled him, but he didn't need to reply. The answer lay in his eyes and in his awkward body language. She smiled. 'As you wish.'

She tugged at the neckline of her dress, then ran her fingers over her chest. 'Is it hot in here or is it just me?' A coquettish smile played on her moist lips.

Dr Lambourn ignored her and returned to his desk. He pulled out a sheet of thick yellow writing paper and dipped his pen into the inkwell. 'I'm going to write to your father detailing your progress. With his agreement, we can then think about ending your certification so that you may return to the family home.'

The well of hope she had dared to create threatened to overflow. She forced herself to remain calm and merely nodded. 'Thank you, Doctor.'

26

As the evenings grew longer, he relished the invigorating walk back to his cottage and the way it allowed his lungs to expel the stale air of his office. The thought of his comfy armchair nestling by the side of the log fire made him quicken his pace. When he imagined the warming glass of claret he would pour, its rich, earthy aroma, he almost broke into a run. He had made it to the bottom of the stone steps, his collar turned up against the rain, when a voice called him back. 'Dr Lambourn.'

He heard the clicking of heels as the breathless voice drew nearer. 'Oh gosh, I'm glad I've caught you.' Student Nurse Crosby patted her chest as she struggled for breath. 'There's somebody here to see you, says it's urgent.'

He pushed up his sleeve and looked pointedly at his watch. 'It'll have to wait, I'm afraid. Tell them to make an appointment as is customary. People need to learn that they can't just barge in and expect me to give them an audience.'

Without waiting for an answer, he strode off towards the main gate, a man on a mission, craving the comfort of his own company at the end of a long day.

'Dr Lambourn, wait.'

He carried on walking, but didn't need to look back to know that the nurse was running after him. She tugged on the elbow of his overcoat.

He glared at her. 'Do you mind?'

'I'm sorry, but the woman is visibly upset, Dr Lambourn, and insisting that she sees only you. She wouldn't tell me what it was about, but she's in a dreadful state.'

He cursed silently. If only he hadn't stopped to re-arrange his desk before he left, he would have been through the gate and out of sight by now.

He stared at Nurse Crosby, her hands in front of her in the prayer position, her puppy-dog eyes pleading with him. He shook his head, his words coming out on an irritated sigh. 'Very well, I'll give her five minutes.'

The woman was sitting with her back to the door as he entered his office, but rose gingerly from her seat as she heard him come in.

He removed his leather gloves and threw them onto his desk. 'How can I help you?' he asked, dispensing with unnecessary niceties.

She dabbed a handkerchief to her nose and held it there, the fabric muffling her words. 'I'm sorry to turn up like this. I didn't know what else to do.'

Spots of rain still beaded on the shoulders of her navy gabardine, and the silk headscarf knotted under her chin was soaked through. Her eyes were hidden by a pair of sparkly-framed sunglasses, which he thought was odd as the sun hadn't put in an appearance for several days. Her fumbling fingers slowly removed the glasses to reveal her blue eyes, puffy and red-rimmed, mere slits in an otherwise pretty face.

He felt a momentary pang of regret that he had been a trifle brusque with this young woman who was obviously in a great deal of distress. He indicated the armchair by the fire. 'Please, won't you come and sit down. The fire's all but gone out, but the embers have a little glow left in them.'

She blew into her hands, trying to coax warmth into them.

'Perhaps I'll put another lump of coal on,' he said, reaching for the scuttle.

She nodded and untied the headscarf, draping it over the fireguard, then forked her fingers through her blond hair, teasing her curls back to life. 'Thank you,' she sniffed.

Dr Lambourn took the chair opposite. His attitude had softened a little, his interest piqued as to why this beautiful, albeit bedraggled girl had insisted on seeing him. 'Why don't you start by telling me your name?'

She raised her chin and frowned slightly, as though the question was a difficult one. 'My name's Carrie. Carrie Sullivan.'

It seemed like several minutes before he was able to speak again. Amy had certainly depicted her stepmother in a different light altogether. This woman was nothing like the image he had conjured up from her rather unflattering, spiteful description.

'Amy's stepmother?' he clarified.

She nodded. 'Peter Sullivan is . . . was my husband.' She clenched her fist and thrust it into her mouth, biting down hard on her fingers.

'*Was* your husband?'

She gulped in some air, her eyes glassy with tears. 'He had a heart attack.' She lowered her voice to a whisper as she fiddled with the sodden handkerchief. 'He didn't survive.'

Instinctively he leaned forward and laid his hand on her wrist. 'I'm so sorry.'

She attempted a weak smile. 'Thank you, Doctor.' She regained some composure. 'Will you tell Amy for me? I would do it myself, but things are a little . . . well . . .'

'Please, I understand. Of course I will let her know.' He hesitated, unsure whether to proceed. 'I wrote to your husband last week telling him of Amy's progress, suggesting that it might be time she came home.'

He noticed the flash of panic in her eyes and raised his hand. 'Obviously I see that may be difficult now. I don't want you to worry. You have enough to contend with at present.'

A timid knock on the door halted the discussion. 'Come in,' he called.

Nurse Crosby crossed the threshold, her shoulders hunched as she supported the weight of the baby in her arms. 'Sorry to disturb you, Doctor, but she's getting fractious. I think she's hungry.'

Carrie's features lifted at the sound of her daughter's grumblings and she held her arms out to receive the infant. Dr Lambourn leaned forward and gazed at the baby's puckered-up face, the long eyelashes framing her deep brown eyes. His throat tightened. 'She . . . she's beautiful,' he managed.

Carrie rocked her daughter from side to side, returning the baby's smile. She stared up at Dr Lambourn. 'Please, Doctor,' she implored. 'You can't let that maniac near my daughter.'

He closed his eyes as he imagined Amy wading into the lake with this helpless little mite in her arms. The responsibility of protecting Carrie and her child lay heavily in his chest, and whilst there was no doubt Amy had made considerable progress under his care, there was no telling how the news of her father's death would affect her.

He picked up the baby's tiny hand. 'Try not to worry, Mrs Sullivan. Amy is here to get better, and you have my word that she won't be going anywhere until she is.'

27

She could hear the doom-laden strains of Chopin's funeral march as she walked behind her father's coffin, the pall-bearers all in perfect step with each other. She clung onto Dr Lambourn's arm whilst he guided her into church and settled her down on a pew. He turned and gave her a thin smile as he took his place next to her. She welcomed the closeness of him in the freezing church, where the cold from the stone floor seeped up her legs. From her knees to her shoulders she could not stop shaking, and her teeth chattered loudly in her head. Sunlight filtered through the stained-glass window, casting a kaleidoscope of colours across the plain coffin. She looked across the aisle at her stepmother, who was hunched over with her head almost on her knees, gently rocking back and forth, her face covered with a thin black veil.

Dr Lambourn patted Amy's knee. 'Are you bearing up?' he whispered.

She shook her head and buried her nose in the hymn book. The yellow pages smelled musty, the thin paper crispy with age.

'"Abide With Me",' she noted. 'My mother's favourite hymn.'

'Very fitting,' nodded Dr Lambourn. 'A nice gesture on Carrie's part, don't you think?'

Amy let out an irritated sigh. 'I'll never like her, so don't waste your time. It's her fault my father's dead.'

He tipped his head back and stared at the rafters. He seemed to count silently to ten. 'Not now, Amy, please.'

The vicar's voice echoed round the sparse congregation. 'Dearly beloved . . .' he began.

Amy closed her eyes and willed it to be over.

She managed to hold it together for the majority of the service. It was only at the mention of her mother that she let out a huge gulping sob that bounced off the walls of the church, causing a few members of the congregation to give her a pitying glance. The nutter who was only allowed to attend her own father's funeral under the close supervision of her psychiatrist.

Outside in the sunshine, she stood over the empty grave, watching her beloved father being lowered into the ground, her stepmother sobbing prettily into a floral handkerchief. There was an awful finality to it and she felt a dreadful sense of hopelessness and utter despair. Dr Lambourn stood head bowed, hands clasped behind his back. The first signs of spring were everywhere. The snowdrops were past their best, but the crocuses and daffodils were already providing a flash of colour, thrusting their way up between the headstones. Everybody was so wrapped up in their own misery that for a minute she considered making a run for freedom, but whilst she knew exactly what she was running from, she had no idea where she would run to.

Dr Lambourn had insisted they go back to the house to pay their respects and partake of a snifter of sherry to toast her late father. Carrie had opened up the front room; it had always been decreed the 'best' room and had seldom been used by her mother when she'd been alive. Amy felt a traitorous pang of guilt as she edged her way into the room and flumped down onto the hard sofa. The curtains were still drawn as a mark of respect, and would no doubt stay that way for many weeks to come. Dr Lambourn handed her a schooner of sherry, which she tipped down in one go, the burning sensation causing her eyes to water.

'How long do we have to stay here?'

'I didn't think you'd be in such a rush to get back to Ambergate, Amy.'

She gazed around the room at the unfamiliar adornments. The plain utility furniture was still there, but her stepmother had seen fit to add some rather garishly coloured cushions, and a rug that had evidently belonged to a sheep in a former life. The Anaglypta, which had previously been painted a rich coffee colour, was now a rather more boring magnolia.

She stood up as Carrie entered the room, the baby

perched on her hip. The ridiculous veil had gone and Amy could see her own grief reflected in her stepmother's face.

'Thank you for coming, Amy.'

The sound of her own name on her stepmother's lips ignited the simmering fury that was never far from the surface. 'How dare you?' she raged. 'You don't *thank* me for coming to my own father's funeral. I came because I wanted to, because he was my father, my *blood* relative, who wouldn't even be dead if it wasn't for you.'

The baby stared wide-eyed at Amy, and Carrie placed a hand over the infant's ear and pulled her close. 'I'll thank you not to shout at me in my own house. Show some respect. Your father would—'

'Don't you tell me what my father would or wouldn't have done.' Amy leaned in close to Carrie's face; she could feel her breath on her skin. 'You . . . killed . . . him.' She spoke with such venom, the baby burst into tears as Carrie fled from the room.

Dr Lambourn, who had remained silent during the exchange, finally spoke up. 'That was rather nasty of you, don't you think?'

'Well I might have known you'd take her side.' She was breathing hard, her bloodless lips white with anger. 'Take me home, please.'

'Home?' he queried.

She paused and stared at him through narrowed eyes. 'To Ambergate.'

*

After completing the journey back in brittle silence, Dr Lambourn pulled up outside the main building. Amy waited impassively for him to come round to her side and open the door. She took hold of his outstretched hand and climbed out. 'I'd like to spend some time in the chapel if I may, Dr Lambourn.'

He nodded. 'Of course. I'll inform Sister.'

The chapel nestled between the main building and the administration villa, its ancient walls green with years of uncleared moss. The iron bell could be seen swinging from the top of the open tower in spite of the early-evening mist that threatened to cloak the churchyard. Amy turned the handle of the thick wooden door and crept inside. Her breath swirled in front of her as she stamped her feet on the bristled mat, the sound resonating around the spartan interior. Two huge candles burned either side of the altar, the brass candlesticks gleaming in the flickering light.

She sat down on a pew and pulled the hassock towards her, her knees cracking as she lowered herself into the praying position. She clasped her hands together, closed her eyes and tried to think of something to say to this omnipresent God who seemed to let her down on a regular basis, bestowing on her misery upon misery. She certainly had nothing to thank Him for. After a cursory muttering of what she could remember of the Lord's Prayer, she heaved herself back onto the pew and gave an involuntary shudder. She had a queer feeling that she was not alone. It was nothing specific, she couldn't see or hear anything, but there was definitely another presence lingering just outside her consciousness.

'Hello,' she called out. 'Is . . . is there anybody there?'

She heard it then for certain: a scraping of feet along the gritty stone slabs to the side of the altar. She glanced towards the blue velvet curtain leading into the vestry, inhaling sharply as it was pulled to one side and a shadowy figure shuffled out of the blackness towards her.

28

'Jesus, Ed!' she exclaimed. 'You nearly gave me a heart . . .' She stopped and checked herself, ashamed that she had nearly been so flippant about the condition that had just taken the life of her father. 'I mean you scared me . . . a lot.'

His dark curly hair had all but grown back, and his boyish face radiated a warmth she could revel in. 'I'm sorry, I didn't want to disturb you while you were praying.'

She patted the pew next to her and he sat down. 'I wasn't really praying. I've got nothing to say to Him, that's even if He exists.'

Ed looked fearfully round the church and then up at the rafters as though expecting a bolt of lightning to pierce the roof. 'Shh, don't say that in 'ere.'

She laughed. 'The worst has already happened. There's nothing He can do to me now that could hurt me any more.'

'What do you mean?'

'My father's passed away. A heart attack, they said, which is no wonder when he was trying to keep up with the demands of a young wife. He was forty-one and saddled with a baby . . . at his age, I mean . . .' She let the sentence trail off and shook her head.

'Oh Amy, I'm right sorry to hear that. Can't be easy for you.'

'I've lost everything, Ed, there's nothing left for me on the outside any more.'

'Don't say that,' he urged, taking her freezing hand and holding it in his own warm one. 'You'll get better and leave this place; you'll meet someone and have a family of your own one day.'

'You're so sweet, Ed. I wish I could believe that.'

She glanced at the blackened rag in his other hand and changed the subject. 'What're you doing here anyway?'

He nodded towards the altar. 'Polishin' them brasses.'

She fell silent for a moment, relishing the calmness of the church and Ed's uncomplicated company. She leaned her head against his shoulder, his rhythmic breathing instantly soothing her, placatory words no longer necessary. In his quiet, healing embrace, she felt a peace she had not known since her mother had died, and years of pent-up emotions, layer upon layer of them, slowly fell away. She closed her eyes and drifted off into an exhausted dreamless sleep.

It was some time later when she awoke with a jolt. It took her a moment to get her bearings. She had no idea how long she had been asleep. She was still leaning against Ed's body, his arm around her shoulders, but something was not quite right.

'Ed?' There was no answer. She turned to look him in the face, but his eyes were unfocused and his pupils dilated. 'Ed, what's the matter? Talk to me.'

His lack of response stirred up the first feelings of panic. She grasped his shoulders and shook him gently, then felt his neck for any sign of a pulse, exhaling with relief when she felt the gentle pumping sensation against her fingers. His face was a death mask, though, his eyes unblinking and his mouth and jaw set as rigid as a statue's. 'Ed, please.'

His whole body began to jerk then, his arms and legs seemingly taking on a life of their own. He rolled off the pew onto the stone floor as he continued to thrash like a man drowning in a whirlpool.

'Ed, what's happening?' she screamed. There was no room between the pews to crouch down next to him to offer comfort or any kind of practical assistance. After what seemed an eternity, the violent twitching ceased and his whole body went rigid before eventually relaxing. A trickle of blood ran out of the corner of his mouth and his face was chalky white and covered with a sheen of sweat.

She stared down at his limp body, his breathing quick and shallow. 'It's all right, Ed, I'm here,' she soothed, bending down to smooth his dark hair across his forehead.

He opened his mouth to speak, but no words came. He pointed to his lips and stuck out his tongue, panting like a dog.

'Are you thirsty?'

216

He nodded and attempted a smile, apparently grateful that she had understood.

She squeezed herself out of the pew, returning a few moments later with a goblet of water she had procured from the sink in the toilet at the back of the vestry. She helped him into a sitting position and placed the goblet to his lips. He took a few tentative sips before his head lolled forward. She sat down crossed-legged in the aisle and gently lowered him down so that his head was in her lap. She smoothed his hair and stroked his face until his pallid colour was replaced with a more healthy glow.

'I'm sorry you had to see that.'

'I'm sorry you had to go through it. You poor, poor thing.'

'I can taste blood. I think I've bitten the inside of my cheek or something.'

She pulled a handkerchief out from her sleeve, dabbed it onto her tongue and wiped the blood from his chin.

He closed his eyes and began to breathe more deeply. 'My head's throbbing and I'm so tired, Amy. I'm always so tired after—'

'Shh, don't try to talk.'

She could still remember how she'd felt after she'd endured a fit during the wretched ECT. Her brain had felt too large for her skull, as though it had expanded somehow and was about to burst through the bones. The blinding pain had made her sick and the tiredness had sapped her of her energy for the following week.

'It's all right, Ed, I'm here now. Just you rest a while, I'm not going anywhere.' She worked her fingers into his hair and gently massaged his scalp until she noticed his jaw slacken with sleep.

After a time, her buttocks were numb with cold from the stone floor, her back ached and her legs were frozen in the cross-legged position. Her empty stomach gurgled and groaned like the ancient plumbing in the ward. She struggled to remember the last time she had eaten. Since the porridge at breakfast, the only thing to pass her lips was the sherry she had knocked back at the wake. She had no idea of the time, but could tell it was dark outside now, the only source of light coming from the two candles either side of the altar. It must be past teatime but she was resigned to missing her evening meal. Ed was peaceful, and no matter how hungry she was or how much discomfort she was in, she would not wake him.

29

Ed was more unsteady on his feet than usual, but his slight frame made it easy for her to support him as she guided him along the corridor back to the ward. An old man, trousers at half-mast, a solitary tooth protruding from his bottom gum, marched towards them. Both his fists were balled and he punched himself in the face, alternating fists in a rhythm to match his stride. Amy covered her mouth, almost retching at the foul stench of urine that emanated from his body.

Ed managed a smile. 'A drawback to the new unlocked-door policy.'

'Mmm, you could say that.' She looked at Ed, intelligent, coherent, a loving mother to care for him at home. It was all so wrong. 'Should you really be in here, Ed? It's not right that you have to mix with nutters like that.'

'Oh, Jimmy the Panda's all right. He's quite a character when you get to know him.'

'Jimmy the Panda?'

'Yeah: he's always got two black eyes.'

'What? Are you being serious?'

He smiled. 'There's all kinds in 'ere, Amy. Most with

very sad stories to tell, people who call this place home and are grateful for it too. I've met some wonderful people and I'll always be thankful for what they've done for me.' He paused. 'Don't be so quick to judge.'

Coming from anybody else it might have sounded like a telling-off, but his smile took the sting out of his words and she merely nodded. Perhaps she could learn a thing or two from Ed.

They stopped at the entrance to his ward. 'I'm fine from here, Amy, but thanks for looking after me, and again, I'm right sorry about your dear father.'

'Thank you,' she whispered. 'And you take care of yourself, d'you hear me?'

'I will.' He held his arms wide, swaying slightly as she stepped into them. They held each other for a few moments, both wanting to preserve this basic human contact that most people took for granted.

By the time she arrived back on her own ward, the curtains were drawn and the lights had been turned out. Sister Atkins was in her office, thumbing through a magazine. 'About time. Where in God's name have you been?'

'Dr Lambourn said he was going to tell you. I've been to the chapel for some quiet reflection.'

'You've been gone for hours. That's a hell of a lot of reflecting, and now you think you can just waltz back in 'ere?' She stood up and slapped the magazine down on the desk. 'I bloody knew this would happen if they unlocked the doors. Patients coming and going as they please. It'll end in disaster, mark my words.' She reached for her cigarettes. 'And don't even think about trying to escape. We'll only fetch you back again and things'll be a lot worse for you.' She sucked in a lungful of smoke and exhaled it dragon-like through her nose.

'It was my father's funeral today.'

Sister stopped mid drag. 'That's as maybe, but it doesn't give you the right to swan off willy-nilly. You've missed tea, so you'll have to go hungry, but perhaps that'll be a lesson to you. Now get to bed before I do something you'll regret.'

Pearl and Queenie were both asleep, Pearl on her back, mouth agape, an annoying rattle reverberating in the back of her throat. Amy peeled back the thin sheet and climbed in. She pulled the pillow over her head and clasped it to her ears. Thank God she would not have to endure this place for much longer.

She heard the springs creak and felt someone plonk themselves down on the end of her bed. She removed the pillow and stared at the figure in the half-light. 'Who's there?'

'Shh, it's me, Belinda.'

Amy pulled herself into a sitting position and folded her arms. She was in no mood for bother tonight. 'What do you want?'

Belinda looked behind towards Sister's office. 'I noticed you weren't at tea, so I saved you something.' She pulled out a bowl from behind her back. 'It's cold now, but still edible.'

Amy took the bowl and prodded the contents with the spoon.

'Stewed apples and custard,' said Belinda. 'Apples could've done with a bit more sugar, but it's better than nowt.'

The thick custard had formed an unappetising yellow skin, but even so Amy's mouth watered at the prospect and she dug the spoon in. 'Thank you, Belinda.'

The other girl grinned and stood to leave. 'Yer welcome.'

Amy scraped round the bowl with her finger, making sure she removed the last vestiges of the dessert. Belinda waved at her from the bed opposite and Amy returned the gesture. Random acts of kindness were certainly scarce in this place and sometimes came from the most unexpected source.

30

The clouds had shifted, allowing the sun to penetrate their stubborn veil. Dr Lambourn looked up at the sky and gave a contented smile. He placed a cushion on each of the white-painted wrought-iron chairs and set a jug of hand-picked daffodils in the middle of the table. Their petals were a little crusty, but the splash of colour brightened up the tiny courtyard. He was proud of his cottage garden, which brought him immense pleasure and provided a welcome respite from the gloomy atmosphere he often had to endure at work. A stepping-stone path led to a small pond at the bottom and the domed heather beds provided a riotous display of varying shades of pink and purple. He held his palms to the sky and, satisfied there was no moisture in the air, went inside to fetch the tray of shortbread.

The harsh frosts of winter had thawed, and as the April sunshine warmed the soil, the grass was beginning to grow again and leaves were unfurling on the trees. He spread his newspaper out on the table, the breeze just enough to lift the corners. He slapped his hand down on the paper and tried to concentrate on the words as he waited for his guest to arrive. At precisely eleven o'clock, two things happened at once. The cuckoo in the kitchen clock shot out of its hiding place, and the doorbell rang. Good, he noted, she was prompt. He couldn't bear tardiness.

He opened the door. 'Good morning, please won't you come in. Go straight through to the back. I thought we might sit in the garden.'

She wiped her feet on the mat, carefully and deliberately taking more time than he thought was absolutely necessary. 'Thank you,' she replied.

She settled herself into one of the chairs whilst he brewed a pot of tea in the kitchen. 'You have a lovely garden,' she called to him.

He came out with the pot and took the other seat. 'Thank you, it's only small but perfectly formed, I always think.'

'Yes, quite.'

Her eyes fluttered about the garden, focusing on anything other than him, her unease evident in the way she shuffled on her seat. The transition from the last time he had seen her was seismic. Gone were the features hollowed out by grief; her once-insipid complexion now radiated health and her hair shone, falling in gentle curls that rested on her shoulders. She cleared her throat to speak and this time looked directly at him.

'This seems a little unorthodox. I wonder about your motives, Dr Lambourn?'

He raised his eyebrows.

'I mean, me coming here to your home when you've a perfectly adequate office in which to meet people.'

He wiped the shortbread crumbs from his mouth with a napkin. 'It's perfectly fine, Carrie. The atmosphere in the hospital can be somewhat stifling, and I thought a more ambient setting would be beneficial to us both.'

'Does my stepdaughter know I'm here?'

'My patients are not party to every move I make. I saw no need to apprise her of the situation.'

'And what *is* the situation, Doctor?'

He offered her the plate of shortbread, but she wafted it away with her hand.

'You are now Amy's next of kin.'

The merest flicker of annoyance crossed her face. 'So?'

'Just before your husband died, I wrote to him about Amy's progress and suggested the time had come for a review of her certification.'

She shook her head. 'I've never seen the letter.'

'That may well be the case, but it doesn't alter the fact that I wrote it.'

She turned away. 'Is that honeysuckle round your door?'

He didn't need his psychoanalytical skills to spot this diversionary tactic. 'Yes, it is. It may be a mass of dead twigs now, but in a few months it'll be resplendent with flowers and their scent will be quite heavenly.' He picked up the teapot and swirled it to agitate the leaves inside. 'More tea?'

225

She shook her head. 'I can't cope with her at home, Dr Lambourn. She tried to kill my baby. It's not right. You can't expect me to take her back.'

'Where *do* you expect her to go then?'

She shrugged. 'I don't know. It's all such a mess. I'm not ready to take her.' She picked absently at a daffodil, tearing off its petals.

'Will you ever be ready?'

'I can't say, Dr Lambourn. I really can't say.'

'Well I appreciate your honesty, Carrie.' He threaded his hands together. 'Look, I'll tell you what we'll do. I'll keep this meeting off the record. I'll continue my sessions with Amy, but you must understand I can't keep her certified without just cause. She's made plenty of progress and I don't want the superintendent questioning my methods. It makes me look bad, as though I don't know what I'm doing.'

'Oh,' said Carrie, dragging the word out. 'Now we're getting to the truth. This is all about you, not Amy.'

He paused, choosing his words carefully. 'If it helps you to believe that, then so be it, but I don't recommend a head-in-the-sand approach.'

'I need to put my baby first, Dr Lambourn. Surely you can see that. She's all I have left now.'

'I understand.' And he did, he really did. 'Let me see what I can do. I promise you that neither you nor your baby will be placed in any danger.'

She visibly relaxed, her shoulders dropping as she let

out a deep sigh. 'Thank you, Dr Lambourn, you've no idea what that means to me.'

He smiled and extended his hand. 'Now, why don't I show you round my garden? I've got some lovely azaleas coming into bloom, and there's a marvellous cloud of frog spawn in the pond.'

Carrie wrinkled her nose. 'Frog spawn?' She studied his face, checking he was serious. 'Go on then, lead on.'

He took hold of her delicate hand, the softness of it taking him by surprise. He was used to the calloused palms of the nurses or the chapped hands of the patients, which he tried to avoid shaking at all costs. He placed his other hand in the small of her back as he guided her towards the pond, catching a whiff of her perfume, the familiar scent at once transporting him back to happier times. He felt possessed by it, unprepared for this sudden invasion of memories that surged unbidden into his head. He shook them away. No good ever came from dwelling on the past.

31

A gentle breeze tickled the tops of the tall poplars that lined one edge of the park. A welcome breeze that cooled the heat of the late-afternoon sun, which had caused her face to glisten and damp patches to form under her arms.

'Feels good to take the air, doesn't it?' Dr Lambourn took a deep breath, his chest inflating with the effort.

Amy had to agree. Anything felt better than scuttling round the grounds of the asylum under the hawkish gaze of the nurses. They walked along the riverbank side by side, the water still high and rushing after the winter rains. Their hands brushed against each other and Amy willed the doctor to take her hand in his. Conscious of her damp palms, she wiped them down her dress just in case he did. The superintendent had introduced a new wardrobe to the ward, and although she appreciated the lightness of the summer dress, her feet felt hot in the sturdy shoes, too tight and cumbersome for such a sunny day.

'Dr Lambourn, would it be all right if I paddled in the river? My feet are very uncomfortable.'

'I see no reason why not.' He pointed a little way ahead.

'There's a bend up there and a small patch of beach. It's the perfect spot for a sit-down.' Amy wondered how he knew this. Who else had he taken to this perfect spot?

They sauntered on in quiet contemplation, the only sounds coming from the swishing of her skirt and the call of a nearby blackbird. They reached the sandy area beneath the shade of a weeping willow and Dr Lambourn spread out the tartan rug he'd been carrying under his arm.

Amy removed the heavy shoes and thick stockings, hoisted up her skirt and gingerly tiptoed to the river's edge. The iciness of the water came as a shock. She had been expecting a soothing tepid flow at this time of year, and she almost lost her balance. But it was more than just the freezing water; it was something she couldn't quite put her finger on, something just beyond the reach of her consciousness. She began to sway as she stared at the water rushing past her feet, holding her arms out in an effort to stay upright, and then she remembered. The horror of it all played back in her mind like a cine film she had seen many times before but had somehow wiped from her memory. She saw herself wade into the water; deeper and deeper she went, desperately craving oblivion. She remembered the screaming, too, hysterical strangulated sobs, and then there was the baby in her arms. The baby she had tried to . . .

She fell forward into the river then, face down onto the shingle, a sharp rock catching her nose. In shock, she gulped in a mouthful of water as she saw a swirl of blood being carried off by the current. Strong hands then, hauling her up and backwards onto the sand, laying her down on the rug; soothing tones, a calming hand on her forehead.

She lay there staring up at the blue sky, at the birds gliding around in aimless circles, her breath coming in shallow gasps.

Dr Lambourn crouched next to her, his face only inches from hers, his breath warm on her damp cheeks. 'You gave me quite a start there.' He dabbed his handkerchief on to the cut on her nose.

'I'm sorry. I'm not sure what happened,' she floundered. 'It was the feel of the freezing water, I think. I was just transported right back to that day when I . . . Oh God, I could hear her screaming. It was as though she was right behind me again, crying out for her baby, it was—'

He placed his finger on her lips. 'Shh, try not to distress yourself.' He hauled her into a sitting position and placed his arm around her shoulders, drawing her close, rocking her from side to side until she relaxed and her breathing returned to normal.

'Look,' he said. 'There's a fellow in a kiosk over there selling ice creams. I'm going to fetch us a couple of cones.' He climbed to his feet and brushed himself down. 'He looks as though he's about to close up for the day, mind, so I'll have to run.'

When he returned with the ice-cream cones, Amy was

feeling much better. She picked bits of weed out of her sopping hair, her damp dress clinging uncomfortably to her skin. She stifled a giggle when she saw the state of his trousers where the river water had seeped up to the knee. He noticed her looking and smiled. 'Well I hardly had time to remove my shoes and roll up my trouser legs, did I?'

He sat down in front of her and she took the proffered ice cream. 'I suppose not. Thank you for this.' She took a lick, savouring the long-forgotten creamy taste on her tongue. He removed his jacket and placed it around her shoulders. 'Here, you're shivering.'

'Why are you doing this for me, Dr Lambourn?'

'I don't want you to catch your death. Your dress is rather wet.'

'I don't mean the jacket. I mean why are you taking me out, giving me all this special attention?'

He seemed to give the question a great deal of thought. 'You intrigue me, Amy,' he replied eventually. 'I like your character, your indomitable spirit, and I don't think you're evil. You've suffered a great deal of loss in your life and it's bound to have had an effect on you, but you've come a long way since that day I first saw you and I want you to be ready when you face the outside world again.'

'Oh, I see.' She popped the end of the cone into her mouth as an awkward silence grew. She had given him the perfect opportunity to express his true feelings towards her. She'd set up the easel and propped up the blank canvas. All he'd had to do was write *I love you*. But he hadn't.

'I think I want to go back now,' she told him.

'Back home?'

'Back to Ambergate.'

'Already? Aren't you having a nice time?'

'I thought you liked me, Dr Lambourn.'

'I do like you.'

'But not in *that* way?'

He sighed. 'Amy, it's quite common for patients to form an attachment to their doctor. It goes with the territory, I'm afraid, but you must understand that any feelings I have for you are born out of my desire to help you, to cure you if you will, to ease you back into society.' He paused whilst his words sank in. 'It's true that I have treated you differently. You wouldn't catch me walking in the park with the likes of Pearl or Belinda, for instance, but I have hopes for you. You're a special girl to me. I've devoted a lot of time to your case.'

She scoffed. 'Is that all I am to you then? A case?'

'Amy, please stop twisting my words.'

She fell silent for a moment. How could she have got everything so wrong? 'I'm twenty years old, Dr Lambourn, and do you know, I've never been kissed.'

For a fleeting moment, he seemed rattled, unsure how to respond. 'Amy, all that lies ahead of you. You're a beautiful young woman; any man would be lucky to have you on his arm. Didn't you notice the way people looked at you when we were walking along the riverbank? You turned quite a few heads.'

'You're just saying that.'

'No I'm not,' he said emphatically.

He leaned closer, tucking a stray curl behind her ear. She almost recoiled at the electrifying touch of his fingers. He let his hand trail along her jawbone, and when he seemed reluctant to withdraw it, she tilted her chin and moved closer to him. She closed her eyes, not wanting to witness his rejection, but she could sense he was still there right in front of her, their warm breath mingling together. She could smell the soap on his skin, the faint whiff of tobacco. Blindly she reached out and touched his cheek, the bristles he had shaved off that morning starting to shadow his skin once more. When she could bear the anticipation no longer, he shifted his weight and then his lips were upon hers, his breathing becoming heavier and more urgent as his hand searched under her clothes.

She stifled a squeal of delight. She'd been right all along; he *had* developed feelings for her and now he was showing her the depth of his affection in a way that could not be misinterpreted. The foundations had been laid for her pathway out of Ambergate. She pulled away and clasped his face in her hands so that he had no choice but to look at her.

'I love you, Dr Lambourn,' she whispered.

32

He was in such a hurry to unlock the door that he dropped the key three times before he successfully let himself in. He kicked the pile of post away and headed straight for the kitchen, turning on the cold tap and letting the water blast into the sink. He rolled up his shirtsleeves, made a bowl with his palms and scooped the cold water over his face. After three dousings, the front of his shirt was soaked through and a puddle of water surrounded his feet. He leaned against the sink, breathing hard, his knuckles white and a pounding in his head that made him want to rip his hair out.

They had walked back to the asylum in silence, neither of them sure what to say, but Amy had definitely been lighter on her feet, almost skipping, in fact, a contented smile on her lips as she clutched his hand. He clenched his fists and banged them down on the countertop. How could he have been so stupid? He had taken advantage of a vulnerable young girl, and no matter that she had put up no resistance whatsoever, he should have known better. She'd even said she loved him. With every fibre of his being he had wanted to say those words back to her, but how could he? He was her doctor. He should have come off her case as soon as he realised he was developing feelings for her, but he couldn't tear himself away. She enthralled him.

He picked up the towel and dried his face, held it there wishing he could turn back the clock. He reached for the bottle of whisky he kept at the back of the cupboard for just such an emergency. Although he appreciated a fine wine, he really wasn't a big drinker, but tonight he would make an exception. He tipped a couple of painkillers into his palm and chugged them down with the whisky. Then he took a second glass into the lounge, ducking to avoid the low-slung beams that crossed the room. He wandered over to the mantelpiece, set the glass down and picked up the silver-framed photograph. He ran his thumb over the picture, clearing the dust from her face. The face of the woman he thought he had truly loved once, the woman with whom he had planned a future, the woman upon whom all his hopes and dreams had rested. Until that awful day when she'd told him that although she loved him, she didn't love him enough. After her, he'd never imagined he would be capable of falling in love again. But Amy had changed all that.

After tea, when the others had retired to the day room, Amy made her excuses and went to lie on her bed. She wanted to relive the afternoon in glorious slow-motion Technicolor, to savour every caress, every kiss, the soft teasing ones and the more urgent passion-filled ones. She'd trembled under his tender touch, every nerve end screaming in anticipation. He'd taken an agonising amount of time, but when the long-awaited moment came, the one that would transport her from a girl to a woman, she was carried off to a place she could never have imagined existed. She'd seen it in his face too, heard it in his laboured breathing and felt it in the frenzied movement of his hips. Of course she wasn't just another patient. She'd known it all along. Now even he could not deny it.

The next morning, she was awake long before the bell sounded; in fact she'd barely slept at all, filled with excitement, making plans for a future that had seemed impossible until yesterday.

'Morning, Amy,' greeted Ellen. 'You're awake early. Is everything all right?'

Amy grinned. 'Oh yes, Nurse. More than all right, I'd say.'

Ellen frowned. 'Well, it's nice to see you in a good mood. It's bath day; do you want to take the first one?'

Normally Amy would have jumped at the chance, but she wanted to savour the scent of him. For as long as she could still smell him, she knew that it hadn't been a blissful dream, one she would wake up from any second, drenched in sweat, with a physical ache at the thought of what might have been.

'No thank you, Nurse.' She gestured across to the other

side of the ward. 'Why don't you let Belinda take the first bath?'

'Well, I must say that's very . . . very kind of you, Amy.' Ellen struggled to keep the surprise out of her voice. 'Very kind indeed. Belinda will be thrilled, I'm sure.' She gave Amy a puzzled look before crossing the room to rouse Belinda and give her the good news.

It was later in the afternoon, as she stood in Sister Atkins's office, that the walls came tumbling down.

'I'd like to see Dr Lambourn, please,' she asked politely but forcefully, knowing that a refusal would be hard to take. She'd been slightly disappointed that he hadn't come to see her, but she supposed he must be busy. He did after all still have other patients.

Sister Atkins looked up from her desk. 'Well you can't.'

Amy immediately felt herself bristle. 'Why not?'

Sister Atkins was engrossed in a file on her desk once more. 'Because I said so,' she replied.

'That's not a good enough reason, Sister.'

'It's good enough for me. Now clear off.'

Amy stood her ground. 'I need to see Dr Lambourn,' she repeated.

'Yes, I heard you the first time. Now get out of my office before I drag you out.'

Unwelcome tears threatened, but Amy refused to move. 'Please, Sister Atkins,' she implored, trying to hold onto her temper. Losing it would only make matters worse.

Sister Atkins exhaled in exasperation. 'You can't see him because he's not here. He's gone away.'

The floor shifted beneath her feet and she grabbed the back of a chair to steady herself. The blood rushed so high up her face it made her scalp tingle. She could barely comprehend what she was hearing. It was as though she was wearing ear muffs. She could see Sister's mouth moving, but her words were distorted and unclear.

'What? No, he can't have done.'

'This conversation has gone on long enough already. You asked me a question, I gave you the answer; now bugger off and leave me in peace.' Sister returned to her file, jotting something down and underlining it savagely.

Amy stood swaying slightly, trying not to reveal too much. 'Where's he gone and when's he coming back?'

Sister Atkins looked up, her eyes narrowing. 'Are you still here?'

'Yes, but . . .'

Sister Atkins rose from her seat and shouted down the ward. 'Student Nurse Crosby, can you please come and remove a patient from my office.' She turned back to Amy. 'Dr Lambourn's been called away on a family emergency, not that it's any of your business. He'll be gone indefinitely.' She placed her hands on her hips. 'Satisfied now?'

Amy turned and shuffled out of the office in a daze, a fog of utter disbelief. She shrugged off Nurse Crosby's attempts to help her and headed straight for her bed, climbing in and pulling the sheet over her head, trying to shut out the sound of the cackling women around her, their nonsensical murmurings an irritant she could do without. Nothing made sense any more. What kind of emergency could have taken him away from her, just when they had so many plans to make for their future together?

She curled up into the foetal position, a single tear sliding down the side of her nose. Everybody she loved always left her one way or another.

33

The weeks dragged by, endless days filled with monotony, petty squabbles and despotic nursing staff. There had been absolutely no word from Dr Lambourn. It was as though he had never even worked at Ambergate. At first Amy had been hysterical, made a nuisance of herself at every opportunity and pestered the nurses relentlessly for information. None had been forthcoming. Instead she had been plied with drugs to calm her down, numb her senses and turn her into a compliant patient who would cease to cause trouble. Except she didn't take the tablets. She'd perfected the art of pretending to swallow, theatrically throwing her head back and gulping down a slug of water, but she now had a pile of pills squirrelled away under her mattress.

One morning, she was out in the grounds with Belinda, walking past the patch of land that had once been the airing courts, now reduced to rubble, ready to be turfed over and fringed with colourful flower beds.

Belinda linked her arm through Amy's and pulled her closer. 'I'm glad you're my best friend.'

Amy took a sideways glance at the girl. She wouldn't

describe them as friends as such. Rather two unfortunate souls who had been thrown together and decided to make the best of it. Other than the fact that they were both certified mental patients, she had nothing in common with Belinda, and if they ever got out of this place, she would cross the road to avoid her. Still, better to have her as a friend than an enemy.

She patted Belinda's arm. 'I'm glad too.'

Spotting Ed over by the chicken coop, basket in hand, collecting up the freshly laid eggs, she extricated herself from the other girl's grip. 'I'd like some time on my own now, if you don't mind.'

'But why? Best friends don't need time apart.'

'Please, Belinda. I just need some time to think. I'll see you back on the ward.'

Without waiting for an answer, she left Belinda staring after her as she made her way over to the only true friend she had in Ambergate.

'Morning, Ed.'

He pulled his head out of the hatching box, two warm brown eggs in one hand. 'Morning.' He held out his palm. 'Look at these two beauties.' He beamed as though he had laid them himself.

Amy smiled. Only Ed could get excited about a couple of eggs. 'Wonderful, I'm sure.'

'How are you?' It wasn't a flippant question. Ed understood her. Although she had not felt able to tell him everything that had happened between herself and Dr

Lambourn, he knew enough to appreciate the pain she felt at the doctor's disappearance, and she found herself leaning on him more and more. In fact, without Ed, she would be unable to endure the agony.

'Oh, you know. Still wondering why I'm here, abandoned by my own doctor, the one person who could have signed me out instead of just leaving me to rot.'

'You don't know that. He's only been gone a short while.'

'Four weeks and two days.'

He held out his arm. 'Come on.'

She stepped forward and took hold of his hand. His face was tanned now, radiating a healthy glow, and she wondered how much longer he would be here. She pushed the thought from her mind.

'I'll just hand these eggs over to Dougie.' He jogged over to where the nurse was standing with a group of patients, trying to explain what he wanted each of them to do in the garden, and the difference between weeds and plants. Amy watched him go. He ran with confidence, his awkward gait a distant memory. She was pleased for him, of course. His road to recovery had been a long one and his determination to get better had been well rewarded, but the idea of him leaving Ambergate was just too horrific for her to contemplate.

It was another hot day. They had been spoiled in recent weeks with scorching temperatures, the only downside being that the nurses were more irritable than usual.

'Let's sit down here.' Ed gestured to a patch of grass in front of the old cricket pavilion and they settled themselves down under the cloudless sky. He lay back and interlaced his fingers behind his head. 'Makes you forget where you are when you just stare up at that.'

She lay down next to him but propped herself up on one elbow so she could study his face. His eyes were closed, his features relaxed and his dimples barely visible. She fumbled around in the grass and plucked a buttercup, holding it underneath his chin. He flapped his arms and sat up. 'Ooh, there was something on me.'

She laughed. 'It was me, you daft 'apporth.' She held up the buttercup. 'I was just seeing if you like butter.'

'Oh, right.' He tilted his chin upwards. 'And do I?'

She squinted at the golden glow on his skin. 'Yes, you do,' she declared.

He picked at the daisies around them, making a halo out of the flowers and placing it on top of Amy's head. 'Beautiful,' he whispered. He leaned forward and lightly kissed her cheek. She instinctively raised her hand and held it against her skin, where she could still feel the moistness from his lips.

He appeared flustered. 'I . . . I'm sorry. I don't know what came over me.'

'Don't be sorry,' she said gently. 'I'm not.'

34

She'd been sent to the stores to pick up a bundle of clothes for a new patient. The implementation of the unlocked-door policy meant that the staff could now get the patients to do the menial tasks they thought were beneath them. Amy didn't mind, though. Any escape from the ward for a while came as a welcome relief. She walked along the endless corridor, trailing her hand along the shiny brown tiles and relishing the time to herself. Another month had slipped by and there had still been no word from Dr Lambourn. When she thought about the way he had used her and then discarded her as though she was yesterday's newspaper, she fizzed with a rage she found difficult to control. In her calmer, more rational moments, though, she knew he had not abandoned her. There had to be a logical explanation. He was after all a caring man, she knew this only too well, so it made sense that attending to a family emergency might take some time.

She tucked the clothes bundle under her arm and decided to take a more circuitous route back to the ward, enjoying the solitude of the long, echoing corridors with only the sound of her own footsteps for company. She quickened her pace as she scurried past the dreaded locked wards. Some lunatics in here would never be trusted with the open-door policy.

She wasn't sure it was a conscious decision, but after a while she found herself nearing Dr Lambourn's office, and her heart quickened as she saw that the door bearing his name plaque was slightly ajar. She stood outside, hardly daring to draw breath as she listened intently to the movements inside. She heard a desk drawer open and close again, and then the sound of another drawer opening as though someone was searching for something. She put the bundle down on the floor, ran her hands through her hair and pinched her cheeks to coax a little colour into them. Then she tapped on the door.

'Come in.'

She hesitated. He sounded older and weary, as though those two words had taken a monumental effort to utter.

She entered the room and saw that he had his back to her as he wrestled with the sash window. The heat was oppressive and the atmosphere in the office was stuffy and stale, suffused with a smell of mothballs and beeswax.

She longed for him to turn round, cross the room and take her in his arms. She didn't care that he'd been away for so long. He was back now and that was all that mattered. He continued to struggle with the window, sighing irritably as it refused to yield.

'I've missed you,' she ventured.

He stopped bashing at the window and turned round. She gazed at him, her mouth open ready to ask if he'd missed her too, but the question stuck in her throat and she could only manage an unintelligible croak.

'I beg your pardon?' he said.

'Where . . . where's Dr Lambourn?'

'May I ask who wants to know?' His tone was polite enough but his features were hard and not at all welcoming. He was much older than Dr Lambourn, the flash of grey at his temples and his liver-spotted hands evidence of his advancing years.

'I'm a patient of his.'

'Were.'

'I'm sorry?'

'You *were* a patient of his. Dr Lambourn has left Ambergate to take up a position elsewhere and I will be replacing him. I'm sure you've been added to my list, so I will make my formal introduction to you when I conduct my ward rounds, but in the meantime, I have rather a lot to do, so if you'll excuse me . . .'

A rushing noise filled her ears, as though her head was underwater. 'Not . . . not coming back? But I need to see him.'

The doctor smiled then, deep crow's feet wrinkling the skin round his eyes. 'I'm Dr Harrison, and I can assure you that I'm just as qualified as Dr Lambourn to look after you.' He spoke slowly, enunciating his words as though he was talking to a deaf imbecile.

'Now then, dear, can you run along back to where you came from, hmm? There's a good girl.' He steered her in the direction of the door and she walked out in a trance.

She wandered aimlessly through the maze of corridors, bouncing off the walls and stumbling blindly through doors. Salty tears stung her eyes and she fought back the sobs that threatened to overcome her. Arriving at the end of a corridor in a part of the hospital she had never even seen before, she barged through the door and out into the sunshine. It was only then that she let go a piercing scream that seemed to come from the bowels of the earth. She didn't see the two male nurses who had come up beside her, but before she had a chance to protest, they had each taken an arm and frogmarched her without ceremony back to the ward.

Sister Atkins threw her arms up in exasperation at the sight of Amy and her puffy-eyed, tear-stained face. 'Where the hell've you been?' She turned to the two male nurses. 'I'll take it from here.'

Amy stared at the floor, not bothering to reply. Sister Atkins grabbed the top of her hair, forcing her to look up. 'I asked you a question.'

'I went to get a new clothes bundle like you asked me to.'

'And where is it?' Sister's face was only inches from hers as she tightened her grip.

Amy looked around, half expecting the bundle to materialise out of thin air. 'I must have dropped it.'

'You must have dropped it,' repeated Sister Atkins. 'What kind of an idiot are you? Can't you carry out a simple errand without messing things up?'

Amy didn't know if she was supposed to answer or not.

Sister delved into her pocket with her free hand, then held her palm open. Amy stared at the pile of white pills. 'Care to venture a guess as to where I found this little lot?'

She bent her head, but Sister pulled her upright again, her grip so tight, Amy was afraid she would pull off a chunk of her scalp. She remained silent. Whatever she said wouldn't be right.

Mercifully, Sister let go of her hair and shoved her hard in the chest instead. 'Get back in there. I'll deal with you later.'

Amy collapsed onto her bed, rubbing at her sore head. Belinda was beside her in a minute. 'They found your pills under the mattress.'

'So I gather.'

'You need to take your pills to get better,' Belinda urged.

Amy regarded the girl with undisguised pity. 'How long have you been here, Belinda?'

'Dunno. 'Bout seven years, I think.'

'And you've always taken your tablets?'

Belinda nodded eagerly. 'Aye, I 'ave.'

'And have they made you better?'

Belinda thought for a moment. 'Yes, of course.'

'Then why are you still here?'

Belinda shrugged. 'Well, I . . .'

'I'll tell you why. You haven't been cured because there was nothing really wrong with you in the first place. The treatments you've had over the years – all the ECT, the insulin-coma stuff, the never-ending cocktail of drugs – were all about controlling you, not curing you. They've deadened your senses, Belinda, turned you into someone who can no longer think for herself. They've institution-alised you, and the worst thing of all is that you're bloody grateful to them.'

Belinda hung her head and picked at a loose thread on her dress. 'But if I did get out, where would I go?' she whispered. 'This is my home.'

Amy rested her head on Belinda's shoulder and picked up her hand. 'And therein lies the tragedy.'

35

Their shift patterns had not been compatible for several weeks, and as Ellen waited for Dougie in the snug of their local pub, she twisted her engagement ring round and round on her finger, admiring the gold band with its trio of tiny diamonds. She'd had no idea how he had afforded it until she thought back on how many extra shifts he had volunteered to do and how he had switched from pints to halves and visited the local bakery to buy up the stale loaves they would otherwise have chucked away. It was all part of his master plan to save money in order to cap off their whirlwind romance with a proposal of marriage.

She stood up as she saw him approaching the table. He rushed forward and buried his face in her neck, kissing her behind the ear and making her giggle. 'Stop it,' she laughed, pushing him away good-naturedly. 'Everybody's looking.'

'I can't help it. I've missed you.'

'And I've missed you too.' She swept his hair from his forehead as he sat down. 'You look so tired, Dougie. Are you sure you're not overdoing it?'

'Don't worry about me. I'm made of strong stuff. You need to be to work in that place.' He took a long gulp of his beer. 'I got some good news today, though. That lad I've been helping, you know the one who was knocked off his bike?'

'Yes, I know the one. What about him?'

'He's going home next week. How about that?'

Ellen hesitated. 'Well, that is good news, I suppose . . . for him, at least.'

'What d'ya mean?'

'Oh nothing, it's just I've got a patient who's really going to miss him, that's all.'

'You mean Amy?'

'Yes, that's the one. They've grown quite fond of each other.' Ellen shrugged. 'Still, people move on, don't they? They're not prisoners.' She thought about Pearl and Queenie and poor old Gertie, who had been incarcerated for years. 'At least that's what they'd have us believe.'

The late-afternoon sky had darkened ominously so that it felt more like evening, and although the rain was welcome after the heat of the last few weeks, the lightning that split the sky over the main building made her quicken her pace. By the time she reached the cricket pavilion, her hair hung in wet tendrils round her face and her thin dress clung to her shivering body. Ed was waiting for her on the veranda. He held out his hand and helped her up the wooden steps.

'Look at you,' he exclaimed. 'Here.' He wrestled himself out of his misshapen jacket and draped it round her shoulders.

Amy smiled. Dr Lambourn had done the very same thing only a couple of months ago. Had it really been that long already? She wondered how it was possible for time to fly by so quickly when she was so miserable.

'Come and sit down,' invited Ed, still holding onto her hand. He didn't let go even when they were seated side by side on the wooden bench, instead loosely holding it in his lap. 'How are you getting on with your new doctor?'

She gave a snort. 'Oh, he's nothing like Dr Lambourn. You know the sort, talks a lot, says nothing. He doesn't care. He treats me the same as he treats all the others, just writing out prescriptions for the pills that keep us all stupefied and compliant.' She looked down at their entwined hands. 'I was really getting somewhere with Dr Lambourn. I was honest about my feelings. It was like popping a cork on a champagne bottle; everything came rushing out and it was helping me.' She saw her own despair reflected in Ed's eyes and shook her head. 'But you can't put the cork back in the bottle, can you?'

Ed looked pained, a deep frown creasing his forehead. 'But Dr Lambourn must have left some notes detailing your progress. Surely they can't keep you here without good reason.'

Amy gazed off towards the main building. The place

was full of people who'd been detained without good reason. 'Oh, they can, Ed. They can.'

He fell silent and stroked the back of her hand as he watched a line of men from the chronic ward shuffle along the edge of the field in their identical ill-fitting suits, heads bowed and shoulders hunched. He knew that a couple of them had been here since the turn of the century.

'What are you thinking about, Ed?'

He turned to her and stared into her face, holding her gaze as he spoke. 'I'm leaving next week, Amy. I'm being discharged.'

His words hung in the air, words that should have been a joy to hear. Ed deserved to go home. She doubted he should have been here in the first place. 'Well, that's . . . . wonderful news.' She forced a note of happiness into her voice. 'I'm so pleased for you, I really am. Of course, I'll miss you, but you—'

'Come with me.' He cut her off, his voice full of conviction and a pleading look in his eyes.

'Come with you?' She laughed momentarily, but then stopped as she saw he was deadly serious. 'But how, where would I go?'

'To my home. There's only Mother and me, we've got plenty of room till you find your feet.'

She glanced around the grounds. 'I don't know. How would I get out?'

Ed scoffed. 'It's not that difficult to get out. It's the

staying out that's more of a problem. As long as you're certified, the hospital has full authority over you. I've no doubt there would be a full-scale effort to bring you back; the police could get involved, possibly the local papers too.'

'Well there you are then. What's the point? It would be hopeless.'

'More hopeless than living out the rest of your life here?'

She thought about the countless men and women housed behind the locked doors who were now so disturbed and dangerous they would never see the outside world again. No doubt they had been as sane as she was when they were admitted a lifetime ago. It was a grim reality that didn't bear thinking about. Then another thought occurred to her. Maybe she would be able to track down Dr Lambourn if she escaped. They would be able to start afresh; she would no longer be his patient and they would be free to be together at last. She turned to Ed, a small smile on her lips. He was waiting for her answer.

She raised a quizzical eyebrow. 'Do you have a plan?'

He winked and squeezed her hand. ''Appen I do.'

36

Her face flushed and her arms heavy, Amy smoothed out the starched sheet, then rubbed her aching back, digging her thumbs into the knotted muscles. She gazed along the ward at the rows of neatly made beds and admired her efforts. Her hospital corners could rival those of Florence Nightingale herself, and the thirty mattresses looked like expertly wrapped Christmas presents.

She heard Pearl puffing behind her. 'Amy, there's two men come to see you . . . here on t' ward.' Her eyes were wide with disbelief. Other than doctors and the occasional male visitor, this ward was not used to men putting in an appearance.

'Thank you, Pearl. I'll be along shortly.'

Whilst appearing unfazed on the outside, she needed a minute to compose herself, taking deep breaths and running through what she was going to say in her head.

Ed was standing at the end of the ward next to Nurse Lyons, who had his arm slung about his young charge's shoulder. The nurse smiled as he saw Amy approaching.

'This young man is on his way home and asked to say goodbye to you.'

Amy stared at Ed. He was in his civilian clothes now: brown trousers that actually fitted him and didn't show off his ankles, and a green checked shirt open at the neck, his rolled-up sleeves showing his tanned arms. He fidgeted with the cap in his hands and looked down at the floor.

Please, Ed, she willed. *Just act normally. Don't give us away.*

'Hello, Ed,' she said breezily. 'I'm so glad you came to say goodbye.'

He looked up but didn't speak. It was as though he didn't trust himself to say anything.

'You look so smart. Ready to go home, I expect?'

He nodded silently. 'Mm,' was all he could manage.

Amy noticed the way his eyes darted left and right. He couldn't have looked more shifty had he been dressed in a striped jersey with a balaclava on his head and a bag of swag over his shoulder. She needed to get him out.

'Well it's been lovely getting to know you, Ed. All the best for the future, and take care on that bike of yours.' She gave a small laugh.

He took a tentative step towards her, opened his arms and gave her a hesitant hug. She pulled him closer, feeling his breath warm against her ear. 'See you tomorrow,' he whispered.

'Are you all right?' Belinda took the chair opposite Amy in the bay window and leaned forward, propping her fist under her chin as she asked her question. She gave the impression she actually cared about the answer.

Amy looked up from her book. 'Why shouldn't I be?'

'Well I know how fond you were of that boy, and now he's gone, I thought you might be a bit sad.'

Amy regarded Belinda through narrowed eyes and marvelled at how far they had come since they had first met, when they had hated each other on sight. 'That's kind of you, Belinda, but I'm fine, honestly.'

This seemed to satisfy the other girl, who beamed her toothy smile. 'Grand, that is. You're so . . . oh what's the word . . . you always seem to bounce back.'

'Resilient?' Amy supplied.

'Yes, that's it. I wish I could be more like you.'

'You're fine as you are, Belinda.' Amy turned back to her book, indicating that the conversation was over.

Belinda didn't seem to take the hint. 'Are you looking forward to the summer ball on Saturday?'

Amy stared at the words on the page as they merged into a mass of unintelligible letters. 'Yes, I suppose so.'

'Will you dance with me?'

The thought of taking Belinda's sweaty body into her arms was repulsive. Just sitting here, she could smell the ripe odour seeping from her pores. 'We'll see.'

'You won't have that boy to dance with, will you?'

'That's true.' She turned over another page, keeping her head down.

'So you'll have time to dance with me, then?'

Amy slammed the book shut, making Belinda jump. She struggled to keep the impatience out of her voice.

'I'm sure there will be plenty of young men willing to dance with you, Belinda.' She knew nothing could be further from the truth. There would be plenty lining up for a quick fumble in exchange for the usual ciggies, but men willing to dance with her would be in short supply.

She was too nervous to eat breakfast, but anxious not to arouse suspicion, she nibbled at the corner of a slice of toast. The greasy slick of margarine on top made her want to retch. She swilled down a cup of stewed tea and glanced at the clock on the wall. Only two more hours of this wretched existence to tolerate and then she would be free. The knot of excitement in her chest made breathing difficult. She wiped away the dewy film of perspiration from her top lip, her fingers beating out an impatient rhythm on the table.

Sister Atkins appeared behind her with a clipboard and prodded her in the back. 'You. Change of plan. Get yourself down to the laundry.'

Amy swivelled round to face her. 'But I'm on beds this week.'

'And now you're on laundry.' Sister Atkins pulled the chair out, causing Amy to stumble to her feet. 'Move it.'

Amy forced herself to calm down. She could still go through with the plan; it would just mean coming up with an excuse to leave the laundry and find her way across to the other side of the hospital where she had planned to meet Ed. Turn left out of the main gate, he'd instructed, then first right, and he would be waiting in the bus shelter. There would be much more ground to cover now, but as long as she wasn't missed before she'd had the chance to make it through the gate, everything would be all right. Ed would have a change of clothes for her; as he'd pointed out, walking out of an unlocked gate was quite straightforward, but patients in their communal garb with the Ambergate insignia stitched into the pocket could hardly be inconspicuous in the wider community.

She made her way along the ward, a thousand scenarios going round in her head. She glanced over at her own unmade bed, the taut corners at the bottom still unruffled. She felt a curious sense of pride. She stopped at Belinda's bed, where the other girl was tearing through her hair with a brush that was next to useless on her thick, matted locks.

'Goodbye, Belinda.' The catch in her throat caught her by surprise, and she swallowed hard as she pasted a smile on her face.

Belinda frowned. 'I'll see you at lunchtime, won't I?'

Amy hesitated. 'Yes . . . yes, of course you will.'

A doubtful look spread across Belinda's face. She didn't believe a word of it.

'Where're you going, Amy?' she asked.

'To the laundry.'

Belinda threw the brush down on her bed. 'I meant after that. When you get out?'

Amy put her finger to her lips. 'Shh, what do you mean?'

259

'You've been acting very strange since your boyfriend left. I'm right, aren't I? You're going over t' wall.'

Amy licked her lips, taking her time to formulate an answer. She could either flatly deny it or take Belinda into her confidence. She looked at the girl's forlorn expression, her puppy-dog eyes and pouting mouth. 'I'm not going anywhere.' She took hold of Belinda's hand and gave it a light squeeze. 'I promise I'll see you later.'

'Good,' said Belinda. 'Because I couldn't bear it in 'ere without you.'

37

The laundry was the place to be in winter. The hot, steamy atmosphere and the comforting smell of the warm linen were certainly preferable to the noisy kitchens. In the summer, though, it was unbearable. As soon as Amy pushed the door open, the rush of heat hit her in the face. It was as though she had walked into a hothouse, except there were no exotic flowers or butterflies here, just vats of steaming clothes and the pungent stench of bodies that worked too hard and went too long between baths. She glanced around the room, relieved to see she did not recognise anyone.

She picked up a pair of tongs and pulled a man's jacket out of the boiling water. She scanned the lapels to check that all dubious-looking stains had been removed, then dipped the garment into the vat of cold water. An old woman sidled up to her, her front teeth missing, her hair almost white except for her yellow fringe, which evidently bore the brunt of her cigarette habit.

'Not seen you 'ere before.'

Amy fed the jacket into the mangle. 'So?' She was in no mood for small talk.

'All right,' said the old woman. 'I was only making conversation.' She reached into the boiling vat with her bare hands.

'What on earth are you doing? Here,' said Amy quickly, brandishing the laundry tongs. 'Use these.'

'When you've worked 'ere as long as I 'ave, you've no need for fancy gadgets like that.'

Amy stared as she pulled out a pair of trousers. The woman's hands were bright red, the skin as thick and crinkly as an elephant's.

Lord above, she thought. *I need to get out of this place.*

The hands on the wall clock seemed to have gone on strike as the time passed agonisingly slowly. She was amazed she hadn't given herself away, the amount of times she must have glanced up at the clock, until mercifully it was time for her to make a move. With trembling hands, she untied her apron, her mouth thick and dry, the apprehension making her fuzzy-headed. Three times she took a deep breath in through her nose and exhaled slowly through her mouth. The adrenalin had kicked in now and she was eager to get it over with. The time had come to begin the rest of her life. Today she would be reborn.

She called to the old woman, who was now elbow-deep in the scalding water, 'I'm just going to the bathroom.' She didn't wait for an answer but instead skipped through the door and into the blessed cool air of the corridor. She moved as quickly as she dared, not wanting to arouse suspicion but desperate to leave this miserable place behind. She kept her head down as she marched purposefully along the corridors, not too fast but quickly enough to deter others from striking up a conversation.

Slightly disorientated, she pushed open the double doors and stepped out into the sunshine. She gathered her bearings. She could see the cricket field and the main driveway beyond, a little further away than she had hoped. It shouldn't matter, though. Ed would wait. Better for her to do things carefully than to rush and end up being caught. She sauntered around the edge of the field, stopping every now and again to pick up a daisy or to simply turn her face up to the sun. Anybody watching from the window would hardly suspect she was about to become a fugitive.

As the main gate came into view, it was all she could do to stop herself breaking into a run. Her heart was pounding so hard she thought it might actually explode. She calculated she had about a hundred steps to go before she would be free. She began to count them off in her head . . . *Ninety-nine, ninety-eight* . . . She thought about her mother, her beautiful, talented mother, who had smothered her with affection. There was no way she would have allowed her to languish in this place. It was her mother who had patiently taught her to read and write during the war years they had spent in Wales, who had taught her to sketch, make Welsh cakes, curl her hair, embroider handkerchiefs. How different things would have been if she'd not died so tragically . . .

Sixty-five, sixty four . . . Amy clenched her fists when she thought about her father. What a weak man he had turned out to be, in the thrall of a much younger woman who had flattered him and given him the baby he should have had with her mother. *Thirty-two, thirty-one* . . . Her eyes misted over when she thought of Dr Lambourn. She refused to believe he had simply abandoned her. They had shared too much for that to be the case, not just physically, but emotionally too. But now she was almost free, and when she found him again, she would give him the chance to explain his actions. She would not get hysterical and he would see they belonged together.

Fifteen, fourteen . . . She was within touching distance of the tall brick pillar at the side of the gate now, and she resisted the urge to look over her shoulder. She'd miscalculated the number, but no matter, she was within a few euphoric steps of freedom. She rounded the pillar, giving a gasp of relief, and only then quickened her pace, a broad smile splitting her face.

Her cry of joy turned to shock as her foot caught on something and she stumbled, falling headlong on the pavement. It took a few seconds for her to realise what had happened. She rolled onto her side and inspected her palms. The heels of her hands were blood-streaked and ingrained with grit. She winced and rubbed them together just as a dark shadow blocked out the sun. She glanced up at the figure standing over her, arms akimbo.

'And where do you think you're going?'

38

She squinted up at the sneering face of Sister Atkins, her red lips curled into a spiteful smile.

'Did you really think you could get away with this?' She kicked at Amy's legs. 'Get up.'

Amy rose to her feet. Her knees were scuffed raw and a trickle of blood ran down one leg. Her left elbow was bruised and she cradled it in her right hand. 'How . . . how did you know?' she whispered.

'As if I'm going to reveal my sources to you.' Sister Atkins grabbed her roughly by the arm and frogmarched her back up the main driveway. With her free hand she rubbed her chin like a cartoon villain. 'How will I punish you, I wonder? I'm going to have to get my thinking cap on and come up with something really creative.' She finished with a manic cackle, but Amy stared impassively ahead, refusing to supply the reaction Sister so obviously craved.

Back on the ward, preparations for lunch had begun. Belinda was helping by spreading the marge on a huge mound of thick white bread. She didn't look up as Amy entered the ward, instead concentrating on the bread as though it was the most fascinating thing she'd ever encountered.

Amy inspected her own bicep, rubbing gently at the bruised flesh. She could see the imprint of Sister Atkins's bony fingers and could feel the heat of bitter anger rising up through her gut until it settled in the back of her throat, threatening to choke her. She approached the table where Belinda was working and took a swipe at the tower of bread. It toppled over, several slices falling to the floor.

'Oi,' said Belinda. 'What do you think . . .? Oh, it's you. How was the laundry?' Her voice was steady enough but her eyes were shifty narrow slits and she fought to keep her trembling hands still.

'I'm going to get you back for this,' Amy hissed. 'Just when you're least expecting it. You're going to have to spend the rest of your time in here looking over your shoulder, and one day, I'll be there, your worst nightmare come true.' She lowered her voice and leaned in to Belinda, their noses almost touching. 'Revenge is a dish best served cold, don't they say?'

Belinda stayed silent, her eyes now round with fear as she wiped Amy's spittle off her cheek. 'I . . . I don't know what you mean,' she protested, but Amy had already turned away, leaving Belinda staring open-mouthed at her retreating figure. She stooped to collect the slices of bread that had fallen to the floor, blew off the bits of fluff and dust and returned them to the pile.

*

Amy lay on top of her bed, a damp towel across her forehead. She closed her eyes and tried to picture Ed, waiting for her in the bus shelter, clutching the bundle of clothes. How many times must he have looked at his watch and gazed down the street, willing her to come round the corner? He had taken a huge risk for her and she'd let him down. Perhaps he thought she'd changed her mind and didn't want to leave Ambergate after all.

She looked towards Sister's office, wondering what the vile nurse had in store for her. She propped herself up on her elbows and wiped the towel over her face. It didn't matter. They wouldn't break her, she decided. Resilient was what Belinda had called her. And she was right. She would not be brutalised into submission. If Sister Atkins wanted a battle, she could have it, and there would only be one winner.

Later, as dusk fell, Amy sat with her book by the open window in the day room, allowing the cool breeze to waft over her face. She absently turned the page, her eyes seeing the words but her distracted brain unable to make any sense of them. Making her wait for the axe to fall was no doubt all part of Sister's plan to prolong the torture. Belinda wandered in carrying a mug from which she took slow, deliberate sips. 'Mmm, this cocoa is delicious. Sister gave it to me as a treat for being such a good girl.'

'Why did you do it, Belinda?'

Belinda wiped her hand across her mouth and gave an almost imperceptible shake of her head. 'I've never had a friend before. Not in 'ere, nor out there.' She gestured towards the window. 'Nobody has ever liked me for just being me. They've always wanted summat from me. You made me see that, Amy. You made me see that I was worth more than that.'

Amy kept her voice level. 'I'm glad you think of me as a friend, Belinda, but I didn't deserve that kind of treachery. Friends don't snitch on one another.'

'But . . . but I didn't want you to leave . . . I . . .'

'What about what *I* want?'

Belinda shrugged. 'I thought you liked me.'

'Well you know what *thought* did.' Amy returned to her book, savagely flipping over the next page. 'Get lost, Belinda, and don't talk to me again.'

Belinda drained the last of her cocoa and slammed the mug down on the table. 'You stuck-up cow. You've always thought you were better than the rest of us, haven't you? Well I've got news for you. You're just like everyone else. Your dad bundled you in 'ere the same as mine did, and no wonder that doctor scarpered. He'd probably had enough of your whining to last him a lifetime.'

Amy swallowed hard, breathing through her nose like an enraged bull about to charge. She slipped her hand down the side of the cushion and groped for the zip. Without taking her eyes off Belinda, she unzipped a gap big enough to get her fingers in. She felt around the foam cushion, prodding the spongy slab until she alighted on what she was looking for. Slowly she withdrew the pointed sliver of china and encased it in her palm with the sleight of hand a magician would be proud of.

Belinda stood over her now, her hands planted on her hips. She evidently had more to get off her chest. 'And why that sweet young boy would want anything to do with such a . . .'

Amy rose from her seat, her right hand behind her back. She stared into Belinda's face, her spiteful, mocking tone inviting a response. Then she smiled, brought her hand up and plunged the shard of china into Belinda's neck. A ribbon of blood arced in front of Amy's face, and Belinda fell to the floor.

39

She lay in the corner of the room, wedged into the angle where the walls met the floor, her cheek pressed into the cold rubber matting and her body curled up like a hibernating hedgehog. She stretched her limbs out one by one and turned onto her back, feeling along the thick walls, spongy walls smooth to the touch. Her finger found a small hole and she dug her nail in and scooped out a chunk of coarse hair. She struggled into a sitting position and rubbed the back of her neck. Her hair was brittle and reeked of the acidic tang of vomit. She glanced over to the steel door, painted gunmetal grey with a tiny square in the middle. Her stomach felt hollow, as though someone had released a valve and deflated her body.

A clang of metal and a squeaking hinge drew her attention back to the door. The small square opened and a pair of wide eyes peered in. 'Morning, Amy. I'm coming in now, so no funny business if you don't mind.'

Nurse Ellen Crosby heaved open the door and reattached the bunch of jangling keys to her belt. She thrust a tray towards Amy. 'I've brought you some porridge.' She glanced at the open door behind her before digging into her pocket. 'I've managed to procure a packet of sugar too. Thought it might make the porridge a little more palatable. You've not been eating much, you know.'

Amy peeled her tongue from the roof of her furred-up mouth. 'Water,' she croaked. 'I need a glass of water.'

Ellen nodded at the tray. 'It's here in this plastic beaker.' She crouched down next to Amy and held the cup to her lips, watching as Amy drained it. 'You were thirsty.'

Amy groaned as she stretched her arms. 'I'm so stiff. What's happened? Where am I?'

With another nervous glance towards the door, Ellen dropped her voice and spoke in hushed tones. 'How much do you remember?'

Amy tried to run her fingers through her sticky hair. She screwed up her eyes and willed her brain to provide a memory. 'I was outside,' she began, her voice hoarse and scratchy. 'It was warm and I was . . . happy, I think . . . excited. I was going to meet someone.' The fog in her memory shifted slightly. 'Yes, that's it. I was going to meet Dr Lambourn. He sent for me. I knew he would.' She tried to get to her feet. 'I need to go and see him now. He'll be waiting. Please help me up, will you, Nurse?'

Ellen placed her hand on Amy's shoulder and pressed down. 'You're not going anywhere just yet, Amy.'

'Please, I need to get cleaned up. He can't see me like this.' She grabbed hold of Ellen's wrist, startling the young nurse. Amy laughed. 'It's all right, I'm not going to hurt you. Now, when can I have a bath?' She grabbed a fistful of her nightdress and stuffed it under her nose. 'And I'm going to need a change of clothes.'

'Dr Lambourn doesn't work here any more, Amy.'

'I know that. I'm not stupid. He's waiting for me on the outside.'

Ellen shook her head. 'No he's not. You're still a certified patient, and after what happened with Belinda, you're likely to remain so for quite some time, I'm afraid.'

Amy stared at her vacantly. 'Who's Belinda?'

'Are you serious?'

Amy didn't answer; just clutched at her stomach as another wave of nausea overcame her. As she heaved, the bile stung her throat and the cup of water she'd drunk moments before was expelled over the breakfast tray.

Ellen took a startled step back. 'Oh no, not again. You've been like this every morning for the past week.'

'The past week?' Amy clarified. 'But I only came in here last night. What are you talking about?'

Ellen shook her head. 'You've been out of it most of the time. You know . . . sedated.' She seemed uncomfortable. 'I mean, we had no choice. You were extremely violent and volatile. Belinda was lucky to survive. It was fortunate that—'

'Every morning?' Amy interrupted.

'I'm sorry?'

'You said I've been sick every morning.'

Ellen nodded slowly. 'That's right.'

Amy gazed down at her stomach and smoothed out

the nightdress, her hand resting on the almost imperceptible swell of her belly. 'Oh!' The word came out on a
breath of disbelief. 'Oh my God.' She looked up at Ellen
and smiled. 'I'm having Dr Lambourn's baby.'

After leaving Amy's padded cell, Ellen scuttled back to
the ward, desperate to find Sister Atkins and tell her this
unbelievable news. She cursed the sheer scale of the place,
with its never-ending corridors and numerous sets of
doors to navigate. Arriving breathless on the ward, she
found Sister Atkins ensconced in her office, listening to
a play on the radio, her eyes closed and her feet up on
the desk.

'Sister Atkins, I—'

Sister held up her hand but didn't open her eyes. 'Shh,
not now.'

'But—'

'Are you deaf or just stupid?'

'Neither, I—'

'Out!'

Ellen hovered in the doorway, biting at her thumbnail.
'It's important, Sister Atkins, I wouldn't bother you ordi-
narily, but it concerns Amy.'

Sister Atkins groaned. 'I might've bloody known she'd
be involved somehow. She's no longer a patient on this
ward and yet here we are still talking about her.' She took
her legs off the desk, switched off the radio and indicated
the chair opposite.

Ellen sat down gratefully. 'I've just taken her some breakfast. I . . . wanted to see how she was this morning. I've always felt a kind of affinity with her, as you know. We both came to Ambergate at the same time, we're the same age . . .'

'Can you get to the point, please, Student Nurse Crosby.'

'Of course. Well, this morning, she was a little more alert. She's been sedated since the attack on Belinda and can't seem to remember anything about it.'

'That's not so unusual, and certainly not important enough for you to disturb me on my break.'

Ellen shook her head. 'No, that's not why I'm here. I'll come straight to the point.'

Sister Atkins glanced at the ceiling. 'Hallelujah!' She lit a cigarette, sucking long and hard.

Ellen leaned forward in her chair and lowered her voice. 'Amy says she's pregnant.'

Sister Atkins stared impassively ahead, her expression difficult to read. She tapped some ash into her saucer. 'Pregnant?'

Ellen nodded. 'That's what she says.'

'And how is that possible?'

'I'm not sure, but she says the baby is Dr Lambourn's.'

Sister Atkins guffawed so loudly, Ellen jumped in alarm. 'Ha, I've heard it all now. Eee, that takes the biscuit, that does.'

'Why . . . why would she lie about a thing like that?'

'Simple. The girl's deluded. She's a certified loony, for

God's sake. You don't even have to take my word for it. I've got the bloody paperwork.'

'But I really think she may be telling the truth. I think she might be pregnant.'

Sister Atkins seemed unperturbed by this. 'In the highly unlikely event that that is the case, I can assure you that Dr Lambourn is definitely not the father.'

'I know it sounds incredible, but he was rather fond of her.'

'You think he'd risk his career for a fling with a silly little girl like that?'

Ellen shrugged. 'Well why would she say it?'

'She's hardly a credible witness. No, if she is pregnant, then my money's on that young lad she was planning on running off with. That makes more sense.'

'I suppose so, but—'

Sister Atkins cut her off. 'Shut the door.'

Ellen frowned but did as she was asked and returned to her seat.

'You've heard of mumps, Student Nurse Crosby?'

'Obviously, but what's that got to do with anything?'

Sister Atkins stubbed out her cigarette. 'I'm going to nip this in the bud, but it stays within these four walls, do you understand?'

Ellen nodded. 'Whatever you say, Sister.'

'Good.' Sister Atkins clasped her hands and laid them on her desk, adopting a reverential tone. 'When Dr Lambourn was a teenager, he contracted mumps, which rendered him infertile.' She waited for her words to sink in before continuing. 'Have you ever wondered why such a good-looking, successful man of thirty is unmarried?'

'No, I can't say I've given it much thought, to be honest.'

'Well, he was engaged once, a few years ago, but when his fiancée found out he couldn't have children, she upped and left.'

'How awful for him.'

'Indeed. So you see, whatever Amy Sullivan says, Dr Lambourn cannot possibly be the father of her child.'

40

The morning air was cold and sharp, and it felt good to take in an invigorating lungful. Amy picked her way along the frost-encrusted lawn, taking care not to slip on the layers of rotting leaves beneath her feet. When she reached the cricket pavilion, she grabbed the handrail and gingerly mounted the wooden steps. Out of breath, she settled down on the bench seat and rubbed her hand over the large dome of her belly, her coat buttons straining over the bump. For the past two days she'd suffered from a dull backache and the familiar dragging sensation she normally associated with her time of the month. She knew it wouldn't be long now. Soon she would be able to hold Dr Lambourn's baby in her arms, and then they would have no choice but to let her out. A baby needed its father as well as its mother.

The last six months had slipped by in a blur of white padded walls, calming drugs that stupefied her to the point of submission and long days spent staring at the ceiling with only foggy distorted memories for company. Dr Lambourn's face was clear enough, though. She could still picture his dark eyes and his even white teeth standing out against his olive skin, which always seemed to sport a smattering of stubble.

She pulled the handkerchief out of her pocket, the one he had given her all those months ago, and held it against her nose. The familiar smell of his cologne, fading now but still just about detectable, transported her back to their sessions in his office, a place where she'd been able to relax and allow him to coax her demons out. She turned around and squinted through the glass into the pavilion, shielding her eyes from the reflection. An old mildewed sofa was wedged against the wall, its stuffing spilling out over the wooden floor, which was speckled with mouse droppings. She frowned as a memory came unbidden, a flash of a smile, a warm brown hand in hers and a thigh pressed against her own.

She turned the handle of the door, and after some gentle persuasion, it creaked open. The air was dank and musty and a spider's web caught in her hair as she crossed the threshold. She felt she'd been inside here before, but her opaque memory refused to surrender a clear image. She ran her hand along the sofa, the pile worn down to the bare wefts of thread. She rubbed her temples and squeezed her eyes closed, willing herself to remember. A name . . . Edward . . . Ed?

From nowhere, a band of pain gripped her round her middle and she emitted a high-pitched shriek, which startled a mouse and sent it scuttling across the floor. She lowered herself onto the battered sofa and breathed deeply as another wave of pain exerted its iron grip. The baby was coming. 'No,' she whispered. 'Not here, not now.'

She struggled to her feet, her hand resting in the small of her back and her heart pumping wildly. She descended the slippery steps and waddled towards the main building as quickly as her cumbersome frame would allow. 'Please, please,' she begged, although she had no idea who she was pleading with.

She stopped as another excruciating wave sliced through her abdomen, causing her body to fold over. The blood rushed to her head, and despite the arctic chill, the back of her neck was pasted with sweat. When the pain had passed, she straightened up and staggered forward again, each treacherous step fraught with danger on the frosted grass. Hot tears scorched her frigid cheeks as she battled to stay upright but she knew deep down that it was a battle she couldn't win. Panic grasped her by the throat, its bony fingers squeezing her airway until the blackness descended as though someone had thrown a cloak over her body. She slumped to the ground, her head hitting the solid turf with a sickening thud.

Somebody had hold of her hand. Someone else was soothing her brow as she twisted her head from side to side. The light above the bed was dazzlingly bright, the sheets cool and clammy and the clatter of instruments too loud in her ears. The metallic tang of blood hovered in the air. Every one of her senses was being assaulted. She raised her head off the pillow and let out a long groan. A nurse she had never seen before was asking her to push hard. Push what? She had no idea what she was talking about.

She lolled back on the pillow. 'What's happening, where am I?'

A voice she did recognise spoke calmly into her ear. 'It's Nurse Crosby here, Amy. You're in a special room in the hospital. Me and the midwife, Sister Brown, are going to look after you. You're having your baby, remember?'

There was no time to formulate a response before another contraction violated her body. 'Aargh, it hurts. It's too much, please, I need . . .'

The pain subsided again and she lay panting, white foam gathering in the corners of her mouth. 'I need some water,' she croaked.

Ellen pressed a glass to her lips and Amy took a grateful sip. 'You're doing very well,' the nurse encouraged. 'It's taking rather a long time, but we're nearly there now, just a couple more pushes and it will all be over.'

Amy gazed down between her open legs to the midwife, who was crouching at the end of the bed. 'How much longer?' she pleaded.

Sister Brown looked up, a slight frown on her ruddy face. Her hand was plunged deep inside Amy's body. 'You can't rush these things.'

'You were lucky,' added Ellen. 'Your waters broke out on the field. It was a miracle that you were found in time and brought inside.'

'Nurse Crosby.' The midwife's voice was light, but her face wore a worried expression. 'Can you come down this end for a minute?'

Ellen placed a reassuring hand on Amy's head. 'Everything'll be fine.'

Sister Brown spoke in hushed hurried tones. 'Something's not right. I think the cord is round the baby's neck. On the next contraction, I expect the head to be delivered. I need you to hook your finger under the cord and wrestle it free. Do you think you can manage that?'

Ellen swallowed hard and panted out a few short breaths as though she herself was in labour. 'I hope so.'

The midwife spoke to Amy. 'Right, on the next contraction, you need to push long and hard. Keep going until I tell you to stop.'

Ellen stared in awe as the baby's head crowned. Then its puckered-up little face appeared, bearing an angry expression, its neck wrapped in the pulsing umbilical cord.

Sister Brown cradled the baby's head. 'Now,' she commanded.

Ellen loosened the cord, slimy beneath her trembling fingers, and with the next contraction the little blue body slithered out.

Sister Brown turned it over and slapped the baby's back with much more force than Ellen thought was necessary. Then she began rubbing at it as though she was kneading dough.

Ellen hovered at the end of the bed, horrified by the sight of the ragged little body, yet unable to tear her gaze away. 'Is he . . . is he going to be all right?'

The midwife ignored the question but carried on rubbing, her whole body shaking with the effort. At last she stopped, shook her head and crossed herself. She looked up at Ellen. 'I did my best, but it took too long.'

Ellen gazed down at the perfectly formed little boy. 'You don't mean . . .?'

'What . . . what's happening?' gasped Amy, propping herself up on her elbows. 'Where's my baby?'

Ellen took hold of Amy's hand, fighting back tears. 'I'm really sorry, Amy, but he didn't make it. The cord was—'

Amy screamed. A long, primeval howl that echoed off the tiled walls. 'No, no, no! You're wrong. Let me see my son. He can't be dead, he can't be. I love him.' Choking on her sobs, she reached out her arms. 'Give him to me,' she demanded.

Sister Brown shook her head. 'I wouldn't recommend it.' She thrust the wrapped bundle towards Ellen. 'You know what to do.'

'No!' Amy was frantic now, flinging off the thin sheet that covered her knees and attempting to get up. 'Let me see my baby. He can't be dead. He's all I've got left. I'm warning you, when Dr Lambourn finds out that you wouldn't let me see our baby, he'll—'

The midwife pressed her down. 'You're not finished here yet. You need to deliver the afterbirth. I'm really sorry about your baby, but sometimes these things happen.'

She nodded at Ellen, not bothering to hide her impatience. 'Take him to the morgue.'

41

September 2006

It was dark by the time Sarah arrived home. She unlocked the front door and called out to her father as she entered the hall. 'Sorry I'm late, Dad. Have you had anything to eat?' She popped her head round the lounge door. He was sitting in his favourite armchair, the newspaper spread out on his lap.

'Yes, I've done roast beef. I've left you a plateful in the microwave.'

'Great, thanks.'

'I've even managed to make some Yorkshire puddings. Followed your mother's recipe and they turned out a treat.'

She returned with her food on a tray and settled down in the chair opposite. 'I'm ravenous.' She shoved a forkful into her mouth. 'It's been a busy day.'

He raised his eyebrows. 'How . . . how's the research coming along, then?'

She stopped chewing and set her knife and fork down. It was the first time he had shown any interest in the project. She swallowed and wiped her serviette over her mouth. 'Really well, since you ask.'

He nodded slowly. 'Good, I'm glad.' He returned to his newspaper.

'Dad?' she began.

He peered at her over his spectacles. 'Yes.'

'You do know I'm only writing a book about Ambergate because you were there?'

'So I gather.'

She shuffled forward, the tray balanced precariously on her knees. 'I was really hoping you would help me, give me some insight into the daily life of the patients. It would make the book so much more authentic.' When he didn't put up any resistance, she ploughed on. 'It's such an important part of our social history. The people who spent time there deserve to have their stories heard.' He stayed silent and she warmed to her theme. 'With your help I could give them a voice.' She paused for effect. 'I could give *you* a voice too, Dad. Your contribution would be invaluable.'

He let his head loll back on the chair and stared at the ceiling. 'I don't know, Sarah. It's all such a long time ago.'

'What's that got to do with anything? People still like to read about the Battle of Hastings.'

He laughed. 'I can't argue with that logic.'

She joined her hands into the praying position. 'Pleeeeeease, Dad.' She was aware she sounded like a mithering toddler.

He shook his head 'I don't know, Sarah, I . . .'

'I found something today that might make you change your mind.'

'Oh, and what was that?'

She chewed on her bottom lip, mulling over how much she should tell him. 'We found some suitcases.'

'Suitcases?'

'Yes, in an attic space.'

'Who's we?'

'Oh, me and this young lad Nathan. He's a homeless guy who sleeps there sometimes.'

'Sleeps in a derelict asylum?' Her father shuddered. 'Rather him than me.'

'Yes, quite. Anyway, there's a pile of suitcases up there. About twenty of them in total. We've been documenting the contents and taking photographs. That's why I've been so long.'

He folded up his newspaper and dropped it onto the carpet. 'Anything interesting?'

She hesitated. 'Well . . . yes, as a matter of fact.'

'Oh?'

'Come with me, Dad. Come with me to Ambergate tomorrow and I'll show you.'

He shook his head. 'Oh no, Sarah. I'm not setting foot in that place again.'

'Why not, Dad? What happened in there?'

'Let's just say it's a part of my life I would rather forget about.'

She stood up, set the tray on the floor and reached into the back pocket of her jeans. She pulled out the note she had found in the suitcase and ran her fingers along the fold. Tentatively she opened it out and passed it over to her father.

He shook his head and put his hand up. 'No, I don't want to be involved, Sarah. Whatever it is, take it away.'

She took the note back and blew out an exasperated breath. 'All right then, as you wish.' She picked up the tray and headed for the kitchen. 'Do you want a brew?'

He looked at his watch for no apparent reason. 'Aye, go on then.'

Later, unable to sleep, she flicked on the bedside light. The duvet was knotted into a tight ball and she struggled to unfurl it. She swung her legs out of bed and perched on the side, then reached for her camera and began to scroll through the photographs once more, her heart quickening at the sight of the treasures she had uncovered. Nothing of any tangible value, but a whole host of interesting memorabilia. And of course, the note. She felt around under her pillow and pulled out the creamy piece of paper. Unfolding it, she read the first four words in a hushed whisper: 'Your baby didn't die.'

42

The library was deserted at this time of the morning. Most of the staff had yet to heave themselves out of bed and the place was eerily quiet, with only the hum of the low-level lighting breaking the silence. Sarah hung her coat on the back of the staffroom door and flicked the switch on the kettle, a routine she had carried out every day since she'd started work here five years ago. She supervised the reference library upstairs, her dedication to local history having been instrumental in getting her the job. She'd written on all sorts of subjects for the local papers and parish magazines, and her features were in demand. Even though the pay was pitiful, sometimes non-existent, she still gained a huge sense of pride at seeing her work in print. Her history of Ambergate was her biggest project to date, though, one that she intended to dedicate to her father.

She poured hot water onto the peppermint tea bag and carried it over to the computer, fumbling around under the desk to switch the machine on. Once it had burst into life and she'd entered the password, she opened her notebook. She found the name and typed it into the search bar. There were over ten thousand results, but she selected the first one, an online encyclopedia.

Millie McCarthy
(6 November 1916–1 September 1947)

Millie McCarthy was an English artist. She was born in Salford and dedicated her career to painting landscapes. The source of her inspiration came from the Pembrokeshire coast, where she spent the war years as a virtual recluse with only her young daughter for company. Such was her talent, she came to the attention of L. S. Lowry, who bought two of her paintings, calling her an exceptionally gifted artist. She was tragically killed in a motor accident on 1 September 1947.

Sarah leaned back in her chair, frowning. She stared at the accompanying photograph. It was black and white, and showed Millie sitting beside her easel, a paintbrush in her hand and her head thrown back in the throes of laughter. She looked happy, radiant even. But there was no mention of her ever being in Ambergate. Sarah pressed another couple of buttons and the printer whirred into life, spitting out a copy of the entry.

Over the noise of the printer, she heard the front door rattling below, followed by a hesitant knock on the glass. She hurried downstairs and stared at the two vaguely familiar figures on the other side as she unlocked the door.

'Story time's not until nine,' she said, glancing at the clock on the wall.

He was apologetic, but the pleading look in his eyes pointed to his desperation. He clutched his daughter's hand. 'I'm really sorry, but could you take her for half an hour.' He smoothed his hand over the top of the little girl's head. 'I've got a conference call with my Hong Kong partners.'

'Can't she wait in your office with you?'

'She doesn't want to miss the start of story time.'

'Well . . . I don't know,' Sarah stammered. 'I don't think we're insured for this kind of thing. Annie's not in until quarter to.'

'She'll be no trouble.' He crouched down and kissed his daughter on the forehead. 'You'll be a good girl, won't you, Maisie?'

The little girl nodded. 'Yes, Daddy, I promise.'

He raised his eyebrows expectantly, bouncing from one foot to the other as he waited for her reply. He was 'easy on the eye', as her mother used to say, his strong jaw speckled with five o'clock shadow, his black hair swept away from his forehead and given an extra sheen with the addition of some sort of gel.

'Go on then,' Sarah relented, opening the door further. It must be important if he was having to make calls on a Saturday morning.

He touched her forearm. 'Thank you, you're a lifesaver.'

'And you are prone to exaggeration.' She tapped her

watch. 'Try to be back by nine thirty if you can. I don't want my boss thinking I've opened some sort of free-for-all crèche.'

He winked at her. 'Now who's exaggerating?'

She laughed. 'See you later.'

She watched as he jogged off down the path, then stopped and turned. 'My name's Matt, by the way.'

Maisie stood clutching her Dora the Explorer rucksack. Her fine blond hair had been clumsily styled into a French plait, wispy loose ends escaping the confines of the bobble.

'Shall we go over and sit on the bean bags in Story Corner?'

Maisie nodded and skipped off. 'Can I choose the story today?'

Sarah followed her. 'Well, that's not up to me, but I'll have a word with Annie, see what she says. I don't work down here, you see. I work upstairs with the grown-up books . . . Would you like a drink?' She mentally ran through the contents of the kitchen cupboard. Tea, coffee, a bottle of single malt they kept for really stressful days. 'How about a glass of milk?'

Maisie grinned. 'Chocolate milkshake?'

'No, not chocolate milkshake. This is a library, not McDonald's.'

Maisie giggled. 'You're funny.' She snuggled down on the bean bag and opened a large picture book. 'Okay, I'll just have the white milk then.'

Sarah returned with the glass and a custard cream and placed them next to Maisie on the table.

'Thank you.' Maisie took a long glug of the milk, leaving a white moustache across her top lip. 'What's your name?'

'It's Sarah.'

'Can you do my French plait again? Daddy's not very good at them and it's all come loose.' She pulled a face and tugged the bobble out. 'Here.'

Sarah took the bobble. 'I don't know how to do a French plait, I'm afraid. Will a plain English one do?'

Maisie considered this. 'Like Rapunzel, you mean?'

'Well, yes, I guess I could manage that.'

Maisie rummaged in her rucksack and pulled out a hairbrush. 'Genkly, please.'

Sarah ran the brush through the little girl's blond locks, careful not to tug at the knots. 'Can your mummy not do French plaits then?'

Maisie turned the page of the book and replied without looking up, 'I don't have a mummy. She died.'

Sarah stopped brushing and took a step backwards. 'Oh gosh, I'm so sorry. I hope I haven't upset you.'

'She was poorly and she had no hair.'

Sarah swallowed and glanced towards the door. She didn't want Matt bursting in on them in the middle of such a delicate conversation. 'You poor little mite.'

'She died when I was nearly four,' Maisie added matter-of-factly.

'And how old are you now?'

'Five and a bit.' Maisie picked up the biscuit and separated the two halves, scraping out the sickly yellow filling with her teeth.

Sarah noticed the little girl's sparkly nails and seized the chance to change the subject. 'I like your nail polish.'

'Daddy put it on for me. He's not very good at hair but he's good at painting nails.'

Sarah separated Maisie's hair into three strands and began to overlap them. 'That's nice. What else is he good at?'

'Well, he's quite good at cooking. My favourite is hoops on toast.'

'Good Lord, I hope that's not the extent of his culinary skills.'

Maisie turned round and stared at her. 'I don't know big words.'

Sarah laughed as she came to the end of the plait and secured it with the bobble. 'You're so sweet, Maisie.' She patted her shoulder. 'All done. Now let's go and choose a story, shall we?'

She was upstairs in the reference library, her back to the door when Matt bounded into the room. The armful of books she was carrying slid to the floor.

'I'm so sorry, it took longer than I expected.'

Sarah patted her chest. 'You startled me.'

He bent down and scooped up the books. 'Sorry,' he said again. 'How was she?'

Sarah smiled. 'She's adorable.'

Matt beamed and held his arms out wide. 'What can I say? She's my life.'

'Well, she's a credit to you.'

'We usually go to the park after story time. You know how kids like routine.'

Sarah nodded, even though she had no idea what kids liked or didn't like. 'That's nice.' She glanced out of the window. 'It looks gorgeous out there, very warm too. Perhaps we're in for an Indian summer.'

He loosened his collar to let in some air. 'Would you like to come with us?'

She hesitated for a moment, feeling ridiculously excited at the prospect of spending some time with him. 'I would like that, yes, thank you.'

He clapped his hands together. 'Great. I'll just go and tell Maisie. It was her idea.'

They sat side by side on a bench as they watched Maisie climb the slide. Sarah took a bite out of her Flake. 'Thanks for the ice cream.'

'You're welcome. It's the least I could do after you helped me out this morning.'

Maisie called from the top of the slide, waving her arms in the air, 'Daddy, look at me.'

Matt was on his feet in an instant. 'Sit down, Maisie, and hold onto the sides.'

He shook his head and returned to the bench. 'She's fearless, that one.'

Sarah glanced down at Matt's wedding ring. 'Maisie told me about her mummy.'

Matt attempted a smile. 'I'm not surprised. She talks about her mummy in heaven as though Lucy has just popped out to the shops. She knows Lucy's not coming back though. I've had to be clear about that. It's hard but she understands.'

'She sounds very resilient.'

'Yep, she keeps me going. Gives me a reason to carry on when it would be all too easy to spend the day under the duvet.'

'I'm really sorry. It must be tough.'

Matt shrugged. 'It is, but what I'm going through is nothing compared to what Lucy suffered. At least I'll get to see Maisie grow up. I was there on her first day at school, I'll get to see her graduate, give her away on her wedding day . . .' He faltered, took a deep breath and turned to look at Sarah. 'I'm sorry.'

'You've got nothing to apologise for, Matt. It's important to talk. Bottling stuff up never did anybody any good.'

'You're so right. When Lucy died, all I wanted to do was talk about her, but that made everybody else around me feel uncomfortable, so I stopped mentioning her. I put other people's feelings above my own because I didn't want to upset them.'

They both fell silent as Maisie ran over to the bench, her cheeks tinged pink. 'Daddy, will you push me on the swing?'

He jumped up immediately. 'Of course I will, darling. Off you go, I'll catch you up.' He turned to Sarah. 'Duty calls.'

She watched as he ran after his daughter, his brown corduroy jacket with reinforced elbow patches flapping in the breeze. Anybody else would look like an aging university professor in that garb but Matt carried it off with effortless chic. Maisie scrambled onto the swing and Matt made sure she was holding on before he pushed her gently.

'Higher, Daddy,' she implored.

Matt shook his head and glanced at Sarah. 'See? Fearless.'

After five minutes Maisie was ready to get off. 'Catch me, Daddy.'

Matt moved round to the front of the swing and as she slowed down, Maisie jumped off into her father's arms. He held her high in the air, spun her round, then buried his face into her neck making her squeal as he covered her in kisses. Sarah watched on, their tender exchange making her smile outwardly but inside she ached for everything they had lost.

She was up in her bedroom when her father tapped on the door later that evening. 'Come in.'

He shuffled into the room. 'I've brought you some hot chocolate.'

She couldn't help her surprise. 'Oh, right, thanks.'

'It's got that squirty cream and marshmallows on, the full Monty.'

She took the mug. 'What have I done to deserve this?'

He sat down next to her on the bed. 'Yesterday, when I asked you about moving out?'

She picked a marshmallow off the top and popped it into her mouth. 'Hmm, what about it?'

'Well, I don't want you to think you're not welcome here. Of course you are. You can stay as long you need to.'

'Thanks.'

'But I'll be all right, you know. You don't need to stay on my account.'

'I know you mean well, Dad. And I will go home soon, I promise.' She glanced around her childhood bedroom with its woodchip-papered walls painted in oranges and browns, her bright yellow eiderdown and the old rocking horse in the corner. She'd brushed that horse's flaxen mane so much that it was now almost bald. Even her poster of David Cassidy still hung over the headboard. The whole room might have been a throwback to the seventies, but she felt safe here. It was her haven. She closed the lid of her laptop and began to gather her notes, which were spread across the bed. Her father picked up the entry she had printed out at the library and squinted at it, the paper quivering in his fingers as he absorbed the information. 'What . . . what are you doing with this?'

She took the sheet from him and put it back in her

bag. 'Oh, it's to do with my research. I found a painting in one of those suitcases I told you about. Millie McCarthy was the artist. I thought it might provide a clue as to why she was in Ambergate, but it seems—'

He cut her off. 'Was . . . was there anything else in there?'

She stopped clearing away. 'I thought you didn't want anything to do with it.'

'W-well . . .' he stammered. 'I don't, but . . . a painting, you say?'

'Dad, do you want to know or not? You're giving me all kinds of mixed messages.'

He considered this for a long while, his voice just a hoarse whisper when he finally answered. 'Go on then, tell me.'

Sarah propped the pillows up behind her back and made herself more comfortable. 'There are around twenty cases up there. Most of them are just full of clothes, knick-knacks and what have you, but some of them are very interesting. There are no names on them, so we have no way of knowing who they belonged to, but in one of the cases, I found a watercolour amongst other things.'

He raised his eyebrows. 'What other things?'

She rummaged under her pillow and brought out the note. 'This.' She thrust it towards him. 'Do you need me to fetch your glasses?'

He opened up the piece of paper and stared at the four words in capital letters with unblinking eyes. 'No,' he said eventually. 'I don't need my glasses.' He ferreted in his pocket and pulled out his handkerchief, dabbing at the corners of his eyes.

'What's up, Dad?'

He folded the note in two again and rose from the bed, his old bones cracking as he stood up. 'I thought I had an inkling as to whose case this was, but now I'm not sure.'

Sarah scrambled off the bed and clutched at his elbow. 'Really?'

He tugged at his ear, a sure sign he was mulling things over. 'Yes, but this baby thing doesn't make any sense at all.' He opened the note up again. 'What does the rest of it say? I can't read that without my glasses.'

Sarah perched her own glasses on the end of her nose. She spoke slowly, deciphering the almost illegible scrawl as she went along. It had certainly been written in a hurry. 'It says, "If you're reading this, then you must have left Ambergate. I'm at 113 Oak Grove, Manchester. Look me up and I'll tell you everything. Sincerely, Ellen Crosby."'

'Is that it?'

'Yes, Dad, that's it.'

He sank back onto the bed and placed his head in his hands. Sarah plonked herself down beside him. 'Dad?'

He closed his eyes and pinched the bridge of his nose. 'This could open a whole can of worms, Sarah.' He shook his head, then fixed her with a determined stare, his voice cold and unwavering. 'I want you to put the note back and forget you ever saw it.'

'That's like telling me to forget my own name.' She patted his knee. 'You don't need to be involved, Dad, but I will be going to that address to find out what all this is about.'

'Sarah,' he warned. 'I said leave it. Nothing good can come from meddling in the past.' He attempted a smile. 'Please, just take the note and put it back where you found it.'

Sarah stood up. 'I'm sorry, Dad. I can't do that.'

43

Sarah stood at the garden gate and surveyed the smart semi with its dark red bricks and white mortar. The lawn's edges were so neat they looked as though they had been trimmed with nail scissors. She smiled at the pair of gnomes sitting by the tiny pond, one of them with a fishing rod in hand. She pushed open the gate, then hesitated as someone appeared from the side of the house carrying a stepladder over his shoulder. His white overalls were splattered with various shades of paint. She guessed he must be in his mid seventies. He spotted her and raised his eyebrows. 'Can I help you?'

She suddenly felt incredibly foolish. 'I'm . . . I'm looking for Ellen Crosby.'

He leaned the stepladder against the wall and advanced towards her. 'And you are?'

She held out her hand. 'I'm Sarah . . . Sarah Charlton. I'm a historian researching a book and I wondered if I might have a word with Ms Crosby.' She cringed inwardly, wishing she hadn't sounded so much like a police officer.

He seemed satisfied with her answer, though, and

offered his hand. 'Douglas Lyons – Dougie. Ellen's my wife.'

Sarah ferreted in her handbag and pulled out her business card from the library. 'Here.'

Dougie took the card, gave it a cursory look and stuffed it into his pocket. 'Come this way, Ellen's inside.'

Wiping her feet on the mat, she waited as Dougie went to summon his wife. The smell of apples and cinnamon wafted through from the kitchen. A woman appeared, wiping her hands on her apron. 'Hello there, I'm Ellen. What can I do for you?'

Sarah stared at her. Maybe she wasn't quite as old as her husband, but she had weathered much better. Her skin was smooth, with only a few lines around her eyes, and her silver hair had been cropped into a fashionable pixie style, which only those with great bone structure could get away with. She must have been quite a beauty in her youth.

'Hi, I'm Sarah. Your brother gave me this address.'

'Our Bobby?'

'Yes, I went to Oak Grove first and he told me you'd lived here for the past thirty-odd years.'

Dougie intervened. 'Why don't you two go through into the lounge and I'll put the kettle on.' He placed his hands on his wife's shoulders and steered her through a doorway. He turned to Sarah. 'Sugar?'

She shook her head. 'Just milk, please.'

In the lounge, Ellen sat down and clasped her hands

on her knee. 'Now, why don't you tell me what all this is about?'

'All right then, I'm writing a book about the history of Ambergate.'

She waited for a response, but Ellen's expression remained impassive and she merely nodded.

'I've been down there numerous times,' continued Sarah. 'Exploring the old place, getting a feel for how it must have been. I'm sure it'll be converted or demolished one day soon, so I think it's important to let the next generation know about these places and how things used to be for people who were mentally ill.' She paused and, feeling the need to give credence to her endeavours, added, 'It's part of my family history too.'

Ellen frowned. 'But how did you know I worked there?'

'Oh, right. You worked there, did you? I didn't know that, all I knew was . . . Hang on a minute.' She rummaged in her handbag and pulled out the note. 'I'm not doing a very good job of explaining myself, am I?'

Ellen looked towards the open door. 'No, I must say I'm a little confused.' She called to her husband. 'Dougie, where are you with that tea?'

He returned with a tray holding three mugs and a plate of digestives. 'I've taken the pie out, love. The timer was about to go off, so I think it's done.'

'Thanks, love.' She cupped her hands around her mug and took a sip. She nodded at Dougie. 'We both worked at Ambergate. It's where we met.'

Dougie sat next to her on the sofa and put his arm around her shoulders. 'We've been married for forty-six years.' He had a slight accent that Sarah couldn't place, but he definitely wasn't from round here, she decided. They were gazing at each other like a pair of lovesick teenagers.

'Anyway, I'll come to the point,' she said. 'Whilst exploring, I came across an attic full of suitcases, about twenty of them.'

Ellen stiffened. 'How . . . interesting.'

'Yes, it's fascinating, like opening a window to the past. In one of them I found this note, and it had your name and address on it. As I mentioned before, I went to Oak Grove but Bobby said you'd moved on.' She passed the note over to Ellen.

The colour seeped from Ellen's face as she gazed at the piece of paper. Her fingers fiddled with the string of pearls at her throat. 'Dear God, I don't believe it.' She passed the note over to Dougie.

'She never got it,' he whispered. 'She can't have got out.'

'What do you mean?' Sarah asked.

Ellen didn't seem to hear her. She was still staring at Dougie. 'If Amy's suitcase is still in that attic, then she must have died in there.'

Sarah settled her mug on a coaster on the coffee table beside her chair. 'Amy? Are you saying you know who this case belongs to, Mrs Lyons?'

Ellen nodded. 'Yes. Yes I do.'

'Are you able to tell me any more about it?'

Ellen glanced at her husband and Dougie nodded slowly. She rose from the settee and moved over to the window, wringing her hands as she gazed out over the lawn. 'Her name was Amy Sullivan,' she began eventually. 'She was admitted to Ambergate about the same time I started working there, November 1956 it was.' She turned to Dougie. 'You remember her arriving, don't you?'

He laughed. 'Sure I do, she was a quite a handful, no mistake about that.'

Ellen smiled at the memory. 'She could be difficult, that's true. I felt sorry for her, though. We were the same age, in the same place, and yet our circumstances could hardly have been more different.'

'Why was she in Ambergate?' asked Sarah.

'Her father brought her in. She'd tried to kill herself, along with her stepmother's baby.'

'Oh God. How awful.'

'She wasn't evil, though, just deeply troubled, and she brought all kinds of misfortune upon herself.'

'She was pregnant then, was she? When she was admitted to Ambergate?'

Ellen and Dougie exchanged another look. 'No,' said Ellen. 'She fell pregnant whilst she was in there.'

'Oh, right. I didn't know that kind of thing was allowed.'

'It wasn't allowed but that didn't mean it didn't happen,'

Dougie explained. 'We nurses were used to turning a blind eye, shall we say.'

'Let me look at that again, Dougie.' Ellen took the note and read it once more. 'It's nigh on fifty years since I wrote this.' She shook her head. 'I used to think about her a lot, wondered what had happened to her, why she never came to my door. That poor girl.' She turned to her husband. 'I did do the right thing, though, didn't I?'

'Ellen, you did more than anyone else would have done.'

She stared out of the window again. 'Perhaps you're right. I mean, what choice did I have?'

'What does the note mean, though?' asked Sarah. 'What's all this about a baby?'

Ellen hesitated. 'Please . . . you mustn't write about this. I know many years have passed, but I don't think . . .'

Sarah held up her hand. 'There's no need to worry, Mrs Lyons. I can see it's a sensitive subject, and I'm not a journalist looking for a scoop. You have my word that I won't write anything you're not comfortable with.' She laid her palm across her chest. 'I promise.'

Ellen gave a small shake of her head, the anguish evident in her eyes. 'I made a promise once.' She waved the note in the air. 'To this girl, Amy. I promised her that one day she would leave Ambergate and a whole new life would be waiting for her. I wasn't in a position then to tell her everything, but I wrote this to ensure that one day she would know the truth.' She held the note up to her nose and inhaled the musty smell. 'I tried my best to keep that promise,' she said eventually. 'But my best wasn't enough, it seems.'

'Do you want to tell me about it?' asked Sarah gently, desperate to hear the story but feeling the need to tread carefully.

Ellen pushed up her sleeve and looked at her watch. 'Yes, yes, I think I do.' She turned to her husband. 'Dougie, go and fetch that pie. This could take a while.'

44

February 1958

Ellen clutched the little bundle to her chest, hardly able to look at the baby's mottled lifeless features. Life was unbearably cruel sometimes and she inwardly raged at a God who had allowed this to happen. Why did He feel the need to keep punishing Amy, not to mention this poor little mite? She quickened her pace, her brisk walk breaking into a jog as, not for the first time, she cursed the long, sterile corridors and endless sets of doors. The baby jiggled up and down in her arms, but she needed to keep going. Up ahead she could see a male patient trudging along the corridor, head bowed as he muttered to himself. Not wishing to alarm him, she slowed down a little and took longer strides as her heart rate subsided. She scuttled past the patient, who didn't even look up, and continued her march down the deserted corridor looming ahead, the silence broken only by the sound of her footsteps pounding the tiled floor.

At first she thought she was mistaken, her ears playing tricks on her. Then she heard it again: a tiny cough, more of a splutter really. She stopped walking and peered down at the baby's face. His lips were now pink and shiny with saliva, his cheeks sporting a rosy glow. 'Oh my word,' Ellen gasped. 'Look at you, you beautiful little fighter.' She raised her gaze to the ceiling. 'Thank you, God, thank you.'

The baby opened his eyes, little slits that could barely focus. A frown creased his forehead as he let out a loud wail, his tongue vibrating. Ellen laughed and placed the knuckle of her little finger in his tiny mouth. He immediately calmed down and sucked hard. 'You're hungry, aren't you?' She turned around and began to retrace her steps. 'Come on then. Let's get you back to your mummy, shall we?'

The baby continued to suck on her finger as she hurried back to the ward. His black hair was pasted down with the sticky white vernix and he moved his head from side to side as he tried to wrestle free from the confines of the sheet he was wrapped in. Ellen tugged at the fabric to give him some room. 'Well you're a plucky one, aren't you? Just like your mummy.' He sprang an arm free and she clutched hold of his tiny starfish hand.

She was giddy with excitement by the time she arrived back at the side room where Amy had given birth. She had not stopped smiling and her cheeks ached. The curtains around the bed had been pulled closed and the smell of disinfectant hung in the air. A mop and bucket had been left nearby, and Ellen looked down at the pink-tinged water. She frowned as she pulled back the curtain. Her instinct was to scream, but she managed to limit herself to a startled gasp for fear of frightening the baby as she gazed at the empty bed and the dark red stain that covered the mattress.

She fled the room and ran to the end of the ward, past half a dozen empty beds. The ward sister's office was empty too; sheets of paper littered the floor and a teacup lay on its side in a saucer, surrounded by dregs. 'What's happened here? Where is everybody?' she whispered to the infant, who now appeared to be sleeping. She touched his neck to check for a pulse. 'Oh thank God,' she breathed.

At the sound of footsteps, she turned to see Sister Brown entering Amy's room. She followed her in and closed the door. 'Where's Amy?' she asked.

'I had to call an ambulance. She started haemorrhaging and there was nothing I could do. She's been taken to the general hospital. We're not equipped to deal with emergencies like that here.' She stopped and pointed at the bundle in Ellen's arms. 'Is . . . is that . . .? Why on earth didn't you take him straight to the morgue? I expressly told you to—'

'Shh,' said Ellen peeling back the sheet and exposing the baby's prune-like face. 'I didn't take him to the morgue because he's alive.'

The midwife stepped forward and touched the infant's cheek. 'Well I'll be damned.'

311

'I know, it's incredible. I ran with him in my arms, and perhaps the motion, I don't know, perhaps it dislodged something, kick-started his breathing.' Ellen leaned down and gave him a kiss on his forehead. 'It's a miracle.'

Sister Brown took hold of the baby's hand, a small smile on her lips. Then her expression darkened and she withdrew her hand as though she had been burned. She tapped her temple. 'He'll not be right, you know.'

'What do you mean?'

Sister Brown shook her head. 'He went without oxygen for far too long. He'll be brain-damaged.'

'Nonsense.' Ellen pulled the baby protectively towards her. 'He's as bright as a button.'

'Just three minutes without oxygen and the brain starts to die. I honestly can't see how—'

Ellen couldn't bear to hear any more. 'I need to reunite him with his mother.'

'Impossible,' said Sister Brown dismissively. 'She's in no fit state.'

'Well what do we do with him? He needs a feed.'

The midwife mulled it over. 'I'll sort out some Carnation milk for it . . .'

'Him,' Ellen corrected.

Sister Brown glared at her. 'I'll fetch some Carnation milk for *him* and then I'll make the arrangements with the authorities.'

'Excuse me?' Ellen pulled the baby closer. 'What authorities?'

'The adoption authorities, obviously. Not only is Amy Sullivan an unmarried mother, she's also a certified mental patient incapable of looking after a child or of making decisions for herself.' She shook her head and added emphatically, 'There's no question about it. This baby will have to be adopted.'

'But—'

'There are no buts, Nurse.' She reached out her arms. 'Give him to me.'

Ellen took a step backwards. 'No, I won't.'

Sister Brown sighed irritably. 'As far as Amy Sullivan is concerned, this baby died. There's no reason to tell her any different. Do you want her to live with the knowledge that her baby is being brought up by somebody else? Hmm?'

Ellen remained silent.

'Think about it. That would tear her apart. Set her right back. There'd be no hope of her ever getting better. Can you imagine telling her that her baby didn't die but we're taking him away anyway? She'd be crushed. Trust me, it's better this way.'

Ellen bit down on her bottom lip. 'But he needs his mum.'

'I agree. He needs a mother who can look after him, nurture him, give him everything he'll ever want.' She paused. 'But that person is not, and never will be, Amy Sullivan.'

'But won't she need to sign something?'

'No, she can't sign anything. She's not of sound mind. As you well know, she's certified. Dr Harrison will have to see to any formalities.'

Ellen gazed down at the little bundle. 'He's going to be forcibly adopted?'

Sister Brown's patience was being stretched. 'Oh for goodness' sake. He won't be the first baby to be taken away from his birth mother in order to give him a better chance in life. There's mother-and-baby homes up and down the country doing exactly that.' She took the baby from Ellen. 'Now, I for one want what's best for this little man, and I would have thought you would want the same.' She raised her eyebrows. 'Well?'

Ellen nodded silently. 'But if Amy believes her son is dead, she might want to visit his grave. How are you going to explain that?' She folded her arms defiantly, a triumphant edge to her voice.

Sister Brown fixed her with a withering stare. 'We don't bury stillborn babies in their own graves. He would've been placed in a coffin with another deceased patient.'

Ellen shuddered. 'How horrible.'

'Better than him being alone in the ground, though.'

'I suppose so. What happens now, then?'

'He'll be transferred to the local maternity hospital and adopted from there when a suitable family is found.'

'What about his birth certificate?'

Sister Brown shook her head. 'Do you ever stop asking questions?'

'Amy is still his mother. Her name will have to be on there.'

'And it will be, along with a blank space where the father's name should be. Place of birth will be recorded as Ambergate Mental Hospital. We've nothing to hide.'

'Except the fact that his mother believes he's dead.'

'Look,' placated Sister Brown, 'one day Amy might be well enough to know the truth, and if that day ever comes, she'll be the first to realise we did the right thing. We have her best interests – and more importantly, the baby's best interests – at heart. We don't know what the future holds for Amy. We can only deal with the situation as it's presented to us today.' She gazed down at the baby's face. 'Besides, we don't know how damaged he is. He may need specialist care for the rest of his life. Do you think Amy could cope with that?'

'I suppose not.'

'In any case, there's no guarantee she'll survive the haemorrhage. She may be dead already, for all we know.'

Later, Ellen lay on her bed staring at the ceiling, mulling over the whole sorry situation. Was Amy really better off thinking her son was dead? She didn't think so. She made up her mind. If the girl was still alive, she would tell her the truth and to hell with the consequences.

315

45

The journey to the Infirmary was only a short one, but it was filled with diesel fumes, hissing brakes and a bus with questionable suspension. Feeling slightly nauseous, Ellen stepped off the bus clutching the bunch of flowers she had bought and made her way to the main entrance. Sister Atkins had received word that Amy had indeed survived the trauma of the birth, but two weeks later she was still not well enough to return to Ambergate.

As soon as Ellen stepped through the door, she noticed the difference. The corridors were airy and bright, there were paintings on the walls and the nurses walked tall, smiles on their faces, as they chatted amiably to each other. Noticing Ellen dithering, one of them stopped. 'Can I help you?'

'Oh, yes please. I'm looking for Ward M8.'

The nurse pointed ahead. 'Through those doors, first on your left, then second right.'

Ellen muttered her thanks, wondering not for the first time why she persevered with working in such a depressing place as Ambergate.

Amy was lying in bed, a bed that bore no resemblance

to the army-style one she was used to. This bed was wide and had lots of space around it, a cupboard for personal possessions and a table that could be pulled across to allow the occupant to eat in comfort. Compared to Ambergate, it was The Midland.

'How are you feeling, Amy?' Ellen stared at the young girl's face. She had a pewter-tinged complexion with a cadaverous look around the eyes. Her lips were cracked and her hair was plastered down to her scalp.

Amy blinked, apparently having trouble focusing. 'Who's there?' she croaked.

'It's me, Nurse Crosby. How are you feeling?' Ellen asked again.

Amy attempted a smile. 'How do I look?'

'Honestly? I've seen you looking better.' She placed the flowers on the bedside cabinet. 'I've brought you these. I'll ask one of the nurses for a vase.'

'Thank you.'

She perched on the edge of the bed. 'You had us all worried there for a moment.'

Amy scoffed. 'I doubt that.'

'We're looking forward to having you back at Ambergate.' Ellen plumped up the pillows as Amy struggled into a sitting position.

'Did you see my baby? Was he beautiful?'

Ellen hesitated. 'Amy, there's something I need—'

'He must have been beautiful. Dr Lambourn's a very handsome man.' Amy dropped her voice to a whisper.

'He was really mad at me, though. When he found out that I couldn't keep his baby alive, he wasn't happy at all. But then he calmed down, said he forgave me and that there was no reason why we can't try again.'

'Wait . . . Are you saying Dr Lambourn's been here?'

'Of course he has. We're getting married.'

'Married?'

'Yes, in the spring. He's already booked the honeymoon. We're going to Paris.' She laughed, then sing-songed, 'Paris in the springtime. How about that?'

'Well, that's lovely,' Ellen said, rising from the bed. 'Can you just excuse me for a minute?'

She hurried over to the nurses' station and approached the sister in charge. 'I was wondering if you could help me?'

'I'll try.'

'Amy Sullivan. Has she had any visitors?'

'Indeed she has. Every evening a gentleman comes in and sits on her bed, reads to her, brings her fruit, although sometimes she's not even aware he's been.'

'Do you know his name?'

The nurse shook her head. 'No, I'm afraid not. She just refers to him as her fiancé. Is there a problem?'

'Every evening, you say?'

'That's right.'

Ellen glanced at the clock on the wall. 'What time's evening visiting?'

'Seven until eight.'

'Thank you.'

Ellen made her way back to Amy's bed. 'Amy, I'm sorry, I've got to go now, but I promise I'll come back later, all right?'

Amy dismissed her with a wave of her hand. 'You don't need to. It really doesn't matter.'

As she waited at the bus stop, Ellen tried to fathom this new turn of events. Dr Lambourn's fiancée had left him when she discovered he was unable to have children, so why did the doctor now think he was the father of Amy's baby? There was only one way to find out. She would intercept him at visiting this evening and ask him directly. If by some miracle he *was* the father, then he would surely want to take care of his own baby and all this adoption nonsense would stop.

46

Ellen walked along the corridor clutching a brown paper bag filled with grapes and cursing the local bus service, which seemed to run on a timetable that bore little resemblance to the one displayed at the bus stop. It was fifteen minutes past the start of evening visiting as she rounded the corner and entered Amy's ward. She hesitated in the doorway when she saw him sitting on Amy's bed, stroking her hand. There was no response from Amy though; her head lolled back on the pillow and her mouth gaped open.

Ellen crept up behind him, her footsteps faltering as she edged closer. 'Hello again.'

He turned to face her. 'Oh, hello . . . Dougie's girlfriend, isn't it?'

Ellen waggled the fingers on her left hand. 'Fiancée actually.'

'Oh, congratulations.' He nodded at Amy. 'She's out of it again tonight. She had another one of her episodes.' He grimaced. 'She became hysterical and they've had to sedate her.'

Ellen settled herself in a chair, the bag of grapes

resting on her knee. 'That's a shame. She'll be sorry to have missed you. Have you been coming every night, then?'

'Yes, every night since I found out. I tried to visit her in Ambergate several times, but I never managed it. Sister Atkins can be very obstructive.'

Ellen passed the grapes over to him. 'Here, hold these for a minute, will you?'

She approached the nurses' station again and pointed to Amy's bed. 'That chap over there visiting Amy Sullivan. Is he the one who's been coming every night?'

The nurse craned to have a look. 'Yes, that's him.'

'And she's had no other visitors?'

'Nope, not to my knowledge anyway.'

Ellen returned to Amy's bed and sat down again. 'Tell me then, Ed, how've you been since you left Ambergate?'

'Fine, it's been seven months now and I get stronger every day. I'm back at work and I haven't had a fit for six months.'

'I'm pleased for you, I really am.'

Ellen nodded to the paper bag. 'Grape?'

'No thanks.'

She took a sideways look at him. He continued to gaze at Amy, her hand still resting in his. 'You planned her escape, didn't you?'

'Yes.' He switched his focus to Ellen, looking her squarely in the face. 'And I'm not ashamed of it either.

She doesn't deserve to be in that place. I can take care of her.' He turned his attention back to Amy. 'I love her.'

'You know about the baby, though?'

He nodded. 'Tragic, isn't it?'

'Did you know she was pregnant when you planned her escape?'

'No, I didn't.'

'Ed . . .'

'Yes?'

'Is there any chance the baby was yours?'

He shook his head. 'But it doesn't matter to me. I still love her.'

Ellen watched as he took out his handkerchief and gently wiped away the drool sliding out of the corner of Amy's mouth. He smoothed her sticky hair and kissed her on the forehead. 'I can take care of her, I know I can.'

'You're a good lad, Ed. She's lucky to have you.'

He sighed. 'Try telling her that. She's got it into her head that Dr Lambourn was the father of the baby and now they're engaged.'

'She's told you that, then?'

'Aye, it's not true, though. I'm the only one who cares about her. I'm the only one who's been to see her.' He squeezed Amy's hand. 'Her future's with me, but she just can't see it yet.'

'She's not well, Ed.' Ellen tapped her own head. 'Up

here, I mean. Perhaps you ought to think about letting her go and move on with your life.'

He stared at her aghast. 'I can't do that. She *is* my life. She's been let down by everybody else and I'm not about to desert her when she needs me most.'

47

September 2006

By the time Sarah had finished listening to Ellen's story, the pie had been demolished and the light was beginning to fade. She leaned back in the chair and gripped the arms. It was no wonder her father was unwilling to talk about his time at Ambergate. A can of worms, he'd said. That was the understatement of the century.

She swallowed hard. 'So you didn't tell Amy about the baby?'

'I couldn't. Sister Brown was right. She was in no fit state mentally and I knew I'd get no support from Sister Atkins. I was just a student nurse with a reputation for having ideas above her station, but I still felt morally obliged to tell Amy the truth.'

'That must have been so difficult for you,' said Sarah. 'Seeing her every day, knowing about such an explosive secret and yet not being able to say anything. How did you cope with it?'

A flicker of annoyance crossed Ellen's face as she sat up stiffly and raised her chin, her voice quiet but determined.

'Please don't judge me, Sarah. You have to look at the whole picture in context. Things were different back then.'

'Oh no, you mustn't think I'm judging you,' said Sarah, mortified that she might have caused offence. 'I was just acknowledging what a burden this must have been for you.'

Dougie squeezed his wife's hand. 'It was too much for her, Sarah.'

Ellen dropped her gaze, her hands absently brushing her skirt. 'I decided to leave nursing shortly after. I really wanted to make a difference but I was fighting against a system that just wasn't ready to change.' She looked up at Sarah and gave a small laugh. 'I was ahead of my time. A few years later, Enoch Powell came to the same conclusion.'

Sarah nodded. 'Yes, I've read about his water-tower speech and how he was instrumental in the closing-down of the old asylums.'

'I remember when he came to Ambergate,' Dougie interjected. 'There was great excitement that the Health Minister was coming to visit and the days before were spent polishing floors, cleaning windows, sprucing up the patients and generally doing everything possible to convince him that Ambergate was an institution devoted to the care and rehabilitation of its inmates. The whole ward smelled of fresh paint and floor polish. Honestly, I don't think we'd have gone to as much trouble for the Queen herself.'

'Dougie,' interrupted Ellen. 'Sarah doesn't need to hear about all that now. Let me finish telling her what happened.'

She turned back to Sarah. 'I left Ambergate a few weeks after the baby was born. Amy was still being cared for in the hospital, but I knew that when she returned to my ward it would be impossible to face her every day knowing I was hiding the truth. Then I had the idea about putting the note in her suitcase. Patients were given back their belongings upon their release, you see. I reasoned that if Amy found the note in her case, that would mean that she'd been discharged and was therefore well again. Well enough to learn the truth about her son.' She turned to Dougie for confirmation. 'It seemed like the best thing to do at the time.'

'It was, love,' he said.

'This was all nearly fifty years ago, Sarah, a lifetime.'

Sarah looked at the note again. 'She never got this, though.'

Ellen shrugged. 'As I said before, I can only surmise that she never left Ambergate and must have died there. A few years after Dougie qualified as a registered mental nurse, he successfully applied for a job as a charge nurse at another hospital and our ties with Ambergate were severed.'

Sarah leaned forward, resting her elbows on her knees. 'Can I ask you something?'

'Fire away.'

'Who do *you* think was the father of Amy's baby?'

'I honestly wouldn't like to hazard a guess. I'm inclined to believe Ed when he said it wasn't him. He had no reason to lie about it. But Dr Lambourn was infertile, so it couldn't have been him either.'

Sarah rose from her chair, the sudden movement making her fuzzy-headed. She grabbed at the door frame. 'Dr Lambourn was not infertile.'

Ellen frowned. 'I'm sorry. How would you know?'

Sarah blew out a calming breath, her voice barely more than a whisper. 'Because he's my father.'

48

Dusk was falling as Sarah drove home. The street lamps were starting to flicker and people were closing their curtains as they settled in for the evening. She was driving too fast, she knew that, and yet somehow it didn't seem fast enough. In a cacophony of screeching brakes and burning rubber, she pulled up outside her father's house and sprinted up the driveway. All fingers and thumbs, she struggled to fit the key in the lock, cursing as she dropped the bunch on the doormat. When she finally entered the hallway, she called out, 'Dad, I'm home.'

There was no response. 'Dad, where are you?'

She ran from room to room calling out his name, although in a house this size he couldn't have failed to hear her. She paused at the bottom of the stairs, bracing herself for what she might find before thundering up to the top. Breathless with panic, she stopped outside his bedroom door. Was it ridiculous to knock, or should she just barge in? She forced herself to calm down and rapped gently on the door. 'Dad, are you in there?'

She squeezed her eyes shut, mentally preparing herself for the sight of his lifeless body, but the room was empty, his bed pristine and his slippers tucked neatly under the dressing table. She ran downstairs, out into the garden, and peered through the garage window, frowning when she saw that his car was gone. He rarely ventured out in the car these days, preferring instead to walk or catch the local bus into town. There had been a minor incident in which he had backed over a bollard, and another one where he had swerved to avoid a cat, mounted the pavement and taken out an old lady's shopping trolley instead. Sarah's ex-husband, Dan, had been insistent that his father-in-law should not be driving any more, but Sarah had not had the heart to take away his independence completely.

She returned to the kitchen and flicked the switch on the kettle. The clock told her it was coming up to seven, and it was apparent that her father had not had his tea. He'd peeled a pan of potatoes, which still sat on the hob ready to be boiled and mashed. This was a slight cause for concern, as he ate at six on the dot every single night. Her mother had started this routine and Sarah had often marvelled at how she had managed to dish up the meal with military precision, not a minute before six, not a minute past. Where on earth had he gone? She pushed away images of blue flashing lights, her father pressed over the bonnet with his arms behind his back as a policeman cuffed his wrists.

She ignored the boiling kettle and reached into the fridge instead. She sloshed some wine into a glass and took a couple of calming sips as she sat down at the kitchen table and mulled over Ellen's revelations. At the unwelcome interruption from the doorbell, she reluctantly heaved herself up. She was in no mood for double-glazing salesmen, Jehovah's Witnesses or anybody with a holdall selling overpriced dusters and chamois leathers. She put the chain on the door and opened it a crack, ready to deliver a stinging rebuke to whoever it was who'd seen fit to intrude on her evening. The words died on her tongue.

'Oh . . . it's you.'

Dan held his arms wide and attempted a smile. 'Surprise.'

Sarah glared at her ex-husband. 'What do you want?'

'It's customary to invite people in.'

She glanced over her shoulder. 'It's not a good time, Dan.'

'Oh, have you got company?'

'No, it's not that. It's too hard seeing you, after everything that's happened.'

He looked down at his shoes, avoiding eye contact. 'I can't keep apologising, Sarah. I know I've—'

'My father's missing,' she blurted out, fully aware that this was stretching the truth.

He looked up. 'What? No, surely not. Let me in, then.'

In the hallway, he enveloped her in a bear hug, the familiar contours of his body making her want to weep once more for everything they had shared and everything they had lost. He took hold of her hands. 'How long?'

'What?'

He spoke more urgently. 'How long has he been missing?'

'Oh, er . . . I'm not sure. He's not *exactly* missing. I just don't know where he is. When I came back, his car was gone.'

He propelled her into the kitchen, reached into a cupboard for a glass and poured himself some wine. 'Trust you to be so dramatic, although him driving around is a concern for other road users.'

'That's the least of my worries,' she said.

She had not seen Dan for several months. His face was leaner, his hair longer and his clothes more suited to a twenty-year-old than a man approaching forty. 'What's with the tight white jeans?'

He looked down as though seeing them for the first time. 'Lauren's idea. She thought I needed bringing up to date.' At the mention of his girlfriend's name, Sarah downed the rest of her wine. 'Perhaps she should have found someone her own age, then.'

'All right,' said Dan. 'I deserve that.'

'Why did you come here, Dan?'

He sat down at the table and ran his finger round the rim of his glass She tried to ignore the irritating whine. In spite of Lauren's efforts to reinvent him, he actually looked older. She leaned over to peer at him more closely. 'Have you . . . have you dyed your hair?' In spite of everything, she had to suppress a giggle.

He looked up almost apologetically. 'I've made a mistake.'

She laughed then. 'I should think so. That colour is way too magenta for your complexion.'

'I'm not talking about the bloody hair dye. I should never have left you. I've been a complete idiot.'

She took a step back, leaving his words hanging in the air, the silence only broken by the quiet hum of the fridge. 'Well you'll not find me arguing with you on that score.'

'Please, Sarah. I don't know what to do. I don't love Lauren. I never have.' Unable to look at her, he stared down at the table and held his head in his hands. Sarah stood behind him, staring at his hunched back, resisting the urge to place her arm across his shoulders and tell him that everything would be all right. Because it wouldn't be all right. It was too late. 'She's having your baby, Dan.'

He leaned back in the chair, his face blotchy, tired rings around his eyes. 'It's a bloody mess, Sarah. I've screwed up big-time.'

How was she supposed to react to this news? Punch the air? Do a little victory dance around the table? But there were no winners here. They'd both lost.

He turned round in his chair and stared up at her, a hangdog expression on his face. 'What am I going to do?'

'You've made your bed, Dan.' If he was expecting sympathy from her, he was going to be disappointed. 'You made your position quite clear when we divorced.' She turned away and moved over to the fridge, thrusting a glass under the water dispenser. She silently congratulated herself on her firm stance when it would have been all too easy to collapse into his arms and grant him the forgiveness he obviously craved. She wouldn't do it, though. Her heart might have been broken, but her dignity was intact. 'Now if you don't mind, I've more pressing matters to attend to.'

'Your father?'

'Yes, and he won't be best pleased to see you sitting at his kitchen table quaffing his wine.'

Dan grimaced. 'He still hates me, then?'

'Can you blame him?'

'It wasn't all my fault. You'd become so focused on having a baby that there was no room for—'

Sarah slammed her glass down on the table. 'Don't you dare start this again.' She stopped, forcing herself to rise above it. 'There's no point, Dan. We're finished.'

'But . . .'

He faltered as they both heard the key in the front door.

'Thank God,' said Sarah. 'He's home.' She went to greet her father in the hallway, calling over her shoulder, 'Let yourself out of the back door if you want.'

Dan stood up. 'I'm not a coward,' he replied.

Sarah returned to the kitchen with her father trailing in her wake. Dan held out his hand. 'Stephen, good to see you again.'

Dr Lambourn ignored him and turned to Sarah. 'What the hell is he doing here?'

'He's just leaving, Dad, no need to get all worked up.'

She peeled the heavy coat from her father's shoulders and mouthed to Dan, 'Just go.'

'So, are you going to tell me where you got to?' Sarah asked later, as they cleared away the pots and stacked the dishwasher together.

'I went to Ambergate.'

She straightened up, a fistful of dirty cutlery in her hand. 'To Ambergate?'

'That's right.'

'Right . . . What for?'

He picked up the towel and dried his hands. 'I brought back the case.' He swallowed. 'Amy's case. I was almost convinced it was hers when you told me about the painting. I had to see for myself.'

'But how did you know where to find it?'

'Sarah love, I know every inch of that place. I spent four years of my life there, don't forget. It took me a little while to get my bearings, I'll admit. Things have changed a lot since I was last there.'

'What're you going to do now? With the case, I mean.'

'Amy was my patient, and if she gave birth in that place, then she deserves to know the truth. I'm not proud of myself. I let her down very badly.'

'Dad,' Sarah began carefully. 'I went to see Ellen Crosby today.'

He seemed resigned and bowed his head. 'I knew you would, but I'd like to tell you my side of the story first.'

She touched his arm. 'I'd like to hear it.'

He indicated the door to the living room. 'Shall we?'

He nestled into his chair and crossed his legs, his movements slow and deliberate. He suddenly looked every one of his seventy-nine years as he removed his glasses and polished them on his handkerchief, his arthritic hands making the task more cumbersome than it should have been. When he spoke, he did so quietly but with conviction, determined that his story should be told.

'When I first met Amy Sullivan, she was nineteen years old. Just a kid really, but she had a certain spark, she was incredibly pretty and I'll admit she enchanted me both on a personal and professional level. She was quite unlike any patient I had ever treated before. I grew fond of her, developed feelings that I shouldn't have, if you know what I mean. She had nobody. She was quite alone, without anyone fighting for her, nobody caring whether she got better or not. I felt a responsibility to her, not only as her doctor, but as a human being. But I shouldn't . . .' He paused, twisting his wedding ring round his finger as he struggled to find the right words. 'I shouldn't have taken advantage of her.'

'Oh dear God, you don't mean you forced . . .'

'No,' he said emphatically. 'Nothing like that, but I was ten years older than her; I was her doctor, for God's sake. I should have known better.'

'What happened?' asked Sarah, inwardly cringing but desperate to know the truth.

He seemed just as uncomfortable as he squirmed in his chair. 'I took her out for a walk along the riverbank, just for some fresh air and a change of scenery. It was late in the afternoon, so people were leaving. It was idyllic really, so peaceful, and a world away from Ambergate. It was just what she needed. I laid the rug down on a sandy patch at the river's edge beneath a willow tree. Amy went for a paddle, but she had a queer turn and fell in the water. I picked her up, settled her on the rug and wrapped my coat around her.' He smiled at the memory, raised his eyes and looked at his daughter. 'It was what she wanted, Sarah. I promise you that I didn't force myself on her.'

'But, Dad, she was a vulnerable mental patient. What on earth were you thinking?'

He shook his head. 'I know, I know. I shouldn't have let it happen.'

'Did you know she was pregnant?'

'No, of course I didn't. But it wouldn't have made any difference. I would not have assumed the baby was mine. I thought I was infertile. I wouldn't have been quite so cavalier had I thought there was any danger of her getting pregnant. I mean, my fiancée had left me because I couldn't father a child.'

'Dad,' Sarah began gently, 'Ellen Crosby told me that Amy always insisted the baby was yours, but nobody believed her; they thought she was deluded.'

He wiped his eyes with the handkerchief. 'That poor kid.'

'And the real tragedy is she was told the baby had died when in fact he survived and was put up for adoption. Somewhere out there, you may have a son.' She paused before adding, 'And I may have a brother.'

'It was a boy?'

Sarah nodded.

He covered his face with his hands. 'Oh God, what've I done?'

Fifty years ago, he'd made a terrible mistake, and it was far too late to rectify it. His pain was difficult to witness.

'Dad, why did you leave Ambergate?'

He inhaled sharply and balled his fists. 'Because I was selfish. I wanted to save my career. If it'd come out that I'd had a relationship with a mental patient, I'd have been certified myself.' He sighed and rubbed his hands over his face. 'So I found a job elsewhere and forced myself to forget all about Amy. I'm not proud of my actions.'

'That's all in the past now, Dad. It's the future you need to think about.'

'You're right,' he said. 'And wherever Amy is, she deserves to know the truth.'

'Ellen Crosby thinks she must be dead,' Sarah said bluntly. 'Why else would her case still be in an attic in Ambergate?'

'It's a possibility,' he acknowledged. 'Perhaps that's where we should start, then.' He heaved himself out of his chair. 'But I promise you, Sarah, if she is still alive, I will find her and make things right.'

49

December 2006

She turned her collar up against the lacerating wind, tasted the salt on her chapped lips. Beneath her feet, the mud had frozen into hard ridges and the shallow puddles of rain had turned to glass. She stamped on one, shattering the ice into tiny fragments, an act of destruction she found therapeutic. She used her stick to propel herself along the coast path. Only the sound of the waves breaking onto the rocks far below was enough to penetrate the howling wind in her ears. She tucked her stick under her arm and blew into her gloved hands before continuing her battle with the elements.

She called out to the dog, bounding on ahead, oblivious to the gale that ruffled her fur and made her ears stand comically upright. 'Jess, wait for me. My old bones aren't built for speed,' but the wind stole her voice and carried it into the foaming sea below.

Back at the cottage, she stamped on the doormat as Jess lapped thirstily at her drinking bowl. She removed her overcoat and hung it on the hook in the porch, tossing

338

her thick mittens into the basket. The woollen fingerless gloves she wore underneath she would have to keep on. It wasn't much warmer inside. She ran her hand down her thick silver plait and brought it round over one shoulder, absently inspecting it for split ends. Someone had once hacked it all off with a blunt pair of scissors, but now, even at her age, her hair was her crowning glory.

'Come on then, Jess. Let's have our brew, shall we?'

As she waited for the kettle to boil, she carved a thick slice of white bread, slathered it with butter and broke off a hunk of Cheddar, tossing a small piece to Jess, who caught it in her mouth like a performing sea lion.

She carried her breakfast through to the front room and settled herself into the armchair, her slippered feet resting in the hearth. Jess placed her head in her mistress's lap and watched her taking bite after bite of tasty bread and cheese.

'Here you are then,' she laughed, giving the last morsel to the ever-hungry dog. Jess gulped down the cheese, then, satisfied that there was no point in begging any more, walked around in circles on the rug before nestling down in front of the fire.

It was Jess who alerted her first. That dog was never truly fast asleep. She raised her head from her paws and cocked it to one side, her ears pricked and her eyes wide and bright.

'It's just the wind, Jess.' Jess sprang to her feet and trotted to the front door, whining and pawing at the wood. 'Stop that, Jess, you'll mark it. How many times have I told you?'

Then she heard it herself. The unmistakable crunch of tyres on gravel. She pulled back the net curtain a little and peered out at the unfamiliar car in the lane. There were two people sitting in the front seats, and they exchanged a few words before the passenger opened his door and with some effort heaved himself out of the car. She squinted at his face, older now of course, but instantly recognisable. With hollow breaths she watched as he fiddled with the catch on the garden gate, heard the squeaking of its hinges as he finally pushed it open. He walked up the path holding onto his hat, which the wind was threatening to carry off. Jess was now frantic, barking at the door and wagging her tail, so there was really no need for him to ring the bell. He did anyway.

She took hold of Jess's collar and opened the door. He removed his hat then and held it to his chest.

A second or two passed before he spoke. 'Hello, Amy.' He attempted a smile, but it withered on his lips. 'How are you?'

She let go of Jess's collar and the dog immediately leaped up at the visitor, her paws reaching up to his chest. He staggered backwards as he patted the animal's head.

'Don't worry, she doesn't bite,' Amy said evenly. She raised her voice. 'Jess, get down.'

'A Border collie, I see. You've always been fond of them.'

340

Amy swallowed hard. There was so much she wanted to say; she'd rehearsed it many times over the years but had long since given up any hope that the opportunity would arise. The passage of time had been kind to him. He stood straight and tall, no sign that his body had begun to crumble, and although his hair was now as silver as her own, there was plenty of it, and his olive complexion still afforded him a slightly sun-kissed look. She closed her eyes. The memory of the last time she had seen him played like a jerky cine film in her head. That afternoon by the river, when she had fallen in, and afterwards when they had . . .

She felt his hand on her arm. 'Amy, I know this must be a shock, but I really need to talk to you. May I come in?'

Fighting every instinct to spit on the floor in front of him and slam the door, she lifted her chin instead and stared into his eyes. 'You're too late, Dr Lambourn,' she said crisply. 'About fifty years too late.'

'Amy, please, I've travelled a long way, and—'

'Have you any idea what you did to me? You think you can just turn up here and I'm going to fall into your arms and forgive you for deserting me?'

'I'm not here for your forgiveness. It's something much more important than that. You've every right to be angry . . .'

'Oh, that's good of you, thank you,' she said, a sarcastic edge to her voice.

341

'Please, Amy,' he implored. 'Let me in.'

She had all the power now. She was in control of her own actions and nobody could force her to do anything she didn't want to. All her life other people had made decisions for her, but not any more.

'Five minutes,' she said, opening the door a little wider.

'Thank you,' he breathed, stooping to avoid the low lintel.

He followed her into the front room and took the chair opposite hers by the fire.

'Just like old times,' he said, settling down.

'Five minutes you've got. I wouldn't waste your time on small talk. How did you find me?'

'It really wasn't that difficult. I know your full name and date of birth. And of course I'd been to your last-known address, you know . . . for your father's funeral.'

She stiffened at the mention of her father and he moved swiftly on.

'But even without public records, I knew you would be here.' He cast his eyes around the spartan room. 'I knew you would be drawn back to this place. The way you spoke about it during our sessions, I knew you would return to the last place you were truly happy.'

'Did you now?' she replied. 'Because you're such a clever psychiatrist?'

He shuffled in his chair. 'Is there any point in me offering an apology?'

'Depends on what it is you would be apologising for.'

'My cowardly behaviour, putting my career before you, deserting you without explanation.'

She turned away, not wishing him to see her face crumple. 'You certainly do have a lot to apologise for, it would seem.'

'If I could turn back the clock . . .'

'Ha,' she guffawed, startling him. 'That old cliché. Well, not even you has that power.' She leaned forward and chucked another lump of wood on the fire. 'Do you remember me asking you what the difference was between God and a psychiatrist?'

He nodded. 'God doesn't think he's a psychiatrist. I've never forgotten that.'

'Really? Well, I was pregnant with *your* baby, Dr Lambourn, and you chose to abandon me.' Her voice rose. 'In Ambergate of all places! You knew damn well that I shouldn't be in there, but you left me to rot in hell. You had the power to release me, but you chose not to.'

As a tear slipped down her cheek, Dr Lambourn fumbled in his pocket and held out the crisp white square of his handkerchief. She stared at it, the years falling away. 'No thank you.'

'I had no idea you were pregnant, Amy. I didn't think I was even capable of fathering a child.'

'And if you had known?'

He shook his head. 'I would have done the right thing.'

'I knew it was your baby. I told them but they wouldn't listen. To them it just confirmed that I was mad. Gave them another excuse to keep me locked away.' She rubbed her face with her hands and looked him directly in the eye, her voice a fierce whisper. 'Our baby died, Dr Lambourn, and there's nothing even *you* can do about that now. Your time for playing God is over.'

He patted his breast pocket, then stood up and walked the two paces to her chair. Kneeling down beside her, he took hold of her hand. 'No he didn't, Amy,' he said gently. 'Our baby did not die.'

50

Sarah drummed her fingers on the steering wheel, then flicked on the wipers. The wind was now driving the rain horizontally, and all the windows in the car had misted up. She ran her palm over the inside of the windscreen, creating an arc she could peer through. 'Come on, Dad,' she urged. 'What's taking you so long?' She glanced behind to the back seat where Amy's suitcase lay, the contents all neatly packed away again.

Not wishing to drain the car battery, she'd turned the radio off, the only sound now coming from the squeaky rubber wipers. She reclined her seat and closed her eyes. It had been a long drive yesterday, and the bed at the guest house had sprouted a rusty spring that had dug into her hip all night.

The metronomic rhythm of the wipers had almost lulled her to sleep when her mobile phone rang. She fumbled in her handbag, read the caller ID and groaned.

'Hi, Dan.'

'Where are you?'

'I'm in Pembrokeshire.'

He hesitated, and she could almost hear the cogs turning. 'Pembrokeshire? What are you doing there?'

'Well, it's a bit of a long story, but . . .' She stopped. 'Actually, it's really none of your business. What do you want, Daniel?'

If he noticed her brittle tone, he didn't comment. 'It's Lauren, she's gone into labour.'

She inhaled a shuddering breath. Her ex-husband was about to become a father, and in spite of everything, he apparently couldn't wait to tell her this news. 'So?'

'It's not due till next month. I'm at the hospital now, the doctor's with her.'

'What do you expect me to do, Dan?' She could hear the echoing of footsteps down the line, and she imagined him pacing the corridor, his hand on his head in despair.

'I don't love her, I don't want this baby. I've told you that already.'

Sarah stared at the cottage. The net curtains prevented her from getting a clear view, but she could well imagine how the conversation was going inside. 'Dan, you cannot walk away from your responsibilities. You don't know how lucky you are. You're going to be a father. Now get back in there and deal with it.' How satisfying it would have been to be able to slam the phone down. The old phone she had grown up with had had a clunky green receiver you could bash down with excessive force, leaving the caller in no doubt about your feelings. She stared at the mobile phone and pressed the red button as fiercely as she could. It wasn't quite the same though.

After five minutes spent inhaling deep, calming breaths, Sarah's pulse rate had returned to normal. The phone rang again and, resisting the urge to chuck it out of the window, she glanced at the screen. There was no name, only a number she did not recognise. Her tone was cautious. 'Hello.'

'Is that Sarah?'

'Erm, yes, who's calling?'

'It's Matt.' He left a pause. 'Erm, you know . . . from the library.'

She swallowed the sudden rush of excitement. 'Oh, hi, it's lovely to hear from you again. How are you?'

'I'm okay. Annie from the library gave me your number. I hope you don't mind.'

She made a mental note to give Annie a huge kiss on the cheek. 'Not at all, what can I do for you?' She groaned inwardly, wishing she hadn't sounded so . . . librarian-like.

He seemed nervous and unsure of himself. 'I was just wondering if you would like to come over sometime. You know . . . to my house . . . for dinner?'

She hesitated. Was he asking her out on a date? 'Well, that would be wonderful, thank you. I'd love to.'

His sigh of relief was audible. 'Oh, fantastic. She'll be so pleased.'

'Who will?'

'Maisie. She's been asking if you can come for ages. She seems to have taken quite a shine to you.'

There was her answer then. It wasn't a date. 'Well, that's nice. I'm fond of her too. I always try to look in at story time and we have a little chat.'

'Is next Saturday okay for you? I'm not what you'd call a gourmet chef but I'm sure I'll be able to rustle up something edible.'

'Next Saturday is pefect.'

'Great. I'll text you my address.'

Her quivering hands held the note as she read it over and over again. Dr Lambourn crouched at her knee, staying silent and watching the impact of those four words. *Your baby didn't die.*

Eventually she turned to him. 'Where did you find this? How do you even know it's for me? There's no name on it.'

He struggled to his feet, his knees cracking as he stood up and settled himself into the chair again. 'It was in your suitcase.'

She frowned. 'What suitcase?'

'The one you took with you to Ambergate. It's in the back of the car. Would you like me to fetch it?'

She held up her hand. 'Wait, slow down.' She squeezed her eyes shut and crumpled the note into a ball. How easy it would be to toss it onto the fire, erasing her painful past forever. The seconds slipped by, counted off by the clock on the mantelpiece, the rhythmic ticking amplified by the silence. She did not want to be reminded of that place.

'Do you know how long I was in there, Dr Lambourn?'

He shook his head. 'No, I——'

'Twenty-seven years.'

She watched as something flickered across his face. Guilt? Shame? Pity, maybe?

'Twenty-seven years of my life were taken from me. My prime years, my *child-bearing* years.' She waited for her words to sink in. 'I was forty-six years old when I left Ambergate. Everything in that suitcase is from another life. A stolen life. I didn't want the case then and I don't want it now.'

'Amy, it contains some precious things, you should——'

She stood up and stamped her foot, clamping her hands over her ears. 'Stop it! Stop talking now. I'm sick to death of people telling me what I should do. I've had a lifetime of it.' She glared at him, her lips white with fury. 'I'm not a certified patient any more, Dr Lambourn. And you . . .' she jabbed a finger into his chest, 'you cannot tell me what to do.' She pulled at his arm, attempting to wrestle him out of his seat, but she was no match for his bulk. 'Get out!' she bellowed. 'I want you to leave now.'

On the verge of hyperventilating, she took short, shallow breaths. 'I need . . . I need some . . . fresh . . . air.' She grabbed her coat from the porch and opened the front door, the wind snatching it from her so that it banged against the wall. A chunk of plaster fell to the floor. 'Jess, come on.' She turned to Dr Lambourn. 'And you had better not be here when I get back.'

The rain had stopped but the wind squalled around her head. The wispy strands of silver hair that had escaped her plait blew across her face. She marched on like someone possessed, taking long strides and using her arms to propel herself forward. Even Jess struggled to keep up. By the time she reached the coast path, she was breathing hard and sweating, her face aglow with anger, her heart weighed down by grief. She stood near the edge of the cliff and stared down at the swirling black sea below, watching as the white horses crashed onto the rocks. She moved closer to the edge and closed her eyes. She held her arms out wide in a crucifixion pose and let the wind buffet her body, swaying gently back and forth. Not for the first time in her life, she craved oblivion. She might not be contained by walls any more, but would she ever truly be free in this life, or would that blessing have to wait until the next?

The wind dropped a little and the howling in her ears abated long enough for Jess's plaintive whine to penetrate her thoughts. She opened her eyes and gazed down into her faithful companion's face.

She caressed the dog's silky ears. 'Oh Jess. What am I going to do?'

She opened up her fist and stared at the note still balled up inside. She unfurled it and read the words again before dropping to her knees, throwing her head back and screaming up at the sky. 'Why? What did I ever do to deserve all this? My baby . . . my poor baby.'

The long-buried sobs came then, from deep within the bowels of her soul, and taking huge gulping breaths, she held out her hand and allowed the wind to carry the note over the clifftop and into the sea.

51

They drove away from the cottage in silence. The line of grass growing in the middle of the narrow unmade lane pointed to the lack of traffic that ventured this far, emphasising the isolation of Amy's existence. Just popping out for a loaf would be an expedition.

Her father stared impassively ahead, his body bouncing up and down as the car's suspension struggled to absorb the undulations of the bumpy track. 'Why did you do it, Sarah?' he asked wearily.

She didn't look at him but instead focused on the road ahead. 'Do what?'

'You knew how I felt about you poking around that asylum, but you wouldn't leave it alone, would you? Put your bloody book before my wishes.' He thumped the dashboard with his fist. 'Damn it, Sarah, why did you have to be so stubborn?'

She gripped the steering wheel so tightly her knuckles turned white. 'Oh no, Dad. You can't blame me for this mess. This is all your doing. It's no wonder you never wanted to talk about Ambergate.' She paused at the

T-junction, giving a cursory look both ways. 'Did Mum know anything about all this?'

'She knew I didn't like talking about Ambergate, but not the reasons why.' He turned and stared out of the side window, his breath condensing on the glass.

'Well I'm glad she's not around. This would crucify her.'

'If she was still alive,' he retorted, 'we wouldn't be sitting here now. She would have forbidden you from digging around in the past against my wishes and you would have listened to her. You always did.'

Sarah blinked back the tears. 'God, what a mess.'

'Amy's still so vulnerable, and now I've left her to cope with a revelation of this magnitude all on her own. I shouldn't have left her; I should have insisted on staying to support her.' He bowed his head. 'What have I done?' he whispered.

'It's not what you've done that matters now. It's what you do next. How've you left it with her?'

'She stormed out and I'm a bloody idiot for not going after her, but she was so angry, I respected her wishes. I've scribbled your number on a scrap of paper so she knows how to contact me. If she doesn't ring, I'll go back tomorrow anyway. I'm not giving up on her again.'

Sarah pulled the car into a lay-by and rested her head on the steering wheel. She felt her father squeeze her arm. 'Sarah?'

She leaned back and closed her eyes. 'Dan phoned whilst you were in the cottage.'

Dr Lambourn harrumphed. 'And what could he possibly want?'

'It's Lauren.' She hated saying her name and pulled a face as though she'd bitten into a juicy apple and found a maggot. 'She's . . . she's gone into labour.'

'What, and he phoned to tell you this?'

'He doesn't want the baby, Dad.'

'It's a bit late for that now.'

'That's what I told him, but—'

She stopped as she felt her phone vibrating in her pocket. The number on the display was unfamiliar, but she recognised the dialling code. She passed it over to her father without answering. 'It's her.'

Dr Lambourn took the phone and squinted at the buttons.

'The green one, press the green one.'

He fumbled with the phone, then brought it to his ear. 'Amy?'

After a few moments, he handed the phone back. 'She wants to see me now.'

52

The suitcase lay on the table between them, the lid firmly closed. Amy ran her fingers over the top and tentatively touched the catch. She looked at the brown luggage label hanging off the handle. No name, just a number. That was all she had been to them. She might as well have been seared with a branding iron.

'Would you like to open it now?' asked Dr Lambourn.

She gave a slight nod and closed her eyes. She heard him fumbling around in his pocket, then felt him take hold of her wrist and gently unfurl her fingers. She opened her eyes and stared at the small brass key, a key that would unlock not only the case, but a lifetime of painful memories. She took a deep calming breath and steeled herself. Fifty years had gone by since she had packed that suitcase, but as she unlocked it and lifted the lid, the familiar smell of her childhood home filled the room and she was transported back to her bedroom. Of all the senses, she found smell was the most powerful when it came to evoking memories. She couldn't even boil a cabbage without thinking of the calamitous Ambergate kitchens and the slop they doled out to patients.

She picked up the floral cotton dress that lay on top and almost laughed out loud at her own naivety. 'Imagine wearing this in Ambergate.'

Dr Lambourn shuffled uncomfortably. 'I didn't make the rules, Amy.'

She threw the dress onto the table. 'You didn't do much to change them either.'

She picked her way through the clothes, placing them in a pile. Her fingers alighted on her mother's hairbrush and she caressed the soft bristles. She tugged the band out of her hair and worked her fingers through it, loosening her plait until her hair fell in soft silvery waves. She pulled the brush through her long tresses as Dr Lambourn watched her in mesmerised silence.

She noticed him staring and dropped the brush on the table. 'I think you can go now. Thank you for the case, Dr Lambourn.'

'Please call me Stephen.'

She frowned and tasted the name on her lips. 'Stephen?'

'That's right, and I'm not leaving you, not just yet anyway. There's a lot to work through.'

'Work through? You're not my doctor any more . . . *Stephen*. You'll have to exercise your psychiatric muscles on someone else.'

He smiled. 'Dear, dear Amy, you haven't changed one bit, have you?'

'No, in spite of everybody's efforts to do just that.'

'Can I use your phone to call my daughter?'

Her voice rose with surprise. 'You have a daughter?'

'Yes, it was Sarah who drove me down here. I can only manage short journeys these days. Sarah's always threatening to take my car keys away.' He looked away in embarrassment. 'There've been a couple of . . . incidents, so I try to placate her by promising not to drive too far. I don't want to give up the car completely, though. I'd hate to lose my independence.'

She stared at him. 'It's not nice when other people think they know what's best for you, is it?'

He regarded her thoughtfully. 'I can't keep apologising, Amy,' he said, holding his hands aloft in surrender. 'But if you're sure you want to be alone, then I'll call Sarah and ask her to come and fetch me. It's your decision.'

'It's all right,' she said, turning her attention back to the case and pulling out the matinee jacket. 'You can stay for a while longer.' She held the jacket to her nose and inhaled the scent of it. It smelled of her father, the whiff of pipe tobacco still ingrained in its fibres. She picked up the hand-knitted teddy bear, its patchwork of mismatched colours testament to her mother's determination to put every last strand of wool to good use. She clutched the bear to her chest. 'This was for my baby brother, the one who . . .'

Dr Lambourn touched her arm. 'I remember,' he said softly. 'This is why I didn't want to leave just yet. I won't tell you what to do any more, but I will be here to support you.' He smiled before adding, 'If you'll let me.'

There were so many memories crammed into this case. It was a time capsule, a window to her past she hardly dared look through and yet was unable to resist. She eased the painting from the bottom of the case and held it up to the light. 'Look at this. My mother painted it in the meadow behind this very cottage. Isn't it stunning? The way she's captured the autumnal colours in the field with just a hint of sunlight shimmering on the sea behind.' She touched the canvas gently and turned to Dr Lambourn. 'See this bracken here?'

He leaned in for a closer look. 'Yes.'

'Can you see the little girl crouched down amongst it?'

He squinted at the painting. 'It's difficult without my glasses.'

'If you look carefully, you can just make out the back of a girl's head, with her long butterscotch hair trailing down her back.' She caressed the image with her thumb, smiling.

'You?' he asked.

'That's right. I begged her to include me in one of her paintings, but she was known as a landscape artist. Then she had the idea of putting me in the painting but hiding me so only we would know I was there. It was our secret.'

She bowed her head and the tears that had been standing in her eyes spilled over. She didn't care. Dr Lambourn would understand. He was the only person who had ever come close to understanding her.

He stepped forward and took her into his embrace.

She didn't resist but instead leaned into his chest and allowed him to stroke her hair. 'What do you think happened to him?' she asked eventually.

'I have no idea, Amy, but together we can find out.'

She peeled herself away and looked up into his face. 'Really? You'd help me do that?'

'He's my son too, isn't he?'

Something between a laugh and sob escaped her mouth. 'I think I'd like that hankie now please, Dr Lambourn.'

He reached into his pocket and handed it to her. 'I've told you . . . it's Stephen.'

53

'It sounds as though the rain has eased off. Would you like to take a walk with me?' asked Stephen. 'I've never walked the coast path before.'

'Really? Then you've missed out. I've been down there twice today already.' Amy scooped the net curtain out of the way. 'I think the sun's even trying to put in an appearance. Come on then, I'll get my coat.'

The sun was indeed making a valiant effort to warm the air, but it was no match for the bitingly cold wind.

'My lips have gone numb already,' Stephen mumbled. 'Perhaps this wasn't such a good idea.'

'Nonsense,' she proclaimed. 'It's bracing.'

They watched as Jess ran along in front of them, nose to the ground, her white-tipped tail swaying like a palm frond.

'Do you remember that other walk we took, down by the river?' she asked.

His cheeks were already crimson with the cold, so it was hard to tell if the memory served to embarrass him. 'Of course I remember.'

They walked a few paces in silence before Amy said

quietly, 'I loved you, Dr Lambourn . . . I mean Stephen . . . How could you not have known that?'

'I did know it, Amy, and I also knew I was falling in love with you too.' He lowered his voice to a whisper and she strained to hear him. 'But our relationship could never have worked.'

'Because I was a certified mental patient?'

'It was more complicated than that, but to my eternal shame I did put my career before my feelings for you.' He stopped and took hold of both her hands, forcing her to look at him. 'You have to believe me when I say that if I'd known there was any chance you were carrying my baby, I would have stood by you, no question about that.'

She stared up at his face, his eyes wide and searching, his brow corrugated. 'I do believe you.'

His features visibly relaxed and his shoulders dropped. 'Thank you, Amy.'

'I nearly died, you know,' she said, matter-of-factly.

'What do you mean?'

'Giving birth.' She clutched at her stomach as though the memory of it was a physical pain as well as a mental one. 'After my baby died . . . after they *told* me my baby had died, I began to haemorrhage. They rushed me to the general hospital, where they saved my life.'

'I'm sorry, Amy. I had no idea.'

'Of course you didn't. You were long gone by then.' There was no bitterness in her voice, just a statement of the facts. 'I wouldn't have cared if I had died. I'd nothing left to live for anyway.'

He winced. 'Don't say that.'

'Why not? It's true.'

He tried to steer the conversation in another direction. 'What about that young boy you were friends with? Whatever happened to him?'

'Ed?' She smiled at the memory. 'He was one of the most special people I've ever met. He came to visit me both in the general hospital and Ambergate. I believe he did truly love me, and I was very fond of him, but it wasn't enough. It wouldn't have worked out because I was in love with someone else.' She nudged his arm. 'You.'

'Yes,' he replied with a half-smile. 'I know who you meant.'

'Anyway, eventually I told him to stop coming. I just didn't have those kind of feelings for him. It may sound harsh, but I had to be honest and he deserved to be with someone who did love him.'

'The course of true love has many detours, Amy.'

She raised a quizzical eyebrow. 'I don't know what that means, but Ed did eventually marry someone else. He sent me a letter enclosing a photograph of the two of them together.'

'A happy ending, then?'

She shrugged. 'He looked happy enough. Happier than I could've made him, anyway.'

He hesitated before asking his next question; the answer

was sure to be a barometer as to how far Amy had recovered. 'Do you have any contact with your stepmother . . . Carrie?'

'Ah, Carrie, Carrie, Carrie. I couldn't bear to say her name once. Do you remember?' She didn't wait for his answer. 'Of course you remember, that's why you asked, I expect. In those days, patients who were deemed fit for discharge were moved to a care-in-the-community programme, into hostels if they had no homes to go to. I didn't want that. Ambergate had become my home. That's what the system does to you.' She took a sideways glance at him. 'But you know all that. You've seen it many times.'

'The system was far from perfect, Amy.'

'Anyway, Carrie agreed that I could go back home.'

'Good Lord, what a turnaround.'

'It didn't come about overnight. Twenty-seven years is a long time. We'd both mellowed. I went to live with her in my childhood home for a few years until I came back here.'

Stephen inhaled a gulp of the salty air. 'It's really beautiful, Amy. I can see why you were so happy here.'

'I love it. The cottage may be a little decrepit, there's no heating and all my cooking is done on the wood-burning stove, but it's mine. All mine, and I can come and go as I please. I don't have to ask for permission to visit the bathroom, I can decide for myself what to wear each morning, and best of all, there're no locked doors.

Only somebody who has been incarcerated for the best part of their life can understand what that truly means.'

'I can only imagine what it must have been like,' said Stephen solemnly. 'Do you still see Carrie?'

Amy shook her head. 'She died a few years back. Susan still comes to visit me, though.'

'Susan?'

Amy stopped walking and turned to stare at the horizon. 'The baby. The one I took into the lake. She doesn't remember any of it, naturally. She's a grown woman now, but she is my half-sister so we stay in touch.'

'That's nice.'

'She's my only living relative.' She paused. 'At least I thought she was.'

Back at the cottage, Stephen stood with his back to the fire, his arms tucked behind him as he tried to warm his hands. 'It's so cold in here, Amy. How do you stand it?'

She pulled at the thick jumper that swamped her tiny frame. 'I'm not cold.' She sat down at the table and picked up a pen. 'We need to make a plan, Stephen.'

'A plan?'

'For the baby,' she tutted. 'You promised to help me find him, remember?'

He pulled out the chair opposite and sat down, placing his elbows on the table. 'What sort of plan?' he asked warily.

'Well, where's he going to go?' She waved a hand around

the tiny living room, her gaze resting on the damp patches creeping up the walls. 'Perhaps you're right, this place is too cold for a baby—'

'Amy,' he interrupted. 'What are you talking about?'

She chewed thoughtfully on the end of her biro. 'Perhaps we'd be better off living at your house.' She stuck out her bottom lip like a sulky child. 'I wouldn't like that, though, oh no, this is my home, it always has been, apart from when I was stuck in—'

'Amy,' he urged. 'Look at me.'

She stared vacantly ahead. 'What?'

'Amy,' he repeated, clicking his fingers in front of her face. His voice was gentle but firm. 'He's not a baby any more; he's a grown man.'

She looked down at the blank page where she'd intended to write down all her plans for their future together. She glanced over at the sideboard, at the crystal fruit bowl containing one hard lemon and a light bulb. Her eyes travelled to the bottle of pills next to it. When was the last time she'd taken her medication? She couldn't remember.

'Amy?'

'I'm sorry. How stupid of me. He'll be, what, forty-nine in February?' She tapped her temple and managed a smile. 'See, nothing wrong with my brain.'

He leaned back in his chair, sighing with relief. 'So you're perfectly clear about this? He's not a baby any more. It's important you understand that if we're going to look for him.'

She nodded her head, her eyes bright once more, her expression alert. 'A momentary lapse, that's all. I'm fine, honestly.' Another thought occurred to her. 'But he might have children of his own, our grandchildren. Wouldn't that be wonderful? They could come here and I could spoil them, take them to the beach, build sandcastles they could stick their little flags into, and after that we could have ice creams and fish-and-chip suppers overlooking the harbour. Not mushy peas, though.' She shook her head. 'Kids don't like mushy peas, do they?'

'Amy, try not to get carried away. I know you're excited, but there's a long way to go before you start making plans like that. Even if he does have children, they're hardly likely to be building sandcastles. They'll most likely be teenagers, or even older.'

She slumped in the chair. 'You always did have a way of bringing me back down to earth.'

'Amy, you've had a big shock today, but I'm here for you. I know I can never make up for deserting you the way I did.' His voice was low, with a gruff edge to it. 'I'm an old man now, but I promise you that whatever time I have left, I will devote to finding our son.'

She managed a small smile, but her enthusiasm of a few moments ago had evaporated. 'Thank you, Stephen.'

'If he's out there, Amy,' he said, his clenched fist showing the extent of his determination, 'I will find him.'

54

Placing the wire basket in the crook of her elbow, she caught a glimpse of her reflection in the big security mirror over the door. Did she really look that slim, or was it just the fortunate angle of the mirror distorting things? The last few months had certainly been hectic for Sarah. She'd moved back into her old apartment, embracing the cool, sterile ambience of her minimalistic kitchen and revelling in cooking up exotic meals for Matt and Maisie. The little girl was always willing to try out new things. She peered at her shopping list. Lemon grass, coconut milk and red chillies. It made a change from the spuds, pork chops and frozen peas she was used to cooking for her father.

She picked up a bunch of bananas for Nathan. He'd disappeared from the asylum a few weeks back with no word at all, until the other day when she'd found a letter from him on her doormat. A letter! What eighteen-year-old wrote letters? Still, without a mobile phone, she supposed he'd had no choice. Apparently he'd been trying his luck down in London but it hadn't worked out. She couldn't imagine what state he would be in after a few weeks living on the capital's grimy streets, jostling for space with all the other down-and-outs, who were no doubt much more streetwise than he was.

She scurried to the next aisle and dropped in a couple of packs of baby wipes. And then she saw him. There was no time to hide behind the heavily pregnant girl beside her, and she wasn't quick enough to bow her head so low he wouldn't recognise her. Instead, she stood there open-mouthed and gawped like 'somebody not right', as her mother would have said.

'Sarah, hi.'

She swallowed hard and attempted a casual nonchalance. 'Dan! Hi, good to see you again. You look well.' It was an automatic response, because he actually looked far from well. His features sagged with tiredness, there were dark circles under his eyes and a splodge of baby sick rested on his shoulder. He had a papoose strapped to his chest, and a tiny head with a covering of downy blond hair peeped out of the top.

She pointed towards his chest. 'Is this . . .?'

'This is Angelica,' he beamed, placing a tender kiss on his daughter's head.

'Angelica? Nice name,' she replied, inwardly grimacing.

An awkward silence descended. Dan was the first to crack. 'You look . . . you look amazing, actually.'

Sarah ran her hands through her hair. 'Thanks.'

He pointed to her basket. 'Baby wipes?

'That's right.' She lifted her chin. 'So?'

'What do you need those for?'

'Well now, that's really none of your business, is it?'

A girl appeared at his side. 'Have you got the formula, babes?'

Babes! Sarah rolled her eyes as Dan turned to her. 'Lauren, this is Sarah.'

Her bleached-blond hair was pulled into an impossibly high ponytail and secured with a leopard-print scrunchie. The skin around her eyes was so stretched it gave her an exotic, oriental look. Gigantic gold hoops dangled from her ears and she wore a chunky ring on every finger, her nails covered in chipped black nail varnish. She pushed her tongue through her chewing gum as though she was going to blow a bubble with it. 'Nice to meet you,' she said without any sincerity at all. She turned to Dan. 'I'll just fetch the nappies.' She swivelled round so dramatically her ponytail caught Dan on the side of his face.

He laughed. 'Isn't she something?'

'Mmm,' replied Sarah. 'She certainly is.'

The baby began to stir, little mewing noises that sounded sweet and kitten-like but would no doubt soon become an unbearable wail.

'Well, I'd better be off. Good to see you again, Dan.'

'You too . . . and Sarah,' he called after her retreating figure. 'Thanks.'

She stopped. 'Thanks? For what?'

He shrugged. 'That talking-to you gave me on the phone – you know, when I was in the hospital and Lauren had gone into labour? You were right.' He jiggled the papoose up and down, trying to calm the baby. 'I am lucky and I am going to be a great father to this little one.'

'And Lauren? How do you feel about her now?'

'She's the mother of my child, Sarah. And I love her for that.'

'I'm glad it all worked out for you, Dan. Truly I am.'

'And you?'

'I'm fine.' She thought about Matt and Maisie and the evening she had planned ahead. An early trip to the cinema, a home-made Thai curry and a bottle of wine. Simple pleasures that most people took for granted. It was only when your life had been ripped apart that you appreciated them. 'In fact I'm more than fine.' She smiled. 'I'm happy.'

On the drive home she mulled over what she had told Dan, forcing herself to confront her feelings. She *was* happy, that much was true. The last three months had seen her grow close to Matt and Maisie and she'd become a big part of their lives. She couldn't imagine her life without them and yet there was something missing. She and Matt had never shared so much as a kiss, never even held hands. The closest they'd come to that was swinging Maisie between them as they took long walks in the woods. She'd been with Matt to see Maisie in the school play and sat alongside him beaming with as much pride as any other parent in the room. They'd taken Maisie to the swimming baths, the little girl going with Sarah into the changing rooms so she could assist with the complicated styling of her hair. Sarah could now do a French plait with her eyes closed. She stopped at a red light and laid her head on the steering wheel, contemplating the possibility that Matt wanted her in his life for his daughter's sake, rather than his own.

Her father was sitting in a deckchair in the back garden. His eyes were closed and his face was tilted towards the sun, the collar of his overcoat turned up to provide some protection from the cool March breeze.

'What are you doing out here, Dad?'

He stirred, groaning in protest. 'Do you mind? I was asleep.'

She glanced at her watch. 'But it's only . . . Oh never mind. Here.' She brandished the newspaper at him.

'Thanks, love.' He rubbed his eyes. 'What are you doing here anyway?'

'Charming. I just thought I'd see how you are. No news from the agency, then?'

'No,' he sighed. 'Not yet.'

She sat on the low wall in front of him. 'Well, no news is good news.'

He raised his eyebrows. 'How do you work that out? No news means they haven't found him. How is that good news?'

She blew out her cheeks. 'All right, calm down. It's just a saying.'

He picked up the paper and opened it wide so she couldn't see his face but could hear him muttering to himself. 'I wouldn't mind a sandwich if it's no trouble.'

She heard him, but the request didn't register and she didn't respond. She was too busy staring at the headline on the front page.

55

It felt strangely good to be back. She surveyed the old building, wondering not for the first time just how many secrets it held within its crumbling walls. Against the blue sky, with the sunlight glinting off the broken windows and daffodils outnumbering the weeds, it didn't look quite so forbidding. She thought of all the poor souls who had been forced to call Ambergate home, incarcerated against their will because they didn't conform to the way society expected them to behave. She moved the security hoarding to one side and squeezed through, cursing as her shoulder bag caught on a piece of wire. She wrestled it free and scurried across the front lawn.

'Oi, you!'

She stopped and looked around for the owner of the disembodied voice. 'Who's there?' she demanded.

'I'll be the one who asks the questions. You're trespassing.'

A man emerged from a Portakabin some distance away, his hi-vis jacket straining to cover his pot belly. He arrived at her side red-faced and struggling for breath, breadcrumbs along his moustache and a blob of mayonnaise on his chin. He lifted his hard hat and wiped his palm over his sweaty bald head. 'Where d'yer think you're goin'?'

Sarah adopted a confident tone. 'May I ask what business that is of yours?'

'Aye, yer can ask and I'll tell you.' He placed his hands on his hips. 'I'm in charge of security 'ere. Building works begin next week, and that place is not safe.'

'Nonsense, I've been in there loads of times.'

He rubbed his chin. ''Ave you now? Make a habit of trespassing, do you?'

She ferreted around in her bag and pulled out a dog-eared business card. 'Here, I'm a historian doing research.'

He glanced at the card. 'I don't care if you're the bloody Queen of Sheba, that building is not safe. It would be a dedication of my duty if I let you in.'

'Dereliction,' she corrected. She thought about Nathan, possibly curled up asleep in a side ward, unaware of the wrecking ball about to smash its way through the brickwork. 'Look, I promise I won't be long. I just need a few more shots of the inside.' She tapped the side of her nose and winked. 'You didn't see me, right?'

He dug his hands into his pockets and kicked at a stone on the ground, mulling over the situation.

'All right, twenty quid and I won't take this any further.'

'You're asking for a bribe?'

'Think of it as an entrance fee.'

Sarah pulled out her purse and thrust the note towards him. 'At least Dick Turpin wore a mask.'

'Nathan,' she called out. 'Are you here?'

His voice echoed off the walls of one of the side rooms. 'Yep, I'm in here.'

He struggled to his feet as she entered the room. 'Hello again. You got my letter, then?'

They stood facing each other for a second, a brief awkward moment whilst they considered whether the situation warranted a hug. Sarah leaned in and embraced him, the ripe smell of his unwashed body making her gag. She looked him up and down, grimacing at his grimy complexion, mottled with spots. His hair was greasy on top but frizzy at the ends. 'You're rocking that tramp look, Nathan.'

'Do I smell really bad?'

She sighed. 'What are we going to do with you, eh?' She pulled out the baby wipes. 'Here, these should help.'

'Oh, cheers, that's very kind of you.'

'When did you last eat?'

'Er, dunno, yesterday I think it was. Bloke threw away half his cheeseburger and I managed to get to it before the pigeons did.'

She could never tell if he was joking or not. 'Nathan, it doesn't have to be like this. Why won't you let me help you?'

He ignored the question. 'I don't suppose you've got anything to eat, have you?'

375

She gave him the bananas and a jar of peanut butter. 'These should fill you up. There're some beef sandwiches too, and a bottle of water.'

He slid down the wall and sat cross-legged on the floor. Sarah sat next down to him, peeling a banana for herself. 'You're going to have to find somewhere else to go, Nathan. The builders are moving in next week.'

He mumbled through his banana. 'I know. I've met the jobsworth from the Portakabin. Cheeky git tried to charge me a tenner to come in. As if anybody's going to fall for that one. I just came in round the back instead.'

'A tenner?'

'I know! Do I look as though I've got a spare tenner? Daylight robbery.'

'Yes, it is,' she replied, wondering if she should ask for a refund on her way out.

'Anyway,' he said, changing the subject, 'what's been happening with you whilst I've been gone?'

She filled him in on Amy's suitcase and the continuing search for her father's missing son.

'Wow,' he marvelled. 'Are you going to put all that in your book, then?'

'I'm not sure yet. I'll have to see how it unfolds, and what my father and Amy want to do.'

She popped the last of the banana in her mouth and took a swig from the water bottle. 'There's something else.'

'What?' Nathan asked.

'Dan's girlfriend has had the baby.'

'Oh, right, I see. And how do you feel about that?'

'I think I feel okay about it, actually. I've moved on.'

She unscrewed the top of the Thermos and poured out two cups of milky coffee. 'Do you ever think about your mum and dad, Nathan?'

'No, not really. They threw me out, remember. I shouldn't think they give a toss about me either.'

'Oh, they threw you out, did they? I thought you said you left of your own accord because of all the arguing.'

He shrugged. 'What difference does it make?'

She took a sip of her coffee. 'I was listening to a radio interview the other day, about a lad who ran away from home. Adam something. He's only fifteen, and his poor mother's frantic. He left her a note saying he couldn't be part of the rat race any more and needed time by himself.' She looked at Nathan. 'He sounds like an ungrateful little sod to me. He had everything: a loving home, a private education. His mother even had aspirations for him to go to Oxford. Now he's thrown it all away because he wants some sort of respite from the real world.' She shook her head. 'Never mind the anguish he's putting his mother through or the resources that are being spent looking for him,' she scoffed. 'It's all right as long as Adam has his little adventure.'

'Maybe the poor kid doesn't want to go to Oxford,' said Nathan. 'Maybe he wasn't happy at the private school when all his friends went to the local high school. Perhaps he was fed up of trying to live up to his mum's lofty expectations. There's more to life than exams and getting top grades, you know.'

Sarah rummaged in her bag. 'The radio interview wasn't the only one his mother gave.' She took out the newspaper and exposed the headline: 'Where is my son?' The article was accompanied by a picture of a fresh-faced schoolboy, his pale skin smooth, his hair neatly combed into place.

Geraldine Clarke is distraught. It is now more than eight months since she last saw Adam, her fifteen-year-old son. As she dropped him off at the school gates, he leaned into the car and enquired about what he could expect for his evening meal. There was nothing unusual about his behaviour that day and there had been no arguments. But nobody has seen or heard from Adam since.

Sarah touched Nathan gently on the arm. 'I think it's time to put your mum out of her misery, don't you, Adam?'

56

'It all makes sense now,' Sarah said. 'I can see why you didn't want me to help you. You didn't want me to find out the truth.' She held his chin, forcing him to look at her. 'I wondered how you managed to keep your skin so smooth without a razor. I bet you haven't even started shaving yet, have you? Eighteen,' she tutted. 'Well, you certainly had me fooled.'

'I'm sorry.' He bowed his head, his eyes riveted on the newspaper. 'Look at this.' He pointed at the article and read aloud, '"I just want him home," said Miss Clarke. "I'm not angry with him. He's a bright boy with a prom-ising future ahead of him. He could be anything he wants to be, a doctor, lawyer, something big in the City."' He flung the paper down on the floor, his eyes wide with fury. 'She still doesn't get it. Even in an interview begging me to return home, she's going on about my future. *He could be anything he wants to be?* Anything *she* wants me to be, more like.'

'She's your mother. She's proud of you, wants you to fulfil your potential.'

'What about what *I* want, though? I'm only fifteen and

I've got two GCSEs already. Do you think I wanted to be revising for exams when all my friends were having a good time? They were learning how to be teenagers, going to festivals, seeing girls, and what was I doing, eh? Soddin' calculus, quadratic equations and Thomas flamin' Hardy.'

Sarah picked up the newspaper and studied the photo of his mother. The agony and desolation were etched into her features. No doubt the newspaper photographer had instructed her to adopt a suitably anguished pose, but her eyes held the despair of a grieving mother who was at a loss to understand what she could possibly have done to drive her only son away. 'It's your mother you should be telling all this to, Nathan . . . I mean Adam.'

He shook his head. 'I can't go home.'

'You can't stay here either.' She picked up his grubby hand. 'Look at the state of you. You're skin and bone, you stink to high heaven and your hair would embarrass Worzel Gummidge.'

He frowned. 'Who?'

'The adventure's over, Adam. It's time to go home.'

He struggled to his feet. 'You can't make me. I'll be sixteen in a couple of months.'

'The last eight months haven't exactly worked out for you, have they?' She gestured around the damp room. 'Holed up in this place, relying on handouts . . .'

He buried his face in his hands. 'Arrgghh, she's just so controlling.'

'What you see as control, your mother sees as love. She only wants what's—'

He held up his hand. 'Don't you dare say it.'

'All right then, I won't, but tell me, where's your dad in all this? There's no mention of him in the paper. I thought you said your parents threw you out.'

He wrinkled his nose and shook his head. 'I don't have a dad,' he said bluntly.

'Oh, okay, I'm sorry, I just thought . . .'

'My mum never talks about him. She went on holiday to Brighton when she was fifteen and came back with more than a stick of rock.' He smiled at her shocked expression. 'My grandparents practically brought me up. I thought Geraldine was my sister until I was about ten. Even though my grandparents did most of the work, I think my mother missed out on an awful lot of school. She certainly didn't fulfil her own potential. It's why she's always pushed me so hard. She's living vicariously through me, revelling in my achievements as though she's the one who sat the exams.'

'Don't you think she's suffered enough now?' Sarah asked quietly. 'You've made your point, Adam. It's time to do the right thing.'

'For who, though?'

'For everybody.'

He stayed silent, picking at a loose thread on his jumper.

'Adam? You know it makes sense.' She took hold of his chin again. 'Look at me. Go home and talk about this like the sensible lad you are. Your mother loves you and this is killing her. Whatever it is you think she's done, she doesn't deserve this.'

He clasped his hands together on top of his head. 'Oh, I dunno. If I go back, it's like admitting I've failed.'

'You haven't failed,' she said emphatically. 'I think you're a fine young man, resourceful, enthusiastic and intelligent, and the way you've helped me with my research, documenting the cases and everything, well . . . I would be proud to call you my son.'

He smiled, reached out and squeezed her hand. 'I wish you were my mum, Sarah. You'd make a really great mother.'

No doubt he meant well, but his words stung. 'It's probably a bit late for me now, but it's not too late for you. You love your mum, don't you?'

He shrugged. 'Suppose so.'

'Well then, your relationship needs a hero, Adam. Is that going to be you?'

'I'm not going back to that school though, no way. I want to go to the local school with my mates, where the teachers don't mind if you show up chewing gum, where you don't get a lunchtime detention just because your shirt isn't tucked in.' He suddenly sounded like the truculent fifteen-year-old he really was.

'Look, I promised my father I would go back to his house. I left in rather a hurry when I saw your photograph on the front page. Come back with me, Adam. We'll get you cleaned up and then you can call your mum. I'm sure she'll be so glad to have you home, she'll agree to almost anything.'

Her father was in his dressing gown by the time she arrived back with Adam.

'Dad, what're you doing dressed for bed at three in the afternoon?'

A damp towel was slung over his shoulders. 'I've just had a bath, if it's all right with you.'

'A bath? Oh God, I hope you've not used all the hot water.'

He noticed Adam then, hovering behind her. 'Who's this?'

'This is Adam Clarke. Adam, this is my father, Stephen.'

Adam held out his hand and Stephen shook it briefly, then, with a look of distaste, wiped his hand down his dressing gown. 'You look a bit grubby, lad. Where've you been?'

Sarah explained the situation, her father becoming more alarmed the further into Adam's story she went.

'Don't you think this should be a matter for the police?' he asked. 'He's only fifteen, you say?'

Sarah touched his arm. 'Give him a chance, Dad. Adam's going to get himself cleaned up and then he's going to call his mum.'

'Well let's hope we don't go down for harbouring a criminal.'

'Dad, for God's sake, you're overreacting as usual. Just let me handle it, okay?'

'Well if you're sure you've—' The ringing of the telephone halted his reply. 'I'll be back in a minute,' he said, making his way to the hall.

Sarah turned to Adam. 'Don't worry about him. He can be a little . . . unreasonable.'

Adam laughed. 'You don't need to tell me about unreasonable parents. I wrote the book!'

'It'll be all right, you know. Trust me.' She nodded towards the hall. 'When he's finished on the phone, you can call her.'

He wrinkled his nose. 'I dunno . . . Will you do it?'

'What's happened to that confident young man I met in the asylum? The one who's managed to survive on the streets for the past eight months?'

He looked defeated. 'That was Nathan.'

'Come here.' She pulled him close and squeezed him hard, rubbing her hand up and down his back, then pushed him away so she could look into his face. 'Okay, I'll call her, but you have to speak to her.'

'But—'

She put a finger to his lips. 'But nothing. I could just be some lunatic phoning up out of the blue as far as she's concerned. *You* have to speak to her.'

He folded his arms, beaten but still belligerent. 'Fine, you win. I'll do it.'

They both turned as they heard the door brush across

the carpet and Stephen re-entered the room. His face was colourless, his jaw slack, and a scrap of paper fluttered in his hands.

'Dad,' exclaimed Sarah. 'What's the matter? Is it bad news?' She rushed to his side.

'That was the agency,' he began. 'They've found him.' His face cracked into a broad smile, the crow's feet around his eyes deepening. 'They've found my boy.'

'But . . . that's wonderful, Dad. I mean . . . is he okay? Where is he? What's his name?'

He eased himself down into a chair and handed her the piece of paper. 'His name is Joseph.'

Sarah turned to Adam. 'Isn't it marvellous . . . Adam?' She looked at her father. 'Where's he gone?'

She heard his voice coming from the hall and popped her head round the door. His back was turned and he was leaning his forehead against the mirror, the phone pressed to his ear. 'I'm fine, Mum, honest. Stop crying, will you.' He straightened up, saw Sarah watching him and gave her a small smile. 'Thank you,' he mouthed.

She winked at him. 'You're welcome.'

She returned to her father and sat on the arm of the chair. 'Well, Dad.' She kissed his head. 'What are you going to do now?'

57

He would have preferred to drive himself. Two hundred miles with nothing to do but think, reflect and plan. It was so frustrating, not to mention demeaning, having to rely on his daughter to drive him long distances. Sarah was insistent, though, intransigent even, and he knew that arguing with her was futile. She was so stubborn. He couldn't imagine where she got it from. He looked across at her in the driving seat, hands gripping the wheel in concentration as the car bounced along the bumpy lane. The hedgerows were coming to life, the thorny twigs now abundant with frothy blossom, birds darting in and out as they collected twigs and bits of sheep wool.

'How're you feeling, Dad?'

Instead of an automatic response, he actually considered the question. It was one he had asked of other people countless times in his professional career. He brought the bouquet of flowers up to his nose and inhaled their sweet perfume. 'Apprehensive, but excited too,' he concluded.

'I really think you ought to have phoned first.'

'Yes, so you said, but I'm not doing this over the phone. I owe her that much.'

She swung the car round a bend and Amy's cottage came into view. He took a deep breath and closed his eyes. 'Can you give me a couple of hours?'

'Hadn't you better see if she's in first?'

He looked at the pale blue front door, wide open, Jess sleeping across the threshold. 'She's in.'

Sarah brought the car to a halt but left the engine running. 'Good luck then, Dad.'

He unhooked the latch on the gate, immediately alerting the dog to his presence. She looked up and sprang to her feet. 'Hello, Jess,' he said, pulling on her silky ears. 'Where's Amy, then?'

Jess circled round him, her tail whipping across his knees. He tapped on the front door and called into the empty hall. 'Amy, are you in there?' There was no response. He tried again, a little louder. Nothing. Clutching the bouquet to his chest, he made his way round to the back of the cottage, stopping abruptly as he saw her familiar figure. She had her back to him, stretching up to throw a sheet over the washing line. It flapped around on the breeze and she struggled to peg it into place. Her long silver hair trailed almost to her waist and her slight frame could have belonged to a teenager instead of a woman who had not long since turned seventy. 'Do you need a hand?' he called.

She swivelled round, her brown eyes opening wide. 'Stephen?'

He moved towards her, holding out the flowers. 'Hello, Amy.'

She took them from him, instinctively bowing her head to inhale the scent. 'What . . . I mean . . . why . . .?'

Her expression was one of confusion, her forehead creased, a questioning look in her eyes. She seemed vulnerable, and all at once he longed to take her in his arms, smooth her hair and whisper reassurances into her ear. The repressed feelings he'd had for her half a century ago bubbled to the surface again. How different her life would have been if he hadn't been such a coward. Because of his selfish actions, she'd spent her best years locked away. He could never make it up to her.

'Stephen?'

He nodded towards a wooden bench, green with moss. 'Can we sit for a while?'

He followed her to the bench and sat down next to her. 'Amy,' he began, picking up her hand. 'The English language has yet to come up with a word to adequately express how very sorry I am. You captivated me all those years ago. Right from the moment I saw you, in fact.' He gave a small laugh. 'But I'm a psychiatrist. I didn't believe in love at first sight. Never mind that you were embedded in my every waking thought. I took this to mean I was infatuated, but not in love. I was wrong.'

'You didn't know about the baby then, though, did you?'

He shook his head. 'No, I didn't. But I ran away from my feelings for you, and that was unforgivable.'

She reached out and touched his cheek. 'You look so

sad, Stephen. Don't be too hard on yourself.' She stood up and held out her hand. 'Let's go inside, shall we? I assume you've not come all this way for nothing.'

He heaved himself off the bench, his arthritic knees audibly complaining as he stood. He placed his hand in the small of his back as he straightened up and faced her. 'No, there's a very good reason for my visit. I wanted to see you in person, to be here for you when I delivered the news.'

'Oh?' The word fluttered out on a sigh. 'Is it . . . is it about our baby?'

He nodded slowly. 'He's been found, Amy. Our boy has been found.'

She grabbed hold of his lapel. 'Honestly, you mean it?'

He reached into his inside pocket and pulled out a photograph. 'Here he is. That's our son.'

She stared at the picture, blinking away the tears. He was sitting in an armchair, staring directly into the lens, a broad beam across his face. His hairline was receding, giving the impression of a large forehead, and he carried a little too much weight around his middle. Behind the thick-framed glasses, his eyes sparkled with obvious affection for whoever had taken the photograph – his wife, perhaps, or maybe one of his children?

'He looks . . . happy,' she declared, flicking the tears from her cheeks. 'He looks really happy.'

Stephen placed his arm around her shoulders. 'You're shaking, Amy. Let's get you inside.'

He pulled her close, supporting her weight as they made their way into the kitchen.

'What did they call him?' she asked, still staring at the picture.

'Joseph. But I believe he's known as Joe.'

'Can I see him?'

'If you're sure that's what you want, we can put the wheels in motion.' He paused to steady his voice. 'And if you don't mind, I'd like to come with you.'

She pressed the photograph to her chest and closed her eyes. 'I'd like that, Stephen. I'd like that very much.'

58

As the train slid silently into Piccadilly station, Amy gathered up the detritus from the table in front of her. For the past six and a half hours she'd shared the company of a young mother and her three-year-old twin girls. Amy had marvelled at the amount of patience the woman had shown as she wiped noses, read storybooks, coloured in endless pictures and made several journeys to the toilet. Now the twins leaned against each other, their eyes closed, pink cheeks aglow from the heat of the carriage.

'Bless them,' Amy said. 'They're a credit to you, they really are.'

The young mother stopped clearing away and beamed at her daughters. 'Look at them, fast asleep now it's time to get off. Typical.'

'They'll be excited to see their father, I expect.'

'Oh yes. Daddy's girls they are. Still, it'll give me a break, or at least a chance to get all this washing done.' She heaved down her suitcase. 'It was really nice meeting you, Amy. And good luck with everything.'

She watched as the three of them stepped off the train, the little girls holding hands and yawning as they tottered along the platform. Amy waited until the other passengers had gone before she retrieved her own suitcase. The brown leather was battered and worn, the stitching around the handle frayed, but this case had history and she would never part with it. Everybody else seemed to have anonymous black cases, with handles you pulled out and little wheels on the bottom, cases that were forever tripping people up or crashing into their ankles. Amy shook her head. No, they wouldn't do for her. She was more than happy with her battered brown one.

She made her way along the platform towards the glass doors, amazed at the number of people milling around in the middle of the day. Didn't they have jobs to go to?

They were standing exactly where they said they would be, next to the circular information booth, the electronic timetable suspended above their heads. Stephen saw her first and moved towards her, arms outstretched. 'Hello, Amy. Welcome back.' He kissed her on both cheeks. How very Continental. When did all that start? she wondered.

'Hello again, Amy,' greeted Sarah, giving her a swift embrace.

'Here,' offered Stephen. 'Let me take your case. How was your journey?'

'It was long, but I shared a table with a delightful family. The mother had taken her twins to Wales to visit their grandmother, and they were on their way home.' She smiled fondly. 'They were a handful, those two, I can tell you, but they made the journey fly by.'

'I would have come to fetch you,' said Sarah.

'Nonsense, I was fine. You've enough on your plate without worrying about an old dear like me.' She looked Sarah up and down. 'There's something different.'

'Oh,' replied Sarah, self-consciously running her fingers through her bob. 'It's the hair. Thought I'd try something new.'

Amy nodded her approval. 'It suits you.'

Stephen took her elbow and guided her towards the exit. 'Come on, the hotel's just a few hundred yards away.'

'Bye then,' said Sarah.

'Aren't you coming with us?' asked Amy.

'No, I'm meeting someone. I'll see you later.'

'Oh?' said Amy, making it sound like a question. 'How . . . lovely. Is it a young man?'

Sarah laughed. 'Yes, as a matter of fact, it is. Now go on, you two. Enjoy yourselves. I'll see you later.'

Sarah waited outside the main doors, the sunshine now warm enough to make her jacket redundant. She stared at the old man sitting cross-legged on the pavement, one arm slung around his dog's neck, the other hand clutching a polystyrene cup. She wandered over and dropped a freshly minted two-pound coin into it. The dog looked at her, its doleful eyes and grey muzzle reflecting its owner's pitiful state.

'Ta,' muttered the beggar. 'I'm grateful to yer.'

She crouched down next to him. 'Are you hungry?'

He smiled, his lack of teeth giving him a manic look. 'Always.'

'I'll be back in a minute.'

She returned with a piping-hot pasty and watched him as he took a bite, then broke off a small piece for the dog. She swivelled round as she heard her name.

'Sarah, hi.'

Had he not called out to her, she would not have recognised him. She could have passed him on the street and not had an inkling as to who he was. His blond hair was even lighter, the long fringe now coiffed into a neat wave, and his once-pallid skin sported a healthy tan. Although he would always be a skinny lad, he had filled out a little, his defined biceps suggesting he'd paid more than a few visits to the gym. 'Adam, oh it's so good to see you again.' She held out her arms and pulled him towards her. He smelled clean, the delicious aroma of freshly laundered clothes.

'You too,' he replied. 'I . . . I like your hair, and you look so thin. I mean in a good way . . . not that you were fat before, but now you . . .'

'Thank you, Adam,' she laughed. 'I do feel much better.'

He turned to the woman beside him. 'Sarah, this is my mum, Geraldine.'

She bore no resemblance to the woman Sarah had seen in the newspaper article. Gone were the haunted eyes and hollowed-out cheeks – the telltale signs of someone who was suffering an agonising wait for news of her only son.

Sarah held out her hand. 'I'm pleased to meet you at last.'

Geraldine's moist palms gave away her nervousness. 'I don't know what to say, Sarah, except thank you. Thank you for taking care of my boy and for bringing him back to me.' She ran a finger along her eyelid, leaving a long dark smudge. 'I can't bear to imagine what would've happened to him if he hadn't met you.'

'Mu-um,' Adam warned. 'You promised not to get all soppy.'

'Adam's a fine young man, Geraldine,' said Sarah.

Geraldine pulled her son closer. 'We've had a lot to resolve, but we're getting there. Adam's at the high school with all his mates now, and doing really well.'

'And we don't focus too much on the academic stuff, do we, Mum? There are other things that're important too.' He pursed his lips and gave a slight shake of his head in Sarah's direction. She detected his exasperated tone and gave him a knowing smile.

'Come on, I've booked a table at a restaurant with a roof terrace so we can enjoy the sunshine.'

Adam pulled out a chair for his mother and she slid gracefully into it. Sitting opposite, and from behind the protection of her sunglasses, Sarah was able to study the other woman. From what Adam had told her, she must only be in her early thirties, and the former wild child who had found herself pregnant at the age of fifteen had certainly matured into a sophisticated woman. Her raven hair fell in bouncy waves, which rested on her shoulders; her make-up was immaculately applied, with no hint of shine in spite of the heat. Her dark ruby lips only served to accentuate the whiteness of her teeth.

Whilst Geraldine exuded effortless glamour, Sarah felt as though she herself was melting in the heat. She picked up the napkin and surreptitiously dabbed at her damp forehead, then called to a passing waitress. 'A bottle of champagne, please, and three glasses.'

Geraldine looked up from the menu. 'Are we celebrating something?'

'You'll see. Do you mind if Adam has a sip of champagne?'

'Ooh,' said Adam, rubbing his hands together. 'My first alcoholic drink.'

Geraldine stared at him, her heavily kohled eyes narrowing. 'No need to be sarcastic, Adam.'

Sarah rummaged in her handbag and pulled out a brown paper bag. She passed it across the table to Adam.

'What's this?'

'Open it.'

Adam peered into the bag, then reached in and pulled out the book. He stared at the glossy cover and the title in large white letters: *Ambergate: A Personal History*. 'Wow, this is cool, Sarah. I can't believe you actually finished it – well done.'

'Well, it's self-published, but it's available online and

my local bookshop has agreed to stock it, and of course there's a copy in the library. I can't see me troubling the *Times* best-seller list, but that was never really the point.'

Adam passed it to his mother. 'Isn't it brilliant?'

Geraldine smoothed her fingers over the photograph of Ambergate. 'It certainly is,' she said quietly. 'Congratulations.'

'Turn to the back page,' urged Sarah.

Geraldine read from the acknowledgements. '"My special thanks go to Adam Clarke. Our serendipitous meeting proved to be a turning point for both of us. I'm incredibly fortunate to count him as a friend."'

Geraldine turned to Adam. 'Isn't that lovely, son?'

The colour had risen in his cheeks. 'Jeez, Sarah, you're a soft one.' He reached across the table and touched her hand, his eyes smiling. 'But thank you.'

59

'How's your room?' enquired Stephen as he pulled the chair out for her.

Amy tucked her skirt beneath her and sat down, spreading the napkin out on her lap. 'Oh, it's marvellous. It has this great big bed, wide enough for a family of four, and all these pillows and cushions. And there's a little fridge tucked away in a cupboard with tiny bottles of whisky and gin and wine.'

Stephen took the chair opposite, watching her with quiet amusement. 'You sound like you've never stayed in a hotel before,' he laughed.

'Well, I haven't.' She looked down and fidgeted with the napkin.

He reached across the table and laid his hand over hers. 'I'm sorry, I wasn't thinking. Let's order some wine, shall we? Red or white?'

She shrugged. 'Why don't you choose?'

He perused the wine list, holding it under the light of the candle. 'It's so bloody dark in here, I can't read a thing.' He beckoned a waitress over. 'We'll have a bottle of the Marlborough Sauvignon Blanc, please.'

'What's the plan for tomorrow then, Stephen?' Amy wrinkled her nose, still finding it odd calling him by his first name.

'I've arranged to meet them in the Pavilion Café in the park. I thought neutral territory was a good idea.'

'You make it sound as though we're at war with them.'

'Not at all. It'll be more relaxed this way. Nobody worrying about whether they've made the tea too strong, or not put out the right biscuits.'

The waitress returned with a bottle, uncorked it and stood with one hand behind her back as she turned to Amy. 'Would you like to try the wine, madam?'

Amy hesitated. 'Oh . . . I don't know much about wine, I . . .'

Stephen gestured dismissively with his hand. 'Just pour it.'

'Well, that was rude,' declared Amy after the waitress had gone.

Stephen looked genuinely perplexed. 'Was it?'

'You haven't changed one bit. Do you possess any self-awareness at all? I remember you used to terrify some of the patients *and* the staff.'

'Nonsense, they loved me.'

'They were in awe of you more like.' She picked up her glass and swirled the wine around, then leaned in and lowered her voice. 'Everybody wanted to please you, everybody wanted you to like them, and you revelled in their fawning.' She leaned back in her chair, waiting for her assessment of him to sink him. 'You were responsible for so many lives in there and I don't think you used that power wisely.' She tipped her head back and stared at the ceiling. 'So many people locked away for years on end, and without good reason. People that *you* certified, Dr Lambourn.' She dabbed at her eyes with the napkin. 'I watched so many of my friends just wither and die.'

'We lived in different times, Amy. I was a victim of the system too.'

She ignored his protest. 'Do you remember Pearl?'

He nodded. 'The big girl with the moon face.'

'How many times did she beg you to let her go home?' When he didn't respond, she supplied the answer. 'Countless times, Stephen. She pleaded with you to let her out. You'd diagnosed her as a mental defective and feeble-minded.' She threw her hands in the air. 'What does that even mean?'

'It means that—'

'Stop it, Stephen. It wasn't enough to keep her locked up for life and you know it. She'd been jilted at the altar by the only man she'd ever loved. She was broken-hearted, that was all. There was nothing wrong with her mind. At least there wasn't when she was admitted. And the others, too – Belinda, Queenie, all of them just left to rot away. I never thought I'd say it, but I was one of the lucky ones. At least I made it out in the end.'

Unable to meet her stare, he laid his palms on the table

and studied the back of his hands. 'You're right, Amy. You're absolutely right.'

His demeanour had changed to that of a broken man, one who had realised there was nothing he could do to rectify the mistakes of the past. A sudden rush of pity for him made her relent. 'You could've made me happy, you know. If there was one person who could have done that, it was you.'

'It's not too late.'

She gave a laugh, but there was no humour in it. 'Oh it is, Stephen, it's far too late.'

He took a bread roll out of the basket in the middle of the table, breaking it over his plate and spreading it with butter. She noticed how his hands trembled and wondered whether it was nerves or just another symptom of old age. He would be eighty later this month, almost ten years older than she was. The age gap didn't seem to matter so much now.

'What are you thinking about?' he asked.

She shook her head to clear the memories. 'Oh, just how different things could have been, that's all.'

'Please, Amy. I—'

'It's all right, Stephen. I've forgiven you. Holding on to all that bitterness, that regret, the anger – well, it's like holding your breath. It ends up suffocating you. I had to let it go.'

She took another gulp of her wine. Already she was beginning to feel hot and light-headed, the back of her neck damp beneath the weight of her hair. She fanned herself with the menu. 'You've redeemed yourself, Dr Lambourn.' She raised her glass. 'And tomorrow, thanks to you, I will meet my son. It may be fifty years too late but I'll always be grateful to you for that.'

60

They chose a table outside in the warm May sunshine, shaded by a huge umbrella. Signs of summer were everywhere. The abundant dark purple flowers of the clematis tumbled over the wall and the scent of freshly mown grass wafted around the courtyard. Stephen pulled a chair out for Amy.

'Thank you,' she said, lowering herself into it and removing her sunglasses. She had agonised about what to wear for days, not that she had a great deal to choose from. She led a simple existence and clothes were not something she gave much thought to, usually pulling on the first thing to hand each morning. Years in Ambergate wearing the shapeless communal dresses had not exactly forged an interest in fashion.

'You look lovely, Amy,' ventured Stephen. 'That colour really suits you.'

She smoothed her hand down the lilac blouse. 'Thanks. I wasn't sure what to go for.'

She had pulled her hair into a chignon, leaving just a few strands loose to soften her face. Stephen had chosen a casual look, his pale pink checked shirt open at the neck, his face clean-shaven and the scent of sandalwood clinging to his skin.

'I think you've got it just right,' he smiled. He squinted at his watch. 'Not long to go now.'

Amy spotted them first and nudged Stephen, and they rose from their seats together to greet them. She could hardly breathe, let alone speak, her mouth a dry cave from which no words would come. She held on to the table for support as she stared at the woman who had become the mother to her own son.

Jean introduced herself to Stephen and he shook her hand warmly. 'Thank you for coming, you've no idea what this means to us.'

Amy hovered behind, happy to let Stephen do the talking. Jean was a small woman with a slender frame, almost birdlike, and a bubble of freshly permed grey hair tinged with blue. Two spots of blusher accentuated her cheekbones, and a slick of pink lipstick showed she had made an effort. She had a kind face that even in repose held a smile. Stephen turned and introduced Amy. Dispensing with a formal handshake, Amy leaned in and gave the older woman a hug, finding comfort in the powdery scent of her skin. Jean returned the embrace and the two women stood locked together until Stephen touched Amy lightly on the shoulder.

Jean smiled and kissed Amy on the cheek. 'I'd like to introduce you to Joe.'

Amy gazed at her son, the boy she thought had died all those years ago. The boy she believed had been chucked into a coffin with someone else and not even afforded the respect of his own gravestone. The boy they told her had not taken a single breath. For most of her life she had tortured herself with the notion that she was responsible in some way, that she had not pushed hard enough during the birth or not insisted that the midwife spend longer trying to revive him.

Jean bent down so that she was level with her son's face. She patted him on the knee. 'Joe, this is Amy and Stephen.' He rolled his head against the back of his wheelchair and gave a small grunt, his mouth stretching into a smile. He lifted his arm, his wrist bent at an awkward angle, and moved it from side to side. Jean squeezed his hand. 'There's a good boy.' She pulled a handkerchief out of her sleeve and wiped his mouth, before kissing him on the top of his head. Then she smiled at Amy, her chest inflating with pride as she held onto her son's hand. 'He's non-verbal, but he understands a lot, so you can talk to him.'

Stephen had briefed her about Joe's condition, so she was prepared for the sight of him in his wheelchair and the involuntary movements he was unable to control. What she was unprepared for was the sudden overwhelming rush of affection she felt for him. He had the same olive complexion as his father, but he had her eyes, huge and fawn-like. She wanted to scoop him up and never let him go. She crouched down in the same way Jean had done and took hold of his hand. 'I'm very pleased to meet you, Joe.'

Stephen moved a couple of chairs out of the way and Jean slid Joe's wheelchair up to the table. She leaned down to talk to him. 'Would you like some cake, Joe? They've got chocolate cake, your favourite.'

Joe rocked his head back and forth, his eyes shining with excitement. Jean laughed. 'Chocolate it is, then.'

After giving their orders to the waitress, Stephen clasped his hands together and leaned forward. 'I was so sorry to hear about your husband,' he said to Jean.

She turned and gazed at her son. 'It's hit Joe harder, to be honest. He doted on his dad and Harold was marvellous with him. Joe just cannot understand where he's gone. He cried for him every night for weeks afterwards.' She sniffed. 'It tore me apart.'

'And how is he now?' asked Stephen.

'It's been almost a year since we lost Harold, and Joe is calmer now. He no longer cries himself to sleep but I worry that he's forgotten him, or worse, that he thinks Harold just abandoned him.' She smoothed her hand over Joe's hair. 'It's difficult to know what's going on in there.'

'Harold sounds like a wonderful father,' said Amy.

Jean smiled fondly. 'He was the best father Joe could have had.' She stopped and looked apologetically at Stephen. 'No offence.'

Stephen raised his palm. 'None taken.'

Joe began to move his arms up and down like an excited toddler, banging them on the arms of his chair. He made a low moaning sound in his throat as he turned his head.

'What is it, Joe love?' Jean asked gently, following his gaze. 'Oh, he's seen the cat. Joe loves animals, don't you, lad?'

Amy rose from her seat to where the smoky grey cat sat in a puddle of sunshine, licking its chest. She picked it up and it rubbed its face against the underside of her chin. She carried it over to Joe and laid it in his lap. Joe's features lifted as he clumsily patted the animal, a wide grin on his face.

The waitress returned with a tray laden with food. A three-tiered serving plate was crammed full of dainty crustless sandwiches and tiny pastel-coloured cupcakes. Joe spotted the huge slice of chocolate cake and waved his arms excitedly as the cat leapt off his knee.

Amy reached for the teapot, lifted the lid and gave it a stir. She picked it up and looked round the table. 'Shall I be mother?' She stopped, at once wishing she could take back her crass words. Her son might be sitting opposite, but she had never felt less like a mother.

Jean unfolded a napkin and laid it across Joe's knee. She cut the chocolate cake into small pieces and popped one into Joe's mouth. He made an appreciative noise and opened his mouth wide like a baby bird awaiting a worm. 'You can do the next one, Joe.' She opened up his palm and dropped a piece of cake into it. Joe brought his hand up and squashed the cake into his mouth. 'Good boy, Joe,' praised Jean. 'Well done.' He held his hand out for another piece, but this time Jean handed him the plate. 'You pick up the next one.' Joe shook his head, but Jean steadfastly held the plate in front of him. 'Go on, Joe,' she said firmly.

Amy watched in agony. It seemed cruel to her, making him pick up the little bits of cake when he obviously had trouble with his fine motor skills. But Jean was immovable, and eventually Joe leaned forward and picked up a piece of cake with his thumb and forefinger. He squeezed too hard, though, and the cake all but disintegrated between his fingers. He managed to shovel only a few crumbs into his mouth, but Jean applauded with obvious delight. 'I knew you could do it.' She leaned over and kissed him on the forehead. 'I love you, you clever lad.'

Joe smiled at her and patted his chest three times.

'That's Joe's sign for "I love you",' Jean explained. 'Harold taught him that.'

At Stephen's suggestion they took a walk around the ornamental gardens, Stephen pushing Joe's wheelchair, Amy and Jean lagging some distance behind. The two women stopped beside a fountain, a cast-iron fish spewing water out of its mouth, the pool beneath littered with coins now turning green. Amy rummaged in her pocket and tossed in a ten-pence piece. She closed her eyes for a second, breathing in deeply, the scent of the nearby lavender bushes filling her nostrils.

'Can I ask you something, Jean?'

'You can ask me anything you want, but I'll not promise to know the answer.'

'Why did you choose my baby?'

Jean smiled and shook her head. 'I didn't, lovey. He chose me.'

Amy indicated the stone bench beside the fountain. 'Do you mind if we sit for a while?'

Stephen was up ahead, bending down next to Joe's chair, guiding his hand to stroke an overexcited golden retriever.

'Of course.'

'Tell me about Joe, please,' said Amy. 'Everything . . . from the beginning.'

She noticed Stephen turning round and starting to manoeuvre Joe's wheelchair in their direction. She shook her head and waved him away. He nodded his understanding.

'Joe was six weeks old when we first saw him,' Jean began. 'Harold and I had never been able to have children, so we'd decided to adopt. There was no shortage of babies back then; young mothers who got pregnant out of wedlock were encouraged, dare I say forced, to give their babies up. They were herded into mother-and-baby homes, and after they had given birth they were allowed to keep their babies for six weeks. That's the part I found particularly barbaric. Giving them the time to bond with their little ones and then just snatching them away. It seemed cruel to me and I didn't feel comfortable taking another woman's child against her will.

'Then I saw Joe, lying in his cot, just staring up at the ceiling. His eyes were huge and so dark. I was captivated immediately. I asked one of the nurses about him and she told me he wasn't to be adopted because he was retarded.' She glanced at Amy. 'I'm sorry, but that's the word they used back then. I asked what was to become of him and the nurse said he would be put away.'

Amy covered her mouth with her hand. 'Put away? My God, how callous.'

'Mmm, quite,' agreed Jean. 'I felt sick to think of this . . . this tiny helpless baby who had no one and was going to be shoved into some kind of institution because he was an inconvenience who had no place in society and needed to be kept out of sight. I couldn't have lived with myself if I'd just turned my back and walked away. I reached down into his cot and touched his cheek. His eyes widened as though he was shocked at this basic human contact, and then his little lips stretched into a crooked smile and he kicked his legs. I looked up at my husband; I didn't even need to say anything. He nodded his head and I bent down and scooped Joe up. The nurse came running then, all of a fluster she was, and demanded I put him back, but it was too late. He'd already stolen my heart and I knew I wasn't leaving that place without him.'

Amy's tears rolled off the end of her chin and landed on her blouse, leaving a dark stain. 'That's so beautiful, Jean.' She glanced along the path to where Stephen was tending to Joe, pulling his hat down to shield his eyes from the sun. 'What a terrible life he'd have had if you and Harold hadn't come along. I've never heard anything so selfless in all my life. I don't know how I can ever thank you.'

'Oh no, I don't need any thanks, Amy. Joe has enriched our lives far more than we have enriched his. I'm right proud to call myself his mother.'

'You've done a far better job with him than I could ever have done,' admitted Amy.

'Don't be so hard on yourself, love. You were never even given the chance.'

Amy turned her face up to the pale sunshine, rolling back the years in her mind. She had never been insane. She'd been traumatised by witnessing her mother's death at such an early age. That was when her life had begun to implode. Even now she could pinpoint the exact second. The image of her mother's broken body spread-eagled across the bonnet of that car was as sharp today as it had been sixty years ago. She hadn't been allowed to attend the funeral, nor cry in front of her father for fear of upsetting him. She'd been forced to repress her feelings, put on a brave face and quietly smother the grief that threatened to swallow her whole.

'Amy, are you all right? You look awfully pale.' Jean's soft voice brought her back to the present.

'I wasn't mad, you know. I should never have been locked away like that.' She held her hands up. 'Oh, I admit I was probably a handful, and attacking another patient with a piece of broken crockery certainly didn't help convince them that I should be allowed out into the wider community, but *they* turned me into someone I wasn't. After my baby died . . . after they *told* me my baby had died, I think I just gave up. I had nothing left to go on for.' She nodded towards Stephen. 'And he had left me.'

'He left you when you were pregnant?'

'He didn't know I was carrying his child. It was complicated. I was a detained mental patient, he was my doctor. You can see how that might be difficult.'

Jean seemed doubtful. 'Even so . . . to just abandon you like that.'

'I've forgiven him, Jean,' she said simply. 'I had to.'

Jean twisted the handle of her bag in her fingers, a frown registering her concern. 'Do you know what I fret about most, Amy? Especially now that Harold's gone and it's just me and Joe.'

Amy nodded. 'What's going to happen to him when you're no longer around.'

'Exactly that,' Jean confirmed. 'I've seen the way he's been since Harold died, the confusion on his face when we sit down for a meal and it's just the two of us. I remember the first time I tried to shave him – he fought me like some kind of wild animal and I ended up nicking his skin. Joe put his fingers to his face and felt the blood.

412

He became hysterical and looked at me as though I'd tried to kill him. Shaving him had always been Harold's job, you see. How's he going to understand it when I've gone and there's no one to reassure him, eh? I'm eighty-two, for goodness' sake.'

'He's got me now, Jean. I'll be here for him.'

'I know you mean well, Amy, but you're no spring chicken yourself.'

Amy managed a laugh. 'True, I can't argue with that.'

'Harold and I have never had much in the way of money. I've never worked because caring for Joe is a full-time job – not that I'm complaining, you understand. It's been a privilege and I wouldn't change a thing.'

The sound of Joe's wheelchair crunching on the gravel made them both turn around. Stephen's face was crimson with the effort of pushing the chair, his forehead shiny with sweat. He took out his handkerchief and dabbed at his brow. 'Phew, it's thirsty work is this.'

'Here's my boy,' greeted Jean, as Joe held out his arms towards his mother. She leaned in to give him a cuddle. 'Your face looks a bit red, Joe. I hope you've not had too much sun.' She delved into her handbag and pulled out a small tube of suncream, then squeezed some into her palm and smoothed it over Joe's face. He closed his eyes and his body relaxed, his jerky movements quietened as he succumbed to his mother's gentle touch.

'You're so good with him,' Amy observed. 'You don't need to hear him say it to know that he adores you,'

Jean sat back and gazed at her son. 'He's everything to me,' she said simply.

'Jean . . .' Amy hesitated. 'I . . . I'd really like to be part of Joe's life . . . if that's all right with you, that is.'

Jean looked from Amy to Stephen, then to her son, his face bright and expectant, as though he knew the importance of the answer. 'Joe and I would like that,' she replied eventually. 'We'd like that very much.'

Sarah stared up at the building where it had all begun. The bulldozers had certainly done a thorough job. All that remained of Ambergate was the Grade II listed front entrance, the clock tower now restored to its former glory and looking resplendent against the cloudless sky. She studied the billboard. *Coming soon – Ambergate Village, a stunning collection of luxury apartments and sumptuous five-bedroom detached homes.*

Matt stood behind her and placed his hands on her shoulders. 'Fancy one?'

It was an intimate gesture and she instinctively leaned back into his chest. 'Never. I know far too much about what went on in this place. I'd never sleep at night.'

'Come on, show me around.'

'Well, there's not much left really.' She pointed across the lawn. 'That's the little chapel where the patients used to pray – it seems to have escaped the bulldozers – and over there is where the cricket field used to be.' She sighed as she thought about Amy and her wasted life. 'I'm just glad I didn't take any notice of my father when he ordered me to stop snooping around. If I'd listened to him, Amy would never have been reunited with her son.'

'You did the right thing,' Matt confirmed. 'And your book is wonderful. I'm so proud of you.'

He pulled her into a fierce bear hug, one that was usually reserved for good friends, rather than lovers. 'Matt?' she asked tentatively. 'What . . . what is this?'

He frowned. 'You've lost me.'

'This. You and me. I need to know how you feel because as fond as I am of Maisie, if you're just looking for a mother figure for her then I'm afraid . . .'

He cupped her face in his hands, silencing her with a tender kiss on the lips. She closed her eyes as she felt his fingers work their way into her hair. He pulled away and locked his gaze on hers as he stroked her cheek. 'Does that answer your question?'

She nodded. 'Things are a little clearer now, yes.'

'Come on,' he whispered. 'It's nearly time to pick Maisie up from school.'

Sarah frowned. 'I don't think so. Doesn't she have art club on Tuesdays?'

Matt smacked his forehead. 'You're right.' He took hold of her hand. 'Whatever would we do without you?'

She stood on her tiptoes and kissed him again. 'Well hopefully you'll never have to find out.'

Epilogue

The room is stuffy and airless. The smells of old furniture, mothballs and body odour combine to make me feel slightly nauseous. A woman on the other side of the room takes hold of a long pole and opens a window high up on the wall. It won't make much difference. The air outside is hot and sticky too; there's not a breath of wind to cool the rising temperature. I stand at the back and stare over the heads of the people seated in the rows in front of me, fanning themselves with whatever they have to hand. My gaze travels along the wall to the front, where my son is sitting in his wheelchair. He catches me looking at him and gives me a wide grin.

Two years have passed since I found him, and it's fair to say that we've become friends. I've accepted that is all we'll ever be, for I can never be his mother. His mother is the person standing behind him now, smoothing his hair and wiping his glistening chin. I watch as she massages his shoulders and absently bends down to kiss his head. I give thanks every day to whoever might be listening that this selfless woman chose my son. Starved of oxygen for so long at birth, he never stood a chance. He's never learned to walk or talk, and but for Jean and Harold, he would have spent his life in an institution. The irony is not lost on me, and I feel physically sick at the thought of him languishing in a home with nobody to love him. And Jean most definitely loves him. But she is not getting any younger. Widowed for three years now, she's eighty-four herself. The future for Joe looks uncertain.

The auctioneer bangs his gavel down so hard, it makes me jump. He adjusts his half-moon spectacles and points to a man on the front row. 'Sold to the gentleman on my right for five thousand, five hundred and fifty pounds. Thank you, sir.'

He clears his throat and adjusts his paisley bow tie. 'Now we come to lot number twenty-eight.'

There are a few rumblings before a hush descends on the room.

'Lot number twenty-eight represents a rare opportunity to acquire a painting by the gifted artist Millie McCarthy.'

I stiffen at the mention of my mother, but a feeling of pride swells inside me and I stand taller.

'Miss McCarthy sold only a few paintings in her lifetime, but L. S. Lowry recognised her talent and two of her works were purchased by him for his own private collection.' He gazed over the expectant faces below him. 'Now, who will start the bidding? Twenty thousand pounds, anybody?'

He pointed to someone at the back of the room 'Thank you, sir. Do I hear . . .? Yes, madam, twenty thousand, five hundred, thank you.'

He stopped and turned to a woman behind him, her neck flushed with excitement. She held up three fingers. He turned back to the audience. 'I have thirty thousand on the phone. Any advance . . . Yes, thank you, I have . . . forty thousand down here . . .' He nodded to his left and raised his eyebrows. 'Fifty thousand pounds . . .'

My head starts to pound, and sweat prickles my armpits. I waft the catalogue in front of my face as the years fall away. It is as though I am back in that meadow watching my mother. Her auburn hair is tied back from her face, her green eyes ablaze with concentration and her tongue sticking out of the side of her mouth as she sweeps the brush across the canvas. I can hear myself asking her to paint me, my childish voice full of indignation when she tells me no. Then she scoops me up onto her knee and tickles my ribs. I squirm with laughter as she nuzzles into my neck and tells me she will paint me into the picture but I mustn't tell anyone. It's to be our secret. I had never felt so loved as I did that day, and I remember thinking I had the best mummy in all the world.

The auctioneer's gavel startles me again and I'm brought abruptly back to the present.

'Sold for one hundred and twenty-five thousand pounds.' He nods to the man still holding up his card. 'Congratulations, sir.'

I feel myself swaying and grab hold of the chair in front of me, catching the back of the person's head. 'Sorry,' I mumble, dabbing my forehead with a tissue. I want to laugh, to cry, to shout out to anyone who cares to listen. My son's future is secured. From across the room Joe catches my eye and smiles. He has no comprehension of what's just happened, but as he looks at me, he pats his chest three times. Tears spring to my eyes, blurring my vision. I can never be his mother, but I can be his friend. I return the gesture, whispering the words: *I love you too, son.*

There's the sound of chairs scraping on floorboards as people stand to leave. Excited chatter breaks out and the crowd begins to disperse. The auction has come to an end, and the story of the troubled young girl who stole a baby and waded into a lake is now at its end too. A young girl who was never evil, never mad or even bad, but who nevertheless had her life stolen. I'm too old now for fairy-tale endings. I'm not married to the love of my life, my son has no idea I'm his mother, but it's an ending of sorts.

I turn to the exit, where Stephen is standing, silhouetted against the bright sunshine outside. He smiles at me and gives me a thumbs-up gesture, mouthing the words *You okay?* I manage a smile in return and nod my head. He holds out his hand and I cross the floor to take it. As he steers me out onto the pavement, his arm now circling my body, I realise that I am happy at last. And it's enough.

Acknowledgements

Writing a book is essentially a lonely business with many hours spent locked away with only a blank page for company. However, I am extremely fortunate to have a wonderful, supportive team behind me. I am particularly indebted to my agent, Anne Williams and my editor at Headline, Sherise Hobbs, who are both instrumental in ensuring that the finished article is as good as it can be.

I would like to thank my family for their continued support, especially my husband Rob Hughes and my parents, Audrey and Gordon Watkin who are always keen to be the first to get their hands on the manuscript. Thanks also to Cameron and Ellen Hughes for leaving me in peace so I could get the book finished.

Whilst researching *The Key,* I read a number of books on this fascinating subject but there was one book which I turned to time and again. *Certified and Detained* by Derek McCarthy is the true account of life in a British psychiatric hospital between 1957 and 1962. Derek was then a student nurse and he tells his story with candour, humility, respect and even humour. I'm so grateful to Derek for patiently answering all my questions and there is no doubt that what I learned from him has enriched my story. Any errors are of course my own.

Finally, I would like to express my thanks to all the readers who have contacted me directly through Facebook and Twitter. I hope I have managed to respond to you all but if not, please be assured that your messages have been read and are much appreciated.

THE KEY

Kathryn Hughes

Bonus Material

Q&A with Kathryn Hughes

What was your inspiration for *The Key*?

The idea for *The Key* is based on a true story. The Willard Asylum for the Chronic Insane was opened in 1869 and is located in Willard, NY. In 1995, after the asylum had closed its doors for the last time, a collection of over four hundred suitcases was discovered behind a locked attic door. The forgotten cases had been stored between 1910 and 1960 and belonged to former patients who had surrendered them on admittance to the asylum. The average stay of a Willard patient was thirty years. Most of the patients never left. To find out more about this fascinating discovery visit www.willardsuitcases.com.

Ambergate Asylum is fictional but is it based on a real place?

For *The Key* I spent a great deal of time researching the history of psychiatric institutions in the UK. During the course of my research, I travelled to the former North Wales Counties Lunatic Asylum in Denbigh. This imposing building finally closed its doors to patients in

August 1995, but even today, some twenty-two years later, this once-majestic building stands abandoned awaiting redevelopment.

The passing of the County Asylum/Lunacy Act in 1845 meant it was compulsory for counties to provide asylums for their 'lunatics'. This ensured the mass construction of over one hundred and twenty county asylums by the end of that century, housing over 100,000 people. No expense was spared in the construction of these magnificient buildings and by the 1950s, one in three families would admit a family member to a mental hospital, often for the most spurious of reasons.

The 1959 Mental Health Act abolished the distinction
between psychiatric hospitals and other types of hospitals
and sought to make treatment voluntary where possible.
In practice though, not much changed and it wasn't until
1961 when Enoch Powell, then Minister for Health, gave
his famous 'Water Tower' speech in which he promised
the elimination of the majority of the country's mental
hospitals. Without the necessary number of community
care programmes though, it would take another twenty
five years for this plan to come to fruition.

When the asylums began to close, many of them were left derelict, awaiting demolition or development. Even some twenty years after closing, there were many asylums standing neglected, falling prey to vandals and arsonists. Many of the buildings' features remained and it was possible, as Sarah does in *The Key*, to wander the corridors, plenty of fixtures and fittings still in place. For a complete list of asylums and what became of them, please visit the excellent website www.countyasylums.co.uk.

Photos of The North Wales Hospital (known locally as Denbigh Asylum), in 2017. © Robert Hughes.

When you start writing a novel, do you know how the story will end?

Of course! I always try to start off with an intriguing prologue which I hope will capture the reader's attention.

I know exactly how I want it all to come together at the end. It's the pesky ninety-odd thousand words in the middle that are the problem! Whilst I know the beginning and the end, it's the route from one to the other that I might deviate from. Nothing is set in stone until the book is rolling off the presses.

Can you describe a typical writing day?

I write from a converted garage in the garden. It's important for me to leave the house because there are far too many distractions there. In my office there is no internet, no kettle and no phone. There is nothing to do except write. If I arrive at my desk by ten, then I consider the day has got off to a good start. I generally read through what I wrote the day before and do some editing. I set myself a target of five hundred words a day but I often write twice that amount which makes me feel like an over-achiever. At lunch time, I wander back into the house and catch up on my emails and then resume writing until around tea-time.

There are some serious themes in all of your books. How do you find a balance between the serious nature of some of the content and the lighter elements within the story?

It's important to find a balance because that's what we do in real life. It's the British way. We can almost always find some humour even in dark situations. Although, I don't want my readers to finish my books feeling thoroughly depressed, I do acknowledge that not every story has to have a blissfully happy ending.

What do you like to do when you're not writing?

When I am writing to a deadline, there is not an awful lot of time for anything else but once the book is finished then I like to catch up with the friends I've neglected, read other people's books and to travel. We have a VW campervan so it's lovely to be able to take off at a moment's notice. Walking is also a great passion and we plan to walk the entire length of the Pembrokeshire Coast Path, which is 186 miles, in 2018. Not only is it stunningly beautiful, but it's a challenge too. By the time, you've finished, you've climbed the height of Everest.

Reading Group Questions

- What do you think is the central theme of the book, and how did it resonate with you?
- The novel's title, *The Key*, can be interpreted in several different ways. Which do you find the most significant?
- What effect did the drama of the novel's Prologue have on your subsequent reading of the book?
- Which of the three women in the novel (Sarah, Ellen, Amy) did you most empathise with and why?
- Which of the three, if any, do you feel is the driving force in the novel?
- How did you feel about the development of the characters in the story? Who do you feel grew the most over the course of the novel?
- What did you think of the character of Stephen Lambourn?
- How did you feel about the ending?

THE SECRET

June 1975

She had first married Thomas Roberts in the school playground when she was five years old. The ceremony had been days in the planning, and when the time came she'd worn one of her mother's net curtains fashioned into a makeshift veil and topped with a halo of daisies, and everybody agreed that she looked just like a real bride. Thomas presented her with a little clutch of hand-picked wild flowers he had collected on his way to school, and they'd stood hand in hand as little Davy Stewart officiated. Davy's speech was impaired by a crippling stammer, and his jam-jar glasses magnified his eyes to the size of a bush baby's, but he was a choirboy and the closest thing they had to a vicar.

Mary smiled at the memory as she turned to one side and admired her profile in the full-length mirror. She ran her hand tenderly over the swell of her belly, admiring the way it jutted out from just beneath her breasts and formed a perfect dome. She placed her hands in the small of her back, leaned forward and studied her complexion for any signs that she might be blooming. The bootees she had bought from Woolworths, a neutral lemon colour, lay on the dressing table. She buried her nose in the wool, but without little feet to warm them, they smelled new and sterile. At the sound of her husband clumping up the stairs, she thrust the bootees back in the drawer and just managed to whip out the pillow from under her dress before he opened the bedroom door.

'There you are, love. What're you doing up here?'

She bashed the pillow back into shape and laid it on the bed. 'Nothing, just tidying up a bit.'

'What, again? Come here.' He pulled her close, nudged her blond hair to one side and kissed her on the neck.

'Oh, Thomas, what if I'm not pregnant?' She tried to keep the whining note out of her voice, but she'd tasted disappointment so many times before that it was becoming difficult to remain positive.

He grabbed her round the waist with both hands and wrestled her on to the bed. 'Then we'll just have to keep trying.' He burrowed his face into her neck, and she detected the familiar lingering smell of coal dust in his hair.

'Thomas?'

He propped himself up on his elbows and gazed into her face. 'What?'

'You will hand your notice in if I am pregnant, won't you?'

Thomas sighed. 'If that's what you want, Mary, yes, I will.'

'I can't look after a baby and run the guest house by myself, can I?' she reasoned.

Thomas gazed at her, a crease of worry lining his forehead. 'It'll be tough, though, Mary. I mean, we've just had a thirty-five per cent pay increase. It's a lot to give up, you can't deny that.'

'I know, love, but it's such a dangerous job and you hate the long commute to the pit.'

'You're not wrong there,' he conceded. 'What time's your appointment at the doctor's?'

'Three.' She stroked a finger down the side of his cheek. 'I wish you could come with me.'

He kissed her fingertip. 'So do I, Mary, but I'll be thinking of you and we can celebrate when I get home, can't we?'

'I hate it when you have to work the night shift.'

'It's not exactly a barrel of laughs for me either.' It was said with a smile that removed any hint of rancour from his words.

As he sat on the bed to pull his boots on, Mary snuggled up beside him. 'I love you so much, Thomas.'

He reached for her hand and laced his fingers through hers. 'I love you too, Mary, and I just know you're going to make a cracking mother.'

Ever since their official wedding night, three years ago, they had been trying for a baby. Mary had not envisaged it being so difficult, and at thirty-one years of age, she was all too aware that time was running out. She was born to be a mother, she knew it, had always known it, and she could not understand why God was punishing her in this way. With each passing month, as the familiar dragging sensation crept into her stomach and the cramps took hold, a little more of her optimism had ebbed away, and her yearning to have a baby had become ever stronger. She was longing to be woken at four in the morning by a screaming infant, would relish having a bucket of terry nappies festering away in the corner of the kitchen. She wanted to look into her baby's eyes and see the future. Most of all she wanted to see her Thomas with his strong arms tenderly cradling his baby – boy or girl, it didn't matter – and to hear him being called 'Daddy'.

She would stare too long at babies in the street and glare at mothers who shouted at their children. She had once pulled out a tissue and wiped the nose of a little kid when his useless mother seemed oblivious to the long candles of snot the child was trying to reach with his tongue. Needless to say, her interference had not been appreciated. Once, on the beach, she'd come across a young boy sitting by the shoreline all alone, taking in the deep, juddering sobs that all children did when they had been crying too much. It turned out he'd dropped his ice cream on the sand after only one lick and his mother was refusing to buy him another. Mary had led him by the hand to the ice cream van and bought him a 99, his beaming face all the thanks she needed.

Her mothering instincts were never far from the

surface, and she was becoming more and more desperate to nurture a child of her own – hers and Thomas's. As she listened to her husband moving round the kitchen downstairs, getting ready for his shift, she prayed that today just might be the day when her dream would start to become a reality.

It was shortly after lunchtime when the train pulled into the station, its screeching brakes causing Mary to cover her ears. Thomas picked up his duffel bag and heaved it on to his back. He hated saying goodbye just as much as she did, but he always tried to remain upbeat. He held her in a bone-crushing embrace and rested his chin on her shoulder. 'I'm sure it's going to be good news at the doctor's, Mary. I'll have my fingers crossed for you.' He tilted her chin and kissed her lightly on the lips. 'And I give you my word that I'll hand my notice in the minute that little one comes along.'

Mary clapped her hands together, her eyes widening in delight. 'Really? Do you promise?'

He made the sign of a cross on his chest. 'I promise, Mary.'

'Thank you.' She kissed him on his stubbled cheek. 'Oh Thomas,' she sighed. 'Parting is such sweet sorrow.'

'Eh?'

'*Romeo and Juliet.*'

He shook his head. 'Sorry, you've lost me.'

'Oh Thomas,' she laughed, thumping him playfully on

435

his shoulder. 'You're such a philistine. Juliet tells Romeo that their sorrowful parting is also sweet because it makes them think about the next time they'll see each other.'

'Oh, I see.' He frowned and wrinkled his nose. 'Makes sense, I suppose. He knew what he was talking about, our Bill.'

He stepped on to the train, closed the door and pulled the window down so he could lean out. He kissed his fingers and pressed them to her cheek. She held his hand in place, struggling to stop the tears she knew he hated so much. 'You take care now, Thomas Roberts, you hear me?'

She wagged her finger in his face and he responded with an emphatic salute. 'Yes, boss.'

The guard blew his whistle and the train eased its way along the platform. Mary ran alongside for a few paces, Thomas waving his white handkerchief and dabbing at his eyes. She knew he was teasing her and she couldn't help but smile. 'I'll see you in a couple of days,' she shouted, as the train gathered speed and retreated into the distance.

The doctor's waiting room was crowded and stiflingly hot. The woman sitting on her left held a sleeping baby, who, by the smell of things, had recently filled its nappy. The man on her right roared a sneeze into his handkerchief and followed it with a violent coughing fit. Mary turned away and flicked through a well-thumbed magazine. It was fifteen minutes past her appointment time and she had chewed her way through two fingernails. At last the receptionist bobbed her head round the door. 'Mary Roberts? The doctor's ready for you now.'

Mary looked up from her magazine. 'Thank you.' She rose slowly from her seat and knocked gingerly on the doctor's door. The minute she entered the room, however, all her apprehension dissipated. The doctor was sitting behind his large mahogany desk, but he had rocked back in his chair, his hands clasped together on his lap, a knowing smile on his lips.

She decided to take the scenic route back to the guest house. A bracing walk along the seafront would put colour in her cheeks, and a lungful of the salty sea air would clear her head. She found she didn't really walk, though; it was something between floating and skipping, and by the time she arrived home she was light-headed and breathless. She played the doctor's words over and over in her head. 'I'm pleased to tell you, Mrs Roberts, that you are indeed pregnant.' Finally, after three years of heartache, false alarms and crushing disappointment, they were going to be a family. She couldn't wait to tell Thomas.

Keep in touch with me

Kathryn Hughes

Sign up to my newsletter for the latest news,
book giveaways and reading group materials
kathrynhughesauthor.com

Join the community on Facebook
@KHughesAuthor

Follow me on Twitter
@KHughesAuthor

He stared at the door long after she'd gone. Then he picked up the brush from the companion set by the fireplace and swept up the shards of coloured glass before returning to his desk and unlocking the top drawer. He mulled over Peter Sullivan's letter again. He chewed the end of his pencil, then made a note on his pad. He read back what he'd written and thought about Amy's words earlier. Perhaps she was right. Maybe he really did think he was God.